*Megan,
Unleash your inner
Sex Kitten!
MSweeney
xoxo*

Breathe In

A JUST BREATHE NOVEL

·

Martha Sweeney

A Kralik Consultants LLC Publication
www.marthasweeney.com

Breathe In (Just Breathe #1) written by Martha Sweeney
Copyright © 2015 Martha Sweeney
Publishing 2015 Kralik Consultants LLC

Copy Editors: Martha Sweeney & Thomas Sweeney
Cover Design: Martha Sweeney
Interior Design and Formatting: Martha Sweeney & Thomas Sweeney

All rights reserved. This book was self-published by the author, Martha Sweeney, under Kralik Consultants LLC. No part of this book may be reproduced in any form by any means without the express written permission of the author. This includes reprints, excerpts, photocopying, recording, or any future means of reproducing text and stories.

If you would like to do any of the above, please seek permission first by contacting the author at: **www.marthasweeney.com**

Connect with Martha Sweeney online:
Facebook: www.facebook.com/AuthorMarthaSweeney
Twitter: @MSweeney_Author
Instagram: www.instagram.com/MarthaSweeneyAuthor
YouTube: www.youtube.com/c/MSweeney
Pinterest: www.pinterest.com/MSweeneyAuthor
Google+: plus.google.com/+MSweeney
Goodreads: www.goodreads.com/MarthaSweeney

Published in The United States by Kralik Consultants LLC
ISBN: 978-0-9862272-4-0

Titles by Martha Sweeney

The Just Breathe Series
Breathe In
Breathe Out
Just Breathe

Acknowledgements:

Thank you, my best friend, my partner, my lover, the love of my life, my husband, Thomas Sweeney, for our relationship that others look at and wonder how we do it. Here's to our love, our laughter and our weird kookiness as we continue this wonderful journey we call life. May others find and enjoy the kind of love we share. I love you!

Breathe In

www.marthasweeney.com

One

As I attempt to lift my heavy eyelids, I discover a hazy darkness surrounding me. Blinking slowly several times, my half-opened eyes won't focus to give me any clear indication of what's around me and where the blurry, flashing lights above are coming from. My body feels heavy. Still unable to open my eyes all the way, I perceive that I'm laying down somewhere. A cool dampness near my left cheek reveals itself as a slight gust of air brushes past my face. Sliding my right arm up the side of my body like a snake, my fingers creep to my lips. Drool — or, at least I hope so.

Two large and oddly shaped figures materialize in front of me. They are so close, only a foot or two away. Voices suddenly emanate from the now more defined silhouettes. Their speech sounds muffled and trails off into the distance even as I try to concentrate on their words. Who are they? What are they saying? Why can't I understand them? One of the voices almost sounds feminine.

Another indistinguishable sound gradually becomes more apparent as it grows louder and the ringing in my ears subsides. It's the engine of a car. My brain finally starts to put the fuzzy pieces of evidence together. I must have fallen asleep in the back seat. A familiar smell creeps into my nose that reassures me — my mother's perfume.

"Mom?" my throat squeezes out in a raw, breathy, hoarse tone.

"We're almost home, dear," her voice replies in a low, sluggish tone.

I internally smile at her comforting words, though her voice sounds peculiar.

A sudden rush of nervousness enters my belly. The car feels as if it's flying down the road like a rocket ship as the speed of the flashing lights zooming above my head all blur into one.

"Mom," I try to shout, but not a single sound escapes my mouth this time. Confused, I try again. "Mom!"

She doesn't hear me. I don't hear me.

A single, bright white light races towards us, growing larger by the second. My mother turns her head towards me smiling. Why doesn't she hear me? How does she not see the light?

Again, with all my might. "Mom . . . !" my voice trails in my head like a deafening siren, stabbing my ears like a knife.

Time stops in this very moment. I can see everything with perfect clarity as I stare in horror into my mother's eyes. My mouth is left open, still screaming without a sound. I can't hear anything except a piercing ring that echoes in my body. Why can't she hear me? Why doesn't she see the terrified look on my face?

My body lurches backward as I attempt to scramble to grab my mother and I suddenly become paralyzed. Then, it happens all at once — I hear the sound of metal hitting metal as it wraps itself around and around. I watch my parents' bodies hurling forward toward the oncoming truck, bouncing around like ping pong balls, getting dented with each blow.

My heart is filled with terror as I desperately try to yell one more time, "Mom . . . !"

Jerking awake, I shout out in despair. The pounding of my heart and heaving of my lungs is only matched by the shaking that racks my body. Whimpers of a dog and the gift of warm, wet licks on my chin and neck draw my attention. Sadie is consoling me. It was just a dream. Yes, just a dream.

Wrapping my arms around Sadie's neck allows me to regain my composure. Mortified, a tear rolls down my right cheek. It wasn't just a dream — it's my mind's attempt to reconcile the death of my parents, even though I can't recall anything.

It's a nightmare that I haven't had in quite some time. It shouldn't surprise me for all the times I've dreamt it, but it does since I don't wake up like that lately near as often. I used to start every morning that way. Now, not so much. Yet, when it does happen, the effect is still the same.

I've been haunted by this vision since the day I regained consciousness in the hospital. Thrashing my body around and pulling out the I.V. the first time caused the hospital staff to sedate and strap me to the bed. It took four more times of the nightmare, plus heavy medication, before my mind and body finally became sedentary and numb enough to allow me to recognize where I was, the devastating pain I felt all over and in my heart, and that the memory was real.

It's not easy to find out from a stranger that your parents died in the horrific vision that keeps reoccurring in your head each time you sleep.

Well, there's no way I'm going back to sleep now, not that I ever did after having that dream.

Kissing the top of Sadie's head before looking directly at her, I half-heartily smile and say, "Looks like it's an extra early morning for us, girl."

Sadie's mouth drops open and her tongue flops out as a sign of relief.

"Who's hungry?"

She licks my chin two more times knowing the meaning of those words and jumps off the bed in excitement. Stopping in the doorway, Sadie looks over her shoulder at me to see if I'm following yet.

"I'm coming, I'm coming . . ." I retort as I slide my legs to the side of the bed, stretch my arms up and yawn.

I prepare Sadie's meals a few days in advance based on what I've picked up at the store, farmers market or had delivered. Her diet consists of all raw meats, fruits, veggies and/or seasonings. On occasion, I get her fresh beef or bison bones to chew on. Only the best for my little Sadie. Grabbing a glass container from the fridge, I dump the contents into Sadie's food bowl and add some turmeric and dried basil for extra flavoring and nutrition.

While Sadie eats, I mix and gulp down my morning routine of water with bentonite clay. There's nothing like cleansing the body before a yummy organic smoothie followed by a vigorous workout. To most, I'm a health nut. My two best friends tease me sometimes at how strict I am with my eating habits. I love food, don't get me wrong, but I love good food and I only eat the best.

I relieve myself before taking Sadie out. She follows me to the bathroom with her leash in tow as if that speeds up the process. Sadie doesn't really need the leash, it's more for the community. The apartment complex likes dogs. They allow pets in the buildings, but because others can't train their own animals properly, which caused an incident, all pets have to be leashed. Even if this rule wasn't in place, most of my neighbors would freak out if they didn't see Sadie on a leash. For starters, I'm a very quiet and private person. They don't know me and my ability to control Sadie. Second, Sadie is a pure breed pit bull. Her breed has a bad wrap for being vicious; a result due to the lack of competent owners only.

Once outside our gated apartment community, the cool winter air nips at my fingers as I unhook Sadie's leash. She stays close to my heels on my right side as we walk to the corner before crossing the street in front of the park. Sadie is trotting with excitement, but remains reserved. It's a part of her demeanor. She's a playful, loving, yet protective three-year-old. I wouldn't have her any other way.

On the edge of the grass, Sadie waits for my command to run. She would never run or leave my side in public unless I give her the signal. I sign for her to go and she takes off to the closest tree to relieve herself. She stays nearby sniffing, watching and waiting for me as I clean up after her. It's too early for the kids to be out playing on the jungle gym, so Sadie is left to playing catch with her favorite natural rubber ball until she tires.

Even in late winter, California is still beautiful and nowhere near as cold as the East Coast. I don't miss the gloomy Spring and Autumn days, cold, bitter Winters or humid Summers. California is home now and has been since I was sixteen. I love how quiet Pasadena is at four o'clock in the morning.

After a long morning exercise session for Sadie, I'm back in my two bedroom apartment with Sadie sitting on the kitchen floor watching me prepare my smoothie, hoping that I might drop something as she gnaws on her naturally harvested deer antler. Her head bounces between my hands and the floor. She wouldn't go after food even if it did drop. Sadie would just wait patiently until I told her to eat it. She's too cute. As I drink my breakfast, a smoothie consisting of banana, strawberries, blueberries, mango, coconut milk, turmeric, cinnamon, and a raw egg, I plop myself down in front of my computer to check emails as Sadie lays at my feet. I love working from home. It makes things so much easier. No LA traffic. No distractions. Well, no distractions other than Sadie, but she's always a welcome distraction. Once I finish checking my emails, I start my workout music playlist and then clean out my cup. Time to stretch and rebound.

I work out longer than usual. Ok, it's not unusual on the days I wake up like I did today, but it's not as common as it used to be. Finally physically drained after about an hour, I stretch again. Sadie decides she needs some attention and lays across my right leg within a few seconds of me getting on the floor. Her full weight is on me and I can't help but laugh.

Reluctant to check the time, I roll my eyes when I find out that it is still very early. Well, not too early for me, but early for most people, including my best friend Jared. I don't think Jared has ever been up this early in the morning, ever, unless he's been up all night and never went to sleep. I decide to text Jared a happy *good morning sunshine* before hopping into the shower.

By the time Jared calls, I've completely showered, dressed, ate a raw organic yogurt and granola with blackberries and figs, played with Sadie for about fifteen minutes, made my to-do list for the next two weeks, responded to inquiries for my business, Naturally Me, started writing outlines for three months worth of blog and video topics, and plotted out what I'd like to see in our social media marketing campaigns that will be used after the already planned and almost completed next quarter.

Before I can even mutter a hello, Jared immediately questions, "Had the dream again?"

Trying to deny it, I reply, "Uh, good morning to you too."

I know he knows. It's obvious with how early I texted.

"It's been a while since the last one," Jared says with concern in his voice. "You okay, *Kitten?*"

Unable to avoid the subject, I reply, "Yeah."

"I'm on my way over to get started on all the stuff you've drafted," Jared replies, knowing my habits. "You know I don't get up this early for anyone else — unless he's naked and in my bed."

"Yes, I know. And, that's why I love you," I profess, trying to butter him up before he sees the mountain of work I've done and have planned.

"Yeah, yeah. I love you too," he says warmly. "Do you need me to pick up anything?"

"Nope."

"Okay. I'll be there soon. Smooches."

He's perky now. That's a good sign for it being almost six-fifty in the morning.

"Smooches," I reply with a smile on my face.

Chapter One

Knowing that Jared's on his way, I decide to stop and take a break for a bit. Sadie joins me on the couch to snuggle, laying completely on my body with her head tucked just under my jaw.

Two

With a jolt, I wake to the sensation of Sadie getting up and rushing to the door. I must have fallen asleep while waiting for Jared. Still foggy, I jump up off the couch to let him in. I feel silly remembering when I'm halfway to the door that Jared has a key.

"Hey boss!" he exclaims when our eyes meet.

"I told you not to call me that," I proclaim with a little uneasiness.

"Seriously? It's been how many years now that I've been working for you and you still can't stand it?" he queries me playfully, wraps me in a bear hug which is a little longer than usual, and kisses me on the top of the head.

He's right. I know he's right, but I still haven't gotten used to it.

After a long comforting embrace, Jared bends down to his knees to give Sadie some love and attention. "What time did you get up today?" he asks, looking up while squatting.

"Just before four," I respond trying to brush it off.

"Thanks for not texting then," he says gratefully with a half smile pressed into his left cheek.

"I knew you'd threaten to quit if I did," I reply playfully.

"Please . . . you'd never let me quit. You'd kill me before I had the chance to utter the words."

"True," I answer slyly.

His smile widens. He's happy to see that my recovery from mornings like this is occurring much quicker than it had when we first met. It would take most of the day for the first year. As the months passed by, it would only take a few hours for the feeling of dread to fade. Now, an extra bout of physical activity works followed by borderline obsessive compulsion like today.

"Well, *Kitten*, you know I do love my job," he declares as his smile stretches from ear to ear. "And, I'd hate to disappoint my fans."

"You aren't one to disappoint," I say mischievously.

His smile is infectious as I return his perkiness.

Jared follows me to the second bedroom of my apartment which has been my office since I moved in a few years ago. Glancing at the clock, I'm surprised to see what time it is. When Jared said he was on his way, I didn't expect him to be here this early. Reaching the front of my desk, I abruptly turn around to him and sheepishly announce, "I'm so sorry Jared. I didn't realize what time it was. When you said you would be here soon, I didn't think you would be here this early."

I know my eyes aren't playing tricks as I check the clock a second time to confirm that it is seven forty-nine.

"Anything for my, *Sex Kitten*," he declares.

"Seriously . . ." I start to protest, but he cuts me off.

"*Kitten*, it's no big deal. You're my girl . . . but, don't tell that to Maggie," Jared affirms while chuckling at his last statement.

Maggie and I are the only girls who have any place in his heart. The rest is for all his male lovers and fans.

"Besides, you should have seen how dead the streets were from WeHo all the way here. I've never seen LA like this. It's creepy," he shares.

I laugh wholeheartedly. Everyone in and out of California complains about the traffic only because they drive during the busiest times. Not many people know when the roads are as still as the aftermath of a zombie apocalypse.

Before I can muffle my laughter, Jared continues, "I just might have to start getting up earlier to travel like I'm *King of the Road*."

"Please," I mutter while trying to subdue my giggle and start shaking my head. "You will never come to the dark side."

"Yeah . . . you're right," he agrees. "But, one can dream."

Our giggles tapper offer as we sit on the white leather couch that's up against the wall across from my desk.

Getting into business mode, I profess, "I know we have next quarter's schedule already laid out and you've got the team way ahead of schedule for development and production . . . which I'm loving since it's almost midway through this quarter . . . ."

"But . . ." Jared chimes in, seeing where I'm going. "You've already started the third quarter's ideas." He smiles, though I can see by the look in his eyes that his worry for me has returned.

"Actually, I have it completely finished," I admit with certainty, but nervous for his reaction.

"Wow. Really?" He takes a breath to process my confession. "How the hell do you do it? I mean, I know how you do it, but . . . ." His eyes soften more as his voice trails off.

I desperately want to ease his concern and move forward.

"Years of practice," I state begrudgingly as I try to brush it off like a joke, but to no avail.

I haven't slept for more than five hours straight a night since the accident. My body shivers at the thought.

"Besides, you know I get phenomenal, intense focus following . . ." my voice begins to trail.

Wanting to keep our attention on the positive, Jared redirects us both, "So, what did you come up with?"

Jared is such a loving friend above everything else. He hates to see me in pain. I've gotten really good at fooling him and Maggie over the years. Not that I want to lie to them, I just don't want them to worry too much. I know what he's hinting at when he tries to praise me for my uncanny attention and ability while leading me back to the distraction at hand. My extreme ability to give my absolute focus to anything I decide is my way of coping. I won't admit it to anyone, not even Jared or Maggie, only myself on some occasions. I just avoid or put up more walls.

I remember vividly the first time I met Jared. Just getting off the train from Newark, New Jersey to Union Square in downtown Los Angeles, California. I was exhausted, frightened and confused thanks to the restless sleep and the more than two-day journey. Not knowing where to go or what to do, I followed the mass of people getting off the train. In the tunnel of the station, I finally stopped, perplexed by which direction to continue. That's when we met.

Actually, he scared the crap out of me when he said "Hello. I'm Jared. You look like you need some help."

I grabbed my bike and tried to put some distance between us. He was too close to me, not for being a stranger, but for my recently acquired fear of men.

"Don't worry, *Kitten*," he said comfortingly. "I'm gay. I'm not going to hurt you."

He must have known what I was thinking by the look on my face and was trying to calm and reassure me. Though he didn't have any glaringly obvious gay traits that are overly embellished in the movies and TV, I honestly believed him. I wouldn't have know from first hand experience since I hadn't known anyone who was gay or openly gay prior to meeting him. There just was a look in his face that I couldn't explain. A look of understanding. I swore I saw myself staring back at me.

He must have seen my expression relax, encouraging him to coax me more by gesturing with his hands as he took a few steps backward away from me through the tunnel to the right. "Come on. Looks like you could use some food. Maybe even some coffee. Do you like coffee?" He paused as his genuine smile grew bigger.

Calmer, I took a step towards him with my bike in tow while shaking my head in response to wanting coffee.

Assuming I was answering his latter question, he confessed, "Coffee's overrated anyhow. How about some tea instead, then?"

I hesitantly nodded as I slowly stepped towards him.

"Great. Follow me," he said as he turned his back to me and started walking. Every few steps he would turn his head over his right shoulder to make sure I was still with him and hadn't run off.

I was at a place in my life where I needed a friend, and for some unknown reason, it was meant to be him. At the time, I didn't know why, but I was grateful and still am. Since the accident almost three months prior, I'd had no one, until Jared.

Jared was kicked out of the house by his parents when he was eighteen. Apparently, according to Jared, they were God fearing, devout bible readers. That was the only book they read and they read it every day. Jared had come out to them the night of his high school graduation, convinced that they would love and accept him. After all, he was their only son. Unfortunately, his father spat venomous words at him as he tried to strike Jared with his belt. The disturbing thing was that it wasn't the first time Jared was ever beaten by his father. He had received lashes in the past as a young boy for being foolish or misbehaving, but that night something snapped in Jared. After taking three blows to the body without flinching, he grabbed the belt on the forth swing, ripped it from his father's hands, and returned the heartless attack on his father. He didn't say a word, but stopped on the thirteenth smack when Jared's mother begged him to stop. She didn't stand up for Jared, ever, and he probably thought to whip her as well, but didn't. She gave him as much money as they had in the house plus a check made out to cash and pleaded for him to pack his bags and leave. I think she was trying to save both of them.

Jared was almost nineteen when we found each other. He had been living on his own in a small rundown studio apartment on the edges of Chinatown. The only time he would leave his apartment before he met me was to go to work. His demons still haunted him too. We were both lost, but then found that day in the tunnel.

As Jared completes his review of what I have written down for the third quarter's schedule, I look to him for his thoughts and suggestions. He seems seriously impressed and it takes him a little longer to verbally respond than I'm used to. It must be the early morning hour that is causing Jared's brain to not fully catch up quite yet.

Glancing at me he says, "Damn. I think this is terrific!" Still with a little bit of shock on his face, "Man, Emma. You've surprised me yet again."

Humbly, I reply with a smile, "Thanks."

Jared adds in some other pointers to add to the Lesbian - Gay - Bisexual - Transgender, or LGBT, section of the website from some recent comments and questions he's collected from our social media platforms and his friends.

Sadie gnawing on her bone catches our attention, and Jared becomes excited again.

"I have and idea!" he shouts.

"What?" I question.

Chapter Two

"It might sound a little silly . . . at first, that is," he cautiously replies.

"Just say it. You know I like ideas," I instruct, prompting him to share his idea.

I'm having trouble understanding his hesitation. Maybe he isn't completely sure of my mood yet. I'll have to do some better convincing.

"You've done a lot already this morning. I don't want to add to . . . ."

"Just spit it out," I politely demand, smiling as I cut him off.

"Ok . . ." he begins, seeming to be more confident now in his decision to bring it up. "We should create a whole section for pets. Mostly dogs to start because of Sadie, but I think we can increase the follower base even more. Sadie would be the face and we write everything from her perspective . . . well, our assumption of her perspective that is . . . what do you think?"

My business, Naturally Me, is a health and wellness blog that focuses on organic and natural products, recipes and the like. When I started it about six years ago, it was to suffice my interest, fascination and experimentation with female health, beauty and food products and questions about alternative health that I started to use when I changed my daily habits after some rocky moments I had while trying to figure out my life during the first two years in California. Jared was a very loving and patient friend from the start, even after learning about my demons.

I was already a computer wiz thanks to being homeschooled and my mother encouraging my learning to be around whatever topics interested me at the time. I was proficient in computer coding and graphic design by the time I was fifteen among other things. I was technically a high school graduate at the age of fourteen. Mom wanted me to have my high school diploma regardless of her thoughts of the ill-effectiveness of the public school system, so she scheduled the testing. The district actually had me take the test a second time, not because I didn't pass, but because my scores were close to perfect and they wanted to make sure I wasn't cheating. Mom was pleased with her teaching ability after the second test results came back practically the same as the first. Not wanting to thrust me into college at my young age, Mom began introducing me to a variety of college based courses until — well, let's not get back into that.

The blog took a little time to get going, but after the first two years, it started to pick up enough that I was making almost twice as much as I was working with Jared at Jensen's Florist. By the third year, I was making even more, almost four times as much money. Not long after the start of Naturally Me's third year, Jared gave me some inspiration for topics to address on the blog from hearing him recount or discuss certain subject matters with me and his other friends. Knowing that I wasn't quite legal yet to get into bars to see and hear everything first hand, I asked Jared to do some recognizance for me. Not understanding why I was so curious, two weeks later he showed up with a fake ID for me. Not willing to use the ID right away, I explained to Jared how I wanted to expand the blog. He instantly loved the idea.

Shortly after Jared's insatiable desire to see what he could find, he and I were quickly overwhelmed by the sheer volume of talking points we could add to the blog. From then on, Jared spent all his free time helping me establish the LGBT division of the blog with him as the face until I could pay him the same amount or more as Jensen's. Proudly, I was able to match his monthly income from Jensen's in just four months.

Currently, Naturally Me offers its readers health and beauty tips, tricks, product reviews, product referrals, homemade recipes along with a section dedicated to cuisine, home decorating, contests and giveaways, and an exclusive LGBT section. The thought of another division is mind blowing . . . but real.

Naturally Me expanded its reach by the end of its fourth year with the use of internet video sharing that allowed the company to instantly start making additional income which grew faster than I believed possible. Now, not only is Jared the main face of Naturally Me, he manages all communication and task completion between me, Naturally Me, and Naturally Me's independent contractors who handle our research, graphic design, video and editing, general inquiries and social media.

"Holy crap, Jared!" I blurt out in sheer astonishment.

"Yeah?!" he hesitantly replies.

"No. Seriously," I exclaim. In shock, then awe and joyous appreciation for the man, I squeal in excitement, "You are a genius!"

"Oh, stop it!" he counters, trying to seem bashfully innocent and humble.

I glare at him with a devilish smile to his response, suggesting that I know what he's doing, but pleased with his brilliance. "We can incorporate the pet section into the third quarter easily. We can hire a few more people to handle it under your direction."

"Sweet!" he shouts with enthusiasm. "Looks like I should be getting a bonus at the end of the year," he says teasingly.

"I'll throw in a night at your favorite strip club if it goes the way I'm envisioning it in my head," I toy with him with a sense of half truth.

"Mmmm . . . You sure know how to please a man," he replies, winking at me with a dirty grin. We both snicker like school girls for a moment before turning back to the project at hand.

Happy with our successful meeting and my true love and gratitude for my friend, I tell him, "I love you, Jared."

He looks at me quizzically for a second. Not sure where I'm going with this suddenly serious tone. He tries to brush it off lightly joking around, "Yeah, yeah. I know. I love you too, *Sex Kitten*."

"No. I'm serious."

He rarely sees the serious and openly emotional side of me, let alone the fact that I don't say those three words loosely to just anyone or in just any context. Appreciatively and affectionately, I smile and repeat myself, "I love you."

Respectfully, he pauses to take in this still unaccustomed moment. Jared, genuinely grateful for the moment, smiles and replies back, "I love you too, Emma." He leans over to embrace me.

We sit, reassuring each other for several minutes and start cracking up when Sadie decides to wedge herself between our arms and onto our laps. Sadie never misses a beat.

We continue hashing out the details for the third quarter's targets to include the pet division while sipping on tea and coffee. I leave Jared to his now coherent and animated concentration to fix him some breakfast. Surprisingly, I can hear his stomach grumble in protest to his second cup of coffee in demand for more sustenance.

A few hours later, content with our goals and objectives, we resolve to bring our business meeting to an end. Any in-person meetings after this will be brief to just review the progress of what's scheduled and the testing of any new products that have arrived, unless it's to just get together and hang out.

"I need to check the P.O. Box for deliveries," Jared admits. "I completely forgot to before coming here."

"That's fine. You were here really early," I reply, letting him off the hook.

He did come over much earlier than regular, two hours earlier.

"How about we check after going out for some lunch?" I suggest.

His eyes gleam with elation. Grinning and pleased, Jared puts his notes and iPad into his bag.

Before we head out the door, I turn off the music streaming from the Baroque classical music playlist on my computer that has been playing since just before I got into the shower. I am disappointed to hear my favorite song, Suite for Cello No. One in G Major by Johann Sebastian Bach, start playing. I almost hesitate to turn it off, but both Jared and I are hungry and need to get out.

If I were musically inclined, I would have learned cello or violin, but alas, I am not blessed with the ability to play. I can dance and follow any beat. Jared and I have taken dances lessons for practically every style of music, but my creative gifts and abilities are the visual arts. Though I can't play an instrument, I have always been able to pick up tones and notes, which help greatly with the variety of languages I speak other than English.

My parents wanted the best for me. They never forced their views, religious beliefs or their particularly desired topics of study. They made learning a game, and I loved it. Though we were never able to travel internationally, we wanted to learn as many languages as possible. Before the accident, I spoke fluent English, Spanish and French, and had four months into learning Mandarin. Each day of the week we would speak only in one dialect regardless if we stayed home all day or went out. It was funny to see people's faces when we spoke in a different language. We got the most looks when we spoke Spanish or Mandarin, but we didn't care.

"Where do you want to eat?" Jared asks as I pick up my purse, keys and hook Sadie's leash onto her collar.

"What are you in the mood for?" I answer with another question.

"Well . . ." he pauses for a second to decide.

Jared knows not to go back and forth with me on asking each other. It could take an hour before he caves in and chooses a place. I always win. As much as I like control, I know I'd be content with any restaurant he chooses.

"I want to go to Stinky Pete's."

Noticing his devilish smile, designed to get a specific response from me, I simply smile and nod.

"You sure?" he inquires, trying to get me to break.

"Sure. If that's where you want to eat," I reply with a relaxed grin.

He will not break me.

"You're no fun," he jokingly whines and sticks his tongue at me as I walk closer to him. "Besides, you know I can't stand their food either."

I smirk as he surrenders easily in defeat.

"Let's have Indian. What was the place we went to last time?" Jared questions.

"Akbar?"

"Yep. That's the one. I loved that place. I think it's my favorite Indian restaurant in town." He closes the door behind Sadie and me.

Though most places in Pasadena have outdoor seating, which is used the majority of the year, Akbar does not. The restaurant is on a side road off Colorado Boulevard which makes dining there more quiet and less distracting. With Jared as the main face of Naturally Me, we occasionally get interrupted at meals, especially if we are dining outside and he's not wearing sunglasses or a hat. My first name and face are used for the business as well, but I try to minimize how much my photo is posted. I don't enjoy being in the public eye as much. By bringing Sadie onboard, that may change.

Since we're bringing Sadie along for lunch, I grab her service dog vest to grant her access into the restaurant. Sadie is not a full-time service dog, but I did have her trained and certified so she can go anywhere with me. With the vest on, Sadie is accepted everywhere.

For our meal, Jared and I share several of my favorite dishes from Akbar. Since he can't remember what he had the last time, he asks me to order. Knowing he's hungry,

Chapter Two

that he can pile a fascinating amount of food into his belly, and that we have the rest of the day to enjoy each other's company, I chose to order a full three course meal.

To start, we treat our taste buds to samosa, mixed green katchumber and the kaske-badamjan. Jared rinses his food down with a glass of water and mango lassi. I just have water. About five minutes after we finish the appetizers, our waiter delivers us tandoori salmon, tandoori chicken, vegetable bhuna and a side of rice suffused with saffron. Jared takes photos of each dish with his cell phone and even has me take a few pictures of him posing to post on his social media for all his adoring fans to view.

As we eat, our conversation bounces around a myriad of topics, mostly memories of glorious excursions we've had together and many of them that included Maggie. We recount our clubbing days in WeHo and all the weird and eclectic types of people who would hit on all three of us. Jared would be hit on by every gay man, whereas Maggie and I would get hit on by the women. Maggie and I never minded being hit on by other women. We felt safe around them compared to men, especially me. "Hey boss!" he exclaims when our eyes meet.

"I told you not to call me that," I proclaim with a little uneasiness.

"Seriously? It's been how many years now that I've been working for you and you still can't stand it?" he queries me playfully, wraps me in a bear hug which is a little longer than usual, and kisses me on the top of the head.

He's right. I know he's right, but I still haven't gotten used to it.

After a long comforting embrace, Jared bends down to his knees to give Sadie some love and attention. "What time did you get up today?" he asks, looking up while squatting.

"Just before four," I respond trying to brush it off.

"Thanks for not texting then," he says gratefully with a half smile pressed into his left cheek.

"I knew you'd threaten to quit if I did," I reply playfully.

"Please . . . you'd never let me quit. You'd kill me before I had the chance to utter the words."

"True," I answer slyly.

His smile widens. He's happy to see that my recovery from mornings like this is occurring much quicker than it had when we first met. It would take most of the day for the first year. As the months passed by, it would only take a few hours for the feeling of dread to fade. Now, an extra bout of physical activity works followed by borderline obsessive compulsion like today.

"Well, *Kitten*, you know I do love my job," he declares as his smile stretches from ear to ear. "And, I'd hate to disappoint my fans."

"You aren't one to disappoint," I say mischievously.

His smile is infectious as I return his perkiness.

Jared follows me to the second bedroom of my apartment which has been my office since I moved in a few years ago. Glancing at the clock, I'm surprised to see what time it is. When Jared said he was on his way, I didn't expect him to be here this early. Reaching the front of my desk, I abruptly turn around to him and sheepishly announce, "I'm so sorry Jared. I didn't realize what time it was. When you said you would be here soon, I didn't think you would be here this early."

I know my eyes aren't playing tricks as I check the clock a second time to confirm that it is seven forty-nine.

"Anything for my *Sex Kitten*," he declares.

"Seriously . . . " I start to protest, but he cuts me off.

"*Kitten*, it's no big deal. You're my girl . . . but, don't tell that to Maggie," Jared affirms while chuckling at his last statement.

Maggie and I are the only girls who have any place in his heart. The rest is for all his male lovers and fans.

"Besides, you should have seen how dead the streets were from WeHo all the way here. I've never seen LA like this. It's creepy," he shares.

I laugh wholeheartedly. Everyone in and out of California complains about the traffic only because they drive during the busiest times. Not many people know when the roads are as still as the aftermath of a zombie apocalypse.

Before I can muffle my laughter, Jared continues, "I just might have to start getting up earlier to travel like I'm *King of the Road*."

"Please," I mutter while trying to subdue my giggle and start shaking my head. "You will never come to the dark side."

"Yeah . . . you're right," he agrees. "But, one can dream."

Our giggles tapper offer as we sit on the white leather couch that's up against the wall across from my desk.

Getting into business mode, I profess, "I know we have next quarter's schedule already laid out and you've got the team way ahead of schedule for development and production . . . which I'm loving since it's almost midway through this quarter . . . ."

"But . . ." Jared chimes in, seeing where I'm going. "You've already started the third quarter's ideas." He smiles, though I can see by the look in his eyes that his worry for me has returned.

"Actually, I have it completely finished," I admit with certainty, but nervous for his reaction.

"Wow. Really?" He takes a breath to process my confession. "How the hell do you do it? I mean, I know how you do it, but . . . ." His eyes soften more as his voice trails off.

Chapter Two

I desperately want to ease his concern and move forward.

"Years of practice," I state begrudgingly as I try to brush it off like a joke, but to no avail.

I haven't slept for more than five hours straight a night since the accident. My body shivers at the thought

"Besides, you know I get phenomenal, intense focus following . . ." my voice begins to trail.

Wanting to keep our attention on the positive, Jared redirects us both, "So, what did you come up with?"

Jared is such a loving friend above everything else. He hates to see me in pain. I've gotten really good at fooling him and Maggie over the years. Not that I want to lie to them, I just don't want them to worry too much. I know what he's hinting at when he tries to praise me for my uncanny attention and ability while leading me back to the distraction at hand. My extreme ability to give my absolute focus to anything I decide is my way of coping. I won't admit it to anyone, not even Jared or Maggie, only myself on some occasions. I just avoid or put up more walls.

I remember vividly the first time I met Jared. Just getting off the train from Newark, New Jersey to Union Square in downtown Los Angeles, California. I was exhausted, frightened and confused thanks to the restless sleep and the more than two-day journey. Not knowing where to go or what to do, I followed the mass of people getting off the train. In the tunnel of the station, I finally stopped, perplexed by which direction to continue. That's when we met.

Actually, he scared the crap out of me when he said "Hello. I'm Jared. You look like you need some help."

I grabbed my bike and tried to put some distance between us. He was too close to me, not for being a stranger, but for my recently acquired fear of men.

"Don't worry, Kitten," he said comfortingly. "I'm gay. I'm not going to hurt you."

He must have known what I was thinking by the look on my face and was trying to calm and reassure me. Though he didn't have any glaringly obvious gay traits that are overly embellished in the movies and TV, I honestly believed him. I wouldn't have know from first hand experience since I hadn't known anyone who was gay or openly gay prior to meeting him. There just was a look in his face that I couldn't explain. A look of understanding. I swore I saw myself staring back at me.

He must have seen my expression relax, encouraging him to coax me more by gesturing with his hands as he took a few steps backward away from me through the tunnel to the right. "Come on. Looks like you could use some food. Maybe even some coffee. Do you like coffee?" He paused as his genuine smile grew bigger.

Calmer, I took a step towards him with my bike in tow while shaking my head in response to wanting coffee.

Assuming I was answering his latter question, he confessed, "Coffee's overrated anyhow. How about some tea instead, then?"

I hesitantly nodded as I slowly stepped towards him.

"Great. Follow me," he said as he turned his back to me and started walking. Every few steps he would turn his head over his right shoulder to make sure I was still with him and hadn't run off.

I was at a place in my life where I needed a friend, and for some unknown reason, it was meant to be him. At the time, I didn't know why, but I was grateful and still am. Since the accident almost three months prior, I'd had no one, until Jared.

Jared was kicked out of the house by his parents when he was eighteen. Apparently, according to Jared, they were God fearing, devout bible readers. That was the only book they read and they read it every day. Jared had come out to them the night of his high school graduation, convinced that they would love and accept him. After all, he was their only son. Unfortunately, his father spat venomous words at him as he tried to strike Jared with his belt. The disturbing thing was that it wasn't the first time Jared was ever beaten by his father. He had received lashes in the past as a young boy for being foolish or misbehaving, but that night something snapped in Jared. After taking three blows to the body without flinching, he grabbed the belt on the forth swing, ripped it from his father's hands, and returned the heartless attack on his father. He didn't say a word, but stopped on the thirteenth smack when Jared's mother begged him to stop. She didn't stand up for Jared, ever, and he probably thought to whip her as well, but didn't. She gave him as much money as they had in the house plus a check made out to cash and pleaded for him to pack his bags and leave. I think she was trying to save both of them.

Jared was almost nineteen when we found each other. He had been living on his own in a small rundown studio apartment on the edges of Chinatown. The only time he would leave his apartment before he met me was to go to work. His demons still haunted him too. We were both lost, but then found that day in the tunnel.

As Jared completes his review of what I have written down for the third quarter's schedule, I look to him for his thoughts and suggestions. He seems seriously impressed and it takes him a little longer to verbally respond than I'm used to. It must be the early morning hour that is causing Jared's brain to not fully catch up quite yet.

Glancing at me he says, "Damn. I think this is terrific!" Still with a little bit of shock on his face, "Man, Emma. You've surprised me yet again."

Humbly, I reply with a smile, "Thanks."

Chapter Two

Jared adds in some other pointers to add to the Lesbian - Gay - Bisexual - Transgender, or LGBT, section of the website from some recent comments and questions he's collected from our social media platforms and his friends.

Sadie gnawing on her bone catches our attention, and Jared becomes excited again.

"I have and idea!" he shouts.

"What?" I question.

"It might sound a little silly . . . at first, that is," he cautiously replies.

"Just say it. You know I like ideas," I instruct, prompting him to share his idea.

I'm having trouble understanding his hesitation. Maybe he isn't completely sure of my mood yet. I'll have to do some better convincing.

"You've done a lot already this morning. I don't want to add to . . . ."

"Just spit it out," I politely demand, smiling as I cut him off.

"Ok . . ." he begins, seeming to be more confident now in his decision to bring it up. "We should create a whole section for pets. Mostly dogs to start because of Sadie, but I think we can increase the follower base even more. Sadie would be the face and we write everything from her perspective . . . well, our assumption of her perspective that is . . . what do you think?"

My business, Naturally Me, is a health and wellness blog that focuses on organic and natural products, recipes and the like. When I started it about six years ago, it was to suffice my interest, fascination and experimentation with female health, beauty and food products and questions about alternative health that I started to use when I changed my daily habits after some rocky moments I had while trying to figure out my life during the first two years in California. Jared was a very loving and patient friend from the start, even after learning about my demons.

I was already a computer wiz thanks to being homeschooled and my mother encouraging my learning to be around whatever topics interested me at the time. I was proficient in computer coding and graphic design by the time I was fifteen among other things. I was technically a high school graduate at the age of fourteen. Mom wanted me to have my high school diploma regardless of her thoughts of the ill-effectiveness of the public school system, so she scheduled the testing. The district actually had me take the test a second time, not because I didn't pass, but because my scores were close to perfect and they wanted to make sure I wasn't cheating. Mom was pleased with her teaching ability after the second test results came back practically the same as the first. Not wanting to thrust me into college at my young age, Mom began introducing me to a variety of college based courses until — well, let's not get back into that.

The blog took a little time to get going, but after the first two years, it started to pick up enough that I was making almost twice as much as I was working with Jared at Jensen's Florist. By the third year, I was making even more, almost four times as much money. Not long after the start of Naturally Me's third year, Jared gave me some inspiration for topics to address on the blog from hearing him recount or discuss certain subject matters with me and his other friends. Knowing that I wasn't quite legal yet to get into bars to see and hear everything first hand, I asked Jared to do some recognizance for me. Not understanding why I was so curious, two weeks later he showed up with a fake ID for me. Not willing to use the ID right away, I explained to Jared how I wanted to expand the blog. He instantly loved the idea.

Shortly after Jared's insatiable desire to see what he could find, he and I were quickly overwhelmed by the sheer volume of talking points we could add to the blog. From then on, Jared spent all his free time helping me establish the LGBT division of the blog with him as the face until I could pay him the same amount or more as Jensen's. Proudly, I was able to match his monthly income from Jensen's in just four months.

Currently, Naturally Me offers its readers health and beauty tips, tricks, product reviews, product referrals, homemade recipes along with a section dedicated to cuisine, home decorating, contests and giveaways, and an exclusive LGBT section. The thought of another division is mind blowing . . . but real.

Naturally Me expanded its reach by the end of its fourth year with the use of internet video sharing that allowed the company to instantly start making additional income which grew faster than I believed possible. Now, not only is Jared the main face of Naturally Me, he manages all communication and task completion between me, Naturally Me, and Naturally Me's independent contractors who handle our research, graphic design, video and editing, general inquiries and social media.

"Holy crap, Jared!" I blurt out in sheer astonishment.

"Yeah?!" he hesitantly replies.

"No. Seriously," I exclaim. In shock, then awe and joyous appreciation for the man, I squeal in excitement, "You are a genius!"

"Oh, stop it!" he counters, trying to seem bashfully innocent and humble.

I glare at him with a devilish smile to his response, suggesting that I know what he's doing, but pleased with his brilliance. "We can incorporate the pet section into the third quarter easily. We can hire a few more people to handle it under your direction."

"Sweet!" he shouts with enthusiasm. "Looks like I should be getting a bonus at the end of the year," he says teasingly.

"I'll throw in a night at your favorite strip club if it goes the way I'm envisioning it in my head," I toy with him with a sense of half truth.

"Mmmm . . . You sure know how to please a man," he replies, winking at me with a dirty grin. We both snicker like school girls for a moment before turning back to the project at hand.

Chapter Two

Happy with our successful meeting and my true love and gratitude for my friend, I tell him, "I love you, Jared."

He looks at me quizzically for a second. Not sure where I'm going with this suddenly serious tone. He tries to brush it off lightly joking around, "Yeah, yeah. I know. I love you too, *Sex Kitten*."

"No. I'm serious."

He rarely sees the serious and openly emotional side of me, let alone the fact that I don't say those three words loosely to just anyone or in just any context. Appreciatively and affectionately, I smile and repeat myself, "I love you."

Respectfully, he pauses to take in this still unaccustomed moment. Jared, genuinely grateful for the moment, smiles and replies back, "I love you too, Emma." He leans over to embrace me.

We sit, reassuring each other for several minutes and start cracking up when Sadie decides to wedge herself between our arms and onto our laps. Sadie never misses a beat.

We continue hashing out the details for the third quarter's targets to include the pet division while sipping on tea and coffee. I leave Jared to his now coherent and animated concentration to fix him some breakfast. Surprisingly, I can hear his stomach grumble in protest to his second cup of coffee in demand for more sustenance.

A few hours later, content with our goals and objectives, we resolve to bring our business meeting to an end. Any in-person meetings after this will be brief to just review the progress of what's scheduled and the testing of any new products that have arrived, unless it's to just get together and hang out.

"I need to check the P.O. Box for deliveries," Jared admits. "I completely forgot to before coming here."

"That's fine. You were here really early," I reply, letting him off the hook.

He did come over much earlier than regular, two hours earlier.

"How about we check after going out for some lunch?" I suggest.

His eyes gleam with elation. Grinning and pleased, Jared puts his notes and iPad into his bag.

Before we head out the door, I turn off the music streaming from the Baroque classical music playlist on my computer that has been playing since just before I got into the shower. I am disappointed to hear my favorite song, Suite for Cello No. One in G Major by Johann Sebastian Bach, start playing. I almost hesitate to turn it off, but both Jared and I are hungry and need to get out.

If I were musically inclined, I would have learned cello or violin, but alas, I am not blessed with the ability to play. I can dance and follow any beat. Jared and I have taken dances lessons for practically every style of music, but my creative gifts and abilities are the visual arts. Though I can't play an instrument, I have always been able to pick up tones and notes, which help greatly with the variety of languages I speak other than English.

My parents wanted the best for me. They never forced their views, religious beliefs or their particularly desired topics of study. They made learning a game, and I loved it. Though we were never able to travel internationally, we wanted to learn as many languages as possible. Before the accident, I spoke fluent English, Spanish and French, and had four months into learning Mandarin. Each day of the week we would speak only in one dialect regardless if we stayed home all day or went out. It was funny to see people's faces when we spoke in a different language. We got the most looks when we spoke Spanish or Mandarin, but we didn't care.

"Where do you want to eat?" Jared asks as I pick up my purse, keys and hook Sadie's leash onto her collar.

"What are you in the mood for?" I answer with another question.

"Well . . ." he pauses for a second to decide.

Jared knows not to go back and forth with me on asking each other. It could take an hour before he caves in and chooses a place. I always win. As much as I like control, I know I'd be content with any restaurant he chooses.

"I want to go to Stinky Pete's."

Noticing his devilish smile, designed to get a specific response from me, I simply smile and nod.

"You sure?" he inquires, trying to get me to break.

"Sure. If that's where you want to eat," I reply with a relaxed grin.

He will not break me.

"You're no fun," he jokingly whines and sticks his tongue at me as I walk closer to him. "Besides, you know I can't stand their food either."

I smirk as he surrenders easily in defeat.

"Let's have Indian. What was the place we went to last time?" Jared questions.

"Akbar?"

"Yep. That's the one. I loved that place. I think it's my favorite Indian restaurant in town." He closes the door behind Sadie and me.

Though most places in Pasadena have outdoor seating, which is used the majority of the year, Akbar does not. The restaurant is on a side road off Colorado Boulevard which makes dining there more quiet and less distracting. With Jared as the main face

Chapter Two

of Naturally Me, we occasionally get interrupted at meals, especially if we are dining outside and he's not wearing sunglasses or a hat. My first name and face are used for the business as well, but I try to minimize how much my photo is posted. I don't enjoy being in the public eye as much. By bringing Sadie onboard, that may change.

Since we're bringing Sadie along for lunch, I grab her service dog vest to grant her access into the restaurant. Sadie is not a full-time service dog, but I did have her trained and certified so she can go anywhere with me. With the vest on, Sadie is accepted everywhere.

For our meal, Jared and I share several of my favorite dishes from Akbar. Since he can't remember what he had the last time, he asks me to order. Knowing he's hungry, that he can pile a fascinating amount of food into his belly, and that we have the rest of the day to enjoy each other's company, I chose to order a full three course meal.

To start, we treat our taste buds to samosa, mixed green katchumber and the kaske-badamjan. Jared rinses his food down with a glass of water and mango lassi. I just have water. About five minutes after we finish the appetizers, our waiter delivers us tandoori salmon, tandoori chicken, vegetable bhuna and a side of rice suffused with saffron. Jared takes photos of each dish with his cell phone and even has me take a few pictures of him posing to post on his social media for all his adoring fans to view.

As we eat, our conversation bounces around a myriad of topics, mostly memories of glorious excursions we've had together and many of them that included Maggie. We recount our clubbing days in WeHo and all the weird and eclectic types of people who would hit on all three of us. Jared would be hit on by every gay man, whereas Maggie and I would get hit on by the women. Maggie and I never minded being hit on by other women. We felt safe around them compared to men, especially me.

Three

A fear of men, heterosexual men, came from my last night in New Jersey. After the accident, the State arranged for me to go into foster care once I was released from the hospital. I didn't have any family other than my parents; they were orphans too. I was in a daze when the whole process began. Eight days after waking up in the hospital, I was turned over to state custody. I would have been handed over sooner, but they were monitoring me to make sure I wasn't a danger to myself anymore. I was placed with a husband and wife who already had two foster girls. Brittany was seven and her sister, Leslie, was five. The State was apparently so bogged down with foster kids, that they weren't as picky with foster parents as they should have been. I had to share a room with the two girls. They slept in one bed and I slept in the other. Though I already was a high school graduate, the State and the foster parents insisted that I attend public school. I just figured they didn't really want to bother with me. The teachers were nice, but I was bored and depressed.

Two weeks into living with the foster family, I started taking care of Brittany and Leslie. Dean and Amber, the foster parents, if you can even call them that, wouldn't really bother with me or the girls. They both drank, were unemployed, watched TV the majority of the day, unless they went out, and it was clear that they were living off of the foster care money. I wondered if the social worker who placed me with them knew that Brittany and Leslie needed me.

I had stopped talking since the day I woke up in the hospital, but that didn't seem to hinder me assuming a motherly role for the two girls. They were young, sweet and never a handful. Since I wasn't really sleeping either, and I was up before the girls from the nightmares, it was easy to make sure they were dressed and fed before walking them to the elementary school which was right across the street from the high school. At the end of each school day, they would wait for me until my school was over. We'd walk home, do homework, and then I'd take them out to play for an hour before going inside to cook dinner. The brutal cold winter weather was much more palpable than the storms of Amber and Dean. After dinner, we'd play some more in our bedroom before I got them bathed and ready for bed. Since I didn't speak, the girls would pretend to read books and describe a different adventure each night from the pictures. They were even able to make me smile a few times.

Our daily morning and evening routine for the week spilled over into the weekends. I would take the girls out of the house for the whole day to avoid the foster parents' drunken fits and rages, which occurred daily. We didn't have

Breathe In

any money, but we always had fun everywhere we went. I was determined to distract them and myself from the miserable house we lived in. Since the foster house was a brick row home in Hoboken, we did have some nearby places to go to other than the park when the days were too cold from the winter gloom. We'd venture around town going to the local bookstore and some of the shops on the block. One of the restaurant owners would invite us in to rest, warm up and even started giving the girls and myself food every time we visited. The owner, Martin, was even nice enough to invite us to the Christmas and New Year's feasts he and his wife would host in their home above the restaurant. I made sure we attended. It was a pleasant distraction. They even gave the girls and me a few gifts, mostly clothing, but we accepted graciously.

On one particularly dreary day, towards the end of January, Dean saw us in Martin's restaurant from across the street. He was picking up his weekly secret ration of liquor that he hid from Amber — I knew where he hid it. Spotting us in the window, he stormed into the restaurant shouting and cursing. Dean accused me of stealing money and sneaking the food we were eating as he grabbed me by my still injured right arm just below my shoulder — when I was released from the hospital, I never received any further care for my injuries. One of the restaurant staff members quickly ran to get the owner.

Martin intervened by placing himself between Dean and me. "She didn't steal money from you, Dean!" Martin shouted loud enough to make his point to Dean while trying not to scare Brittany and Leslie. "Get out of my restaurant. You are not welcome here. The girls are, but you aren't." Martin nodded to Conor who was behind the counter and Conor picked up the phone.

"Don't you tell me what to do," Dean's mouth slurred.

"I gave the girls the food. Let them be and go home," Martin insisted, taking a step closer to Dean.

"Who the hell do you think you are?" Dean blurted out with a breath that reeked of whiskey that I could smell even six feet away.

"This is my restaurant. Get out before I call the cops," Martin demanded.

"Fine, but they're coming with me," Dean barked as he reached to grab Leslie's left forearm, but Martin blocked him.

"No. I'll bring them home later after they are finished and you've calmed down," Martin sternly commanded.

Dean glared at Martin with rage. Suddenly, Dean went to strike him, but missed as Martin easily moved out of the way, causing Dean to fall to the floor.

I wondered if he saw the punch coming.

Chapter Three

"That's it . . ." Dean muttered as he tried to stand up straight several times. He repeated his attempts to strike Martin; each time Martin ducked and Dean fell.

The police station wasn't far, so the police arrived just after one of the times Dean got to his feet, still stumbling from intoxication.

Once the police removed Dean, the girls huddled on my lap. Martin and Conor cooperated with the police and gave statements. The police tried to get me to talk, but Martin told them that I was mute. So instead, they just asked questions and I nodded or shook my head.

The girls and I finished eating slowly out of complete amazement and shock of what had just occurred. I cringed at the thought of what would happen when we got back to the house that evening. I prayed that they would keep Dean locked up until morning.

When Martin and his wife, Celia, dropped the girls and me off at the house, they parked the car and followed us in. The house was dark and empty. They hugged us goodbye and Celia gave me their phone number just in case anything should happen. I nodded my understanding and appreciation.

I picked up Brittany and Leslie and carried them upstairs. I knew they were exhausted and scared from what had happened with Dean, so I only had them change into their pajamas. Instead of tucking them into their bed, I climbed in and gestured for them to join me. I sat up against the wall as Brittany and Leslie fell asleep with their heads on the pillow I had placed across my lap. Nervous about Dean's state when he finally comes home, my eyes stared unblinking at the wall across the room.

The need to leave was evident — good thing I never really unpacked my stuff from my two bags when I first arrived. Once the girls were asleep, I quickly and quietly snuck out of their bed. I stuffed the rest of my things into one of the bags and took them both to the backyard. I strapped one to the front of the bike and left the other one on the ground next to it. It would be on my back when I was ready to leave. Then, I returned to girls. I couldn't just leave them home alone without any adult supervision, but I was scared.

The sound of a door being slammed roused me and my head jerked up. I blinked my eyes rapidly to clear them as I listened. I slowly crept off of the bed, trying not to stir the girls, but desperate to know who had arrived. I tipped toed to the door and cracked it open slightly. I heard Amber mumble something and my heart settled a little.

As I turned after shutting the door quietly, time stood still as a roaring sound got closer. Dean's boots stomped up the stairs as he took them two at a time — I've seen him do it a number of times to know the echo.

"What the hell, Dean?" Amber shouted after him.

The door swung open just missing my back by a few inches, and before I was able to turn all the way around, his cold, rough hand was around my neck. My feet lifted slightly off the floor as he propelled my body into the bookcase behind me on the wall and held me there. My eyes, wide with fright, got even wider when the girls screamed in terror. Deans right arm hooked and caught me in my stomach. I clawed at his hand on my neck, gasping for air. Brittany suddenly jumped at his free hand as he swung back to give another excruciating blow. He flicked her off his arm like she was an ant, and during that brief moment of distraction, I was able to clip him in his groin with my right knee. Dean slumped to the floor wailing in pain.

Still gasping for air, I saw Amber standing in the doorway frozen and watching. I stumbled to Brittany to help her up when one of Dean's hands seized my right ankle and yanked it, swiping my feet out from under me. I fell onto my still injured right shoulder with a thunderous sound, just missing Brittany by an inch or two. The pain in my right arm subsided, most likely due to the rush of adrenaline coursing through my veins, as I quickly rolled and shoved my left foot into Dean's face.

I ran to the doorway and shoved Amber out of the way. She was still standing frozen like a statue. I stumbled downstairs to get the phone. Before dialing, my eyes were drawn to Amber's body that thudded heavily down the stairs followed by Dean staggering in delight. My eyes searched for things to throw at him as I pressed 9-1-1-send. I tossed the phone towards Amber's limp body at the base of the stairs just as Dean lurched for the wrist of that hand. Suddenly, pain exploded in my head. I was on my back on the floor. Dean towered over me and my eyes flickered to see Brittany grabbing the phone from behind him. Good, he didn't see her.

"You fucking bitch!" Dean howled at me. "You fucking bitch! I'm going to fucking kill you." Dean hovered over me as I tried to shake the dizziness from my aching head. We locked eyes and my body froze at the expression on his face. "But first . . ." a sinister voice oozed from his mouth. "I'm going to have a little fun with you."

As he lowered his body over mine, I scrambled to get away and kicked furiously at him, almost clipping him in his manhood again, but he deflected my attempts. He pinned both of my hands above my head with such force that I felt the rug burning my skin. I screamed out in horror.

"That's it. Scream. Fight. It will make this all that more enjoyable," he growled his intent.

Chapter Three

Trying to unbuckle his pants in his drunken stupor — Dean must have refueled himself after Amber bailed him out of jail — my left arm broke free and I jabbed my thumb into Dean's right eye. He yelped in pain as both of his hands shot to his eye. Feeling me scurry away, he swung his left arm as he tried to focus and find me with his only good eye. I swiftly kicked him again in the groin and down he went.

I took a few steps back to give myself distance from him as I plotted my next attack. Brittany caught my attention and nodded, waving to the phone as she and Leslie embraced each other. I nodded back. She pointed to the closet at Amber's back and my eyes lit up, remembering the baseball bat.

I grabbed the bat and handed the girls their coats and boots as I escorted them to the front door. I unlocked it for them to leave, but turned around abruptly when I heard Dean trying to crawl at us.

"Get back here, you bitch!" he grumbled,

I raised the wooden club above my head, poised to whip it down into the side of his skull.

"Emma?" Leslie uttered meekly.

I looked back pained, realizing that Brittany and Leslie were still in the house. Lowering the bat, I thrusted my foot into the side of Dean's head. He was out cold after that.

Compelled by a vengeful thought, I went over to Dean's hidden liquor stash and found eight bottles of whiskey, five bottles of tequila, and four and a half bottles of vodka along with several boxes of cigarettes. Dean doesn't smoke — I never saw him and never smelled it. Picking up one of the boxes, I was surprised to see wads of money stuffed in them. I opened one box all the way and it was packed full of one hundred dollar bills. I took all of the loose cigarette boxes and a full carton that were hidden at the bottom.

I rushed back to the girls who were still standing in the front door while Dean and Amber lay unmoving. Without saying a word, the girls knew my intentions and hugged me. I could hear the police cars in the distance and knew the clock was ticking for me to get away. I gave Brittany four of the six packs of money along with a piece of paper. Brittany hung up the phone on the police dispatch. I punched in the number for Martin and Celia and held it to her head.

"Martin," she said confirming more than questioning as the phone rang on the other end.

I nodded.

We embraced and for the first time since the accident I spoke, "Take care of each other." They sobbed as I led them out front before I turned to leave; they probably knew we would never see each other again.

I snuck out the back to my bike after grabbing my coat from the closet. I hoped that the police would handle the situation at the house for the next few hours and not bother looking for me right away. With pain seeping back into my bones, I rode to the Hoboken train station, got on the arriving shuttle and rode it to Union City station near the home I grew up in. The neighborhood was dark and motionless at four o'clock in the morning and an empty feeling crept into my heart.

My house was lifeless when I found the spare key under the back step and unlocked the door to let myself in. Nothing had changed. Nothing had moved. The State hadn't done anything to it yet. Thank God.

I went into the house only to collect a few things. I knew that I couldn't stay. My eyes remained dry the entire time as I went throughout the house grabbing what I needed and wanted. I switched out some clothing, grabbed some non-perishable food from the kitchen and opened the safe my parents had hidden in the wall of the closet at the top of the stairs that no one would be able to find — unless you knew to look. The safe was there for emergencies. This was an emergency.

My parents weren't rich, but they were smart and they made sure to pass that on to me. There was ten thousand dollars cash, our social security cards, birth certificates, and even passports that we never got to use. I grabbed it all before fastening it closed again.

I left the house with nothing other than a few family pictures, a few of my mother's books, my laptop computer, Mom's first aid kit to help with my injuries, and never looked back as the door closed shut. A single tear found its way down my face that night, but it was the only one.

Still aching, I biked back to the train station that let me off eight blocks from the house. I knew I had to get away, far away, or else the State would thrust me into another questionable situation. This time, I rode to the Newark station and bought a one-way ticket to California. It was several hundred dollars more for a private room, but I didn't care. It was a small price considering the amount of money I had on hand. I stopped in the twenty-four hour convenience store that was across the street to pick up a few minor things before hiding in the restroom of the station until boarding to make sure I wouldn't be spotted — just in case the police were looking for me. While in the restroom, I cleaned myself, used some of the stuff from my Mom's first aid kit and ate some of the food I had in the bag.

Chapter Three

I looked in the mirror and knew that another step needed to be taken before leaving the restroom, using the materials I purchased from the convince store. When I finally stepped out to board the train, my naturally dirty blond hair that flowed just below the middle of my back was now jet black and shoulder length. I blended with the small group of passengers easily. The sling for my injured right arm would stay hidden under my jacket until I got to my private cabin.

The journey went smoothly. I stayed in my cabin for most of the ride across the country, only exiting my accommodations to eat a few times or use the restroom. After my first round of sleep and food, I counted the money Dean had hidden in the cigarette cartons several times. I was shocked to find out that I had nineteen thousand, four hundred and seventy-eight dollars total, including the ten thousand I had gotten from my parent's safe. I rolled up the majority of the money in small wads and hid them inside my bike frame. No need to have that much exposed. The cash would buy me time to find a place to stay and get a job. Unable to sleep consistently for the rest of the trip, eating or reading became my main distraction while awake.

A weight was lifted from my heart and gut when I stepped off the train and breathed in the sunny, cool air of California. Though I didn't know where to go or what to do at the moment, I didn't care. I felt free.

That's when I met the man that sits before me today, sharing with me this wonderful meal, this wonderful moment. He is not just a friend. He has become family. He has become my brother. Other than my parents, he and Maggie are the only two people who truly have my heart — and who could break it.

Before heading back to my apartment after lunch, Jared and I decide to walk Colorado Boulevard to do some shopping instead of going to the P.O. Box right away. We take a break on Miller Alley to get some gelati and to give Sadie some more water and a little snack before resuming our stroll. We both find a few cute items in Banana Republic and J. Crew that are on sale. We figure we owe ourselves a little shopping spree after our successful morning. Jared complains at the lack of accommodations Kate Spade has for gay men before continuing on.

Our last stop is at Tiffany's. I'm not a big jewelry kind of girl, but all that sparkle is sure fun to drool over. They do have a beautiful pair of ruby studded earrings that I decide to purchase. I convince the salesman to give me a good discount by flirting with him. Jared tries to sell me on the ruby teardrop set that are encrusted with diamonds, but I politely decline. I may have money, but I never go anywhere that would warrant wearing those gorgeous accessories.

Dropping us off at the gate, Jared kisses both Sadie and me as we say farewell. Returning to the apartment, I find a place for each of my new items. Snuggling on the couch with Sadie, I read a book to kill some time before dinner, then some business research and streaming a movie before bed.

Four

A few days later, I spend the entire day cleaning my whole apartment from top to bottom. Mia, my cleaning lady, would have a conniption fit if she found out that I was doing her job. She's been working for me since I moved into the Arc Apartments that overlook the Del Mar Train Station four years ago. Every week on Thursdays, Mia comes. She has a key for the times when I'm not home, which is the case the majority of the time.

Two weeks ago, I told her that I was giving her a paid day off for this week's worth of work. She knows that this time of year, every year, I give her time off, but she never knows why. Mia is a sweet young woman not much older than me. She speaks little English, but that isn't a complication since I'm fluent in Spanish. What's most important is that Mia is a person I can trust and my trust has to be earned before it is ever given.

There is only one day a year I partake in this obsessive cleaning habit and that is in preparation for the upcoming Chinese New Year. I learned about all of the Chinese traditions, old and new, from Maggie and her family. Her parents moved to America when Maggie was barely one-year-old.

Maggie is my other best friend. Jared and I met her a few weeks after I came to California. It was my second day on the job at Jensen's Florist with Jared when he and I decided to have some lunch at the Peking Wok Chinese Restaurant that is across the street and on the opposite corner from Jensen's in downtown Los Angeles. Maggie's parents, Mr. and Mrs. Li, opened their restaurant shortly after they had moved to America. Maggie didn't normally work at the restaurant during the day because of classes, but school was closed due to a national holiday.

Maggie greeted us at the door with a beautiful, bubbly smile that was infectious. We were seated just as their lunch crowd was dying down. Over the course of a few weeks, Jared and I stopped in for lunch or dinner at the Peking Wok and we ran into Maggie several times. Jared and Maggie did all of the talking since I still hadn't started speaking. I would nod in agreement when necessary.

When Maggie found out that we lived on the outskirts of Chinatown, she became instantly excited. Her family lived in Chinatown. Evenings or weekends when she was free from school or working at the restaurant, and when Jared and I were not working at Jensen's, the three of us would get together. One night in May about four months after I started living with Jared, Maggie came over to celebrate Jared's nineteenth birthday. Both Maggie and

Jared were shocked when they heard me speak for the first time. Their eyes opened wide and their mouths hung in astonishment after they heard me wish Jared happy birthday with a voice that sounded like sandpaper.

"Holy Shit!" Jared cried out, running over to hug me. "And, here all this time, I really did think you were mute."

After that night, if I spoke, it was to them and to them alone. Over time, I opened up to both of them more. Eventually I would speak to other people, but I kept quiet, reserved and guarded. We became best friends. We became family.

Turning on some music through my computer, I get to work cleaning the apartment with the occasional break to eat, play with Sadie or take her out for a walk. Cleaning the home before the New Year in Chinese tradition is a ceremony. It creates a fresh, clean environment to welcome the coming new year. Sweeping the dust away represents a wish to put away old things and bid farewell to the passing year. I find myself singing some of the Chinese songs I've learned over the past eight years from the Li family. They're comforting and reassuring as I go through this cleansing journey.

I don't follow every Chinese tradition that I have learned from Maggie and her family, but this cleansing ritual is one of my favorites, other than New Year's Eve and New Year's Day themselves. There is a feeling of healing that takes place for me each time I do this and I hope that the cleaning helps to rid me of my nightmares.

From sun up to sun down I keep cleaning, finally finishing by about eight-thirty at night. With everything back in place, I begin to sage the entire apartment as I say certain chants and prayers in Mandarin. The sage helps to ward off any negative energy as well as to bless the confines of my home.

The next day, both Jared and I are in Chinatown helping Maggie and the Li family prepare for the New Year. Shops and buildings are being decorated and certain streets are already marked as no-parking zones since some of them will be shut down for the parade. There's a feeling of excited chaos in the air.

Mǔqīn, Maggie's mom, is in the kitchen with Nǎinai, Maggie's grandmother and Amy, Maggie's cousin, organizing for the feast that will last from New Year's Eve night until late New Year's Day. Amy is two years older than Maggie and married to Eric Liu. They have a happy and adorable baby boy named Jet, who is eight months old and on the kitchen floor playing with pots, pans and wooden utensils. Eric is helping Fùqīn, Maggie's dad, at the Peking Wok.

We all pitch in to help. There is a ton of food to be prepped as well as decorations to be hung. The food for the Chinese New Year, also known as the Spring Festival, is very important and symbolic beyond the gathering of family. Every item is made from scratch. Dumplings made of minced meat and finely

Chapter Four

chopped vegetables are wrapped in a thin dough, spring rolls are stuffed with vegetables, a variety of fresh fish are cleaned and readied to be boiled, steamed or braised, followed by vegetables readied to be steamed while rice and noodles are set aside for soups and side dishes.

Năinai is singing as she rolls out the dough for the dumplings and cuts them. Maggie and Amy chime in from time to time as they wash dishes. Mŭqīn is placing the dumpling stuffing in the middle of each dumpling dough circle as Jared and I pinch the dumplings closed and shape them in our hands. Sadie is on the floor next to Jet acting as babysitter.

Everyone is only speaking Mandarin since Năinai doesn't speak English. I think she knows and speaks more than she lets on, but I'm not one to divulge her secret. Jared's Mandarin has improved immensely over the years. He still understands more than he can say, but he gets his point across. Every so often, Jared uses a slightly different inflection for a word which will cause us girls to giggle. That slight change in tone can change the whole meaning of a word.

At one point, Năinai stops singing and asks us all if we have met Maggie's new *love?* We all stop and stare at Maggie.

"Năinai!" Maggie shouts, thoroughly embarrassed.

"Who is he?" Mŭqīn exclaims with angered panic.

Mŭqīn wants her daughter married — happy too — but married, and still clings to her meeting a nice, Asian man.

"Don't worry, Mi. He's Chinese!" Năinai says with a proud grin on her face as she looks at Mŭqīn and Maggie.

Maggie's mom's name is Mi, but we all call her Mŭqīn which is the Mandarin word for mother, except for Năinai, who calls her daughter by her first name.

"What?!" Mŭqīn is clearly in shock.

"We aren't dating," Maggie argues. "He's been into the restaurant a few times the past couple weeks. We haven't even spoken to each other yet."

Maggie's habit is to tell Jared and me about a guy she's interested in once she feels that he's interested in her, which usually occurs after the second date, so I'm not surprised that she hasn't mentioned it prior.

"Liar," claims Amy. "I saw you talking to him yesterday and the day before that, and the time before that . . . ."

Jared and I just sit back enjoying the action that's unfolding before us. We've seen this scenario too many times before, but we're curious to see how this plays out with Mŭqīn because Maggie has never been interested in a guy who is Asian. Maggie wasn't allowed to date all through high school and when she started dating in college, she had a number of non-Asian suitors, whom Mŭqīn was not happy about.

Everyone's eyes are on Maggie waiting for her to explain.

"We didn't talk. Ok, I didn't talk much. I was in shock."

"Well, then what did he say?" Năinai chimes in before anyone else can say anything.

"He said *hello*," Maggie starts to share, but then pauses.

"And . . ." Amy presses her to continue.

"And, nothing really," Maggie says, trying to blow it off. Getting a look from Mŭqīn, Maggie sighs and proceeds, "He introduced himself. His name is Henry."

"Henry what?" Mŭqīn questions.

"I don't know. He didn't say," Maggie replies.

"Then what?" Năinai questions.

"He asked if I was going to be at the parade. I told him yes." Maggie's excitement about sharing the story is starting to stir despite her audience.

"So, is he going? I want to meet him," Mŭqīn says sternly.

"I'm not introducing anyone until I find out if he's interested," Maggie timidly asserts.

"He's totally interested. If he wasn't, he wouldn't have asked if you were going to the parade, Mags," Jared interjects.

"You think?" Maggie's giddy now.

Everyone looks at her in surprise. By this point, I think Maggie has done a mental head slap.

"So, where and when are you going to meet him?" Năinai queries.

"I'm not telling. It's a secret. Besides, I don't want to jinks it," Maggie announces with some tentativeness in her voice. "And, that's that. I'm not discussing it anymore." She looks to me and Jared reassuring us that we'll get the juicy details later when the rest of the family isn't around.

"Well, you know he needs to pass the friend sniff test before he's even considered to meet the rest of the family," Jared proclaims teasing her.

Mŭqīn is pleased. If anyone will give her insight to Henry, Jared will. She knows better not to press me for information. Mŭqīn does not scare me, but she sure does scare Jared.

Chapter Four

A few minutes go by before anything else is said. Nǎinai starts singing again to help take the edge off the paranoid anticipation hanging in the air and I join her this time. Mǔqīn and Nǎinai smile sweetly at me and everyone else starts singing too, even Jared, though he's not sure of most of the words.

The next day, New Year's Eve is met with the finishing touches of food and decorations along with a lot of silence and prayer before starting to enjoy the feast. Though it is not part of any tradition, Nǎinai starts to pray and bless the whole house and each person individually while giving gratitude for all the joys we have all brought to each other this past year. I think Nǎinai has created her own tradition as a joining of old and new. She respects her family and ancestors, but also accepts the beauty of change eagerly. She is a beautiful, loving, yet spunky, older woman. I don't dare call her old. She has the life force of a twenty-something.

Maggie and Jared come home with me tonight for New Year's Eve. I think Maggie's nerves are getting to her about Henry and Mǔqīn is not helping. I've always been able to calm Maggie and distract her when she needs it.

After taking Sadie to the park for one last little stroll before calling it a night, the four of us pile into my king-sized bed after putting on our pajamas. As the night rolls over into the new day, we toast to the new year with glasses of champagne under the covers. Maggie refrains from telling me where she and Henry are meeting at first. She's afraid that Jared will tell Mǔqīn, not like it's really a big deal.

"I'm not going to tell Mǔqīn," Jared says for the sixth time trying to reassure her. "I love your mom, but you are my girl. I wouldn't do that to you."

"I know," Maggie replies meekly.

"If he tells her, I'll kick his ass for you," I assure — we all know I can kick his ass.

Jared introduced me to self-defense classes not long after meeting him, but I was fanatical about it. I never wanted to not feel safe, secure or in control after my run in with Dean. Thanks to my obsession, I'm well versed now and not afraid of anyone.

"See! Emma's got your back too," Jared presses.

"Ok. Fine." Maggie takes a breath. "We're meeting in front of the library."

"Ooo, how romantic," Jared taunts in his usual manner.

"Stop it," Maggie tries to command in a hurt tone.

She's not good at faking or lying.

"Be nice you two," I scold playfully.

"Will you come with me, Emma?"

"Me? Why?" I say confused. "You've never needed me with you when you've met guys before."

"I know. But . . ." Maggie hesitates temporarily. "I don't know. It would just be nice. Besides, I can't bring Jared along. Henry might think we are dating."

"If I tag along, he would probably just think I'm dating Emma."

"True," Maggie nods her head in agreement.

"Ok. But, I swear, if you tell Mŭqīn . . . ."

"I know, I know. Emma kicks my ass," Jared answers for her.

"You know, he might like that too much. I'm going to have to find another scare tactic," I comment grinning.

"That could definitely be a big possibility," Jared confesses.

We all laugh. I think the champagne has gone to our heads.

A few minutes later, we kiss each other goodnight, even Sadie. Jared lays in the middle of the bed with Maggie on his right and me on his left. Sadie is across the bottom of the bed with her upper body strewn over my legs.

"Here is to a great new year full of happiness and new beginnings for us all," I declare, turning off the light.

"Here, here," Jared responds.

"I love you both," Maggie states with a yawn.

"Love you, too," Jared and I say in unison.

Sleep falls upon us easily and quickly.

Five

Even fast asleep surround by the two most important people in my life, the only two people I really trust and feel safe with, I wake after having the nightmare of my parents death. Thankfully, I don't wake screaming. I don't know if the accident really occurred the way that I dream it, but because of it's timeless unchanging depiction, I fear that it did.

I roll slowly to check my phone that sits on the nightstand, careful not to rouse Jared or Maggie. Right on schedule. Only five hours of sleep as always. Sadie and I exchange glances before getting out of bed. I change into my workout clothes, feed Sadie, have my morning clay water, and then we make our way off to the park.

I check on Jared and Maggie when Sadie and I return. They're still resting peacefully. Sticking with my morning workout routine, I hit the rebounder that sits in the office as Sadie watches. Today, I close the door to minimize the sound from disrupting the sleeping beauties in my bed, and I also strap my phone to my arm to listen to music through headphones. About an hour later, my stomach begins to grumble as my energy level starts to feel depleted. As I stretch, Sadie takes her turn on the rebounder. She mostly just lays on it, but the thought of getting her on a larger trampoline and what she would do humors me. Looks like my turn around from the nightmare is even faster.

I still can't make my smoothie without waking the maidens in my room, so I settle for some fruit, raw yogurt and mix my power greens powder into coconut milk to tide me over until I finish showering. Letting my hair air dry, I put on sweats to wear until its time to leave. No need risking getting dirty the cute outfit I picked out for the day as I make breakfast for everyone. I do have an apron, but I always manage to get food on myself somewhere.

It's after six thirty now and Maggie and Jared are going to need to get up soon, so I start making a little noise in the kitchen as I prepare breakfast. I make a lot of food for us knowing that it's going to be a long, but fun day. I set out some smoked salmon, bagels, cream cheese, cut up some apples, pears and kiwi and put them onto a plate along with dried cranberries, dried mango and nuts. I add in two times as many ingredients in my blender for a smoothie, enough to be about eight ounces for each of us. Last, I get some free range turkey bacon cooking as I put some fresh, homemade cinnamon toast slices in the broiler that will be topped with some non-pasteurized butter. Just before hitting the on button for the blender, I tell Sadie to go wake up Jared and Maggie. Seconds later, I hear them grumbling.

"Mom. I don't want to go to school today," Jared whines, trying to be cute.

"Happy New Year!" I shout from the kitchen.

Both of them stroll in with their hair tossed a mess and rubbing their eyes.

"Ooo, Mom made us food!" Jared sings.

I give him a playful glare and smile.

"I don't know why you won't date, Emma. You'd be a great mom," Maggie claims.

I choose not to respond and just ignore her statement. Jared and Maggie watch closely for my reaction, but I refuse to give them the satisfaction.

I know that Maggie just wants me to be happy, and because she will be happy being married with kids of her own, I think she believes that I would be too if I'd just give it a try.

I don't date. I've never dated and that's by choice. I'm not a virgin by far. I've had a number of men that I've slept with. Okay — I've slept with a lot of men, but I don't do relationships. I simply use men for sex. A girl has needs too.

I won't sleep with just any guy, I have certain criteria that need to be met before a man is even considered. For starters, it has to be a man that I don't know. I'm not into the whole one night stand thing, though a few of them turned out fine, however, I'm not interested in knowing a guy too well. I like my privacy and my distance. Guys have to be more like an acquaintance of a friends' acquaintance so I have little to no interaction with them once I've had my fill. He needs to be handsome — attractive. I need to be physically turned on by the man enough, but how he speaks plays a huge roll. I've slept with some dumb ones, the male model type who have braun, but barely any brains. They are the easiest to lie to about what I do and where I live, but they are the ones who usually get attached the quickest, so I'm only able to use them about three or four times maximum. I stay away from the jock brains or the jocks with too much muscle that they can barely move — their type just doesn't do it for me. I've slept with a few cute geeky guys, but I like men with more meat on their bones. A physically fit man has a bit more stamina. I tend to sway towards the average guy. The type that are easy on the eyes, decent build, and who usually get overlooked at first glance by most women. The only challenge with them is that they have a tendency to want a relationship too, like the models, but the average men last about two to three times longer.

Chapter Five

There are also edicts that I've established for myself to minimize any casualties. I have several golden rules that I haven't swayed from since I started sleeping with men. One, no dating or going out on dates. Two, never let them know where I live. Lie if I must. Three, never pick up a guy in a particular social setting where I may frequently attend. Or, never sleep with a guy whom I have the chance to run into on a regular basis. Four, never have a guy over to my place for any reason. Jared is the only exception — and maybe a few of his gay friends, but they don't count. Five, end things before they start to want more. Six, always use protection. Seven, never sleep over at their place. Once we've finished, I get dressed and leave. This usually shocks them. I guess I act more like a guy than they expect. Eight, always have more than one exit strategy.

"What time does Mǔqīn need us today?" I ask, chewing on some fruit.

"She needs us around nine," Maggie confirms as she stuffs a huge bite of her bagel topped with cream cheese and salmon into her mouth.

"Good. Then we've got enough time for you two to get ready and head down on the train without rushing," I say to keep them focused on some semblance of a schedule. I gulp down my smoothie.

"What time are we supposed to meet *Romeo?*" Jared harangues Maggie while taking a few bites of turkey bacon.

Maggie looks at him with her eyes squinting a little and her mouth scrunched to one side in what appears to be her contemplating how to respond, "Twelve-thirty."

She tries so hard to appear angry, but Maggie has never really done angry well. Actually, I've never really seen her angry.

Jared and I chuckle a little.

"I hope you aren't going to wear sweats today, Emma," Maggie says, trying to change the subject.

"No. Of course not. I planned on changing after we had breakfast. Besides, I can dress however I want. I'm not the one meeting . . ." I attempt to pick on her too, but I fall short of calling Henry *Romeo*.

"Ha ha . . . very funny," Maggie tries to shrug off my lightheartedness while still trying to be offended when Jared snickers.

"What did you bring to put on?" I question to ease her nerves.

"I know it will be cool, yet warmer than usual, so I brought a cute new red dress. Amy helped me pick it out." Maggie's excitement is returning. "What are you wearing?"

Breathe In

"I've got a red, silk, long sleeve, fitted blouse and jeans that I was going to wear with those red velvet flats I bought when we went to the outlets a few weeks ago," I reply.

"Are you going to wear those new ruby studs you got too?" Jared questions.

"Yep. That's why I got them," I answer.

"When did you get ruby studs?" Maggie asks.

"When Jared was here last week going over the Naturally Me schedule. We did a little shopping afterward to celebrate the pet division," I explain.

"That's right. I remember you telling me," she recollects.

"How about you, Jared?" Maggie inquires. "What are you wearing?"

"I'm keeping it simple this year. Just a new red long sleeve henley shirt with jeans and my brown slip-on dress shoes. I felt like going relaxed this year," Jared responds.

Red is a symbolic color in the Chinese tradition. It's a color of luck which is why each one of us is wearing it in one form or another for the day.

"Well, one of you needs to get into the shower," I interject after checking the time.

"Yes, Mom," they say simultaneously.

They help me put away any food we didn't eat and rinse the dishes before putting them into the dishwasher.

Jared lets Maggie shower first since his hair doesn't take as long to dry. I bounce back and forth from my bedroom to the bathroom getting dressed and fixing my hair and make-up while Maggie showers. Jared sits on my bed updating me on the latest news of his fans reactions from the past week. Once Maggie is done in the shower, she leaves the water running so Jared can hop in. We feel completely comfortable being naked around each other. Jared's gay, so there's no weirdness there. He admires the female body, but has never been turned on by it. Women like Maggie and me have no challenge being naked in front of each other for a variety of reasons.

Once we're done getting ready, I grab Sadie's dog bag that is full of some of her basics; dog bowls, biodegradable relief bags, snacks and some toys. Mǔqīn has plenty of food in the kitchen, so I don't need to pack Sadie anything. We head down to the train platform that is in the middle of my apartment complex and jump on the next train heading South. A few stops later we're in Chinatown.

Chapter Five

Before leaving with Maggie to meet up with Henry, the three of us gather with Maggie's family; Năinai, Mŭqīn, Fŭqīn, Maggie's dad, Fŭqīn's brother and Amy's parents Jie and Jiao, Amy, Jet and Eric, Eric's parents P'eng and Xiu, Eric's older sister Kim, Kim's husband Peter and their two children Jade and Rey.

The children are given their Lai See first. Lai See, which means Good Luck, is a Chinese tradition which involves giving money in red envelopes from the senior members of the family to the junior members. Pretty much, married couples give Lai See to unmarried relatives, friends and colleagues. All three children, Jet, Rey and Jade receive Lai See. This is one of my favorite traditions, not for receiving any money, but because I can give the children a substantial amount of money each year for their future. The whole family says I always go a little overboard, but the Li family has given me so much, more than money can buy.

Năinai says several prayers welcoming in the new year, followed by specific and special blessings for each of us. When Năinai gets to Jared she bestows upon him happiness and love, but specifies love for Jared in the same sex realm of things. Mŭqīn and Fŭqīn shake their heads disapprovingly at Năinai's little show, but don't say a word. The whole family knows Jared is gay. They don't judge him and have considered him a son because of the friendship he has with Maggie and the rest of the family. I think Năinai was just making sure that everyone was paying attention to her. Then, Năinai turns to Maggie and bestows her with happiness, love and marriage and outwardly states that the family would be grateful if it is with Henry. Mŭqīn mutters under her breath. Fŭqīn chooses to just ignore her. Then, Năinai gets to me. She wishes for me to find full happiness and love, not just with the family that sits around me, but with my own family — a loving husband and children. She emphasizes the words husband and children. My eyes are as wide as they can get as I'm mortified and distressed at her proclamation. She's blessed me to be happy and to find love, but she's never specifically uttered the words husband or children before. She gives me a kiss on the top of my head as her hands hold me on either side over my ears.

"Looks like love is coming your way too, Emma," nudges Jared.

We know that Năinai is never wrong with her blessings.

"Not funny, Jared," I mutter under my breath while looking down at the floor.

"Maybe Henry has a cute friend. Wouldn't that be funny!" Jared announces, getting louder for the whole family to hear.

"Oh, that would be so much fun! We could date together! There were a few times he came into the restaurant with a friend or colleague," Maggie shouts with excitement.

Nǎinai smiles at me, pleased with herself. All I can do is purse my lips to stifle any kind of a reaction or response. Jet, who was playing on the ground with Sadie, suddenly decides to try to pull himself up using my pant leg. He is a much-welcomed distraction and aids in easing me out of the embarrassment I feel.

Unfortunately, Nǎinai decides to use Jet as confirmation for her blessing, "See how Jet is with you and you with Jet. You're a natural."

Jared and Maggie crack up at Nǎinai's continuation.

Fǔqīn scolds Nǎinai in my defense, "Leave Emma be."

Fǔqīn rarely intervenes and I nod my appreciation.

"Oh, Emma knows I'm just playing. Right, Emma . . ." Nǎinai retorts a little too proud of herself.

"Sure," I calmly reply back as my focus turns back to Jet who is sitting on my lap and playing with a strand of my dirty blond hair as he tries to reach for the red sparkling studs in my ear lobes.

Conversations continue as Jade and Rey play on the floor with Sadie until lunch which we eat earlier to make it to our seats for the parade. While we eat, Nǎinai is talking the entire time with food in her mouth, and I watch in amusement at everyone's interactions. Maggie is picking at her food more than really eating it. She's clearly nervous and anxious about meeting up with Henry. I hope he's not like the other guys she's dated before. I don't want to be pessimistic. I really just want her to be happy. Maggie falls in love easily, a little too quickly, only to be dumped after a few months. She recovers pretty quickly, but heartbreak is painful none the less.

Maggie taps her watch discreetly at me to indicate that we need to get to the library to meet Henry.

Nǎinai catches Maggie out of the corner of her eye and blurts, "Are you running late for a date, Maggie?"

"What? No," Maggie bashfully tries to deny.

"Don't lie. I know when you're lying," Nǎinai alleges as she wags a finger at Maggie. "Are you going to see Henry?"

"No. We, umm . . . the parade will be starting soon. We should head out to our seats," Maggie declares.

Jared tries hard to suppress a smile and giggle. Nǎinai watches Jared, Maggie and me carefully.

Chapter Five

"Oh, just go already," Mŭqīn shouts in desperation.

We always walk down to the parade together, so my guess is that Mŭqīn knows what's going on. You can't sneak anything past her.

"Thanks, Mŭqīn. Love you!" Maggie squeals as she jumps up out of her seat.

She practically runs to the closet by the front door to get our coats. I grab Sadie's leash and hook it on after I put on my jacket.

Once on the street heading towards the library, Jared questions, "So, how do you want this to go down, Mags?"

"What?" Maggie's definitely clueless to what Jared is talking about.

"Do you want us standing right there? You know, like you're obviously with us or do you want us to stand off to the side talking?" Jared explains.

"I don't know. Why?"

Maggie's anxiety has just gone up a few levels. I can see it in her eyes.

"Well, it all depends on what kind of a vibe you want to give off. Do you want him to know you're here with friends or not. Do you want to intimidate him a little with us being there or not?" Jared explains.

"I . . . I don't know," Maggie says with worry in her tone as she stops.

"Stop freaking her out, Jared," I defend, punching him in the arm.

"I'm not trying to freak her out. I just want to know how she wants us to approach the guy. Should we go right away or wait for her signal?" Jared replies. He is honestly trying to help her, but his timing is horrible.

"How about we'll play it by ear and if she wants us to move away before he gets there, she'll let us know," I offer.

"I like that," Maggie express, calming a little.

Approaching the library about ten minute early, Maggie suddenly stops in her tracks.

"You okay, Maggie?" I ask with concern.

"Yeah . . ." she reacts as her voices trails off.

I notice she's in a dead stare and follow her eyes. There are two men standing at the base of the stairs to the library talking. The Asian guy looks and stops too. His friend's back is to us and they are too far for us to hear their conversation prior to them stopping.

Maggie moves forward toward who I assume is Henry while at the same time he instinctually moves toward her. Jared and I proceed to follow Maggie, but stay a few steps behind her to give some space. Clearly there is a connection between the two of them, there's no denying it. They stop about a foot away from each other, eager to talk and touch bodies, but refrain themselves from physical contact.

Henry is as tall as me and his five foot eight inches stature towers a little over Maggie's five foot three inch petite frame. He's slim, but you can tell that he is muscular even under his lean, dark brown jacket, white with thin, red pin stripped button down dress shirt, dark khaki pants and brown casual dress shoes. I can tell his clothes are high quality without seeing the labels.

My attention is abruptly pulled away from Maggie and Henry chatting when my gaze falls upon the face of Henry's friend who is following Henry a few steps back. I pause for a brief moment as we lock eyes. I regain my movement forward when I realize that I had suddenly stopped.

"You alright, Emma?" Jared asks.

Unable to pull my eyes away for a second, I finally look to Jared, finding a weird look on his face, and respond, "Yeah. I just wanted to give them a little more space."

"Good idea," Jared replies as he drapes his arm around my neck and whispers in my ear, "So do you think he's gay or straight?"

"Who?" I question, confused as I try to retain my awareness and focus on the present.

"The friend," Jared states playfully.

My eyes shift back to Henry's friend and it feels like he never looked away. He smiles a half-cocked grin that curves up on the left side of his face. He too is wearing high-quality clothing in the form of a light blue button down dress shirt that makes his eyes sparkle, along with dark blue slacks and a pair of brown slip on casual dress shoes. His navy blue jacket is draped over his arm. This man is stunning. He has physical qualities that would allow him to be a male model if he choses, but he's got an air of confidence and something else that I can't quite make out in his stare. Luscious, thick dark brown hair adorns his head, but has flicks of what I would think is natural light brown highlights. He's taller than me, but only by a few inches, and he is only about an inch or two shorter than Jared. This man is yummy, causing my lady parts to react.

"Definitely not gay," I answer quietly.

For a gay man, Jared has miserable gay-dar. I'm his default detector.

"Damn," he states, revealing his disappointment.

I force myself to pay attention to Maggie and Henry, but this guy's ocean blue eyes have me mesmerized. The sound of Maggie's voice mentioning my name brings me back to the moment and I force my gaze to meet her's and then Henry's.

"This is Jared and Emma."

"Nice to meet you. I'm Henry," he offers, shaking Jared's hand and then reaches for mine, though I do not return the gesture.

I have a thing about touching strangers.

"This my good friend, Joe," Henry continues politely, almost sensing and understanding my uneasiness with physical contact and does not seem offended by my rudeness.

Crap. I have to look at his friend again. Compose yourself, Emma. I watch Joe and Jared shake hands and when Joe looks to me, I simply smile and nod. A look of disappointment appears on his face when I don't shake his hand. Typically, I don't care what others think of my habits. I shouldn't care, yet for some strange reason — this time, I kind of do.

"You'll have to excuse Emma. She's not very personable with strangers," Jared cuts in before the moment becomes too awkward and squeezes my shoulder into his body.

"Who is this?" Joe squats down to his knees to make himself eye level with Sadie, but keeps his attention on my face. His enigmatic smile has returned and he looks even yummier than before.

Instinctually, Sadie knows to place herself between me and anyone new. I don't like getting too close to anyone I don't know. She sits with her eyes glued on me watching and waiting for direction.

"That's Sadie," Maggie introduces for me.

Henry is a little timid to bend down like Joe. Joe doesn't move to touch Sadie and seems to be waiting for permission from me or her. I'm not sure.

Looking back down to Sadie, I can tell she's a little uneasy, which she is getting from me. I signal to her that it's okay to greet and Joe is her first target since he's right in front of her. He is the first person outside of Maggie, Jared and Maggie's family whom she bares her belly to on first contact. I'm in complete shock. Joe pets her vigorously from head to toe as if he's used to dogs and Sadie loves the attention. Sadie stays focused on Joe and keeps her body up against his like she's hoping that he will keep petting her as she greets Henry. She senses Henry's apprehension and goes easy on him.

Before Henry reaches to pet her, Maggie exclaims, "Sadie won't hurt you! She's a big softy and is great with my niece and nephews."

The tension in Henry's body relaxes a little as he reaches his hand forward to let Sadie sniff him.

"Here," Maggie encourages Henry and Sadie by putting her hand next to his slightly touching it. "She'll smell me mixed with you which will make it easier for you both."

Sadie sniffs his hand and gladly lets Maggie guide Henry's hand over her head.

"See, she likes you," Maggie says reassuringly.

"We should walk and talk to make it back to our spots on the street," Jared suggests.

Everyone agree and start moving towards the parade route. I'm surprised that they are both joining us. Maggie never introduces a guy to her family this quickly.

Maggie and Henry are in front, talking to each other. They seem very calm in the way they speak as if they've known each other for a long time. As we cross the street, I notice that Henry purposefully puts himself between Maggie and the street. Jared, Joe, Sadie and myself follow closely behind them not talking. Jared is closest to the store entrances as our arms are entwined, Sadie is between myself and Joe and Joe is along the curbside mirroring Henry.

We easily find Nǎinai and the rest of the family about fifteen minutes before the parade starts. Nǎinai gleams with enthusiasm, not for the parade, but at seeing Henry and Joe. Maggie makes introductions to the whole family in English. She explains who's related to whom and Jared adds how he and I tie into the whole family, pretty much as brother and sister to Maggie. Maggie and Henry stand side by side followed by myself with Jared behind me, then Sadie and Joe. The whole family listens intently to Maggie and then begins asking Henry a few questions.

"My parents are somewhere here. This is our first time seeing the parade in Chinatown, usually we're either back home in China or up in San Francisco to celebrate," Henry answers openly.

"What are your plans for the rest of the day once the parade concludes?" inquires Nǎinai, testing the boundaries of Maggie's new love interest.

She doesn't ask if he speaks Mandarin. It's assumed since he refers to China as back home.

"Nothing, really. Since we aren't familiar with the celebrations here, we figured we just follow along with what others were doing. We aren't here with any other family members currently," Henry replies back in Mandarin to Nǎinai.

She's very pleased that he speaks her native tongue. "Great! Then you, *Blue Eyes* here and your parents can join us for dinner," Nǎinai insists.

Chapter Five

Jared chuckles at Nǎinai, knowing who she is referring to by calling him *Blue Eyes*. Mǔqīn and Fùqīn are pleased that Nǎinai has invited Henry, Joe and Henry's parents and urges them to join us. They are clearly curious about Henry and his family.

Though she's giddy from all of the excitement, I notice that Nǎinai is cold, so I take off my jacket to cover her.

"Thank you, Emma," Nǎinai says gratefully.

I smile and nod.

"Now *Blue Eyes* can get a better look at you and your voluptuous body," she adds, grinning.

I take a deep breath, shake my head and try not to roll my eyes at her. I know what she's trying to do and I really hope that Joe doesn't understand Mandarin.

Jared does not contain his laughter as he hugs me from behind to keep me warm.

"Not funny, Jared," I scold him as I quickly look from him to Joe to catch Joe's reaction.

Maybe I can find out if Joe knows Mandarin too since he is Henry's best friend. He just looks at me and grins like he does each time our eyes meet.

"He doesn't know what I'm saying, " Nǎinai claims, slightly taunting me as she sees me studying Joe's face. "Look at him. He's been smiling the whole time and his face hasn't changed. I could tell him you're madly in love with him and want to have his babies and he'd just smile and nod."

I look back at Joe to find his smile hasn't changed — at least I don't think it has. God, I hope he isn't just being polite and really doesn't understand her.

The music begins as the parade commences, interrupting Nǎinai's goodhearted cajoling at my expense. We stand or sit watching, smiling and having a great time. After a while, Jade and Rey are running around our group playing and imitating the dancing that is taking place. Rey, who is only three, pretends that he is either a dragon or a lion. I'm not quite sure which. He's chasing after his older sister Jade, who is six.

Jared snatches up Rey, which Rey loves. "Uncie Jay," Rey shouts giggling. "Shoulders!"

Happy to fulfill Rey's request, Jared hoists him up.

I shiver at the disappearance of his body heat. Suddenly, I feel warmth blanketing around me. Joe has placed his jacket around my shoulders. It smells sinfully delicious and feels cozy.

Turning my head to Joe I say, "Thank you."

Joe leans into my right ear. "You're welcome." His warm breath is refreshing against my cheek. Our eyes meet again as he slowly pulls his face away.

"Looks like you have an admirer," pokes Jared.

I ignore him other than bumping him with my hip.

Jade stays near her brother holding onto my waist. I can see it in her face that she wishes she could be held up like that too. She's petite and I could easily holder her myself — I've done it before.

I offer to hold her, but Jade declines. "You look really pretty today, Emma," she says. "Not that you never don't look pretty. I just don't . . . ."

"I can hold you up if you'd like," Joe offers with a smile before Jade finishes her sentence.

Jade, though shy, immediately answers by moving over towards Joe, holding her arms up to him. Out of the corner of my eye, I see Năinai watching us.

"Look Emma, he's even great with kids. My blessing of love and marriage has come to you early this year!"

"You've given me the same blessing the past two years Năinai," I retort back in Mandarin. "And, it didn't happen then."

There is no way her blessing is coming true anytime soon if I have anything to do with it.

Năinai regards me and comments, "It will happen. I didn't bless you with a husband and children in the past."

My mouth opens as I'm about to rebut, but there's a look in her eye that I've never seen before. A sense of unshakeable definitiveness. It's a little creepy and I decide not to continue this conversation by closing my mouth.

At one point, Joe leans over to me and says something that is drowned out by all the music and noise. Since I can't hear him, I'm forced to lean in to hear him better.

"What?" I say, shifting towards him.

His eyes widen and his smile opens more, showing some teeth as he repeats himself, "Did I miss the memo about wearing red today?"

Aware of what he's trying to do, I choose not to be rude. "In the Chinese culture, red is considered good luck."

I guess his best friend failed to inform him. I wonder if this is his first Chinese New Year.

Overhearing us, Jade leans down and asks if he's ever celebrated New Year before.

Chapter Five

"Yes . . ." he replies, "But, not a Chinese New Year."

Jade giggles and then leans over to me and whispers, "Can we get him something red? You know, for good luck."

I look at Joe first as if I'm considering it. He gives me an inquisitive look indicating that he didn't hear what Jade said to me, and because there is no way I'm turning down this beautiful little girl, I smile at her, reach into my purse and give her a twenty dollar bill. "You choose. Just don't go too far," I instruct.

Jade beams and asks Joe to be let down. She stays within view as she stops over at a cart that is about fifteen feet away. I notice that Joe keeps his attention on her as well. A minute or two later, Jade comes bouncing back with something. She holds out her one hand to give me the change and I tell her to keep it. Her happiness turns into a full ray of sunshine as she shoves the money into her jacket pocket before anyone sees.

Keeping what she bought hidden in her other hand, Jade directs Joe, "I need your wrist, but no peeking."

Joe gladly obeys and fixes his gaze on me.

"There . . . all done," Jade exclaims after tying it on. "Do you like it?"

Joe's attention stays on me for a split second longer before looking down at his wrist. Jade found a beautiful, red beaded bracelet with a gold Chinese coin.

"It's perfect. Thank you," he confirms with a full smile directed at Jade. He takes her hand and kisses the back of it. "Ready to go back up?" he asks.

Jade nods, reaches her arms up, and in one fluid movement, she's back up on his shoulders. For a moment, I can't take my eyes off of him. When he starts to turn in my direction, I immediately look up at Jade to throw him off before I return my attention to the parade.

As the parade continues on for the next several hours, we all watch in amazement. At one point, I place my arms through the sleeves of Joe's jacket. I purposefully resist from looking in Joe's direction other than to look up at Jade only a few times. He's bouncing up and down as she waves her arms in the air.

Once the parade is finished, Jade and Rey join some other children playing in the street. All of the children are picking up the pieces of paper confetti and then throwing them back up into the air. Maggie announces that she's going with Henry to bring his parents back to the house. I ask if she wants us to join them, but she refuses my offer. She clearly wants some privacy with Henry. Kim starts to call Rey and Jade to join the family back at the house, but I tell her that I can stay with them so they can play until Maggie and Henry come back this way. Nǎinai grins deviously as she hands me my jacket and I take off Joe's to return it to him. Everyone else heads to the house except Jared, Sadie, Joe, Rey, Jade and me. I stay near Rey as Jared starts running around with Jade and copies whatever she does. Joe stays within a few feet of me. I'm not sure why. He doesn't strike up small talk, nor do I. Oddly, the silence isn't uncomfortable between us. Is he quiet like me, or just doesn't know what to say?

Suddenly, Jade and Jared are running toward us playfully screaming as they throw confetti at Rey, Sadie, Joe and myself. We grab some that fall to the ground and throw it back at them as Sadie tries to catch them in her mouth.

About fifteen minutes later, Maggie, Henry, and Henry's parents arrive. Henry makes brief introductions in English after finding out that the rest of the family has gone to the house. Everyone walks quietly except Maggie and Henry who are talking with his parents. Rey is starting to fall asleep in my arms, Jared is to my right, Sadie is on my left and Jade has found her perch on Joe's shoulders again who is standing on the other side of Sadie.

Back at the house, after more introductions, everyone sits down to start eating. The meal is slow and long, but entertaining. Everyone is speaking to each other in Mandarin during the entire meal but Năinai, Mŭqīn and Mrs. Wú are doing most of the talking with the exception of Fŭqīn, Henry and Mr. Wú on occasion.

Mŭqīn and Fŭqīn find out that they indirectly know Henry's parents, Lin and Nuo Wú, through mutual acquaintances and share pleasant stories of their friends and the differences between living in China and America. Later into the meal, the conversation eventually steers over to Maggie and Henry and then over to general topics for discussion. Everyone talks from time to time, even Jade and Rey except for Joe and myself. Mr. and Mrs. Wú question how Jared and I became a part of the family and all eyes turn to us.

I know that Mŭqīn, Fŭqīn and Năinai are being respectful by allowing Jared and I to tell our own stories, especially me since I'm not generally one to speak about myself. If we were all more familiar with the Wú's, I know that Năinai would be adding some of her own points. Jared instinctually knows to take the lead. I add in a sentence or two here and there, showing my respect to the Li family's guests, though it's uncomfortable for me. By the look on their faces, Mr. and Mrs. Wú seem impressed with the level of Mandarin both Jared and I speak.

Jared explains that he and I had met on my first day in California and that we became instant friends. His lack of a full explanation as to how I came to California comes up and he only mentions that I had just traveled across the country by train from the East Coast. He left a number of details out which

Chapter Five

he knows not to disclose. There is still a bit of information Maggie's parents don't know about me — I should say, I don't think they know about me, unless Maggie has filled them in.

Jared goes into describing how I started working with him at the florist shop that is across from the Peking Wok in downtown LA and how we met Maggie. He adds to his story how I was very shy and didn't speak much. He teases how Mǔqīn and Fǔqīn instantly fell in love with me because the first words that I spoke to them were in Mandarin. This creates smiles all around the table and Mr. and Mrs. Wú nod acceptingly of us. Jared jokes how Maggie's family was a little suspicious of him at first, but when they found out he was gay and not interested in dating Maggie, he was instantly accepted. Jared is not in the closet, but confirms who he is to certain people who may question it as well as to see how receptive they are to his orientation. Mr. and Mrs. Wú seem pleased with Jared's story telling and don't pry for more details.

Nǎinai asks how Henry and *Blue Eyes* know each other. I guess she feels it's only fair for them to share their story since Jared told ours. Before Henry begins his story, I look to Joe to watch for his reaction — nothing but smiles. Henry briefly explains that he and Joe had met their freshman year of college. They were roommates and have been like brothers ever since. Henry kept his story simple and short as well, obviously leaving out many details like where they went to school, what they were studying and other incidentals.

Later, as most of us finish eating, everyone continues sitting around talking and Jade joins me by sitting in my lap. She loves everyone in her family, but she usually singles me out at some point or another when we're all together. Her legs are on either side of my lap as she faces me and twiddles with a lock of my hair.

"Do you think he likes his gift?" Jade asks me in Mandarin.

"Who?" I question to make sure I know to whom she's referring.

"Joe silly," She indicates with a giggle.

"I would think so. He's wearing it isn't he?" I encourage, smiling back at her.

"Yeah . . . but that doesn't mean he likes it," Jade states with a little disbelief.

"Then, ask him," I politely instruct.

Jade turns her attention to Joe who is sitting across from me and poses her question.

"Yes. Very much so. I'll keep it forever and ever," Joe replies in Mandarin with a smile.

Everyone who hears Joe's response stare in astonishment since he spoke Mandarin.

Crap. He knew what Năinai and I were talking about this whole time. It makes sense. No one ever asked him or Henry if he spoke Mandarin let alone ask him anything in Mandarin to hear his response. Everyone who didn't know him just assumed he only spoke English.

I start to panic, knowing that he heard every single world Năinai was saying to me about him. I am mortified, but skillfully refrain from displaying my shock, other than my eyes widening momentarily. My mind races to recount everything that Năinai said and my responses. I'm safe with what I had said, nothing incriminating. Then, I get a little mad at how he kept himself composed and quiet the entire time.

"Well, look at that," busts Năinai. "*Blue Eyes* does speak Mandarin."

The rest of the families' attention is on Joe now, not completely understanding Năinai's declaration. If I'm not mistaken, Joe blushes slightly.

"Of course," Mrs. Wú says nonchalantly. "Joe knew Mandarin before he and Henry met at in college."

"And, here we thought he was just as quiet as you, Emma," Jared chimes in.

I give Jared a slightly scolding look to avoid drawing to much attention my way. Thankfully, no one else adds their thoughts or opinions.

"I like to listen more than I talk," Joe shares.

"Indeed," confirms Mr. Wú. "Joe is very much like his father, John."

"Well, he's perfect for Emma," Năinai proposes.

I inwardly wince and for some reason I look at Joe who is just grinning from ear to ear.

We sit for about another hour gathered around the dining table. After finishing her dessert, Jade gets daring and tries to steal some from Jared. She's able to snitch a bite or two before they play a game of swords with their spoons. Jared usually lets Jade win, but not when it comes to Năinai homemade confections.

Still wanting more, Jade searches for a new target. "You gonna eat that?" She asks Joe in English.

"What?" he playfully inquires.

"That," she says, pointing to the rest of his rice pudding. "Are you going to finish it?"

"Yes," He smirks. "Why?"

"Doesn't look like you're eating it," Jade states.

"I am . . . slowly," Joe answers as he takes a small scoop and surrounds it with his gorgeous lips.

Chapter Five

Jade laughs a little as she gives Joe a devilish look. He pulls his bowl closer to himself as his grin stretches outward. Kneeling on my legs, Jade gathers more courage and leans across the table, stretching her right arm out holding a spoon. Joe pulls his bowl in just a bit more, takes a spoonful to his mouth very slowly as his eyes shift to me for a few seconds and then back to Jade as she reaches farther. This has turn into a full on game of the battle of wits and I'm curiously watching to see who wins. Jade has been know to win simply by persistence.

Unable to reach without drawing attention from Kim or Peter, Jade backs away and slowly creeps off of my lap. Joe watches her out of the corner of his eye while he peers at me. My eyes dart back and forth between him and Jade's movements. Joe shifts in his seat which gives Jade a clear shot to his rice pudding, pretending he doesn't see her.

Last second, after Jade scopes some up on her spoon, Joe grabs her arm, startling her a little. "Hey," he says, laughing and smiling.

She giggles in return as he raises her spoon to his mouth. "Hey!" Jade says softly as not to get caught by her parents.

Joe is obviously pleased with himself for tricking her.

"Take it," he says to her reassuringly. "I'm done. You can have it."

Jade beams with happiness as she takes the bowl quickly to make sure he wasn't still teasing. She returns to my lap to enjoy her sweet victory.

Joe's watches Jade as she enjoys his leftovers. Several times, Joe looks up at me before noting, "I have a niece Rey's age and a nephew Jet's age."

I hope I don't have a look of surprise on my face from his statement. Joe's face doesn't give me any indication to if I do.

As the group starts to break up in the house between clearing the table and having tea and smaller conversations, we younger adults migrate in one area as the senior adults congregate in another. Maggie, Henry and Jared are doing most of the talking while Joe and I stay fairly quiet. On occasion, I glance in Joe's direction while I pet Sadie and I catch him looking at me. This is not good.

Jared mentions to Henry that the three of us were going to play some volleyball at the beach next weekend and invites Henry and Joe to join us. Maggie jumps in, insisting they come.

Henry looks to Joe and Joe replies, "I don't have any plans. So, I'm in if you are."

So it begins — socializing with Maggie's new love interest and friend. A regular routine that I should be used to by now.

I excuse myself first from the celebration since I've got to be able to catch one of the last trains before they stop for the night. As I finish saying farewell to everyone who is awake, the children have all fallen asleep, Jared offers to walk me to the station. Maggie, Henry and Joe proclaim that they'll join us which makes me a little uncomfortable. No one has escorted me to the station in a long time, not unless they're joining me for the ride.

As we're walking, Henry asks why I don't just drive home.

Without thinking, Maggie blurts out, "Oh, Emma doesn't drive. She hates cars."

I spin sharply at her slip and glare. My discomfort is written in my eyes as I chide, "Maggie."

"Oops. Sorry," she sincerely apologizes.

"Why do you hate cars?" Joe asks with a hint of concern.

"No reason," Jared interjects. "Besides, the train is the fastest way from here to Emma's."

We all climb the stairs to the platform and I wave my TAP card upon entering.

I can only hope that my two best friends keep their mouths shut and don't disclose anything else about me after I leave. I prefer that they don't talk about me at all, I don't like strangers knowing too much — and my friends know that.

The train arrives just a few minutes later after some awkward silence. I kiss and hug Jared and Maggie farewell. Everyone pets Sadie and I wave to Henry and Joe from a distance as I walk to get on the train. Henry and Joe seem to be easier with the fact that I'm not embracing them in some way.

"See you Saturday," Henry reminds me.

I smile and nod as the doors close and I take a seat.

Six

The week following our New Year's celebration is busy — good busy. The team has been doing a wonderful job on all aspects of Naturally Me and have about three weeks left of finishing touches for the next quarter's scheduled pieces. Yesterday, we spent the entire day filming a few videos for the third quarter of product reviews, cooking recipes and home made products right in my kitchen and dinning area. Now, these videos sit in line to be edited. Everyone would rather film a bunch of stuff all at once rather than break it up in a two to three-day span. Since filming for several short videos takes a whole day, I always make sure I feed Jared and the team; Connor, Vanessa and Ian, as a small thank you for all their hard work. The best part is that the food used for the cooking segments get eaten for lunch or snacks and we leave the cameras on while eating. We've had some really great feedback from our audience when they see the team actually eat what was just prepared. Once the day concludes, I give them each product samples for them to take home to use and review.

Maggie is back to work on my other business, Raven Media, which is a social media management services firm I started a few years after social media platforms started showing their effectiveness in connecting with current and potential clients for Naturally Me. Maggie is the chief operating officer of my firm and oversees operations for our staff of fifteen associates who handle social media for the company's clients. We use a single internet cloud-based software system I created that enables Maggie to communicate and supervise the staff anytime, day or night, and allows the entire team to work remotely. All associates are independent contractors since they work from home and many of them work in a different state. Reports are generated automatically from the system and sent to us and our clients on either a weekly, bi-weekly or monthly basis for monitoring purposes. Raven Media also provides content creation, social media marketing planning and consultation, as well as general business consulting services that are available in addition, on an as needed basis. My company is a small, yet successful firm that touts itself for having direct and personable interaction with our clients.

This morning, Maggie and I are reviewing the progress the associates are making and the overall stats for our clients. Since I was home all day yesterday filming, I hop on the train to meet up with Maggie at the Chinatown station. Once together, we continue to downtown LA, getting off at Union Station a few blocks from the Peking Wok to conduct business before opening hours and then stay to have lunch.

Breathe In

The Peking Wok has been a client for the past two years, though at first Mŭqīn was apprehensive about it and needed some coaxing. She doesn't bother with technology outside of the restaurant other than a television or radio on rare occasions. Maggie knows the ins and outs of the family restaurant and started up some social media profiles for the Peking Wok not long after she started working for Raven Media, all before Mŭqīn agreed to become a client — Maggie knew Mŭqīn would respond to results. Sure enough, within two months, the Peking Wok was getting busier during their usually slower times.

We didn't tell Mŭqīn right away about what was happening on social media. Then one day, a young couple gave their compliments directly to Mŭqīn and Fŭqīn. The couple explained that they had seen all the great reviews about the restaurant online, that it is one of the few places in LA County with real Chinese cuisine, which they loved and had to visit since they had spent some time in China and missed the food. The couple even took some pictures of the food and the restaurant, and shared their glowing reviews online. Since Maggie was assisting with the restaurant that same day, Mŭqīn mentioned what had happened. Though Mŭqīn didn't completely understand everything, Mŭqīn and Fŭqīn sat down later so Maggie could explain. Once Maggie filled them in on what Raven Media has been doing online for the Peking Wok, showing them all the reviews and photos people were taking, not just of the food, but of themselves eating, Mŭqīn understood. That was the turning point in Mŭqīn's and Maggie's relationship with each other. Though she knew her mother loved her, Maggie told me it was that day when Mŭqīn started treating her differently and stopped questioning her about anything business related for the Peking Wok. I was so happy and proud of them when Maggie told me.

Even though the Peking Woking is open only from lunch to dinner, the staff is already there putting away fresh food deliveries and prepping as early as eight o'clock in the morning. Maggie and I arrive just after nine and seat ourselves in one of the back, circular booths we prefer. Raven Media has just brought on a new client and there are a lot of things to discuss with her and eventually the client.

As our meeting is drawing to a close, Amy enters the restaurant with Jet and Rey and joins us temporarily. Amy is a stay at home mom who loves motherhood and helps out Kim whenever she needs Rey and Jade looked after. Amy regularly comes to the restaurant to help out too. Mŭqīn and Fŭqīn have a little play and nap area connected to their office for the children when family visits. Amy and the kids stay at the table just long enough for the boys to eat before Amy takes them to the back for their naps.

Chapter Six

Putting my stuff into my briefcase, Maggie stands up, appearing to stretch. A second later I hear her call, "Over here!"

The corner of my eye finds Henry and Joe walking toward us. Great, our girls lunch has now turned into something I was hoping wouldn't occur until after the weekend. Maggie does this with every guy she meets. If a guy is going to be a part of her life, he needs to get along with her family and friends. It's very important to her. I was just hoping to have a little bit more time observing first in a larger group setting before having open discussions to get to know Maggie's new boyfriend. Actions speak louder than words to me and Maggie greatly respects my ability to pick up on people's character. I saw the connection they had when we met Henry at the library, but I'm a little surprised to see her rushing the process. I guess I shouldn't be too surprised. Her usual boyfriend scanning protocol has been changed since he did meet the family already.

Henry greets Maggie more warmly than when I last saw them together. They hug and he kisses her on her cheek and Joe follows suit.

"Hey, Emma," says Henry as he releases Maggie. "It's great to see you again." He reaches forward to shake my hand.

I consider the contact but refuse and he's not disappointed, more understanding. "Hello, Henry. Likewise," I politely respond.

Taking the cue from my interaction with Henry, Joe simply greets with a smile, saying, "Hello, Emma."

"Hi," I reply while returning his smile.

Yep, he's still yummy.

"Sit, sit," Maggie instructs.

I return to where I was sitting on the far right of the booth cushion. Maggie scoots in beside me knowing to separate me from the two men I hardly know. Henry follows in behind her and Joe sits next to Henry which is directly across from me on the other end of the booth.

"I hope we weren't interrupting you ladies," Henry adds once we're all seated and looks to me.

Before I can answer, Maggie jumps in, "Oh no. Not at all. We actually just finished up our business meeting a few minutes ago."

"Good, glad to hear it," Henry confirms.

From the sound of his answer, Maggie has already informed Henry about the meeting we were having prior to them joining us. I guess today will uncover exactly how much she has divulged. I mentally cringe at the idea.

"What kind of business?" Joe questions, looking directly at me.

"Well, Emma actually has two businesses, but I help with her social media firm," Maggie eagerly shares. "I guess I should let Emma explain what she's comfortable with. I'm just so excited you guys were able to have your lunch with us."

Maggie's statement confirms a bit of information for me. If the two of them are on their lunch break, that means they work here in the city and probably pretty close. No one drives to lunch in downtown LA unless they're not returning to the office right away, if at all. Yet, today is Thursday and not Friday, so I would deduce that they are most likely heading back to work which would confirm the idea that their offices are nearby.

"My first business is an online website. It's a health and wellness blog. The second, as Maggie explained, is a social media management services firm. Maggie does more than just work for me, she's the COO for the entire company." I finally get to answer for myself, giving just enough information while leaving out a lot of detail.

"They are expanding Naturally Me in the third quarter to add a pet division. Jared had the awesome idea and they've already been making arrangements for it. Sadie's going to be a star," Maggie adds enthusiastically.

She has never been known not to be enthusiastic.

"Naturally Me?" Joe and Henry question at the same time.

"That's the name of her wellness website," Maggie interjects before I have the chance to comment.

I see a look of revelation from both Henry and Joe that this is typical behavior for Maggie as I just sit patiently and wait for her to finish.

"I like the name," Joe firmly states, widening his smile. "So, I would speculate that Jared manages Naturally Me for you since Maggie manages . . ." he pauses, obviously looking for the name of my media company.

If Joe is making an assumption that Jared manages Naturally Me, I hardly believe that it's from just finding out that Maggie managers Raven Media. My friends must have revealed some information after I left on New Year's.

"Raven Media," Maggie answers Joe's lingering question of the name of the company.

"Sounds like we have a smart business woman in our presence, Henry," Joe express with interest and intrigue.

"I think so," agrees Henry.

Maggie smiles at us speaking freely and sits quietly hoping it will continue. I think she's pleased with herself. She thinks I don't know what she's doing. Should I play along? It's still up for debate.

Chapter Six

"Do you have your MBA? If so, did you attend or are you attending UCLA? I'd love to get a fresh perspective on the school and it's program," Henry excitedly asks me.

"No. I hear it's a great school, though. It's in the top tier of MBA colleges," I politely respond without giving any indication to the extent of my educational background. "Why?"

Now it's my turn to ask some questions.

"Joe and I just started at UCLA this year. One semester under us isn't enough to know. I figured if you, or anyone you know has attended, that might give us some insight or assistance," Henry answers. His personality seems a bit like Maggie's, eager, enthusiastic and very friendly.

"No. Sorry," I apologize. "Are you required to work and study at the same time?"

"Yes, though classes aren't intrusive to our work schedule. A lot of the classes and teachings are based on us already having experience working with a company to a certain degree. The learning is supposed to work in tandem with our everyday tasks at our jobs and vice versa. Kind of like work and use what you learn at the same time kind of thing and share ideas and experiences in class."

Henry is definitely a talker like Maggie. This is good. I can keep my questions simple and flowing and he'll just keep talking, revealing more.

"Interesting," I reply.

I am genuinely interested, but I want to know more about this guy who my friend has the hots for.

"So what companies do you both work for?" I inquire.

"I work with my parents in the family business. We have several businesses overall, but our main industry of business is manufacturing. We have facilities in both China and here in the US and they create a variety of products or product parts from vehicles, to clothing, to technology." he answers openly.

I can tell from the way he speaks and his body language that he's happy to share. I don't know if this is just who he is yet or if Maggie preempted our meeting by warning him of what Maggie and Jared call *Emma Interrogation*.

Silence falls upon us momentarily. Actually, I'm waiting for Joe to answer, but the hush drives Maggie crazy and she clearly doesn't realize what I'm trying to do.

"Emma never went to college!" she nearly shouts.

"Really?" counters Henry as Joe sits back with attentiveness.

"Yep. She's one smart cookie. All self taught," she offers.

For a brief moment, I wince at the thought that she might go into more detail. Thankfully she doesn't.

"Obviously," Henry agrees, appearing to want to know more, but doesn't press.

"And you?" I challenge Joe since he didn't respond after Henry while I try to divert any other question away from myself.

One way to know a guy is through his friends, and I'm not letting Joe sit on the sidelines during this meeting. Besides, I figure that he's getting to know me just by sitting back and watching Henry and I talk, and I refuse to be opening up that much and let him keep most of the mystery.

"What about me?" Joe returns playfully, grinning more.

His lips are so inviting. Focus Emma, focus.

"Yes, you. What company do you work for?" I press politely.

I know the game he's playing. It's the very same game I'm playing. This is going to be fun and I can see from the looks on their faces that Maggie and Henry are already enjoying themselves as this moves along. They are trying to set Joe and me up. I'm onto them.

"I thought this meeting was for you and Henry to get to know each other?" he questions, trying to avoid answering as a sparkle shines in his eye.

Yep. He's definitely toying with me.

"Well, then I would have to ask what you are doing here?" I firmly push back.

At least someone can keep up with the witty banter.

"I couldn't send my friend in alone to possibly be slaughtered by you ladies now, could I?" Joe seems impressed with my quick wit and how I don't easily falter at being provoked.

Enjoying that he's playing along, I reply with a grin, "That or you're a sadistic voyeur."

"Maybe I'm both," Joe says, clearly trying to lure me in further.

"Regardless, you are a means to an end. A piece in the game, the mystery," I say, baiting him back.

"How am I a piece in the mystery?" Joe inquires while the look on his face exposes his desire to continue.

"One way to get to know someone is through the company he keeps," I reveal.

"Interesting . . ." he says teasingly. "So you're just using me?"

Chapter Six

Is he flirting with me? I wonder if he's in on Henry's and Maggie's little game. Oh honey, I can play this game for as long as you want.

"Exactly." I honestly, but mischievously verify as my smirk expands a little and my eyebrows lift.

Joe chuckles a little as he reveals his full smile. God, is he sexy. I'm extremely attracted to this man, but I know my rules and boundaries and need to keep them in check. Nothing should come from this. I mean, nothing will come from this.

"I work with my father who owns a few businesses as well. I'm mostly familiar and currently working in real estate and hospitality," Joe remarks with truthfulness in his voice. "However, I'm looking to branch out the family's business assets with more modern industries like technology."

"What areas of technology?" I inquire interested.

"Not sure. I'd like to have at least one division dedicated to renewable resources," he replies.

I nod in response processing and enjoying our little game as well as cataloging all of his and Henry's direct answers. His eyes narrow slightly as if he's looking for something more in my response. Or, maybe he's looking to see if he's off the hook. I don't reveal my intention, but I am rather curious as to the extent of his business knowledge and if he's forward thinking or not. His brain is starting to pique my curiosity.

Maggie and Henry are on the edge of their seats watching us. When Maggie and I make eye contact, she gives me a look. It's a look I'm all too familiar with that has so many meanings as she bites her lip and smiles with the inquisition that lays blatantly in her gaze. She's never really seen me banter like this with a guy before and it looks like she's reading way too much into it. Maggie frowns when I shake my head at her investigation. Pouting doesn't work on me.

She tries to nonchalantly tip her head in Henry's direction, knowing to move on. I smile at her, nodding reassuringly that this meeting is going well so far. Maggie always runs guys and potential boyfriends by me first. There has obviously been a slight change in the procedure since Henry and his family joined us for New Year's, but I appreciate her still going through this boyfriend screening. None of her past boyfriends have passed my tests before, not that I would ever tell Maggie that, but Henry is showing some real promise.

She releases a breath as if she's been holding it this whole time. The two men sitting with us watch Maggie and me intently, trying to decipher our nonverbal communication.

Kevin, one of the waiters who has been working at the Peking Wok since the restaurant opened comes over with menus for the guys. Maggie and I know the menu inside and out.

"Apologies for not getting to you sooner," Kevin says to Joe and Henry.

"No worries, Kevin," Maggie answers. "We were just getting more acquainted and they wouldn't have had time to look at the menu."

"Just let me know when you're ready," he instructs.

"Thank you," Joe says followed by Henry.

Kevin nods and moves onto one of his other tables.

Maggie and I sit in silence for a few minutes to give Henry and Joe time to look over the menu. She and I exchange a few more nonverbal glances of conversation and I see both Joe and Henry looking back and forth from their menus to us as if they are going to miss something. It's actually quite comical.

Before Kevin returns to take our order, Amy comes over with some water and tea. She's obviously trying to see what's happening. I bet she's reporting back to Mǔqīn and Fùqīn. I wish I knew what they thought about Henry and his parents. Trying to secure a return to the table, Amy asks us if anyone wants anything else to drink. Amy shows her disappointment when everyone courteously declines. I don't feel too bad for her since I know Maggie will fill her in later anyway.

Prior to resuming the interrogation of my two victims, I purposefully don't speak for several minutes just to torture them. I can see that I'm driving Maggie crazy with the look she's giving me, but Joe and Henry seem to be playing it cool as I sip my tea.

"So, how did you two meet again?" I probe, finally starting the conversation with an easy and light question directed at Henry while nodding in Joe's direction.

"We met our freshman year in college at Dartmouth," Henry replies, happy to resume our conversation.

Maggie sighs with relief as if I was going to ask something really invasive or rude.

Kevin returns to take our order, ceasing our chat momentarily.

"Dartmouth," I repeat, having the name dance around in the arena of my game before continuing on.

"Yes," henry confirms not catching on.

I look to Joe briefly and I can see him trying to suppress a smile. He knows what I'm doing.

Chapter Six

Before I ask my next question, Henry offers more information, "My parents wanted me to attend an American school since we were already doing more business here in the States."

"I wouldn't give that much validity and credit to the American educational system," I reply strategically. "But, what do I know. I didn't attend college."

They all seem a little surprised by my offering.

"So, which Coast do you prefer?" I ask, wanting to lighten things up a little as Maggie's anxiety increases.

Joe sits relaxed.

"Definitely the West Coast. The weather is nice and the people are friendlier," Henry comments, smiling as if he appreciates an easy question.

"Any brothers or sisters here or back in China?"

"No. I'm an only child," Henry answers.

"Just like Emma!" Maggie throws in.

I bet she's been dying to talk this whole time. I smile and nod even though I'm not pleased with her eagerness to share more about me.

"Any pressure then to have children?" I go right in for the kill to test the waters and see if Henry waivers.

Joe smirks at my directness.

"No. Though they'd like to see grandchildren, probably sooner than later," Henry reports honestly while Maggie stares off into the distance in disbelief at my question.

I know she's dying to know the answer. Besides, I needed to get her back for giving them information about me so freely.

"Do you like children? Do you want some of your own?" I push further.

I might as well go in for the kill with this one.

"Yes and yes," Henry answers without any hesitation and with a degree of clear certainty. "Family is important to me."

"I appreciate your honesty," I reply genuinely.

To help ease some of Maggie's tension, I excuse myself to use the restroom. Without hesitation, both Henry and Joe stand up when I do. Are they going as well? When I step out of the booth, I see that they sit back down after Maggie gets up to join me.

"I need to use the ladies' room as well," Maggie mentions. Almost to the bathroom, Maggie freaks out, "What the hell was that?"

"What?" I respond, playing it cool.

Breathe In

"The question about children!" she exclaims.

I think she may hyperventilate.

"What? Like you weren't thinking it?" I throw at her.

She stands in astonishment at my response, blinking a few times. "Well, yeah . . . but that doesn't mean I want that out right off the bat."

"Were you happy with his answer?" I coax her to realize where I was going with it.

"Yes, but . . ." she replies, tripping over her own thoughts.

"Then, you're welcome," I return proudly.

All Maggie can muster is a shocked smile.

"Besides, he didn't even hesitate when he replied, which says a lot," I point out.

Her face lightens up at the realization. "Thank you," she admits shyly as we enter the facilities.

"Your welcome," I answer. Wanting to bring her back down from cloud nine, I stipulate, "Though, don't let it go to your head. It's still really early in . . . well, whatever the two of your are calling this."

She giggles a little, "I'll try."

We each take a stall next to the other and relieve ourselves in peace. Maggie is rarely speechless and this is the second time I've rendered her that way today. Man, am I on a roll. I wish Jared was here to witness this. I can't wait to tell him.

We return to the guys who stand again as we approach the table and then sit back down once we are seated. This gesture is perplexing me. I've seen it in movies, but I don't understand it.

Sometime later, Kevin comes over to the table to serve our meal. For the first few minutes, we dine in silence as I plot my next round of examination. Maggie is sitting a little closer to Henry this time which seems to be a comfortable behavior for the two of them. Joe watches me without losing an ounce of allure in his smile.

Halfway through the meal, Joe asks, "So, beach volleyball, in February?"

"Yes!" declares Maggie. "It's a great time to play here. The weather is perfect, not too hot, not too cold."

"Is this your first winter here in California?" I probe, speculating that it is.

"Yes. I've visited once or twice in the summer, but never in winter . . . if you can call this winter," Joe replies earnestly.

Chapter Six

"To those who have lived here all their life, it is winter. Having experienced the East Coast weather, Southern California only has three seasons to me. Spring, Summer and Fall. That is, unless you are up in the mountains . . . there's probably snow there right now," I say in a friendly manner.

"I've spent a bit more time here in California than Joe since my family has a few properties as well as for business. The weather down here is much more mild that San Francisco this time of year. There is definitely a difference. I think I prefer the winter here compared to Northern California. It would be fun sometime to see how the mountains are here. Is there enough snow for skiing?" Henry searches.

"Oh, yes!" Maggie replies. "There's skiing and tubing. The San Bernardino mountains aren't too far either. We'll all have to go next year!"

She's clearly testing the waters on her own now.

"There are snowy mountains near here?" Henry asks with a little disbelief.

"Yeah. They're only about two hours east on Route Two-Ten. You've heard of Big Bear, haven't you?" Maggie offers.

She appears to be too excited to finish the last few bites on her plate.

"I didn't realize Big Bear is that close. I just figured that the skiing areas would be more in Northern California. Yes, we'll definitely have to go next year!" Henry mentions with eagerness.

Maggie beams at his promise of future activities.

"Next year, then," Joe adds as he stares right at me, taking another bit of his food.

Is he looking for me to agree?

The rest of the meal I refrain from any further prying, deciding to put the rest of my testing on hold for Saturday. I don't want to scare Henry off too much, but I also want to throw him and Joe off the scent of my plans. I ask one or two little questions or add commentary, but I leave Maggie and Henry to their own devices of fervent talking for the majority of the time. On occasion, Joe adds a comment as well, but his behavior mostly models mine.

Before leaving to head back to their offices, Henry and Joe inquire about the check for lunch because one never came to the table. Maggie explains that it has already been taking care of, which is met with objections from both of them. They insist that they pay and Maggie refuses. Henry quickly insists that he gets our meal on Saturday when we are all scheduled to play volleyball and Maggie agrees.

I mention that I need to get back to Sadie and they all offer to walk me to the train station. Appreciative that they weren't offended by my fun during our lunch, I respectfully decline. However, I do offer my hand to Henry when we officially say farewell to head in our separate directions. This peace offering gets a temporarily startled responses from the guys and an instantaneous sunny response from Maggie. I offer my hand to Joe last, who instead of shaking it, raises it and kisses the tips of my knuckles. I've never had a man do this before. Joe's supple lips send electric sparks instantaneously to my sex, turning my body temperature up a few degrees. I've never had this intense of a reaction to a man's touch and I'm conflicted by how much I like it.

Returning home from the engaging morning for both business and pleasure, I decide to take Sadie out for an early afternoon romp. I've got the local taxi company on speed dial for when I do need to take a car when my friends aren't around. After changing into a sports bra, light blue colored, organic cotton v-neck shirt that doesn't entirely hug my torso, black yoga capris that form to my entire body, and a my black moisture wick running jacket that has pockets perfect for jogging that hold keys and other little necessities, I then pack a small bag with three thermoses filled with filtered water, a pack of trail mix, a few doggy treats and a small folding bowl to pour water into for Sadie. After putting on my sneakers, Sadie and I head down to the cab and are off to one of the local hiking trails that are a few miles away up on the edge of the Altadena mountains, Eaton Canyon.

I hate cars — correction, I loath them after loosing my parents — but, sometimes they are necessary for getting around California. As much as I try to prep myself mentally, the experience is always the same, no matter who is driving. My heart races, my body temperature increases, usually causing me to perspire a little and one or both of my knees rapidly shake. Sometimes I'm able to minimize the stress and anxiety by distracting myself with my phone, but motion sickness can set in if I'm on it for too long. When I'm with Maggie, Jared and Nathan, one of them always holds my hand which helps and they talk to me the entire time to keep my focus off of the ride. If Sadie is with me, I usually pay lots of attention to her, however, she picks up on my nervousness which just heightens mine.

The afternoon drive in the cab goes quickly and there aren't too many red lights before getting to the park entrance. Since I started using the cab company, I always request to have Charles. He has a nice, non-aggressive driving habit that I appreciate, and we get along well. Instead of heading back down the mountain, Charles sits and waits for me. Knowing my routine at the mountain, Charles always turns off the meter. He gets a quiet break and nap while I'm out as well as an additional forty dollar tip for waiting. We have a

Chapter Six

mutually beneficial relationship that we've established over the past two years that has turned into a nice friendship. We chat on the drive as he updates me on how his children and wife are doing as well as thanking me again for my generous Christmas gifts I gave him and the family. A while ago, he had mentioned that he and his wife wanted to take a week's vacation with the kids to Disneyland, so I arranged for them to spend a week at Disney World. They are scheduled to go during his children's spring break from school this year. I covered their flights, hotel stay and park passes. Every kid needs to visit Disney World at least once in their life — that is one of my fondest memories of my parents when I was little.

It takes a moment for me to adjust to the higher altitude. The air is thinner and takes a moment to get used to even for a physically fit person. Getting out of the taxi, I add my keys and phone into a zipper compartment on the inside of my jacket. My phone won't be of any real use here because we are in the middle of several small mountains, but I bring it none the less — maybe I'll listen to some music. I keep my jacket half zipped and toss the bag on my back.

"Ready, Sadie?"

She wags her tail ferociously, anticipating where we are going.

The hike is great for both of us, getting some fresh, cool air, warm sun and time out in nature to decompress everything that has been going on since the New Year. There aren't too many people on the trails today which makes it easier to just enjoy the scenery. About thirty minutes later, Sadie and I arrive at the first waterfall. We sit quietly drinking and having our snacks. We watch a few people come and go as we relax and I try some mild meditation.

Unfortunately, my thoughts wander back to the lunch I had today and Joe's lips on my hand. Damn it. Pull yourself together, Emma. Why is my mind going to him? Thinking for a moment, I realize that it has been a while since I've been with a guy and masturbation can only do so much. Maybe it's time to find another guy to play with for a while. I'll see if either Maggie or Jared is free tonight or tomorrow to help take off the edge. I grab my phone, and as I'm about to call, I realize I don't have cell reception. Great! I think it's time to head back.

Sadie and I return to the Charles and the cab in twenty minutes. I took ten minutes off our walk back?! Wow! I definitely need some action — preferably tonight. Once we hit the road at the bottom of the mountain, I group text Maggie and Jared, about going out tonight or tomorrow while sitting at a red light.

"Got the itch?" Jared texts back with a winking emoticon.

"Ha ha," I write, trying to brush it off.

"Can we invite Henry and maybe Joe, too?" Maggie texts back.

"No!" I shout back at her in writing.

The last thing I need is to have two strange men tagging along.

"You can handle one day without Henry," Jared comments to Maggie.

"She saw him for lunch today after our meeting!" I return, hinting to Jared about the morning's events.

"Really? Was *Blue Eyes* there too?" Jared heckles.

"I thought it would be a great time for Emma to get to know Henry better," Maggie interjects, trying to defend herself.

"Man, you must really like this guy, Mags," Jared pokes.

"More than me. I didn't know they were joining us," I retort, still a little peeved.

"You owe her then, Mags. I'm good for either," Jared texts back.

"I can do either," Maggie notes. "It wasn't definite if Henry and Joe could join us, so I didn't think to really mention it."

Before I can even write back, Jared confirms, "Tonight, then. How about dinner and dancing on Sunset?"

"Terrific!" I text.

"Awesome!" Maggie affirms.

Charles notices that I've perked up a bit as he pulls up to my apartment complex. "Got good news?"

"Yes. Thank you," I cheerfully respond, handing him the money I owe him plus a little extra for his tip.

"This is too much, Emma," Charles scolds a little unease.

"Not for you," I reassure him. "Send my love to the family!"

"Will do. Thanks again. See you soon!" Charles announces.

Waving farewell, I beam with anticipation. Hurrying, I empty my pockets on the kitchen counter and start getting Sadie's dinner together. Once she's finished eating, we head out to the park. Sadie only relieves herself and then comes back over to me. She must be tired from the hike which gives me a few extra minutes to get ready.

Back inside the apartment, I'm peeling off my clothes before I hit the bedroom. I have about thirty minutes to shower and get dressed before Maggie arrives to get me. Sadie lays across the bed, watching me as I dart back and forth from the bedroom to the bathroom a few times. My hair is air drying as I've now got my makeup on. Time to choose an outfit. Standing in front of my walk-in closet, I peruse my vast selection. I easily rule out a number of items due to the cooler night air as I select fitted, black dress pants that tighten down

Chapter Six

to my ankles, a shimmering, light silver, plunging neckline tank top adorned by a simple contoured black blazer that rests at the small of my back and the sleeves stop in the middle of my forearms. After throwing on a pair of four-inch heels that cutout on the arch side of my foot, I accessorize with diamond crusted hoop earrings and a simple diamond necklace that rests right a the crux of my cleavage.

Maggie texts that she has arrived right as I finish transferring my purse necessities into a simple, shiny silver clutch. I kiss Sadie goodnight and tell her to behave and not stay up too late.

"Sexy!" Maggie shouts as I climb into the passenger side of her car. "Maybe I should be the one who takes you home tonight and have my way with you."

"If there aren't any options tonight, you just might have to," I confess.

"Fine by me," Maggie confirms, giggling at the thought.

Maggie and I aren't joking and I'm almost half tempted to text Jared that we aren't meeting him and to party on without us. I lost my virginity to Maggie and her's to me. When we were eighteen, we decided that we wanted to get the whole anxiety about having our cherries popped out of the way to make it easier for if and when we did sleep with a guy.

I'm not your typical bisexual kind of girl. The only girl I've slept with is Maggie. She's beautiful and I am attracted to her. I love her, but I'm not in love with her. I never have and never will be. We kind of fill a need for each other during the interims of finding a male partner while making each other feel safe, secure and free. Maggie and I have fun, a lot of fun, but my body really craves the sensation of a man.

After parking, we head to Katana's to meet Jared for sushi. I am pleased when I see that Jared invited Nathan along to join us. Nathan became friends with him not long after Jared and I met. They have never dated, but have an unspoken partnership that fulfills needs for each other, even if just sexually. I think they love each other and will eventually be in an official relationship, but right now neither of them is ready.

"Nathan!" Maggie yells as we approach the table. "I'm so glad you joined us."

"Hello, darlings," Nathan greets hugging and kissing her on each cheek. "Don't you look delicious! Where is your new man? I was hoping to meet him."

Maggie blushes at his compliment and at the mention of Henry. "Just us girls tonight," she answers. "Besides, you'll meet him Saturday."

"And, here is the reason we are all out tonight!" Nathan beams as he looks to me.

"Hi, Nathan," I reply, hugging and kissing him too.

"I sure do love when the Sex Kitten get's the itch," Nathan expresses rather buoyantly. "I get to see my two favorite ladies and my favorite man."

"I keep telling Jared to bring you along more," I say earnestly. "But, I think he just wants to keep you all to himself. He just doesn't want to admit it." I take the seat next to Maggie which is across from Jared.

"And, he would if he would just ask," Nathan retorts, regaining his seat and glancing at Jared who is blushing.

Jared, Maggie and I hang out together with Nathan at least once a month. Sometimes Jared and Nathan get together just the two of them. We're all friends and Nathan is just as much of a friend as Jared and Maggie are for me. I think that Jared tempers how often he invites Nathan out because of their on again off again semi-committed relationship.

"So, do tell, Mags. I want all the yummy details!" Nathan is eager to hear all the particulars of her new catch. "Is he amazing in bed?"

"We haven't had sex yet," Maggie bashfully admits.

"Seriously? Then what the hell are you doing here? You and Kitten should be having your ways with each other to temper the lionesses within," he asserts in astonishment.

"If Emma doesn't find a suitor, we will," Maggie affirms.

"Shit, then let's just have some dinner and head back to either Jared's or my place. I've always been curious as to what it looks like to see the two of you go at it since Jared told me about your little deflowering adventure," Nathan remarks, insinuating that he wants to get Jared naked too.

I roll my eyes and shake my head during my response to Nathan's statement because moisture surges between my legs. "Please, you just want to get Jared naked," I say, calling his intentions out.

"Can you blame me?" he inquires, looking to Jared.

Surprisingly, Jared is more playful than usual in public with Nathan and places his hand on Nathan's shoulder.

The waiter comes over and we place our order immediately. We are hungry, but we've dined at Katana's enough times to know the menu. Besides, we usually order a variety of items and split them.

"So spill it," Nathan commands. "I want to hear about Henry."

Chapter Six

I cringe a little at the thought of hearing the recounting of all things Henry, especially with what happened earlier today. Tonight was supposed to be about sufficing my raging need for sexual relief. I quickly correct my thoughts. There is no way I'd be able to fulfill my aching need while eating dinner with two gay men. Though, Maggie could take the edge off if we just take a long trip to the restroom. Then again, if we get started, we might not ever leave the bathroom.

"Is his friend gay?" Nathan questions at some point during Maggie's diatribe.

"No, unfortunately," Jared verifies. "He's gorgeous . . . but, completely straight. I saw him staring incessantly at Emma on New Year's. He's completely into her."

"What?" I refute in shock.

"Please, *Kitten*. He totally wants you. *Blue Eyes* wants to make mad passionate love to you!" Jared jabs with a sense of knowing that gives me chills.

"No, he doesn't," I argue, trying to not allow the idea of Joe to arouse me, but my lady parts tingle.

"Yes, he does!" Jared insists in a commanding tone. "Deny it all you want, but *Blue Eyes* has the hots for you."

"I can't wait to meet these men Saturday," Nathan declares with delight as our food arrives.

"It will be interesting, to say the least," Jared comments.

"Why don't you just use *Blue Eyes* to indulge your need, Emma?" Nathan urges with a hint of torment.

"You know my rules," I hold stedfast in my conviction.

"Rules are made to be broken," Jared rebuts with a smirk on his face as he takes his next bite of sashimi.

I glare at the two of them with mounds of discomfort, mostly stemming from my loins. They do have a point to some extent, though I would never admit it to them. They've been able to show a working *friends with benefits* relationship. Yet at the same time, I can see that each of them wants more. It's in their eyes when they look at each other when they think no one else is paying attention. Jared has mentioned to me that he has yet to find anyone who can please him more sexually than Nathan. He even hinted one time at the idea that it's probably because they know each other's bodies so well.

Maggie knows my body and I hers, but that will be coming to a screeching halt here soon. I always back off when she starts dating a man. Her friendship and happiness means more to me than the fun sex we have. Maybe that's

Breathe In

why my itch is so apparent, my body knows what's coming and I'm starting to get back in the habit of withdrawing? Well, at least I have until they start having sex.

Since I choose not to respond to Jared's stipulation about my rules, the conversation goes back to Maggie describing what has happened and what she thinks about Henry. I interject on occasion, revealing my antics at lunch today which still gets an embarrassed look on Maggie's face. Nathan and Jared crack up and give me high fives for my interrogation.

Once I've added my jabs, I sit quietly pretending to listen as I continue to eat. My thoughts keep going back to what Jared said about *Blue Eyes*, I mean Joe, and my yearning increases.

One would think that masturbation on a regular basis would suffice — apparently not. I'm not a sex addict, but I'm definitely a horny girl. If, and I mean if, I would ever entertain the idea of a friend with benefits with someone other than Maggie, it would have to be a man who can not only arouse me, but bring me to full climax. None of the men I've slept with have been able to make me cum without me having to touch myself.

Settling our tab, the four of us head out to Ayana's that just opened about six months ago. It is a beautifully sculptured building that was constructed after several of the buildings on Sunset Boulevard were torn down. The interior is extravagantly designed for a nightclub, but it was tailored only for those with money in mind. The VIP rooms are usually rented out by celebrities and there is a one bottle minimum per table that starts at four hundred dollars. If you aren't a celebrity or going in with one, then you're pretty much stuck out in the line that trails out the door and wraps around the block all night. Most people never get to see the inside of this exquisite palace.

Fortunately, Jared's local celebrity gets us right in the door, though some of the people working there know me too. The head bouncer, Garrett, has had the hots for Jared since they met at a bar in WeHo a few years ago. Garrett is a sweet and handsome man, but definitely not Jared's type.

Ayana's owner, Caleb Henderson, has been trying to seduce me into his bed since we met at Ayana's opening night. Though Caleb is a mouthwatering piece of meat that any woman wouldn't mind hopping on, I would be breaking at least one of my rules to shack up with him, plus, as soon as he opens his mouth, I'm turned off. Caleb is a bit of an arrogant prick who thinks he's God's gift to women.

With a line out the door, there are only about two hundred people scattered between the dance floor, the tables circling along the walls and the VIP sections. The hostess, Molly, escorts us to a corner table that is about twenty feet from

Chapter Six

the edge of the dance floor which is backed by a stage hidden by plush black velvet curtains — looks like there's no live band tonight.

"What would you like to drink?" Molly inquires with a beautiful smile outlined in red hot lips after waiting for us to take our seats.

I've met Molly a few times in WeHo. She's a beautiful black haired and green eyed vixen who I actually wouldn't mind exploring for a night with the way my sexual itch is increasing. I know she has the same idea about me and Maggie as she looks both of us up and down with a flirting smile.

"A bottle of Cristal, please. Thank you," I reply, returning the same look.

She nods and licks her lips before turning to leave. Thankfully, no one in my group notices.

"Hey, I was thinking you girls should come over tomorrow so we can catch up. Stay the night and we'll be good to hit the beach in the morning . . . maybe party the whole weekend." Nathan suggests, hoping we will.

It's been a little while since we've all really gotten together, and he lives in downtown Santa Monica which is not too far from the volleyball courts.

"I'm in," I indicate.

I really would love to get to hang out with Nathan. We connected right away when we met, just like I had with Jared and it's been a while since we've just spent time together outside of business. Maybe that's why I'm wishing they end up together. They complete each other even in their many similarities. He's become a brother, like Jared.

"What about Henry . . . and Joe?" Maggie cautions.

"What about them?" Jared interjects. "You are just starting to get to know Henry and you don't want to come across too desperate, do you?"

Jared is right as he tries to empower Maggie. She gets's so insecure and loses confidence too quickly with any guy that shows interest.

"They can find their way to the beach," I protest. "They're big boys."

"Come on, Mags?" Nathan urges with puppy dog eyes.

"Ok, fine," she tentatively confirms.

"Yay!" shouts Nathan with genuine excitement as he dances in his seat. "It's a girls night! Oh, and guess what? I've officially just started working on details for a women's line to air in the fall. So, I need all of your feedback."

Nathan has been interested in fashion since he was a teenager. He attended the Parson's school in New York, and a few years later after working with a few top designers, started an all men's line boutique in WeHo named Nathaniel's. The man sure knows how to dress men, gay or not. I'd be really curious to see his take on women's wear. If he's as good with women's clothing as I suspect, then I'll be happy to back him to get that division going.

Molly returns promptly with our bottle, chilled in a bucket of ice and four glasses which temporarily halts any further conversations about Nathan's news. She hands us each a glass before proceeding to pop open the bottle. Maggie and I get winks as Molly pours our glasses which both Jared and Nathan witness.

After Molly returns our bottle to the bucket and leaves, Jared inquires with loads of curiosity, "What was that?"

"What?" I question, denying everything.

"The look between you and Molly?" Nathan adds.

"She's a sweetheart!" Maggie expresses with some naivety in her tone.

"She is a sweetheart, but I said what was that not who was that?" Jared clarifies.

He's insistent on getting an answer — I wonder if I gave a look without realizing it.

"What was what?" Maggie questions as she's lost to what Jared and I are discussing.

"Emma just flirted with a lesbian who is lusting after your two beauties," Jared says, confronting the small elephant in the room that Maggie missed completely.

Nathan doesn't comment, he just sits back and watches while sipping his champagne as if we're live television.

"What?! I didn't know she was a lesbian," Maggie utters with genuine astonishment before stopping and thinking for a moment, considering the events that took place.

"I'd do her," I state very matter-of-factly, glancing in Molly's direction and take a sip of my wine.

"She's hot, I wouldn't mind giving her a go," Maggie chimes in, finally catching up with the conversation.

"You'd screw almost anyone right now given your current state, Kitten," Jared affirms.

"Yep. I won't deny it," I confirm before taking a sip of champagne.

The three of them crack up at my revealing statement of need.

Trying to contain his laughter, Nathan suggests, "Maybe we should get a VIP room so you two can go at it unless you want to make it a threesome with Maggie."

"That would be fun!" Maggie exclaims in excitement.

"Don't tempt me," I scold with a devilish grin.

Chapter Six

My statement gets more laughter which is borderline hysteria from Jared and Nathan. Maggie only blushes at the image as she considers the idea.

Suddenly a voice from over my right shoulder chimes in, startling me. "What's so funny?"

I pause for a very brief moment to compose myself before looking back and find Caleb Henderson just two feet away.

Before any of us answer, Caleb is bending at the waist and kisses me on my right cheek. God, even he smells divine. So many choices and temptations tonight.

"I haven't seen you in a while. It's wonderful to have you back," Caleb confesses as his attention stays glued on me.

"It's nice to be back," Jared shares.

"Definitely!" Nathan chimes in.

"Is it just the four of you tonight?" inquires Caleb.

"Yes," Maggie confirms.

"I have a small group of friends here whom would love to meet you ladies. Why don't you join us in the VIP room?" Caleb persuades us knowing that Jared and Nathan will be the first to bite at the offer.

"Sure!" replies Nathan before I can even muster an excuse.

I grimace at Nathan once he can no longer avoid eye contact with me.

"Well, then follow me. I'll have Molly bring up your bottle, which is on me of course." Pleased with Nathan's response, Caleb directs us to the stairs that are on the other side of the room. He ushers Maggie with his left hand while placing his right on the small of my back, which makes me a little uncomfortable and disappointingly aroused, as we ascend the stairs.

Thankfully, Caleb wasn't joking and actually did have several friends in a VIP room. They are all men and perk up at the sight of Maggie and me arriving. Before introductions are made, I notice a peculiar look in the their eyes and glance over to Caleb. I catch him slightly shaking his head.

Did he just try to claim me in front of his friends? Seriously?! Oh no! I don't think so. I am not anyone's property.

Seeing the look on my face, Jared immediately knows what had just happened. Before Jared has the chance to swoop in to diffuse the situation, Caleb introduces Maggie and me first to Chris, Robert, Elliot, and Marcus, all of whom I am familiar with, not in the sense that I know them all personally, but because they are actors with varying degrees of success. I do remember meeting Chris two different times a while back. We met at Ayana's opening the first time and he still looks just as yummy and possibly even more muscular for a recent job.

Maggie shakes each of their hands and beams while I just smile with a seductive look in my eye towards all of them — especially Chris. Each of the handsome men seem a little apprehensive when greeting me, not because I didn't shake their hands, but most likely because of Caleb.

Without restraint, Jared steps forward to greet them, introducing himself and Nathan while grabbing a hold of my hand as I reach out to him. If anyone is going to stake any kind of claim, I would only allow Jared. The men's faces ease a little though still confused by Jared's and my actions.

Lightening up the mood, even though she was completely unaware of what had just happened, Maggie starts gushing over the four new acquaintances. She may be interested in Henry, but that isn't going to stop her from flirting and chatting — I am proud of her in this moment for doing so.

Chris motions for us to sit while keeping his eyes mostly on me. Between Jared, Maggie, Nathan and myself, we know how to flawlessly move about, around each other like a fluid dance, positioning ourselves in an intricate manner that would be missed by the naked eye during conversation. The four stunning actors sit across from us as Maggie is to my left and Jared and Nathan are to my right, completely blocking Caleb from having any kind of access to me.

"So . . . are you boys just finishing some work, or getting ready to head out to some?" Maggie begins.

Though she is attracted to these men, she only fumbles her words and wits when she's in the presence of a man whom she is utterly smitten with. If given the opportunity, I don't doubt she would seriously consider sleeping with one of them. I sure as hell would and am considering it, especially to dispel Caleb's actions.

"Just finishing," Chris eagerly answers.

"Same here," beams Robert.

"Me too," replies Elliot.

"I'll be starting in a few weeks," answers Marcus.

"How wonderful! Isn't that wonderful, Emma?" Maggie playfully muses.

"Indeed," I say, floating my eyes to each man and then staring at Chris.

I watch Chris glance slightly at Caleb to get a reaction, but he instantly stops when I lick my lips. Caleb obnoxiously pulls over a chair to sit alongside Elliot, trying to get into my line of sight, but I refuse to give him the satisfaction.

Chapter Six

"Anything else lined up, or are you guys taking a break?" Jared directs towards Chris, Elliot and Robert.

Chris, Robert and Elliot each respond that they have projects lined up, but don't need to leave for another several months. Conversations continue and lots of flirting between Chris, Robert, Elliot, Marcus, Maggie and myself continue on as Caleb scowls. We're pleasantly disrupted by Molly who has brought up our bottle of champagne and several other drinks. Later, I'm relieved when Molly comes back and informs Caleb of something that requires his attention, forcing him to leave the room.

With Caleb gone, we all instinctually move about the room more freely and our chatting becomes more relaxed and friendly. After a while, I get up to stretch my legs and peer out the tinted glass window that overlooks the dance floor. Draping my arms across my chest and holding up the wine glass near my mouth, I stroke my lips with the tips of my fingers. The champagne is heightening my arousal and I'm weighing my options and their possible circumstances.

Chris and Robert join me while Elliot and Marcus stay focused on Maggie, Jared and Nathan. A fleeting thought of taking them both at the same time amuses me and would surely make several statements. It would let them know I'm not looking for anything other than a little fun and most importantly, that I do not belong to Caleb.

"Do you live around here?" Chris initiates with a hint of nervousness in his voice.

I turn with a widening grin, "In LA County. Yes."

"How long have you known Caleb?" Robert delves into the lingering question on their collective minds.

"Just since the opening like you, Chris," I say, taking a small step towards them. "I've only seen Caleb a few times after that when my friends and I have come into the club."

We stand in silence for a bit. I'm curious to see where they want to go with the conversation and I think they are almost a little intimidated as well as not quite sure what to make of me.

I've never been with two men at the same time, but I am seriously considering it. They are both lucky that we aren't already alone, because I'd probably have one of them straddled by now if we were.

"Would you like more champagne?" Chris finally slips in with a husky tone, breaking the awkward silence.

"No, thank you," I return in a low voice as I caress my fingers across my lips.

Both men appear to be slightly uneasy at my directness. I wonder if they've ever had a woman be so forward with them — that, or their uncomfortable because of Caleb's claim.

Deciding to press forward with my intentions, I inquire, "I was wondering if you would escort me to the ladies' room? I'm not sure where it is up here and I'd rather not get lost."

Both Robert and Chris look like deer in headlights. It's almost comical.

"Umm, sure . . ." Chris hesitantly replies.

I bite my lip as I look to Robert for his response.

"Chris can show you . . ." he answers uncomfortably, not getting my hint or uneasy by the idea.

"Hmm . . . looks like you've got me all to yourself," I deviously assert. "Are you sure you don't want to join us, Robert?"

The realization settles on their faces about my implications as they both stare at me in bewildered astonishment. Chris looks at Robert to see if he's joining us as he shifts and reaches his elbow for me to grasp. I'm impressed.

Giving Robert one last chance, Chris pauses. Waiting a few seconds, I announce to Maggie and the rest that Chris is escorting me to the ladies' room. Nothing but wicked grins smear across Maggie's, Jared's and Nathan's faces.

"I'm glad someone is making sure you don't get lost," Jared goads, grinning at Chris and nods.

Moments later, Chris is guiding me down the upper hallway away from the stairs that lead to the dance floor. A fleeting thought of concern passes over me, not because of what I'm about to do, but because the idea that he actually is taking me to the restroom enters my mind. My excitement races as I see Molly heading toward us, suddenly signaling us to follow her. To my delight, she leads us into a non-window room marked with a private sign that has two small couches across from each other inside it. Before closing the door, Molly and I make eye contact and I jerk my head, signaling for her to join us. She checks both ways before entering the room and locks the door. Before he can say anything, I reassure Chris that she's joining us because I invited her. I'm not sure how much Molly will interact with him, but I might as well suffice my need with two options.

I press my body into Chris as I gently nudge him to move backwards until his legs meet the couch behind him, forcing him to sit. My ardent lips thrust upon his as I mount his lap.

"She's more here for me than you," I reassure him. "You don't mind, do you?"

Chapter Six

A wicked smile dances across his face as he registers my intent. All he can do is shake his head as he presses his mouth to mine and his hands grip my backside. My left hand reaches for Molly as Chris continues to massage my tongue with his. He's a pretty good kisser compared to some of the men I've made out with.

I break my lips from his and Chris groans in disappointment before he finds my neck. I find Molly watching as she kneels next to us on the couch. She leans in and as her sweet, soft lips embrace mine, a moan escapes my throat. Shifting her body, she's now pressed up against my back as our lips stay locked. In one effortless movement, she removes my blazer, only breaking physical contact to drape it over the other couch. My lips find Chris' as his right hand cups the back of my neck and Molly's hands slide down my shoulders and over my breasts.

The three of us dance our bodies on and around each other's for several minutes as we build up the momentum and take our clothes off. I glide between the two of them, kissing their lips as Molly's hands explore my body and parts of Chris'. Chris explores more of me and slowly ventures over onto Molly, who accepts it naturally.

Molly assists me to put the condom on Chris before helping me to slide out of my own pants. By this point, we are all completely naked. Prior to assisting me to lower onto Chris, Molly massages my breasts and nipples as Chris observes with eager anticipation, caressing my thighs and licking my navel. Molly's hands slip down my front and glide over my waxed lips several times before returning her fingers to her mouth to taste. My hands have been intermittently rubbing her, enticing her since before she undressed me.

I mount Chris and Molly guides my hips up and down over his shaft as her mouth licks and sucks my neck and shoulders. Chris' tongue is on my nipples as Molly's and my mouths meet and my fingers return to her folds. Molly's left hand dips down to my nub as she shifts her body slightly to gain more access. She accepts Chris' hand on her waist as I continue to pulse three of my fingers into her saturated cave. Molly and I stroke each other as I repeatedly ride up and down on Chris. My tongue creeps over Molly's right nipple and I continue to plunge my fingers into her as she moans louder. Chris is now thrusting harder inside of me as Molly and I continue to manipulate each other's sex. Within a few more thrusts into her, I have Molly writhing in climax shortly followed by Chris. Molly quickly regains her composure, assisting me to reach climax by putting her mouth onto my clitoris as Chris proceeds to thrust into me trying to stay hard. I grip the back of her head as I move closer to orgasm until I finally cum with the thought of Joe popping into my head. What the hell!

Molly and I kiss as my breathing slows while licking my fingers from her taste. Chris' face is buried into my neck. "God, you are so hot," he professes.

I smiled politely, though indifferently.

Two seconds later, I'm peeling myself off of him and start to get dressed. Molly and I pass each other our pieces of clothing as Chris watches in amazement at how nonchalant we are. Being the first to dress, Molly kisses me on the cheek and rushes out the door.

As I finish fixing my hair and makeup in the mirror on the wall, Chris finishes getting dressed with a look of trepidation on his face. "So, you definitely don't have anything going on with Caleb?"

"Hell no, though I know Caleb wishes," I answer honestly.

This gets a furrowed brow response from Chris. "So, can I see you again?" he uncomfortably requests.

"You're cute. I had fun, but I don't do relationships. Never have, never will."

He seems shocked by my response. "Really?"

"Yes, really."

"I don't know what to say to that," Chris truthfully answers as he walks up behind me and places his hands on my hips and whispers in my ear. "I like you."

"You like your idea of me," I retort with a slight chill. "I don't doubt you're a great guy and all. Don't take it personally. Like I said, I don't date."

The bummed look on his face confirms my theory about actors being too vain, needy or insecure, or a weird combination of the three.

"We had a fun time. No strings attached in any way," I state calmly.

With a look of concern on his face, Chris asks, "Are you going to tell Caleb?"

"It's none of his business," I say frankly.

Chris seems relieved as I turn my body to face him with a reassuring smile. He leans in to kiss me and I allow him. If we ever ran into each other in the future, I'd sleep with him again. Hopefully next time, he'll last longer — I wonder if that was is first threesome?

We venture out of the room arm in arm to head back to our friends. Caleb gives Chris and I an angry glare as we enter the room. I kiss Chris on the lips in front of everyone before sitting down on Nathan's lap which seems to infuriate Caleb even more.

"Any good?" Nathan whispers.

"Decent," I mutter. "Especially since I was able to get Molly to join us."

Chapter Six

Nathan snaps his head back for a moment to see my whole face before laughing. He leans in close to my ear, "I want details later."

"Of course you do," I whisper.

Jared tilts in to where his face is almost touching mine and Nathan's. "Satisfied?"

"For now."

"Looks like *Sex Kitten* has only taken the edge off," Jared quips.

I nod in agreement.

Maggie stands up and announces to me that she wants to go downstairs and dance, so I oblige. Everyone in the room, including Caleb, follows us to the dance floor. Maggie and I proceed to dance facing each other as Jared, Nathan, Chris, Robert, Marcus and Elliot surround us. As we continue to dance, Maggie prods a little to see how my trip to the ladies' room went. She gasps when I mention that Molly joined us and Maggie insists on getting all of the juice details later when she stays over. Aside from wanting to know what happened, it's obvious that Maggie is in the mood now too. I think she needs it just as much as I do since I know she hasn't started sleeping with Henry yet.

At one point, most of the guys head to the bar to get drinks for everyone leaving Maggie, Chris and myself in the middle of the crowded dance floor. Maggie and I both dance up on Chris now since he's the only guy of our group left with us. A few moments later, I see Maggie swatting off a guy behind her. Chris tries to get the guy to back off, but he shoves Chris.

"You've got your own to dance with," the guy shouts.

I step in between Maggie and the guy and inform him, "Back off, she's with me!"

This gets the guy riled up and grabby with me. Two seconds later, right as the rest of our group is heading back to join us, and before Chris can even process that the guy has put his hands on me, I immediately grab and manipulate the offending oaf's arm, twisting his entire body and forcing him to drop down to his knees. I have his wrist pinned in such a way that all I need to do is jerk my hand and I would break his arm in two places.

"Get this crazy bitch off of me!" he shouts, wincing in pain.

Two bouncers preceded by Molly are heading in my direction. I've definitely made a new friend tonight.

After the temporary scuffle, I get cheers from all the ladies on the dance floor. Chris, Robert, Marcus, Elliot and Caleb all gape in shock and disbelief followed by pure arousal. I shoot a fierce look right at Caleb, wanting to put him and his claim on me in its proper place.

"That was so hot," Robert announces with fervor as he moves closer.

Elliot nods in agreement as Chris flushes and returns his hands to my hips.

"How did you do that?" Robert continues.

"Years of martial arts classes," I reply while advertising my dominance to Caleb. "Why is that such a shock, guys? You've seen women do that in the movies you make."

"The movies are fake. This was real," Robert broadcasts. "I should have joined you guys . . ." he says with his voice trailing off.

Chris smirks leaning more into my body and kisses the nape of my neck, "Definitely your loss, man!"

We dance a little more into the night before calling it quits. Jared and Nathan escort Maggie and me to her car that is parked below Katana's. Maggie and I drive back to my place, get naked and make sure one another are utterly, sexually satisfied before passing out in my bed.

Seven

Maggie, Sadie and I make it to the Li family home by around ten the next day so Maggie can pack before we head over to Nathan's. Like me, Maggie packs a variety of options to choose from for the weekend since anything is possible after playing volleyball. Though she borrowed some clothes, Maggie decides to hit the shower at her house before changing and invites me to join her. I agree, knowing we're the only ones in the house and happy to have another sex session before the weekend.

Maggie's definitely starting to get impatient from not having sex with Henry — I saw the look last night when we had sex and again this morning. From what she told me last night, it's been about three weeks since they met, and though I know she's put herself out there, Henry has only made out with her. My initial reaction is to question what is wrong with him. Maggie is a beautiful and intelligent woman, and any other guy she was interested in the past would have slept with her by now. The thought that he might be a virgin comes to mind, but I can't see how a handsome man like him hasn't even had one fling, even if it was with a somewhat serious girlfriend.

After our shower, we text Nathan before heading out to Santa Monica in Maggie's Tesla. We are able to beat most of the LA traffic on Route Ten which gets us to Nathan's in about forty minutes.

Nathan lives in a newly purchased and renovated three bedroom and two and a half bath condo on the west side of Ocean Avenue in downtown Santa Monica. He wasn't able to afford the penthouse, but even on the fifth level, he has breathtaking views of the beach from several rooms. The complex is very posh as well as the interior of his condo that he has yet to decorate since he bought it a few months ago on short-sale. Nathan must be ferociously working on the finishing touches for his Spring collection and his upcoming Summer line to neglect decorating his home — which is not like him.

"I still can't believe you bought this much space," I comment as we step into his foyer after being buzzed in.

Sadie bounces in excitement to see her uncle.

"I have aspirations and I got tired of stifling them in my one bedroom with noisy neighbors," Nathan remarks, greeting us with hugs and kisses. "Besides, I had to have the view."

Jared pops up from the couch behind Nathan, catching me by surprise.

"Hey you," I say with a slightly shocked look. "Did you stay over last night?"

Breathe In

Jared's sheepish grin gives him away.

"Boy did he," Nathan goads.

I shake my head at the two of them as they help Maggie and me with our bags.

"Do you ladies need to do any work?" Nathan checks.

Maggie and I reply in unison that we don't.

"Great, follow me! I want to see what you think," he continues, leading us up to his mezzanine above the kitchen.

"These are stunning," Maggie disclose with definitive awe as she walks into Nathan's workspace before me. "I want!"

"Wow," I add when my eyes fall upon the fabric and pictures.

"You think?" Nathan nudges with a hint of uncertainty in his tone.

"Yes!" Maggie and I exclaim.

Our lack for words substantiates our impressions of his work.

"Really!" Nathan blurts with absolute giddiness.

"Do you have anymore," I inquire, hungry to see them.

"No, but I have sketches. I didn't want to go into a full line if I didn't get good initial feedback," he says cautiously. He opens his sketchbook to show me the colors and styles for the women's line.

Cutting to the chase, I offer what he will never ask. "Do you need more financing to get them out and noticed?"

"Oh my God, are you serious, Emma?" Nathan's voice has now gone up an octave.

I shoot him a look for questioning my interest.

"I couldn't. You've already done so much."

"Yes, you can," Jared endorses, knowing what I'm getting at as he pets Sadie.

"My first round of investment in you was because I believed in you, and I still do. You know I wouldn't offer if I honestly didn't mean it." I share with love and a hint of business acumen attached. "We don't have to go over the details now. We'll sit down and you can show me what you need and go from there."

"I love you!" Nathan shouts, grabbing and kissing me all over my face.

"I love you too, sweetie," I respond, wrapping my arms around him to get him to stop his assault of affection.

Suddenly, Jared and Maggie are hugging us too.

"Ooo, a four-way," Nathan jokes.

Chapter Seven

We all laugh.

When Nathan was getting his boutique started in WeHo, I was able to help as a financial backer and he insisted on me being a partner. I agreed to be a silent partner and only assist with any business aspects that he didn't understand. Nathaniel's has been showing promise for its first year and a half. It's in the green, which is not typical for any business within the first few years, though it's not enough green to take on a second line. Naturally Me started openly pushing Nathaniel's three months before the opening and Jared has been wearing some of the clothing on camera which has been a nice boost for sales each month. Maggie has had two team members from Raven Media working on the social media marketing for Nathaniel's which has been the strongest proponent of Nathan's fashion success.

"Once you get the women's line going, you're going to need to consider a diva pet line as well," Maggie excitedly suggests. "Can you imagine, pet's matching their owners?"

"That would line up perfectly with the pet division for Naturally Me with Sadie too," Jared adds.

"Oh, my! That's an awesome idea. I've got a bunch of ideas already running through my head," Nathan shouts with absolute delight.

"One step at a time girls," I politely chide. "We need to know that the current men's line and what's coming out for next season gets positive feedback as we dip into the women's line before even entertaining the idea of pet fashion."

"She's right," Nathan agrees without a change in his tone. "But, I'll start dreaming and designing it all."

"I wouldn't expect anything less," I encourage.

"Are you girls hungry? Did you eat lunch?" Nathan asks.

"No, we came right here," Maggie answers.

"Good! Jared and I just went shopping after breakfast, so we're all stocked up for the weekend whether we go out to eat or not." Nathan informs us, excited to entertain.

Nathan has been vigorously following many of the nutrition topics posted on Naturally Me and he's mentioned how different he feels. He was never fat to begin with, but Nathan's become leaner, stronger and more energetic. He mentions how the energy helps with his clarity and focus while designing and it's obviously evident in the women's line he's been creating.

"You boys had breakfast?" Maggie mocks, finally being able to harass Jared.

"I was so excited about this weekend that I could barely sleep," Nathan confesses.

"I couldn't even tire him out," Jared shares with a blushing grin.

"Wow!" I say rather impressed.

Being the two main cooks in the group, Nathan and I get to work on making lunch for the four of us while we all chat about incidental topics. We decide on making grilled cheese sandwiches with two different kinds of raw, organic cheese topped with a delicious homemade mustard mayonnaise spread I love to make, spinach, avocado, onion and tomato. Instead of butter, we use raw coconut oil on the cast iron skillet. We also have homemade lemonade with fresh peppermint leaves from Nathan's little herb garden, a side salad with all the fixings and organic roasted red pepper and tomato soup.

A variety of topics enter our conversations while we cooking and eating lunch. Though I'm not a complete kiss and tell kind of girl, I do give most of the juicy details about my encounter with Chris and Molly.

"Would you sleep with him again," Nathan asks.

"Most likely if I saw him again, but I'd have to be careful," I answer truthfully.

"Because of Caleb?" Maggie inquires.

"God no. Please, I can handle him," I firmly insist.

"He's into her. Wants more than just a couple of good fucks," Jared declares.

"Really?" Nathan questions.

"I saw it in his face every time we saw him since Ayana's opening and again last night, especially after they returned from their adventure," Jared confirms.

"Yep," I validate Jared's statement and observation.

"Why not just date the guy," Nathan challenges.

I reply with a *you're kidding me right* look.

"Yeah . . . Emma date. When Hell freezes over . . ." Jared chuckles and I quickly join his amusement.

"You really still don't want to date," Nathan says with a slightly worried tone.

"Nope," I affirm with sternness.

"You don't think you'll ever date, even when the three of us are married and with kids?" Nathan probes.

I shake my head in response causing the mood to become a little cloudy.

I know that anything can be possible, especially the thought of Nathan and Jared being married at some point — even if it's not to each other. However, the thought of letting anyone in that close freaks me out. The idea of even just losing the three of them terrifies me to no end. I don't know what I would do if I lost one of them. I'm not heartless, I just don't want to allow any chances of my heart being broken for any reason.

Chapter Seven

Oblivious to the shift in the mood, Maggie chimes in, "What about Joe? He's cute and totally into you."

Jared cracks up at her suggestion as I just eyeball her and remind her of my habits. "Seriously, Maggie? You know my rules."

With a confident smile, she throws at me, "Well, rules are made to be broken. Besides, Nǎinai has blessed you with *love*, a *husband* and *children*."

I cringe at the memory.

"That's right," Jared adds, proud of Maggie's moment as he hugs her.

"Nǎinai is never wrong, Emma," Maggie affirms while getting more laughs from Jared and Nathan.

"End of discussion," I instruct, a little miffed at their statements.

I know they mean well overall, but I'll decide my love life.

The rest of the day, the four of us and Sadie go out to spend some time at the park before shopping. When we eat dinner back at the condo, we curl up together to play some board games and then watch a movie. I am surprised at the three of them wanting to keep it low key for the evening as the night progresses. I'm more surprised with Nathan and Jared than Maggie. They must really want to be on their game tomorrow for volleyball — that or they plan on having more sex.

Jared joins Nathan in his room after the movie and Maggie and I move to the bedroom that we're sharing. I wonder if things are starting to change between Nathan and Jared again. They've always been so cool and calm around each other, but there's something different. I don't know how to explain it. Regardless, I'm happy for them.

While Sadie falls asleep in the middle of the bed, Maggie and I sit up for another hour before turning off the lights. She's trying to recount all of her conversations with Henry for me. I'm not really in the mood, but I know it's more because she's trying to see if there's anything that I might pick up. I do my best to counsel her regarding his actions and what he has said directly to her, in person or in text messages. Compared to all of the other guys she's met and dated, Henry seems legit. I think he genuinely cares for her which I share with her openly.

Inwardly, I keep my concern for what a relationship between her and Henry means for our friendship. She's been elated when dating a guy before, but with Henry she's different. I'm just worried that things between us will change too much. I know we won't engage sexually over time, which is fine. I've been able to manage in the past. But, what if they do get married and have kids? Will she move away? Will we still see each other as much? The one thing I'm not willing to accept is that these are all things in my life that I can't control and it pisses me off while simultaneously scaring the living daylights out of me.

Eight

As I attempt to lift my heavy eyelids, I discover a hazy darkness surrounding me. Blinking slowly several times, my half-opened eyes won't focus to give me any clear indication of what's around me and where the blurry, flashing lights above are coming from. My body feels heavy. Still unable to open my eyes all the way, I perceive that I'm laying down somewhere. A cool dampness near my left cheek reveals itself as a slight gust of air brushes past my face. Sliding my right arm up the side of my body like a snake, my fingers creep to my lips. Drool — or, at least I hope so.

Two large and oddly shaped figures materialize in front of me. They are so close, only a foot or two away. Voices suddenly emanate from the now more defined silhouettes. Their speech sounds muffled and trails off into the distance even as I try to concentrate on their words. Who are they? What are they saying? Why can't I understand them? One of the voices almost sounds feminine.

Another indistinguishable sound gradually becomes more apparent as it grows louder and the ringing in my ears subsides. It's the engine of a car. My brain finally starts to put the fuzzy pieces of evidence together. I must have fallen asleep in the back seat. A familiar smell creeps into my nose that reassures me — my mother's perfume.

"Mom?" my throat squeezes out in a raw, breathy, hoarse tone.

"We're almost home, dear," her voice replies in a low sluggish tone.

I internally smile at her comforting words, though her voice sounds peculiar.

A sudden rush of nervousness enters my belly. The car feels as if it's flying down the road like a rocket ship as the speed of the flashing lights zooming above my head all blur into one.

"Mom," I try to shout, but not a single sound escapes my mouth this time. Confused, I try again. "Mom!"

She doesn't hear me. I don't hear me.

A single, bright white light races towards us, growing larger by the second. My mother turns her head towards me smiling. Why doesn't she hear me? How does she not see the light?

Again, with all my might. "Mom . . . !" my voice trails in my head like a deafening siren, stabbing my ears like a knife.

Time stops in this very moment. I can see everything with perfect clarity as I stare in horror into my mother's eyes. My mouth is left open, still screaming without a sound. I can't hear anything except a piercing ring that echoes in my body. Why can't she hear me? Why doesn't she see the terrified look on my face?

My body lurches backward as I attempt to scramble to grab my mother and I suddenly become paralyzed. Then, it happens all at once — I see the face of the truck driver before I hear the sound of metal hitting metal as it wraps itself around and around. Maggie? I watch my parents' bodies hurling forward toward the oncoming truck, bouncing around like ping pong balls, getting dented with each blow.

My heart is filled with terror as I desperately try to yell one more time, "Mom . . . !"

Jerking up, I shout out in horror. My heart is pounding, my lungs are heaving and my entire body is shaking.

"Emma?! Emma, are you alright?" Maggie searches for the light next to the bed as Jared and Nathan barge into the room in response to my screams.

Sadie is whimpering and scrambling to comfort me as well.

Wrapping his arms around me, Jared pulls me into his chest, draping my legs across his lap like a parent would for their child, "It's okay Emma. It's okay." Jared's actions are routine from the years of us living together.

Nathan sits across from me, stroking my hair while Maggie presses her forehead into my back. Sadie wedges herself between Nathan and me, placing her head on my leg as Jared rocks us gently back and forth while repeating his soothing words, "It's okay, Emma. It's okay."

My body trembles as I recount the nightmare to myself. The vision has always been the same until now and my mind is disturbed by the image of Maggie's face as the truck driver. I bury my face into Jared's chest and shake my head, trying to rid the pictures from my memory. The tears just keep flowing as I keep seeing in my head the image of Maggie driving the truck.

I must have passed out over time because I wake with all five of us spread out a little on the bed and to the sound of Jared, Nathan and Maggie talking softly.

"Has it always been like this," Nathan whispers with a shaky voice.

"No," Jared answers with fear. "It hasn't been like this in a long time."

Jared has experienced the brunt of my nightmares since we met. It took months before I stopped waking up screaming from them. He's the only one I've told what I see.

"I've never seen her this bad," Maggie adds cautiously with a shaky tone.

"I thought they weren't this bad anymore. She had one a few weeks ago, the morning of our meeting, but she seemed fine when I got there. I'm not

Chapter Eight

sure why they're happening again. She's gone months without having them," Jared discloses as he pulls me in tighter.

"What's causing them to come back?" Nathan searches.

"I honestly don't know," Jared admits with a sniff like he's been crying. "How was she last night when you two went to bed?"

Pausing to think, Maggie responds, "Fine. Like normal. Nothing different."

I can feel Jared nod his response. I'm not sure why I'm having them either and I hope they don't ask when I finally let them know I'm awake.

I wait for what feels like ten minutes later before shifting like I'm waking up. "Since when are you guys into an orgy?" I say with my best fake groggy morning voice.

I feel Jared breathe in and out as some tension in his body releases.

"Only if they're all men," he replies with strained emotion.

Maggie and I chuckle when I hear what sounds like a slap on skin. Nathan must have hit Jared for his comment.

Before letting them question me, I ask, "What time is it?"

"It's just after six," Maggie answers with her perky, soft voice.

She's clearly happy to hear me joking.

"I've got to feed Sadie," I continue, rising and trying to move on from earlier.

Jared catches my eye and I know he's not convinced by my little act, though Maggie and Nathan buy into it. I can tell Jared is hesitating to say anything for which I'm very grateful. If we're going to have a discussion, I don't want to do it now, let alone in front of Maggie and Nathan. I've always been able to talk to Jared about this. It's not easy, but it's easier than with anyone else.

They all follow me into the kitchen, watching me closely, wondering if anything should be said and trying to find out if I might share. I start my morning process by feeding Sadie and then drinking my glass of clay. Nathan has a glass as well while Maggie and Jared make tea.

"What time are we meeting *Romeo*?" I tease Maggie with a smile.

"Ha ha," she shoots back with a grin, lighting up at my playfulness. "I told them to meet us at the courts for eight-thirty."

"Cool. We have plenty of time to get ready," I continue with a bounce in my voice.

Jared watches me cautiously as Maggie and Nathan start chatting about their excitement for the day. As I finish my drink, I rinse out the cup and walk over to Jared to give him a reassuring hug and kiss.

With a tentative tone, he whispers, "Glad to have my *Kitten* back."

My grin widens seeing him ease. "Me too."

"You rebounding this morning?" Nathan directs at me.

"Just to loosen up. I want to be on my A-game for kicking some butt in volleyball," I reply.

"That's what I was thinking," Nathan shares. His smile widens, "I figured you haven't lost your competitive side."

Nathan has had a rebounder since Christmas. It was a gift from me when he had vocalized several times that he wanted to start improving his overall health.

"Nope," I confirm.

"Be nice today, Emma," Maggie comments, as if I'm never nice.

"I'm alway nice," I mock.

Jared and Nathan giggle.

"You know what I mean," she counters, waving her finger at me.

Laughing, Jared taunts, "She's serious, Emma. She's even using Năinai's finger wave. You better watch out."

I shake my head at all the fun while deciding on if I want to add to their morning entertainment.

"Why don't you start jumping while I take Sadie out," I suggest to Nathan.

Jared joins Sadie and me for a walk on the beach, obviously concerned about this morning. "You okay, *Kitten*?"

"Yeah . . . yeah . . . I'm fine," I uncomfortably agree.

Jared and I both know that I'm lying.

"Want to talk about it?" Jared gently pushes.

He knows I hate talking about the dream and he always treads lightly when we do.

"Not really . . . but, I know you do."

"It's been a while since you've had them . . . and then you had one a few weeks ago before our meeting, and then this morning," he reminds.

"I know . . . and this one was different," I accidentally blurt, crossing my arms in front of me.

"Different?" he quickly questions.

"Umm . . . shit," I comment.

"Different, how?" he confronts.

Chapter Eight

Jared's demeanor changes as he gets into protective mode.

Taking a deep breathe, I admit what I saw. "Everything was exactly the same . . . except . . . ." A shiver slides down my spine.

"Except . . . ?" Jared pries.

"I saw the truck driver . . .his . . . her . . . face . . ." I hesitantly reveal.

"Seriously?"

"Yeah . . ." I confirm. " . . . but, not how you think."

"What do you mean?" Jared stops us, placing his hands on my upper arms.

"It was . . . Maggie," I begrudgingly confess, not wanting to look him in the eye.

"Maggie?" Jared repeats, confused and bewildered.

"Yeah . . ." I unwillingly verify. "Please, don't tell her."

Jared doesn't say anything. He doesn't need to. He just pulls me into his body, hugging me, reassuring me. We stay embraced for a little while until Sadie insists on one of us throwing her ball again.

When we resume walking back towards Nathan's, Jared breeches the subject again. "So, why Maggie's face?"

"Don't know . . . and, I don't really want to know," I confess.

Jared nods his understanding and during the rest of our walk, we stay connected by holding hands.

By the time Jared, Sadie and I return from our walk, Jared jumps on the rebounder first. "I really need to start using this more," he announces as he jumps off. "I can feel the difference with just ten minutes." He sits down on the floor to stretch. "And, look at Nathan . . . he's gotten sexier just using it these past few months."

"And, you wonder why you have a challenge when we go trampolining," Nathan adds playfully.

I laugh because it's true. We go to some of the local trampoline places between Santa Monica and Pasadena. They have large trampolines in rows across the floor that allow you to jump from one to the other. We go when they have their free jump times and Jared gets tired after about thirty minutes into our hour long paid session.

"Emma's like the freakin' *Energizer Bunny*," Maggie comments as I hop on for my turn.

It's true, I jump every morning on my rebounder for at least thirty minutes, usually more, and that doesn't count when I do the same thing in the evenings.

At least two days a week I head over to the trampoline facility in Glendale to take their morning hour long rebound classes on the large trampolines.

Today, I'm inclined to keep jumping, but I have to control my tendency to continue after having the dream. I'll need to relieve the rest of my tension when we play volleyball.

"She's the *Energizer Sex Kitten*," Nathan laughs out.

This gets all three of them laughing and a hearty giggle out of me.

By the time we hit the showers, Nathan and Jared are in one and Maggie and myself are in another. We've got about forty-five minutes to eat and dress before getting to the courts by eight-thirty to meet Henry and Joe. Luckily, dressing isn't as big of a deal for the boys and they are dressed in record time as I finish packing the soft coolers with water, coconut water, fruit, trail mix and a few snacks for Sadie. Maggie isn't helpful packing the coolers since she's more concerned with texting Henry. We all gulp down the smoothies I prepare before we're out the door.

"Which Tesla should we take?" Jared asks. "Yours, mine or Maggie's?"

Not looking up from texting, Maggie replies, "I left me keys upstairs."

All she brought was her phone and small clutch purse which she stashed in one of the outside pockets of the blue cooler.

"Alright. Your's or mine," Jared states to Nathan with a seductive undertone.

"Oh, God. Please don't start now or we'll never leave," I poke.

"Mine then," Nathan says, taking the high ground before smacking me on my ass.

"Cute. Just hope we aren't on opposite teams today," I threaten deviously as I put the coolers in the trunk on top of the beach chairs.

We're at the volleyball courts in just five minutes since there's nobody on the Santa Monica roads this early on a Saturday morning.

"They should be here any minute," Maggie shouts as Jared and Nathan put out three folding chairs onto the sand near one of the nets and I start setting up the umbrella.

"Yay," Jared yells in a mild mocking tone, jumping up and down and clapping his hands.

Maggie sticks her tongue out in protest while Nathan and I laugh.

When the boys and I finish getting the umbrella situated, we turn to see Maggie running to the entry way of the fence towards the parking lot.

"They're here," Jared squeals into Nathan's ear while wrapping one of his arms around Nathan's shoulders.

Chapter Eight

As Maggie, Henry and Joe approach the fence, Sadie whines, so I signal her that she can go greet them. Sadie gets to Joe first and is met warmly by him. I'm still perplexed at her response to him — she only bares her belly with the people within our little family. Henry has to let go of Maggie's hand to pet Sadie, but immediately returns his palm to hers as they resume their way over.

Henry and Joe immediately hug Jared and then Jared makes introductions to Nathan who openly hugs Henry and Joe.

Approaching me, Henry holds out his hand and I shake it happily, "Good morning, Emma."

"Good morning, Henry," I return warmly.

My attention goes to Joe next, who can wear workout clothes as well as he wears a suit.

"Hi, Joe," I initiate with the same smile I gave Henry.

"Good morning, Emma," Joe returns with a full, elated smile as he reaches to shake my hand.

My lady parts tingle at his warm touch as he lifts my hand to his mouth again.

"Is it just the six of us," Henry questions.

"For now . . . but we usually pick up a few more as the morning passes," Nathan replies.

"Cool," Henry acknowledges.

Joe nods in agreement.

"I'm on Henry's team," shouts Maggie.

I swear that Jared, Nathan and I all roll our eyes and shake our heads at the same time.

"Should we have the girls on different teams to make it fair?" Joe questions, which is immediately met with laughter from Nathan and Jared.

I deliberately choose to not respond which could work to my benefit.

"Sure," Jared eludes in agreement. "We should definitely make it fair." He and Nathan continue to crack up as Joe appears a little confused.

The air is still cool this early in the morning, but I decided to take my dark grey running jacket off leaving me only wearing a tight white v-neck cotton tee shirt, that makes my natural c-cup sized breasts pop, even in a sports bra, and dark grey spandex capris. I'm always barefoot when I play beach volleyball.

"Hey Joe! Do you want a front view or back view while we play?" Jared inquires loudly.

I glance over at them when I hear Jared's remarks and spot Joe looking away. Was he just checking me out?

Nathan roars with laughter as Joe blushes a little. Joe was checking me out and I almost blush myself. Maggie and Henry seem too preoccupied in their own conversation to notice.

"You're right," Nathan agrees. "He's totally into her. But, then again, what guy wouldn't be?"

I shake my head in protest and mild irritation. I should be used to this by now from Nathan and Jared.

We divide up into our teams of three and begin playing. Henry, Maggie and Nathan are on one team and Jared, Joe and myself on the other. With one person up front and two in the back, we volley for the serve as I stand in the back left position. Jared is in front me and purposefully misses the ball when he and Nathan jump up at the net, letting Nathan win. Man, does he have it bad for Nathan.

Henry serves first in my direction. I pop the ball up for Jared who lobs it over the net.

"Come on man. Play the game. Stop flirting with Nathan," I yell playfully, not letting my competitive nature out too quickly.

"What?!" Jared retorts.

I glare at him. "You know you're getting laid tonight regardless, so you better play," I chide with a smile.

Jared's eyes look to Nathan who nods in agreement.

Maggie, Henry and Joe look at me a little in shock at my blatant announcement. I'm only this vocal when I'm surrounded by my friends and I seem to not care with two others present. Maggie's only shocked because Henry is here.

"Emma," Maggie scolds with embarrassment in her voice.

I smile proudly. Oddly, I find my gaze heading to Joe as I take my position to the left of him.

By the time I get to serve, it's five to three and my team is losing.

"This one is for you, Dartmouth," I shout to get Henry's attention which is on Maggie.

I hurl the ball into the air and jump to hit it with my fist. The ball spirals towards Henry's feet faster than he expects, causing him to miss the ball.

"Four-to-five!" I broadcast as I look for Joe's response before the ball is returned to me for my next serve.

His smirk has returned.

Chapter Eight

"Be nice, Emma," Maggie scolds.

"What?!" I reply. "I'm just playing the game. It's not my fault if he's not going to pay attention."

She shakes her head at me.

"Fine," I agree.

Aside from my competitive nature, my eagerness to get the tension out from the nightmare from this morning is going to need to be tempered a little.

"Let the torture begin," Jared proclaims as he raises his arms above his head.

"Don't encourage her," Maggie warily shouts.

Nathan laughs and directs to Maggie, "You better bring your A-Game now, girl! This is no time to be all cutesy for a guy."

Maggie's face flushes a little as her eyes widen. Though she's short, Maggie can play a mean volleyball game when she wants to. She's nowhere near as competitive as I am, but she starts to get the look in her eye that she's not going down without a fight.

"There's my Mags," Jared coaxes her.

"It's on," Maggie confirms with determination.

I serve four more times bringing the score to eight-to-five with my team in the lead before we falter. Maggie sends a sharp serve over that causes Joe and I to almost collide.

"Call it!" Jared shouts.

Joe and I nod in agreement.

"Six-to-eight," Maggie announces, pleased with herself before her second serve.

Nathan pops the ball up, forcing me to line the ball to the net for Joe to send over towards Maggie. The ball falls to the edge of the court, staying in play by a couple inches. Jared boasts as we win the point.

We continue playing until my team wins by one point, fifteen-to-fourteen. After Jared serves the winning point, I jump up on him with my arms and legs wrapped around his body, almost knocking him to the ground. Everyone has a good laugh at our celebration.

Taking a break, everyone starts hydrating and adds some natural suntan lotion to their exposed skin. Sadie eagerly greets everyone, looking for attention. I pour her some water and a few snacks into her mesh bowls.

Maggie's team triumphantly wins the second game by two points. Getting ready to start our third game, all of the guys are shirtless. Trying not to directly stare, my peripheral vision allows me to enjoy the sight of Joe's body. There's not an ounce of fat on the man with his rippling muscles from his shoulders to his lower abdomen. For an East Coast boy, he's got a slight tan and no sign of tan lines. His muscles sparkle as a hint of sunlight bounces off his sweat. Joe's got a little bit of chest hair that tappers down into a happy trail all the way to the edge of his shorts. I feel an increase in moisture between my legs as a small gust of wind lightly swirls around me. Focus, Emma.

A group of four guys join us just as we take the court again, making it five people per team. The new teammates take their turns flirting with Maggie and me, but Maggie tries to ignore them. I, on the other hand, thoroughly enjoy the attention and flirt back, even adding Joe to the mix so he doesn't feel left out.

My team wins again, by two points.

By the end of the forth game, Maggie's team has won and we decide to call it a draw. The four guys who joined us are sad when our group explains that we are done for the day. I guess they were hopping to see Maggie and I bounce around a little more. They ask for my phone number, but I refuse politely.

"Henry and I are going for a walk on the beach," Maggie discloses after speaking privately with him and folding up the beach chairs.

"Good idea. Wanna go for a walk, cutie?" Jared questions Nathan mischievously.

"Of course," Nathan answers with a gleam in his eye.

The four of them head away as Joe, with an adorable smile, states the awkward and obvious circumstance we're left with. "Looks like it's just you and me."

"Yep," I confirm.

He helps me get the chairs, umbrella and coolers packed into Nathan's car as Sadie bounces around us.

"I like your car," Joe states.

"It's not mine. It's Nathan's," I reply.

"Oh, sorry. I just figured it was yours," he says nervously. "That's right, you don't like cars."

I wince a little at his words and he catches me.

"Sorry . . . I, uh . . . that didn't come out right," he stutters.

Joe seems sincere, so I let him off the hook. "It's okay," I say, hoping he doesn't inquire why. I grab Sadie's ball and look to Joe, "I'm taking her out to play a little?"

"Do you mind if I join you ladies?" he asks.

"Sure," I return, not sure if it is a good idea.

Chapter Eight

We start walking in the opposite direction from the rest of our group. There are fewer people, so it's easier to give Sadie more room to run and fetch. We walk quietly all the way to the water's edge tossing the ball for Sadie each time she brings it back, staying far enough away from the ocean since it's chilly.

"I didn't mean to be rude earlier . . ." Joe starts as he scratches his head. ". . . when I was asking if we should split you and Maggie up for teams."

"It's okay. No big deal," I reply.

It's obvious that Joe means what he says. The trait of honesty seems fully seated in his personality and I appreciate that. This idea only bothers me since my attraction for him is more than I anticipated.

He continues as he still seems a little rattled, "I didn't think you girl's couldn't play . . . I . . . ."

"Don't worry about it," I reassure him. "No hard feelings."

This brings a relieved smile to his face as he nods.

I take a few more steps before saying timidly, "Please don't think I'm . . . not a nice person."

"Why would I think that?" he questions with his eyebrows raised before picking up the ball this time to throw if for Sadie.

"I know I can seem a little gruff and mean, and I wasn't very nice when we first met and . . . ."

Cutting me off, Joe turns towards me to respond, "Not at all. I can see that you're just protective of your friends. I admire that."

My eyes soften under his gaze. "Thanks."

Aside from my sexual attraction to Joe, I actually feel very comfortable with him. It's a similar comfort I felt with Jared and Nathan when I first met them, though I know Joe is not gay. What is happening?

We decide to sit in the sand after a little bit as Sadie bounces into the water chasing the waves on occasion and then runs back to us. Anytime there is silence between us, it isn't awkward for me and it doesn't appear that way for him.

"No interrogation for me today," he teases as he bumps my shoulder.

I get the feeling that he wants me to question him. "No . . . not now, anyway," I reply with a smile, aware of the bait he's laid out for me.

"Do you mind if I ask a few questions?"

I inwardly cringe at the thought, but relay an expression as if I'm considering it.

"Nothing too intrusive. Just a few little questions," he nudges gently.

"I guess . . ." I say with my voice trailing off as our eyes meet.

He hesitates for a moment, considering on what question to ask first. "Henry is like one of my brothers. I only want to see him happy. So, I guess . . . I was just wondering, from your perspective, what does their relationship mean to Maggie?"

I'm shocked at his question. He seems protective of Henry like I am of Maggie. I like that a lot, but feel defensive of Maggie at his subtle implication.

"She's not a heart breaker or a gold digger, if that's what you're worried about."

Bashfully, he responds, "I wasn't trying to imply . . . ."

I cut him off before he can continue, "It's okay . . . Maggie is the type of girl who falls for guys easily just to have her heart broken." After another beat, I add, "I can see there is a connection between the two of them. A connection I've never seen her have with any other guy. . . ." My thoughts and where they are leading cause me to stop short of saying them out loud.

"Good. I mean . . . I'm sorry. That came out wrong," Joe replies while trying to recover.

He really is trying to be respectful towards both of them. It's sweet and I find myself liking him more.

"Relax," I say with a little chuckle which seems to ease him.

I'm excited to hear we both feel the same way about our friends.

After a few more minutes of quiet, Joe asks, "So, should I be worried about your boyfriend seeing us talking. If he's the jealous type?"

He just went there and the funny thing is that I'm not really surprised or offended. "No. No boyfriend."

"Really?" he declares with awe. "I can't believe for one second that a woman as beautiful as yourself doesn't have a boyfriend."

He's totally hitting on me and I'm enjoying it more than I should.

Trying to control myself, I reply, "Really?!"

"Well, I'd ask about a girlfriend, but that was ruled out at New Year's by Nǎinai," he jokes.

Carefully considering how I want to answer, I glare at him with a grin before responding. "Do you really think flirting with me will help your case?"

"Is it working?" Joe inquires with a large smile.

He's clearly not afraid to hide it.

"No," I sternly reply, holding my ground. "Besides, I don't date."

"Must be your pleasant personality when people first meet you," he teases, bumping his shoulder into mine again.

"I'm not going to respond to that," I declare as I shake my head and push his shoulder away a little.

Yep, definitely all muscle. Yum.

He sits laughing under his breath at his little victory as I look away, trying not to smile. I can't let him see that he's gotten to me. I oddly find myself more turned on.

Sadie bounces back from the water to us, staying close while we sit in silence, and on occasion I swear I can hear Joe laugh when I don't look at him. Our eyes meet for a moment and his gaze captivates me.

Joe's eyes suddenly dart up, and before I can respond, Jared wrestles and pins me to the ground. Jared's temporary victory doesn't hold me long as my reflexes from the years of training kick in. Within just a few seconds, I've got Jared pinned in a Jujitsu move that I know he can't get out of.

"Shit!" Jared whimpers.

Jared has been strong since we first met and is the person who introduced me to self-defense. Though he had about a year on me in training, I caught up pretty quickly. Jared was always willing to practice at home, and we'd spend a lot of free time sparring. We finally reached a point where the skill was thoroughly engrained in us and everything became instinctual. It was like breathing. We just do it. However, I continued to train. I loved to learn new things aside of my compulsion to feel safe and secure. Jared knows as much as I do, because whenever I learn something new, I show him. The only difference between us is that I practice more often.

Nathan is laughing profusely at our entanglement.

"Should we break them up?" Joe says with a little concern.

"Not at all," Nathan reassures him. "They do this all the time. Kind of like a big brother, little sister thing."

"Say it," I command.

"Never," shouts Jared.

"Would you two stop it! Somebody's going to get hurt," Maggie yells at us like we're children fighting as she and Henry stroll closer.

"Never," Jared repeats. Frustrated with his position, Jared tries anything and everything to get free. "Get ready, Nathan!" Jared presses his fingers down causing me to yelp and release him. Before I can compose myself from being tickled, Nathan grabs my legs and Jared has my arms secure behind my back.

"The only way you ever win is by cheating! Don't think I won't get even!" I yell in defiance.

The two men proceed to stand up and head towards the water.

"Don't . . . you . . . even think about it," I shout in warning, aware of their intention.

Though they're both strong, I've got more body awareness and control from all of my compulsive exercising. I start thrashing my body up and down, bending at the waist in an attempt to break free. Nathan tries to pull a little on my legs to sturdy himself while temporarily hindering my movement.

"Leave her alone," Maggie commands in the distance.

I appreciate that she's trying to help, but it's already beyond the point of words. We're all having fun and I doubt she realizes it.

I call for Sadie, but all she does is run around us as we get closer to the water. Seeing that we're on the water's edge, I give a sudden thrust with my entire body knocking all three of us down into the oncoming wave.

"Shit!" Jared yells, scrambling to his feet, soaked all the way up his back.

"Damn that's cold," Nathan shouts, crawling out wet from the waist down.

"Serves you right for trying to mess with Emma," Maggie chides as she rushes to help me while trying to avoid the freezing water.

"Yooooooou . . . sssssssuckkkkkk!" I stammer as I slowly creep up out of the water, exposing my drenched, shivering body. Immediately, I place my arms across my chest not concerned that I'm wearing a wet, white shirt, but simply because the water in California this time of year is that cold, especially when the wind gusts along incessantly.

"We weren't really going to throw you in," Jared proclaims walking towards me hesitantly. "Honest."

"Shame on us," Nathan announces, still laughing.

I can't help but smile at them. It was funny — though I was the one who got wet the most. At least I got them a bit too.

The wind is making the chill worse, so I peel off my shirt exposing my six pack abs and my more prominently erect nipples that are pushing through my white sports bra.

Joe moves toward me as he takes off his shirt and hands it to me, "Here. I have extra in the car."

"Thhhhanksss . . . bbbbbbut I'mmm fffine," I confess, too proud to cover up from the cold as my teeth chatter.

Chapter Eight

Joe grins while biting his bottom lip. I watch his eyes travel down to my breasts. I smile back at him not caring at this point.

"I'll take it," Maggie says as she drapes the shirt around my shoulders. She wants to help, but doesn't like the idea of getting wet.

"Do we have any towels?" Jared asks.

"They're in the car," I advise with my teeth chattering less.

Maggie's body heat is helping to warm me and I savor her touch.

"Where are the keys?" Henry asks. "I can go get them."

"Hooked on Sadie's leash." I point in the direction of where I left it.

Henry grabs the keys and jogs to the car as we begin to follow. Henry reaches the car first, but the rest of us are shortly behind. Maggie grabs one of the towels from Henry and drapes it over my shoulders. Nathan and Jared giggle as they watch Joe and Henry stare with stunned looks on their faces as Maggie's hands rub me down, including my breasts, rear and thighs. Though I protest, she ignores me. I don't think she realizes what's happening, so I start to laugh at her innocence.

"Looks like we should change before heading to lunch," Nathan states the obvious while trying to direct everyone's attention away from Maggie's actions.

"Yep," I agree as my suppressed laughter returns. "Maggie, I'm good. Thanks."

"What? Oh, okay," she replies. After a few more pats, Maggie leans in and asks, "Do you mind if I ride back with Henry?"

"No," I chuckle, taking the towel from her hand to stop her.

Maggie smiles eagerly. She's so cute.

I put my running jacket back on as Jared opens the door for me. Does he really think that an act of chivalry will win him back into my favor? I signal for Sadie to get in after putting the towel on the seat to minimize the amount of moister from both of us. Nathan jumps behind the wheel and starts the car as Jared climbs in. Two seconds later the right back passenger door opens.

"You joining us?" Nathan says as more of a statement than a question.

"I figured I should give them a little privacy. Just in case," Joe say, sliding across the seat still topless.

We all nod and I purposefully fix my gaze to the front of the car, not wanting to stare at Joe's half naked body.

Joe looks over to me with a smile, "How are you feeling?"

"Better. Thanks," I reply, keeping my eyes forward.

Nathan turns on the heat before pulling away from the parking spot and up to the street. Jared reaches back to hold my hand for the ride and I graciously take it.

"I've got the car registration and insurance in my bag," I announce to Nathan. "Don't let me forget to give it to you."

"Why didn't you give it to me yesterday?" he inquires.

"Wasn't thinking about it. It popped into my head just now," I confirm.

"Why do you have his car information?" Joe queries.

Great! Now here's another item about me that shouldn't be disclosed. What was I thinking?

"She technically owns it," Jared explains.

"No, I don't," I protest.

"Okay. My bad. Actually her company owns it," Jared corrects himself. "They're all company cars."

"All?" Joe searches.

"Yep. Nathan's, mine and Maggie's," Jared confirms.

"Smart . . ." Joe comments. ". . . but, funny."

"What's funny?" I inquiry.

"You hate cars, but technically own three," Joe replies with a chuckle. "I understand why. It's just funny."

"I know. Right?!" Nathan adds.

I don't say anything because there is truth to the irony of it all.

Back at the condo, Nathan escorts Joe and Henry to the third bedroom which is on the other side of Maggie's and my room that is divided by a joining bathroom. "You guys can stay the night, or weekend, if you'd like. We've got plenty of room and food."

"Thanks," Henry and Joe reply.

I shudder at the thought of Henry and Joe joining us as I make my way to the bathroom. Maggie is going to be obsessed with Henry the whole time.

"Nothing fancy," Jared instructs with regards to clothing. "We're just hanging out."

"What do you boys like to eat?" Nathan questions.

"I'm not picky, " Joe responds.

"Me either," Henry agrees.

Chapter Eight

Looking to me as he opens the door further from the third bedroom into the bathroom where I am, Nathan inquires, "Where should we go to eat?"

"RFD?" I question back.

"Ohh, I haven't eaten there in a long time," admits Nathan.

"There's only two and half bath here boys, so you'll need to wait for the girls to finish showering before you can jump in," Jared instructs.

"Unless you want to . . ." Nathan begins.

"Don't even go there," I reprimand him as I snap a towel on his backside. "Go rub each other down and leave us be," I dictate with a glare.

"Okay, okay," Nathan sheepishly retorts, grabbing Jared's hand and leads him out the door.

"You girls can shower first," Henry offers.

"Thanks," Maggie says with bubbly enthusiasm. She gives me a look to see if I want to go first.

I know she wants to spend more time with Henry, so I don't mind. Plus, I'm still a little chilled from Jared's and Nathan's dunking.

The shower is absolutely invigorating. I stand soaking for probably five minutes under the steaming hotness before moving to wash. There are no plans to have sex with anyone for the next couple of days, and since I got waxed a week ago, I'm good in the hair removal department. I start with shampoo, leaving it in while I lather up my body. As I rinse the soap off, my entire body tingles all the way down to my loins. If I knew I wouldn't be heard and that I had time, I'd masturbate. I finish with conditioner, letting it sit for a few extra moments as I keep my body under the water.

Getting out of the shower, I towel dry my hair. There's no need to blow dry it since there are three more people to take turns. Securely wrapping the towel around my body, just in case there are people in my room or the bedroom door is open, I head to Maggie's and my room. I'm relieved to find the room empty and that the door is closed, allowing me to begin changing.

Santa Monica is typically about ten degrees cooler than Pasadena, so I dress in blue jeans, a cotton white tank top and a sky blue v-neck cashmere sweater. I put my makeup on, brush and dry my hair a little more before going out to the living room.

"Got kicked out of your own room?" I question Joe when I find him on the couch, still shirtless, with his iPad and Sadie.

Why is he still shirtless? I am shocked to see Sadie laying with him instead of being in the room waiting for me. This is new.

"How can you tell?" he responds with a hint of sarcasm.

I nod, rolling my eyes, not surprised.

We both look over towards Nathan's room suddenly as we hear some soft moans echoing through the wall.

I laugh at the sound. "They must have forgotten to close the bathroom door."

Joe nods in agreement but doesn't seem flustered or irritated.

"Do you have access to your stuff?" I ask, wanting to redirect our attention to something else.

"Yes. I left my bags just over there. I figured I might be on the couch tonight. Why?" he says.

If he's got access to his stuff, why hasn't he put on a new shirt?

"Might as well take your turn in the shower," I suggest. "I doubt that Maggie or Henry will be next. There are plenty of towels in there too."

"Thanks," he says, rising to get his bag.

I show Joe where everything is in the bathroom. Turning around to give him privacy, I almost bump into his impeccable, naked chest. "Apologies," I offer trying to keep my composure and not show signs of being flustered. "Let me know if you need anything."

A wicked grin forms on his face and he works hard to stifle it. "I should be good. Thanks."

I head to Nathan's door first, to hurry the boys along as well as to encourage them to muffle their sounds of pleasure. Pounding a little on the door, I give them fair warning and they immediately take the hint. I turn to head towards the room where Maggie and Henry are and I catch the sight of Joe standing in the doorway to my bedroom with nothing but a towel around his waist.

"Everything okay," he questions.

It takes me a second or two to respond. "Yeah. Just giving them their warning. They know what it means. Sorry."

He nods, smiles, and leaves the doorway. I take a deep breath in and out. I lost myself there — my mind imagining what was under his towel and what I would like to do to him. Focus, Emma. Breathe.

Our conversations are light and fun as we dine at Real Food Daily, our favorite organic, vegan restaurant in Santa Monica. We arrive just before the lunch crowd starts filling in, which makes it easy for us to get a table right away. We share a few appetizers, have entrees and now we're considering our dessert options. Maggie declines, but all of the guys are in for something sweet. I happily join them.

Chapter Eight

"How can you eat all of what you ate and more, and . . . um . . . ?" Henry asks amazed. A small flush rises in his cheeks.

Joe snickers as he finishes the rest of Henry's question for him, "And, have the body she has?"

This gets laughs from Nathan and Jared as they look to me for my response. Maggie tries to suppress a giggle.

I compose myself and my answer as I let their laughs die down, "I'm a very physically active person."

More laughter stirs from Nathan and Jared. I know that their idea of my physical activities is not limited to only sports. But then again, they probably see sex as a sport as well.

"She loves to trampoline," Maggie adds eagerly.

"Trampoline? Where do you trampoline?" Henry inquires.

"I have a rebounder, mini trampoline, at home and I go about two or three times a week to one of the local places that have larger trampolines lined up side by side. You can jump from one trampoline to the other," I inform him.

"It's so much fun," Maggie shares. "We go all the time."

"It sounds fun!" Joe states.

"Definitely," agrees Henry.

"We should all go tomorrow then," Nathan recommends eagerly. "Now you boys have to stay the night."

As excited as I am to go trampolining, I'm not happy with the idea of them sleeping over, but it is Nathan's home and he's the host. Maybe this is a good thing. With Joe here too, I doubt that Maggie will sleep with Henry let alone share a bed with him. Plus, this allows us all to get to know each other a little better, and I wouldn't mind getting to know Joe more. Henry. I mean I wouldn't mind getting to know Henry more.

"Did you have the class or free jump in mind?" I inquire.

I know they won't want to get up that early for the hour long intense workout.

"Free jump, of course," Jared express with a hint of disbelief at the fact that I even dared to ask.

All I can do is laugh. Aside from the classes starting as early as 6:30 in the morning, I know Jared can't handle too much of the intense workout.

"Fine," I retort back, acting a little hurt and disappointed.

"What's the difference?" Joe investigates with avid curiosity.

"One is you jump how you want in the different areas. Only Emma likes the classes," Jared explains.

Breathe In

"I like the classes too! I've gotten much better," Nathan interjects a little defensively. "You don't like them because you don't jump enough."

Jared narrows his eyes at Nathan in a playful manner as he decides how he wants to continue, "Free jump is better for newbies. That way you don't get scared off by it. There's the pit and everything. You'll see tomorrow!"

"A pit?" Joe questions.

"The pit is awesome," Maggie confirms.

"Sounds interesting," Henry comments with an earnest smile.

Our desserts arrive and our conversations come to a halt, save everyone commenting on which dessert they like better since we're all kind of sharing. I got the stone fruit blackberry crisp ala mode, Jared and Nathan are sharing the Faux-stess Cupcake, Henry ordered chocolate ice cream and Joe got the salted caramel ice cream.

"Would you like some, Emma?" Joe asks, pushing his bowl towards me after the others already had a bite.

Before I can even answer, Jared interrupts, "Don't give her any. That's her favorite and she'll eat it all."

"Gee thanks," I return with slightly squinted eyes.

Nathan insinuates, "If you're lucky, maybe she'll eat you all up too!" Nathan roars with laughter while Maggie giggles and Joe blushes.

I see contention in Jared's face knowing Nathan went a little too far. Henry has a somewhat serious look on his face that appears he's hoping I would confirm Nathan's statement in the positive.

Smirking and taking another bite of my dessert, I comment, "He wishes."

My statement prompts Joe to blush more as a smile dances on his face and I tingle with delight. A little playful banter never hurt — or did it? My playfulness causes an eager look in Maggie's eyes as she craves for my response to be true. I disappoint with a head shake as Nathan and Jared almost choke on their cupcake. I nearly snort my bite through my nose as I watch Jared and Nathan.

After lunch, we head toward the Third Street Promenade.

The walk allows everyone's meals to settle, sparking a groan from Jared. "Ooh, I ate too much."

"Good thing we're going jumping tomorrow," Nathan nudges.

"What are we in the mood to do?" Maggie inquires.

"A movie?" Nathan suggests.

Everyone nods in agreement.

Chapter Eight

We start heading past the shops with Jared and Nathan in front, followed by Maggie and Henry, and Joe, Sadie and me bringing up the rear. Each couple is holding hands other than Joe and I.

"What about Sadie?" Joe asks with a little concern.

"She's got her service dog vest on, so she can go anywhere," I answer.

I don't always like to use the vest, but it definitely helps for long days when I'm away from home and don't want to be concerned about leaving her locked up all by herself.

"Oh, that's what that is," Joe says. "Why do you need that?"

"When I adopted Sadie, I immediately signed her up for classes. She's fully trained and certified, not because I need it, but because I wanted people to look at her breed differently as well as be able to take her anywhere I go," I reply.

"Wow. That's awesome," Joe says. "I haven't had a dog since I was a teenager. I just couldn't get another one after Duke died." Joe catches me trying to conceal a giggle. "What's so funny?"

Crap, I just got caught. "Oh nothing . . ." I try to reply, subduing a laugh. "I'm sorry about your dog dying . . . it's just that . . . I can't believe you named him Duke."

"Why is that funny?" he says as I curl my lips into my mouth.

"Nothing . . ." I mutter.

"Just say it," he insists. "Get it out."

"Is Duke short for something?" I say with a little more control.

"No. Why?" he pushes.

"For some strange reason, I pictured that you named him Duke Wellington III or something," I answer, loosing control and giggling.

Joe shakes his head and says, "Just Duke. Why would you think that?"

Shrugging my shoulders, I smile and declare, "I don't know. I guess I just expected a weird name like that. You are a Manhattanite."

Joe flirts, "So you're checking up on me?"

"Just making sure you and your friend aren't creepy," I poke.

"Creepy?"

"Yeah. Creepy. I've heard stories about all you boys who come from billionaire families. Weird names and fetishes," I retort.

I know I'm right and he knows it too.

Rolling his eyes at me with a smile, he mentions, "There are a few creepy ones. I'll give you that. But, Henry and I are not them."

"I'll be the judge of that," I quip back.

Joe and I walk in silence for the next block, only looking back and forth at each other, smirking while watching Maggie, Henry, Jared and Nathan. Joe's fun, not like other straight guys I've dealt with or the weird friends of Maggie's ex-boyfriends. We actually can have a conversation and he doesn't get on my nerves.

"Which movie?" Jared asks the group when we arrive at the theater.

"Romantic comedy!" Maggie shouts.

"That's all you ever want to watch," I complain a little.

"I like being happy and they make me happy. So, that's my vote," she replies, sticking her tongue out at me.

"Mature," I bait, sticking my tongue out back at her.

"What do you boys like?" Nathan asks Henry and Joe.

"I'll watch anything," Henry says.

"Me too. I like romantic comedies," Joe adds, taunting me.

"How about a sci-fi?" I suggest with a fake smile.

"I'm picking or else we'll never agree," Jared announces.

Jared gets tickets for the next showing of a romantic comedy that starts in just over an hour. I give him a look when he hands me my ticket. Jared seems pleased with himself.

Not excited with the movie selection, I hint, "Remember, paybacks are still coming for earlier and this just adds to the pile."

He gives me a pleading hug and kiss in an attempt to sway me.

We bounce between a few stores to kill some time. Maggie and Henry are talking the entire time, practically ignoring us. Nathan is checking out some of the clothing stores to see if they hint to anything about the upcoming Summer Season as well as to get some ideas for his women's line.

"Try this on for me, please," Nathan says, shoving a dress to my chest.

"Seriously?" I whine softly.

"Yes, seriously. I need to see it on a woman's body and your body happens to be right here," he directs. "Jared will watch Sadie. Go." He shoos me away as Jared takes Sadie's leash and sits on the padded bench in front of the dressing room.

Chapter Eight

Joe stays nearby as Maggie and Henry are lagging behind in their own little world.

Rolling my eyes, I grab the dress and head to the changing room. "I need a different size," I state without coming out of the room once I have the dress on.

"Why?" Nathan inquires. "It should fit your proportions."

Other than myself, Nathan is the only one who would know my size.

"It does, all but one," I wince as he opens the door, exposing me to everyone in the store.

"Damn girl, did they get bigger!" Nathan shouts as his eyes inflate and he pokes one of my boobs repeatedly.

I swat his hand away as I blush a little. "No. It's the dress," I say.

"You look hot, Emma!" Jared announces loudly. "Doesn't she look hot, Joe?"

I blush as every straight man within earshot stares. Joe doesn't say anything, he doesn't have to since his eyes are glued to my chest and the expression on his face says everything. Good thing I'm completely comfortable with my body.

Nathan requested for me to try on a black halter dress that accentuates my breasts, has a triangular cutout below my boobs causing my upper stomach to be slightly exposed, fits snuggly to my frame all the way down just below my knees and has a deep open back.

"Put these on," Nathan says handing me a pair of black platform pumps.

"I don't wear platform heels," I demand, refusing to take them and crossing my arms in front of my chest. Realizing that the gesture only makes my breasts pop out more, I immediately lower them.

I never where platforms. I don't like the look and to me they look like stripper shoes.

"Fine," he says, putting them back and grabbing open-toed stilettos.

I take the shoes from his hand, and hold onto his shoulder while slightly bending forward, lifting one foot at a time behind me to get them on. Nathan takes my hand and leads me to a mirror a few feet away. I stand with my hands on my hips as he inspects every seam. He never touches me or the dress, except to gently guide my hands up from my hips momentarily. Snatching his phone out of his pocket, he takes a few pictures, both from a distance and up close.

After what feels like an eternity I ask, "Are you done?"

"Yep. Thanks," Nathan confirms.

I rush into the changing room and hand him the shoes and dress once they're off.

Breathe In

I'm in the midst buttoning up my pants when Jared says, "You should totally get the dress, Emma."

I wait to respond until I'm finished changing and leaving the dressing room. "No."

"Why not? Every girl needs a couple of little, black dresses in her closet," Jared challenges with furrowed brows.

"I have enough black dresses," I calmly reply.

It's true. I like dresses, don't get me wrong, but I don't really need another black one.

"You don't have *that* black dress," Jared contends.

"I wouldn't wear it to the places we go," I argue, thought my statement is not completely true.

"I bet Joe could think of a few places to take you to get you in and out of that dress," Nathan pushes with a devilish smile. "Right, Joe?"

Clearing his voice and blushing, Joe mutters, "Definitely." His eyes go to me and then he quickly looks away as he scratches his head.

This is not good. I know we've had some playful banter, but it feels like it's gone beyond innocent flirting. Okay. Maybe it hasn't been completely innocent, but it's crossing a line I'm not comfortable with. A line that shouldn't be crossed, because if it is, I break my rules. My rules cannot be broken.

I choose not to respond and take Sadie's leash from Jared, then head over to Maggie and Henry. I'm relieved when Maggie and Henry don't say a word about the dress and what had just happened. From the looks of it, they didn't see or hear any of it.

Looking at her phone as if she's been here in reality this whole time, Maggie announces, "We should be heading over for the movie."

I won't admit it openly, but the romantic comedy is actually very good. I don't mind those movies. I just don't feel comfortable watching them with a guy whom I'm attracted to, a guy I can't have sex with, but part of me is curious about what it would be like, a guy who is openly flirting with me, and a guy who is friends with the guy my best friend is dating. The thought of sleeping with him enters my mind. Maybe if I just get it out of my system I'll be fine. I've never been really impressed with any of the guys I've slept with, so maybe the same thing would happen with him. However, what if it's better than I expect? Or, what if things got weird because it is or isn't and then I have to be around him all the time because our friends eventually get married. No. I need to control this. I need to control myself. We're friendly and that's all it will ever be. Just friends.

Chapter Eight

Back at the condo, Nathan starts setting up his new grill for dinner. Jared and Joe are helping Nathan and Maggie and Henry are on the couch cuddling and talking. I feed Sadie and take her out for a walk, wanting some distance and personal space before helping with dinner. Deciding to take a longer walk than usual, I notice Sadie is moving slowly towards the end. She must be tired from the day. I sit on a bench along Ocean Avenue as Sadie stands with her front paws on the bench enjoying me scratching her behind her ears.

My phone chimes, so I take it out of my pocket to read the text that just came in from Jared, "I can see you!"

I wave my hand in the air without turning around.

"I see you waving! You okay?" he writes back.

"I'm fine. Just enjoying the view," I text with a smiley emoticon face.

"I think the grill is good to go," Jared mentions.

I giggle at the thought that it took two gay men and one straight guy to figure out a grill this whole time while I was out with Sadie. I can understand why Jared and Nathan have a challenge with a machine like that because they've never used one, but Joe? Well, I guess they don't really do any cooking or grilling themselves in high society.

"Sounds good. On my way back," I reply and push send.

Back at the condo, Jared, Nathan and Joe seem a bit surprised at the fact that we need to wait for the grill to heat up enough before cooking. They literally just turned the thing on about five minutes before I came in. It takes all the strength I can muster to stifle any kind of laughter at their innocence and not to comment. This is technically their first barbecue. I suggest that they help prep the food while it warms. We make grass-fed burgers stuffed with feta cheese and spinach, cut potatoes into wedges to be roasted with garlic, sea salt and oil, make a quinoa and cranberry salad, a salad with fresh strawberries and a strawberry vinaigrette, and chocolate mousse with fresh, handmade whipped cream. We add a dish with extra toppings for the burgers including pickles, olives, fresh fried onions, tomatoes, onions, and pepperoncini.

Everyone sits at Nathan's dinning room table, eating, sharing stories, joking and laughing for several hours. At one point during the meal, I sit back and watch how naturally everyone gets along and enjoys each other's company. It feels like our little family is growing which makes me happy and sad at the same time. I smile at a comment Henry makes as I glance around the table. Locking eyes with Joe, I get the distinct feeling he knows what's going through my head as he gives me a comforting smirk. I need to make sure I don't show my feelings outwardly.

Breathe In

Stuffed, we wait a little before having dessert. Everyone helps clean up the table and food before changing into pajamas and heading to the couches for a night of board games. Maggie and Henry sit on the love seat side, Jared and Nathan sit in the middle of the couch. Joe takes a spot on the chaise end closest to me. He offers several times to switch seats, but I'm happy to sit on the floor with Sadie while playing. I've got a pillow under my butt, my back is against the chaise and I've got Sadie's head resting on my lap. I'm content.

Playing for hours, the sun had already set by the end of dinner, a few of my friends appear to be getting sleepy. Most of us didn't even bother to eat dessert. Nathan and Jared call it a night first, but I know they're off to have sex. About ten minutes later, Maggie and Henry venture into the third bedroom while Joe and I are left to ourselves in the living room.

Breaking the silence, I figure now would be a good time to get to know Joe a little more. I shift onto the middle of the couch and Sadie places herself between Joe and me before I begin my mild interrogation.

"How many are in your family?" I ask quietly.

With a devious grin, Joe states, "For every question you ask, I get to ask one too."

Pondering my options, I agree. I doubt he'll ask too many questions that I don't want to answer and if he does, I just won't response.

Smiling, Joe questions, "Do you want the short description or the long description of my family."

I pause to think for a moment, a little suspicious of his long description, "Whichever you prefer sharing."

Joe shifts, moving a few inches closer and leans, supporting his head with his arm that is on the back of the seat. "There are my parents, John and Elaine. My grandparents on my mom's side, Leonardo and Magdalena. My father's father, Angelo. My father's mother, Viviana passed a few years ago. Then there's my aunt, my mom's sister, Olivia, who is married to Uncle Ben. My father's two brothers, Gabriel and Alexander, who are married to my aunts, Elizabeth and Cecilia, and five cousins between the two of them, my six brothers . . . ."

"Six brothers?" I question cutting him off, shocked at his statement. "Seriously?"

"Yes," he says with a chuckle. He waits a second to let all of his already lengthy description sink in a little before continuing, "John Junior, my oldest brother and his wife, Emily, and their two children, Lily and John I. Then

David and his wife, Charlotte, who is pregnant. Daniel, David's twin, and his wife, Isabella, who is also pregnant. Then, there's Anthony, Thomas, James and his boyfriend, Allen, and then me. That's the immediate family."

He gives me a moment to process. "So you are the youngest?" I question with eyes wide open and barely blinking.

"Yes." Giving me another moment, Joe then peruses, "So, what about your family?"

"My family? You've met them."

"No, I didn't," he says confused.

"Yes, you did. At New Year's," I answer truthfully.

"I'm talking about your real family."

"They are my real family," I insist.

Pressing gently, he says, "I mean your biological family."

I look down at Sadie, stroking her lightly while trying to decide what I'm willing to share and how to present it. "They're in Jersey." Avoiding any further prying, I proceed with my next question, but it comes across more as a statement, "Your girlfriend must not like you being all the way out here on the West Coast."

He grins. "No girlfriend."

"So, you're a heart breaker, huh?" I taunt.

"No. I just hadn't found the right one yet," he admits.

"So, are any of your other brothers involved in the family business?"

"No. Just me. That's two more questions I get to ask." he teases.

"No." I contend.

Crap. He's right, though I don't want to admit it. I want to keep the inquires off of me and my life.

"So, how often do you see your family in Jersey?"

"Not as often as I used to," I disclose carefully.

"I'm sure they miss you," he says rather than questions.

"It's not a big deal." Wanting to move the conversation forward, I ask, "So, what did you study in college?"

I'm caught off guard by his willingness to answer my questions as I avoid his, which leaves me temporarily without my next question.

"How is it not a big deal? They're your family."

"Because it isn't," I insist.

"I'm sure they want to see you . . . ."

"It doesn't matter."

"Sure it does," he coaxes.

"No, it doesn't," I demand, gritting my teeth while rising from the couch.

"How?" he searches with soft eyes and a concerned expression.

"Because they're dead," I quietly lash out and storm to my bedroom slamming the door behind me after Sadie enters. I rest my back against the door trying to regain my composure.

I'm not really mad at Joe, I know that. I'm mad at having to explain myself — that I exposed myself. Why did I say anything? I told myself that I wouldn't share. I could have just told him to ask a different question.

A tender knock on the door startles me. I don't move, but I turn my head in the direction of the knob.

"Emma . . ." Joe whispers. "Emma . . . I'm sorry. I didn't know. I didn't mean to make you upset."

Nine

As I attempt to lift my heavy eyelids, I discover a hazy darkness surrounding me. Blinking slowly several times, my half-opened eyes won't focus to give me any clear indication of what's around me and where the blurry, flashing lights above are coming from. My body feels heavy. Still unable to open my eyes all the way, I perceive that I'm laying down somewhere. A cool dampness near my left cheek reveals itself as a slight gust of air brushes past my face. Sliding my right arm up the side of my body like a snake, my fingers creep to my lips. Drool — or, at least I hope so.

Two large and oddly shaped figures materialize in front of me. They are so close, only a foot or two away. Voices suddenly emanate from the now more defined silhouettes. Their speech sounds muffled and trails off into the distance even as I try to concentrate on their words. Who are they? What are they saying? Why can't I understand them? One of the voices almost sounds feminine.

Another indistinguishable sound gradually becomes more apparent as it grows louder and the ringing in my ears subsides. It's the engine of a car. My brain finally starts to put the fuzzy pieces of evidence together. I must have fallen asleep in the back seat. A familiar smell creeps into my nose that reassures me — my mother's perfume.

"Mom?" my throat squeezes out in a raw, breathy, hoarse tone.

"We're almost home, dear," her voice replies in a low sluggish tone.

I internally smile at her comforting words, though her voice sounds peculiar.

A sudden rush of nervousness enters my belly. The car feels as if it's flying down the road like a rocket ship as the speed of the flashing lights zooming above my head all blur into one.

"Mom," I try to shout, but not a single sound escapes my mouth this time. Confused, I try again. "Mom!"

She doesn't hear me. I don't hear me.

A single, bright white light races towards us, growing larger by the second. My mother turns her head towards me smiling. Why doesn't she hear me? How does she not see the light?

Again, with all my might. "Mom . . . !" my voice trails in my head like a deafening siren, stabbing my ears like a knife.

Time stops in this very moment. I can see everything with perfect clarity as I stare in horror into my mother's eyes. My mouth is left open, still screaming

Breathe In

without a sound. I can't hear anything except a piercing ring that echoes in my body. Why can't she hear me? Why doesn't she see the terrified look on my face?

My body lurches backward as I attempt to scramble to grab my mother and I suddenly become paralyzed. Then, it happens all at once — I see the face of the truck driver before I hear the sound of metal hitting metal as it wraps itself around and around. Joe? Suddenly, I see my mother's and father's bodies hurling forward toward the oncoming truck and bouncing around like ping pong balls getting dented with each blow.

My heart is filled with panic and fear as I desperately try to yell one more time, "Mom . . .!"

Jerking up, I shout out in horror. My heart pounds, my lungs heave and my entire body shakes. Sadie is whimpering and scrambling to calm me down as my eyes search for something familiar other than her. Where am I? I'm not at home.

The door to my right flies open just a split second before the one in front of me, both causing a thundering sound to echo in my ears. It's too dark to know who's standing in either doorway as a familiar voice rings through the air and the bed under me shifts.

"Emma?" Maggie yells with fright, wrapping her arms around me. Looking to the silhouette in the other door, she instructs, "Go get Jared."

Rocking my shaking body, Maggie strokes my hair trying to calm me, "It's okay. It's okay."

I hear another voice that sounds vaguely familiar approaching but it's muffled, causing me to not be able to decipher it.

"She'll be fine . . . once Jared gets here," she soothes.

Less than a minute later, Jared is on the bed to my left and wraps me in his arms as he always does. The sensation of his familiar touch brings peace to my mind and body, starting to still my pounding heart.

"She'll be fine," Jared announces quietly.

I'm not completely coherent yet to know who exactly he's talking to other than Maggie.

"This is too often," Nathan whispers with a shaky tone.

"Not now, babe," Jared directs.

I hear sounds in the background, but I stay focused on the sound of Jared's beating heart that is pressed up against my left ear. The lights go off and I'm consoled by the presence of my friend, my brother, until sleep over takes me again.

Ten

I wake to find Jared and Nathan sleeping next to me and Sadie perched across my belly. It happened again. I don't understand why, which scares me, especially since I just had one yesterday. Why did it change again? Yesterday, the driver was Maggie and today it was — Joe.

I shift gently to check the time on my phone that I left on the nightstand. It's five thirty-three in the morning and I'm wide away. Sneaking out of the bed, Sadie and I head to the bathroom and I grab some clothes on the way. After relieving myself, I change into workout clothes and turn off the light before I open the door to the bedroom. Good, Jared and Nathan are still asleep and Jared has repositioned himself by spooning Nathan.

Tiptoeing to the kitchen to make Sadie's breakfast, I move slowly as my eyes adjust to the dimly lit condo. I gulp down my clay as Sadie munches down her food. Once we both finish eating and drinking, Sadie follows me when I head to the bathroom one more time before going for our walk.

Careful to close the door quietly as I head back into the living room, I don't notice Sadie walk away from me until a noise from the couch catches my attention.

"Hey Sadie," Joe says in a hushed, sexy, gruff tone. "What are you doing out here?"

Sadie snuggles her head up on his chest, tucking her nose under his chin.

"Sorry," I whisper, walking over to get Sadie.

"It's okay," he hums as I get Sadie off of him. "I don't mind. She can stay."

"I doubt that you'll want her to. She just ate and I have to take her out."

"I'll join you," he replies, rushing to get up and find his shoes.

"No, it's okay. Go back to sleep," I encourage.

I'm really not in the mood for company other than Sadie right now.

After checking his phone, Joe answers, "No, it's okay. This is when I usually get up anyway."

I nod in agreement despite not liking the idea at all.

At the park, Sadie relieves herself before Joe and I head down the stairs to the beach for a short stroll. I'm tempted to jog, but I refrain since we'll be trampolining in a few hours. Instead, I take out Sadie's ball so she can at least run and get out this morning's tension. This will give her time to stretch before she's stuck in the condo for a few hours. Neither Joe nor I speak as we stroll alone in the brisk, morning air. Santa Monica is peaceful early in the morning just like Pasadena.

"So, trampolining . . ." Joe begins, finally breaking the silence as we're halfway back up the beach towards Nathan's. "I'm excited and a little nervous."

"Yeah," I confirm and my body relaxes.

I'm getting the feeling that he's not going to question me about earlier. While Jared keeps my personal life private, Maggie has the tendency to share on occasion. I'm really hoping that she doesn't divulge my secrets even though this morning was unusual.

"You must really like it," he says.

I nod in response and my body continues to release the anxiety. "Do you workout?" I question, immediately chiding myself for asking.

He obviously does. God, look at his body. You can see his muscles under his shirt. That was such a stupid question. My brain is obviously still not fully functioning yet.

"Every day," he politely replies. "I like to run and lift weights. I love to play any sport that I'm decent at so I'm not stuck in indoors or doing the same thing all the time. I practice Wing Chun and I also know Jujitsu."

"Interesting," I respond.

My appreciation for the sight of his half naked body yesterday stirs inside. Well, maybe this will be the way for me to come out of my funk.

"I can show you some Wing Chun sometime if you'd like. Not that you necessarily need help," he snickers a little. "But, if you're interested in knowing more options . . . and, you can teach me what you know."

I ponder his suggestion for a moment, not sure and surprised at the mix of emotions stirring inside of me. "Sure. I'd like that," I say.

I really would like to learn another style of martial arts. The thought of having more control over my body and what I can do with it intrigues me immensely. The idea of being closer to his body is a bit enticing too.

Sadie bounces up and down a good stretch of the beach chasing after her ball and returning it to either Joe or myself to throw it. Joe and I don't talk anymore, just stand or walk in calm, peaceful silence.

My level of comfort with Joe is increasing, despite the sexual tension. This man perplexes me. He's got a very confident air to him, but not cocky. There's something else that I can't quite put my finger on. He's young, rich and handsome. How does he not have a girlfriend?

Chapter Ten

My mind wanders back to our conversation last night about what Joe said. Did he say he hasn't or hadn't found the right one? I can't remember. Hadn't. He said hadn't. What did he mean by that?

After taking turns showering in Nathan's room since Nathan and Jared are still asleep in my bed, Joe and I sit on the patio talking quietly as we lay on the two lounge chairs and eat some fruit and yogurt to tide us over until breakfast. Sadie is curled up between my legs with her head on my belly.

Our conversation is light, general stuff and nothing intrusive. We get to know each other on a different level and find ourselves laughing half the time. Okay, I get to know him more than he does me because he is telling me stories about his brother's and himself. It's delightful to listen and I only ask a question here or there since he's really willing to keep talking. He seems happy to share and I'm enjoying the sound of his voice.

When I ask, Joe openly shares about his parents. His Mom, Elaine Kensington, comes from the Kensington family who have a long, successful reputation in the shipping industries since his mother's grandfather, Lord Byron Kensington built the family empire when he was a young man in England. He branched out into real estate and hospitality soon after moving to America with his young, pregnant wife when he was in his early thirties. Elaine was learning the family business while attending Yale as her sister, Olivia, was finishing high school. Elaine was being groomed to take over the family business after her father.

Joe's father, John Covelli, didn't come from money, rather an honest, hard-working, blue collar family. His parents owned a small Italian restaurant, called Angelo's, in a middle-class section of New York that John was expected to take over. While helping the family with the restaurant, John attended NYU for business — John's college was paid for by scholarships. In his second year at college, John ran into Elaine when she and a few of her friends stopped into Angelo's to warm up from the cold streets of New York late one snowy night just before closing. It was love at first sight for John.

Over the next few years, John courted Elaine from a distance, believing her family would never approve of his social status until he proved himself. Eventually, Elaine didn't care and dated John openly despite her family's protest. Without anyone's help, and using all of the money he saved from working at Angelo's since he was ten, John began purchasing small, rundown hotels on the edges of the middle-class and upper-class sections of New York. Properties the rich overlooked, but John had a vision. Buying the first few with mortgages, he'd fix them up and name them after his love. They were each named Elaine's of whatever street or street corner they were on. Also, they were each styled differently, giving them their own personality and varying degrees of affordability. He wanted to cater to all levels of the working class with the design and feel of the opulence he believed everyone deserved to experience. By the time he bought his fourth building, John had just graduated college, as did Elaine. John had all the mortgages for his first three hotels paid off and he bought his fourth, fifth and sixth properties with cash. Just before buying his seventh property, John scheduled an appointment with Mr. Leonardo Kensington himself, Elaine's father, with the assistance of Elaine, of course. The two of them visited Mr. Kensington together, and to Eleanor's surprise, John asked Mr. Kensington for his permission to marry Elaine. Still not pleased with his pedigree, Mr. Kensington apprehensively agreed. Though John did not come from the same status, Mr. Kensington was rather impressed with John, his business sense and his determination to make a name for himself. Just after their honeymoon, Mr. Kensington began to recognize what Elaine had seen in John and overtime was reassured by John's continued successes. Through his actions, John proved himself a worthy suitor not only for his daughter, but also potentially for the family business. Now, Elaine and John run the family empire together with the approval of Mr. Kensington. Since John's involvement, he and Elaine have tripled the family's assets and income.

Joe's older brother, John Jr., is involved in politics in New York, while his wife, Emily, is a happy, stay at home mom with their children, Lily and John I. Then, there's David and Daniel who are twins, each married with a child on the way, and they've started their own private airline company. Anthony is the fourth oldest and most boisterous and somewhat of a womanizer. He bounces from girlfriend to girlfriend and hasn't quite found his niche in life. Anthony is the life of the party, or brings the party to you. Thomas is the fifth oldest, who is single as well, but not as bad as Anthony when it comes to women. He loves cars but hasn't decided on what aspect of the car industry he wants to pursue. The sixth oldest is James who is blissfully gay and in love with his partner Allen. James and Allen own and curate an art gallery in Manhattan. Joe is close with all of his family, but he explains that he and James have a special bond. The last of the Covelli boys is Joe. Out of all of the brother's, he's the only one, who at an early age, had interest and desire to help with the family empire which is not typical for the youngest. Usually, the first born is the one who takes over.

The age differences between Joe and his brothers are staggering. John Jr. is thirty-six. David and Daniel are both thirty-four. Anthony is thirty-one. Thomas is twenty-nine. James is twenty-eight and Joe is my age, twenty-four. Obviously, they come from happily married parents.

Chapter Ten

Though he and his family come from money, they actually sound happy and content compared to all of the depictions of high society in television and movies. From how Joe describes them, and what he implies, they seem like a group of people who are friendly, lively, and joyous — people I'd be excited to meet.

"Looks like you two are having fun," Nathan sings as he pulls open the sliding door.

Joe and I smile in response.

"Is everyone finally getting up?" I ask, hoping I can get breakfast going.

"I think so," Nathan replies lowering himself on the chair I'm on and snuggles up to me. "Jared is in the bathroom and I think I heard noises from the other room."

"Noises?" I inquire, though I don't really want to know what type of noises.

Giggling, Nathan whispers, "Not those kind of noises, you dirty Kitten you. Where is your mind this morning?"

"Not where you're thinking," I rebut with a grin, nudging him.

"So what's going on here?" Nathan questions devilishly, pointing back and forth between Joe and me.

"What are you talking about?" I reply, knowing full well what he's suggesting.

"We're just talking and becoming more acquainted," Joe says with a smile.

"Acquainted?" Nathan whispers with a playful accusatory tone.

All I can do is laugh and shake my head.

With a smirk and a chuckle, Joe answers, "Yeah. We're becoming friends. There's nothing wrong with two people being friends, is there?"

"No. And, there's nothing wrong with two people being more than just friends," Nathan adds.

"Enough, Nathan," I say, demanding he stops. I glance at Joe and catch him trying to hide a smile.

"Fine," he caves. "You're no fun."

"Who's not fun?" Jared inquires, popping out of the patio door.

Nathan makes a face as he looks at me, tilting his head. "Emma," he whines. "She won't play along. It's not like she hasn't been laid recently."

I glower at Nathan's comment while attempting not to blush at his openness with Joe sitting right next to me.

"Stop meddling," Jared playful scolds. "Emma's been friendly to some of Maggie's past boyfriend's friends."

"Not this friendly," Nathan insinuates.

"I'm not going to be rude when they disappear and you two disappear at the same time," I say, defending my actions.

Jared changes the subject as he wraps his arms around Nathan and kisses him on the cheek. "I think we need to get breakfast started. What do you think, Emma and Joe? I bet you two have been up for a while."

"I agree," Joe confirms. "I'm hungry." He looks to me and I nod in agreement.

"Cool. Let's get the lovebirds up and we'll have another feast," Jared announces.

We get up and make our way inside. Jared yanks Nathan by the hand to follow. Joe gestures for Sadie and me to go first.

"What time did everyone want to go jumping?" I ask, wanting to move the conversation away from Joe and I as the main topic.

"We should probably go earlier this morning to beat the kid crowd," Jared replies.

"The kids won't matter. I'll call and reserve the private court," I say.

"Sweet," Maggie answers bounding out of the second bedroom behind us. "I love watching the kids and all, but they do make it a challenge sometimes when there are too many of them."

"Good morning," Jared, Nathan, Joe and I say in unison.

"Good morning," she answers, taking turns hugging each of us.

Feeling my stomach grumble, I leave everyone chatting and head to the kitchen to start breakfast. Nathan quickly follows and we hop behind the counter, enjoying the groove we fall into naturally when we cook together. Maggie and Jared set the dining room table and Joe plays with Sadie waiting to help. My friends and I turn Joe down when he offers to assist. Each time Jared enters the kitchen area, he's overly affectionate with me and hovers. To diffuse his concern, I purposefully smile and joke around.

As Nathan gets the stovetop warming for eggs and turkey bacon, I turn on the waffle maker.

Henry cheerfully comes out of the bedroom and all eyes are on him. Stopping in his tracks to the hush that falls upon the condo, Henry questions, "What?"

The elephant in the room has arrived. Did they or didn't they? I really don't want to know the answer.

"Good morning!" we all serenade as Maggie bounces over to him.

We dine with great conversations and lots of loud laughter as we enjoy eggs, bacon, toast, fruit, smoothies and waffles. Just like the night before, we all settle into a mode that feels like we've been doing this with each other for many years. Nothing but comfort, ease and joy. Though I see this regularly when I'm with Maggie's family, with this small group of people, it feels different — a good kind of different. I get a shiver as the thought that this scenario will be playing out before me for years to come. This feeling invigorates me, but also intimidates me.

After our energetic meal, everyone helps to clean up before getting dressed into workout clothes. Jared, Nathan, Joe and I change pretty quickly and I only need to rush Maggie and Henry along once before they emerge from the bedroom ecstatic for the morning's activities.

Eleven

"That was fun," Henry exclaims as we are leaving the trampoline facility. "I would love to do that again."

"Me too," adds Joe with a smile. "I never knew jumping around like that would be so much fun and a great workout. I see why you like it, Emma."

"And those flips she was doing . . ." Henry adds with astonishment.

"I know, right," Joe says.

"Thanks," I reply with a bashful smile. To direct attention away from myself, I commend to Nathan, "Looks like you've gotten a lot better."

"I know. I have so much more control," he answers with delight.

"He's sexier too," Jared adds with a wink.

Piling back into Nathan's Tesla, I hear a few moans from the vigorous workout. Maggie holds my hand discretely for support with my car jitters. Her gesture helps, but my leg still pulses a little from my nerves.

Everyone is quick to shower. Jared and Nathan jump into one shower, as I head to the other, confident that I'll probably get into the kitchen to begin lunch before Nathan. Maggie surprisingly joins me in the bathroom as I turn on the faucet. Thinking she just wants to talk a little, I'm surprised when she gets undressed. Now, I'm not sure if she wants to talk or needs to take the edge off.

"You okay?" I ask with a little concern.

Beaming, she replies, "I'm great. Just figured this would be faster and I'm starving."

I shrug my shoulders and shift out of the way so she can get under the water. As she stands there, I grab the sea sponge and soap and begin to wash her back.

"Thanks," she responds.

I don't say anything as I wash her body and hair, patiently waiting for her to offer what she's willing to share.

"I had so much fun last night," she begins. "We talked until we feel asleep."

"That's cool. I'm happy for you," I encourage.

She turns to rinse the shampoo from her hair before taking the sponge and turns me around. "You okay?" She questions.

"Yeah, why?" I lie, convinced she's referring to this mornings episode.

Maggie doesn't say anything and studies me carefully after I turn to face her before she answers, "Nothing. Just checking." She steps aside to allow the water to rinse my back as I hear the snap of a bottle lid opening. Moving closer, Maggie starts to wash my hair. "Sorry for ditching you last night," she confesses.

"It's okay. I'm a big girl," I deliver, wanting to ease her concern.

"I know," she reveals with a touch of guilt. "I just don't want you to think . . . ."

"Mags. We're good," I comfort her, taking her hands in mine.

"So, did you talk to Joe?" she questions.

I know she's looking to see if I've discovered anything about Henry. He seems almost too good to be true, but so far I haven't picked up a single warning flag.

"I think Henry really likes you," I say bluntly.

My instincts are never wrong about people. I'm not thrilled at the idea of losing time with Maggie, but I'm happy that she's happy. Who knows, Henry just might be the one.

"Really?" Maggie says excitedly.

"Really," I reassure.

She doesn't say anything else, but I can feel her smiling from ear to ear behind me. Maggie's glowing and I can feel her body heat rising on my naked skin. She moves to let me rinse my hair and when I finish, Maggie hugs me.

We finish showering and dry off in silence. Maggie has her towel secured first and just as I'm tucking in my towel in front of me, Maggie opens the door to the boys' room and offers, "We're done."

I spin around sharply, gripping my towel in my fist to see both Henry and Joe standing in their room wide-eyed and paralyzed. I swear the color drains from both of their faces while the look of confusion, disbelief and arousal swarms within them at the same time. I'm going to kill Maggie.

"Who's next?" Maggie inquires innocently.

"Wanna go?" Henry quietly mutters to Joe.

"Sure," Joe replies, altering his expression.

Once showered and dressed, everyone eats in silence for the first five minutes as they shovel food into their mouths. The guys have a glazed look in their eyes that slowly dissipates with each bite. They must have been really hungry. Maggie and I glance back and forth to each other as we watch in amazement and giggle. Chatter suddenly erupts and the rest of the meal is lively.

Chapter Eleven

After cleaning up the dishes, everyone slumps on the u-shaped sectional in the living room. Jared and Nathan cuddle in the middle. Henry and Maggie are on the love-seat side and Joe offers me the chaise as he positions himself closer to Nathan. Nathan puts the television on to minimize the need to talk and to allow those who need it to sleep.

I wake first around an hour later to five sleeping bodies and a wide awake Sadie. I only needed to nap because of the rocky morning from the nightmare. If I had my full five hours of straight sleep, I would have been the only one awake the whole time. It's comical seeing all of these grown adults comfortably asleep around each other.

I take Sadie out for a little walk around the block to stretch before resuming my place on the couch with a book. Instead of laying with me like before, Sadie chooses a different spot and places her head on Joe's chest this time. I sit and stare at Sadie and Joe in amazement, still puzzled by her interactions with him. He breathes rhythmically as his stunningly handsome features remain soft and sweet. I wonder if he knows how striking he is, not just physically, but also his personality. Anytime we were out in public this past weekend, I watched women of all ages gawk at him and he never seems to notice. His lips and eyes are the most intriguing parts, especially when he smiles.

Suddenly, Joe shifts and I peel my eyes off of him in just enough time to pretend that I've been reading.

"Hey," he whispers in a low, sexy greeting.

I make sure I pause for just a brief second before looking at him. "Hey," I softly reply.

Our eyes stay locked on each other for a few seconds before I return my eyes to my book. Out of the corner of my eye, I watch him inspect the sleeping bodies around us while he scratches Sadie. Continuing to pretend to read, my attention follows him as he gets up, stretches and heads into the bedroom.

"Hey," he whispers to get my attention and tilts his head toward the patio door.

I half smile and I nod.

Sadie, Joe and I hang out on the patio in the late February, warm, Southern California air while our friends rest. I eye him as he moves the two lounge chairs closer together before gesturing for me to sit.

"So we can talk more easily and not wake them up," he suggests.

I internally question his actions and find myself flattered and curious to see what else he tries.

"So, how are you liking California?" I ask politely after sitting down.

Love it," he eagerly replies. "The weather is awesome, the people are friendly and the food is great. What's not to love?"

"Do you miss the East Coast?" I continue.

With a smile, Joe answers, "Yes and no." He pauses before continuing, "I don't miss the weather, but I do miss my family."

Smirking, I tease, "So, you're a family man, huh?"

His grin widens. "Yes." Taking his turn, he asks, "Do you miss it?"

I feel the expression on my face change as I breathe in for a second before responding, "No."

"I guess you wouldn't really, not if you don't have anything to go back to. I understand why," he states with soft sincerity.

"Nope," I agree.

"So, what's your favorite color?" he says in a playful voice.

He's obviously trying to keep things light and I appreciate the courtesy. It's like he knows when to stop pushing automatically.

"Why?" I say with a giggle, not sure what he's trying to do with a question like that.

"Just figured it would be a valid question. Not too intense, I hope . . ." he replies.

I contemplate a second before answering, "Blue. And, you?"

For some reason, the color of his eyes is alluring and the exact color of blue I'm referring to. I don't dare tell him.

"Same," he answers without hesitation.

I tease, "I don't think we can get any more intimate than that."

His grin extends from ear to ear before he agrees, "I don't think so either. So, where do you live?"

He's fishing for more information about me, which for some reason, is exhilarating. I'm not sure if I want to tell him, but I know that it will come up eventually if Maggie's and Henry's relationship really is that serious.

I take a deep breath as I consider answering truthfully, "Pasadena."

He watches me for a moment, trying to figure out if I hesitantly told him the truth or was trying to lie, "Pasadena. Where is that?"

Accepting that I just allowed that door to be opened, I confirm, "It's just north of downtown LA off the One-Ten."

"Maybe, sometime you can show me around Pasadena," he says with a flirtatious hint to his voice.

Chapter Eleven

With my eyebrows slightly raised, I question, "Just the two of us?"

"No. Well, not unless you want it to be."

With a little laugh, I answer, "I'll consider it."

My comment gets his smile to return.

"Pasadena. That's where the Rose Bowl is and the Rose Parade takes place, right?" he continues after a minute of silence.

"Yes."

"I missed it this year. Maybe we all can get together for next year?" he comments, implying a long-term relationship for Maggie and Henry.

That's a good sign — I think.

"Sure," I agree while suppressing a smirk.

The patio door slides open and Jared joins us. "Hey, you two."

"Hey," Joe and I answer at the same time.

"Everyone still sleeping?" I question.

"Yeah, but . . . I think Nathan will be up next," Jared offers as he slips onto the lounger with me.

Sadie moves over to Joe's chair for more room. The four of us sit quietly enjoying the usually quiet Santa Monica Sunday afternoon.

Once everyone is finally awake, we decide to stroll around Santa Monica, giving Henry and Joe more of a tour before deciding on a restaurant for dinner. More great food and conversations flow as the night falls upon us. Henry and Joe decide to leave when Maggie and I do, seeming to not want to overstay their welcome even though Nathan insists that they're welcome several times. Unfortunately, Henry and Joe follow Maggie and I back to Pasadena, which unnerves me a little. Maggie can't invite Henry back to stay with her since she lives with Fūqīn, Mǔqīn and Nǎinai in Chinatown. She knows better not to ask for them to join us at my place. I deduce that she'll be telling her parents that she's staying with me, but will be going to Henry's.

I have Maggie drop me off at the curb to my apartment complex instead of pulling into the underground parking. As we open the trunk to get my bags, Joe and Henry are out of their car and standing behind us. I was really hoping to not make a scene saying farewell.

"Thanks for letting us crash your weekend," Henry says, moving in to hug me.

I try my best to not look uncomfortable, let alone make the moment awkward since he catches me off guard.

Breathe In

"I really appreciate you and your friend's allowing us to join you," Henry adds, with his arms still wrapped around me.

"Sure," I answer uncomfortably, tapping him on his back.

I catch Maggie beaming when Henry finally lets go of me.

"Nice to see you again, Joe," I begin, afraid Henry will hug me again.

"Definitely," Joe answers offering his hand.

I'm relieved when he doesn't try to hug me, though the thought of his smell piques my interest.

"Let me get those for you," Joe insists, reaching for my bags.

"No. Don't worry about it. I got it," I politely contend.

"He's being a gentleman, Emma. Let him help," Maggie interjects.

Letting out a sigh, I accept, "Fine."

"It's okay," Joe replies, noticing my uneasiness and backs off.

"No. It's okay, she doesn't mind," Maggie presses.

I give her a look, but I really don't want to drag this situation out any further.

"Help would be nice," I reply with slightly gritted teeth and a forced smile.

Joe grabs my bags and follows me to the gated entrance that is around the corner of the first building. Aware that we can't be seen anymore, Joe courteously offers, "I'll let you be here and just wait a minute or two before heading back to them."

"Thanks." I smile in appreciation before turning to unlock the community entrance.

Joe places my bags on the other side of the gate and says farewell to Sadie first. Awkwardly standing, he pauses before saying, "Thanks for the great weekend."

I smile and nod in response.

"I look forward to next time," Joe adds.

Before I even get a chance to respond, Joe leans in and kisses me on the cheek. His soft, warm lips linger on my skin and send tingles of delight to my sex.

Shocked, I mutter, "Goodnight."

We stare at each other for a moment before I will my body to move.

As I walk away from the gate that is now behind me, I hear Joe say, "Goodnight, Emma."

Twelve

Since the first weekend with Henry and Joe at Nathan's, I haven't had the nightmare again and the weeks become typical for me; taking care of my businesses, meetings with Nathan about expanding Nathaniel's and the new women's line, connecting with Maggie and Jared about business, working out, reading, being with Sadie, and hanging out with my friends, including Henry and Joe occasionally. All six of us are together most weekends, going somewhere — like mini adventures. We visit San Diego, Las Vegas, Palm Springs and Ojai when we don't stay in LA County. We eat and drink. We laugh. We surf. We dance. We see shows. We gamble. We visit spas and do anything that looks fun and interesting.

One day of each weekend together is a relaxing day, while the other is filled with some kind of physical activity or sport. The relaxing day is more for the two couples to have bedroom time with each other, not like they don't get enough during the week, while Joe and I find something to do away from them with Sadie.

The relationship between Maggie and Henry has progressed rapidly. They had sex for the first time that Sunday night after we spent the first weekend at Nathan's — just as I predicted. She's told me all about it, of course — she didn't leave out a single detail.

Nathan and Jared have been seeing each other more, but they haven't official declared that they're dating. I'm curious to see if they take things farther this time with their relationship.

Being the non-couple of the group, Joe and I have started to become more like friends, especially during the weekends when we're actively avoiding the sounds of sex coming from our friends', particularly when they don't stay in their assigned rooms. Joe is the first straight guy that I feel comfortable around. He and I have a lot in common with our personalities and openly discuss a wide variety of topics, including business. I, of course, still leave out a lot of details about my family and past, and he doesn't ask, which is fine by me. I'm not sure if he's being respectful or if information has been disclosed by my friends. I'm hoping that it's not the latter.

Joe and I have spent some time learning each other's level of martial arts mastery and spar. I can tell Joe is holding back when we fight, and I'm grateful. Not that I can't handle the sparing, but there have been a few close encounters that have caused our full bodies to touch for more than just a few seconds.

Whenever our bodies come into contact that much, I become a little distracted. He's a handsome, sexy man. What woman wouldn't get distracted being that close to him from time to time?

Today, Maggie and I just had our monthly in-person meeting for Raven Media. Everything is running smoothly, and with needing less time to talk business, we're able to chat more about personal stuff just between us girls. I'm excited to have my friend back — not that I really lost her, but more because she's my only girlfriend and there are certain things I just don't discuss with Jared — somethings you can only discuss with another woman.

Trying to break the ice, Maggie pries, "So, what's going on between you and Joe?"

I look at her quizzically, first because I'm confused by her question, and second because I seriously can't believe she's asking. "What are you talking about?"

"I swear there's chemistry between you two . . . " she nudges.

"No. Don't even start," I warn.

Looking genuinely shocked at my response, Maggie replies, "Seriously? Nothing? Why not? He's cute. He's available. He's . . . ."

"He's . . . a . . . friend. Nothing more," I enunciate each word for her to clearly grasp the concept.

She tries to refute my declaration by adding, "Why can't you be open to the possibility?"

"There is no possibility of anything other than a friendship. You know that. We've been through this with several times now, Mags," I insist, steaming a little.

"Ok, fine. I just don't understand why you don't want to be happy," she pleas with concern.

"I am happy. I'm happy with how I choose to live my life, and I'm happy that you are happy with how you choose to live yours. I just wish that you would be happy for me too," I explain honestly.

"I am happy for you . . . if you are really happy." Maggie hangs her head a little. "He likes you, you know?" she suddenly throws in to stoke the fire more.

"Mags, please," I whine with mild irritation at her decision to press the issue.

"That's all I wanted to say," she confesses.

Part of me wants to believe her and I'm oddly flattered knowing I've caught his interest.

"I see him like I see Jared or Nathan. Just friends," I return, hoping to seal the vault to that topic forever.

Chapter Twelve

I'm not interested in a relationship, and I still don't think I ever be. If, and this is a really big if, I ever changed my mind, Maggie would be the first person to know aside from Jared. I just can't bring myself to let anyone in like that.

There is sexual tension between Joe and I, I'll admit that, but only to myself. Yes, it seems to be building a little bit more, but it's only lust, a physical desire. As much as I want to put out that fire, I still refuse to break any of my own rules. I'm not sure to what extent Maggie means that Joe likes me, but to whatever degree that is, it would just make things weirder if we did do anything.

"I have a confession to make," Maggie adds, still holding her head low, barely peeking up at me with just her eyes.

"What?" I say, suddenly nervous about the subject of her confession.

What now? What is it that she wants to tell me?

"I . . . um . . . " Maggie searches for words.

"You didn't hint to Joe that he might have a chance with me, did you?" I demand while trying to remain calm.

"What? No. God, no," she confirms.

Her response validates it's truth. I know she didn't when she says it. Maggie is a horrible liar.

"I . . . um . . ." she searches how to tell me something.

I cringe, not knowing where she's going.

She obviously sees the panic in my face and blurts, "I told Henry about us." Her face reddens and her eye bounce between my face and the floor.

I sit frozen for what feels like hours. Did I just hear her correctly? Did she just admit that she's told Henry about her and me? She's never told any boyfriend about us and our sexual encounters. My eyes begin to sting a little, so I flicker my eyelids a few times. I must have stopped blinking.

"You . . ." I pause, not knowing what I want to say. My mouth feels dry like a desert and I try to regain even a little bit of moisture by swallowing hard once before continuing. "You, what?"

Wincing at my words, Maggie repeats herself, "I told Henry about us. Please don't be mad at me."

An uncontrollable giggle leaves my mouth before I repeat her. "You . . . told Henry . . . Wh . . . Wh . . . ."

"We're serious, Emma. And, if he's the one. He needs to know me, accept me and love all of me," Maggie announces with a dignified manner.

I completely agree with her. Any man that deserves her must love and accept her unconditionally. I've told her that since we became friends and she started dating.

"He knows it stays between us. He's not to say anything to anyone."

"I . . . would . . . hope . . . so," I mutter, still trying to wrap my head around what's occurring.

Cheerfully, Maggie adds, "He's completely accepting. He's even said that if you or I ever need to, that we have his full support. He's not looking to interact with you . . . ."

Cutting her off, I reply, "I would hope not."

I would never sleep with any man she has dated, is dating, and now possibly, dare I say, eventually marrying. My body shivers at the thought. The last thing I would want to do is make our friendship awkward in any way.

"You're funny. You know I would never ask that of you. I know where we stand, Emma. And, I love you for that," she pauses for a brief second and then continues. "He's willing to do whatever we, you and I, feel comfortable with."

"I can't believe you are telling me this," I profess still dazed.

A little surprised, she replies, "Why wouldn't I tell you this? We are family and of course I would tell you. I wanted to tell you first that I was planning on telling him, but it just came out the other day."

I take a deep breath before continuing, "I'm just surprised that you're telling me about this . . . now . . . just before we are supposed to go have lunch with him and Joe."

"Oh," she bashfully states as her eyes widen. "I thought it would be weirder if he knew and you didn't during lunch. And, if I waited, you'd kill me."

Another giggle escapes my mouth as I reply, "I just might kill you anyway."

"Emma. Come on," she pleas.

I hear the worried strain in her voice.

Pinching the skin at the top of my nose between my eyes, I shake my head. Fear and dread surround me. I understand why she told Henry and I truly appreciate that she informed me. But seriously? Now? Right before we're supposed to have lunch. Couldn't she have given me some time to process all of this?

"What's done is done," I express while trying to compose myself.

Maggie hesitantly moves towards me. I know she wants to hug me, console me and herself, so I let her. Stepping towards her, I lean in to let her know

Chapter Twelve

that I'm not mad or hurt. I knew this day would eventually come, but I was just hoping to have more time. Patting her on the back reassuringly, I provide comfort as she sighs with relief.

Standing, holding each other warmly for another few seconds, we release each other and she kisses me on the cheek. Grabbing Sadie's leash, I keep taking in deep breaths, trying to prepare my mind and body for seeing Henry. I think it would be a lot easier if Joe wasn't going to be there, but then again, maybe he'll be a nice distraction and keep any conversation from going in any awkward direction.

As we walk toward Colorado Boulevard to one of my favorite restaurants, La Pain Quotidien, Maggie texts Henry that we're leaving a little early. Seconds later, her phones chirps. Henry and Joe apparently have been in Pasadena for the last fifteen minutes and are heading over to meet us.

The four of us and Sadie meet in front of the restaurant at the same time and exchange greetings. Luckily, since we are early, we're able to get a seat outside on the patio. I watch and listen to Henry closely, but I don't notice any odd behavior from him. This is comforting. Curiously, I watch Joe as well. If he and Henry are such good friends, even though Maggie told Henry not to say anything, that doesn't mean he won't necessarily tell his best friend. That's how Maggie operates and I know that she's already informed Henry of her habits.

After ordering drinks and meals, our conversations remain light and friendly as usual for us at this point. Maggie opens up a new topic for discussion eagerly, "So, Henry and I have made arrangements for a trip for all of us next month for our three month anniversary."

I look to Henry when she makes this statement and he doesn't flinch. If anything, he's just as excited at the announcement as Maggie. Creepy. Most guys would be running by this point.

"We're all going to . . ." she pauses temporarily for a dramatic affect. "Hawaii!" Maggie's bouncing in her seat as both her's and Henry's eyes sparkle with elation.

"Awesome," I respond animatedly, though a little disturbed by their equaled enthusiasm.

"I know, right," Maggie eagerly adds. "It's going to be so much fun. We can hike, swim, sail, jet ski, and so much more . . . ." Her voice trails off as her eyes glaze over dreamily.

I try really hard not to smirk at her comment and Henry's equally enthusiastic stare. Good thing, Henry and her have their attention on each other. Bad thing, Joe catches me and restrains himself from snickering as well.

Breathe In

"Does Jared know?" I inquire, forcing Maggie and Henry to break their intimate moment.

"No, not yet. I was going to tell them later today," Maggie confirms.

I nod in agreement still try to suppress my smirk.

The rest of the meal, Maggie continues to talk about Hawaii and everything she's learned since she and Henry started planning the trip. I listen contentedly, excited to go to Hawaii. I've never been, but my enthusiasm does not match the level of Maggie's, especially for a three month anniversary.

My mind starts to wander a little as Maggie sustains the topic of her and Henry's anniversary. I start reviewing what she told me earlier before we left for lunch and start to study Henry's face more closely. I'm relieved after another ten minutes of coming up with nothing, no uneasiness. This completely baffles me. Other topics float in and out of my mind as I nod and hum fake responses to Maggie's diatribe.

The books. I have the books for Joe and Henry.

When Maggie takes a sip of her drink, I'm allotted enough time to interject. "I've got something for the two of you," I offer looking to Henry and then Joe.

Their questioning faces are funny, including Maggie's. I think Maggie is more in a state of shock.

"What?" Joe questions.

"You got them something?" Maggie adds with a puzzled look that has a hint of concern.

What? Have I ever given her cause for concern? Would I ever give her cause for reservation? Okay, maybe. I laugh inwardly at the thought.

"Here," I say, handing them each packages wrapped in blue and white striped wrapping paper.

"I didn't realize that you cared so much," Joe taunts wickedly. As Joe reaches for the gift, I teasingly pull my hand back just enough to keep it out of his reach while eyeing him, sparking a chuckle out of all three of them.

Joe and Henry both take the items from my hands, confused by my actions and what the packages could be. Has Maggie said something to them at some point to have them question my intentions too? I've joked around on occasion, but I've never done anything down right mean.

"They might help with your classes," I offer as they unwrap them at the same time.

"Ooh, that's a great book!" Maggie shouts. "Emma made me read it before I started managing Raven Media."

Chapter Twelve

"Wow. Thanks, Emma!" Henry expresses with genuine appreciation.

"Thank you. This is awesome," Joe adds, equally grateful. "I heard one of the guys in my class mention this book the other day — said it's been helping."

Maggie is beaming at my generosity, which concerns me a little. I've never given anything to any of her previous boyfriends, let alone their friends. Did I just openly accept Henry and Joe too soon? Damn. I should have made her sweat it out a little longer. Oh well.

Both Joe and Henry get up from their seats and move towards me. I'm not sure what to make of their actions. Getting to me first, Joe leans down and plants a kiss on my cheek and whispers, "Thank you."

I temper my facial reaction to his low, sultry voice. The sexual tension has just increased ten fold. I'm pleased when he doesn't linger and Henry offers the same gesture. To my delight, I'm glad that Henry was second. He completely squashed all of the sexual desire I had for Joe and replaces it with complete awkwardness for me. Damn Maggie for her confession. I'm still wishing she hadn't told me.

We continued chatting at the restaurant for a short period after we finish eating. Henry covers the check as he always does, unless Joe beats him to it. I'm not used to anyone else picking up the tab, not this much. Over the years, Maggie, Jared, Nathan and I have always altered who takes care of the bill. Now, with two other people in the mix, it's not horrible, just awkward because they always insist on paying. I'm not sure what to make of this habit. I've never experienced it before with anyone. None of Maggie's past boyfriends ever did this. Is this an ego thing or a male dominance thing? I'm still not sure I like it and sometimes I even argue with them about it, but today, I deliberately choose not to say anything.

The guys and Maggie insist on a tour of Pasadena, so I begrudgingly agree since I'm outnumbered. We walk around Old Pas for about forty-five minutes before we hop on one of the local Metro buses to head east on Colorado to show them the Pasadena Playhouse and continue by foot to the South Lake Avenue section. Maggie insists on showing them some more sites including the famous Rose Bowl and local museums. That means we'll be in a car and I brace myself for the trip. We get back onto the Metro bus to head towards Henry's car which is parked near where we ate. Henry holds the front passenger door for Maggie at the same time Joe holds the back left passenger door for me. Well, I do need to give Maggie some credit, she did finally pick a gentleman this time around.

Maggie knows Pasadena as well as I do, so I relinquish any navigation or sightseeing suggestions to her. Sadie lays stretched out over the middle of the back seat with her head on my lap and her rear against Joe. Joe's hand rests comfortably on Sadie's hip, scratching her with his fingers as I pet her head.

My mind begins an internal conflict with itself as the car glides over the streets. Outwardly, my body typically displaces the battle my thoughts engage when one of my legs shake rapidly. With the weight of Sadie's head, my tension is released instead by tapping my right thumb on the side of my clutch repeatedly. My eyes take turns peering between the top of Sadie's head, where my left hand rests, and the buildings moving past us through the window. Even knowing we are driving at a leisurely city speed, it does not reduce my anxiety in the slightest bit. My brain floods with chatter and noise which adds heat to the battle brewing inside me.

Suddenly, my attention is pulled away from its increasing dismay. My gaze finds a hand draped over mine with a thumb brushing lightly back and forth over my knuckles. Looking up, I catch a calm, soothing expression on Joe's face adorned with a soft, gentle smile and kindness in his eyes. The discomfort inside me subsides immensely at his gesture. I turn my hand to grasp his to keep me here in reality which pleasantly distracts me from the war inside.

I don't want to mislead Joe and the thought presents itself temporarily. I squash it with the belief that he's just being friendly. Joe's large hand is warm and soft, but firm as it embraces mine. I welcome the desire that stir inside me from his touch; it's a much more bearable sensation than the fear and thoughts of my anxiety for being in a car. I smile warmly at him in appreciation.

Our hands stay clasped during the entire drive and neither one of us seem to mind. Thankfully, Maggie and Henry don't turn around enough at any point to catch us hand in hand. As soon as we stop out front of my apartment complex, I immediately let go of Joe's hand. He accepts the release and doesn't show disappointment before rushing around to open the door for me.

We say our farewells at the curb with the knowledge that we'll all be together again tomorrow with Jared and Nathan. This weekend we're staying local for our outings; Universal Studios on Saturday and the beach again on Sunday.

Later that night, Sadie and I hop on the Gold Line and then the Red Line to the Hollywood and Vine exit where Jared picks me up every time I go to visit. Staying the night with him will make it easier for the six of us to get together first thing in the morning to be ready for Universal when the doors open. Nathan and I cook, we eat and relax for the rest of the night. We chat and watch movies on Jared's bed while Nathan sketches from time to time. Jared and Nathan fall asleep halfway through the second movie, which makes getting them up early in the morning much easier. I turn off the lights and curl up next to Jared with Sadie on my left.

Thirteen

We have a fantastic day at Universal Studios in Hollywood. The weather is perfect and the crowd is small for an early weekend in April. Maggie, Jared, Nathan and I have been there several times, but it was Henry's and Joe's first time. The six of us joke, laugh, scream and shout throughout the day depending on the ride or attraction as we also take lots of pictures with our phones.

Maggie and Henry, in Henry's car, follow Jared, Nathan, Joe and myself back to Jared's apartment in West Hollywood to pick up Sadie and our bags before heading to Nathan's for the night. Once at Nathan's, everyone gets settled as I feed Sadie and take her out for a good run on the beach. Joe joins Sadie and me to avoid being left with the two hot and horny couples.

Heading back up from the beach, I text both Maggie and Jared giving them fair warning that Joe, Sadie and I will be returning in five minutes. Thankfully, everyone has their clothes on when we open the condo door. Within fifteen minutes, we leave to have dinner.

After dinner, as soon as the door to Nathan's condo opens, Maggie and Henry rush off to the third bedroom for the night. Nathan turns on the television for a movie, but his main intent is to prevent moaning from being heard. The four of us and Sadie pile onto the couch to watch a movie and in less than fifteen minutes, Jared and Nathan are making out. Before I need to say anything, they excuse themselves for the night, each kissing me on the cheek on their way to bed.

Joe and I sit quietly during the rest of the movie as we both pet Sadie. Once the movie is over, I wince at the noises we suddenly hear when I turn off the television and catch Joe doing the same thing.

"Come on," I instruct him, tilting my head towards my room.

"You sure?" he asks.

"Yeah," I answer nodding and rolling my eyes to the moaning and groaning that seems to be getting louder.

In the bedroom, I make sure both doors to the joining bathroom are closed and turn to see Joe shutting the one behind him. I pull out my Bluetooth speakers and start playing some music on my phone. No need to overhear anything from the adjacent room.

"Where's your stuff?"

"My bags? They're out there. Why?" Joe returns, unsure of my question.

"I doubt that you'll want to go back out there anytime tonight," I offer.

Looking confused with a brow lifted, Joe asks, "Are you suggesting that I sleep in here?"

"Yeah," I confirm.

He chuckles, "Wow. I didn't know that our relationship is that serious."

Blankly looking at him, "We aren't having sex. We're two adults sharing the same bed. Besides, I know you aren't a serial killer or rapist."

Laughing hard, he teases, "You sure?"

"Yes. I'm sure." Shrugging my shoulders, I add, "Even if you did try something, Sadie would have your throat in her jaw before I would even need to defend myself."

Joe laughs as he quickly leaves the room to get his bags and darts back in within seconds. Eyes wide, he comments, "It's gotten louder."

We both stand giggling for a minute before getting situated.

We've become friends over the past two months and I feel more comfortable with Joe, more than I have with any straight man. In the past, I deliberately haven't allowed myself the chance for any kind of a friendship to happen with other men, but our friendship has developed out of necessity when we are the third and fourth wheels to our friends dating. Thankfully our personalities line up and anytime we hang out it's fun. The sexual tension is still there with Joe — I continue to admit to myself only, to make sure I adhere to my rules, of course. The fact that he's about to share a bed with me tonight makes me a little jittery and nervous because I desire him — and, I'm horny. I've never had the notion not to adhere to my rules in the past when it came to friends of Maggie's previous boyfriends. It was easy then. They were dumb or annoying, therefore immediately expunging any possibility of desire. Be strong, Emma.

Returning from the bathroom with his pajamas on, Joe graciously says, "Thanks, Emma."

Glancing up from my book, I smile and say, "You're welcome."

I continue reading to avoid watching him get to the other side of the bed and slide in. Placing my book down for a second, I move a pillow longways in the middle of the bed. Sadie shifts up to rest her head in the center. With a book in hand, Joe laughs.

"What?" I demand.

"Nothing," he rebuts with a smile.

Chapter Thirteen

We read in silence for a while, and as I cover a few more pages, I peek from the corner of my left eye at Joe. With my attention back on my book, my left hand caresses Sadie several times before it bumps into something unfamiliar. I immediately look over and see Joe's hand as I run my fingers back up Sadie's body — his goes in the opposite direction. He never flinches and continues to read while maintaining his even, fluid strokes. With a mind of its own, my hand heads back down Sadie's body. Luckily, I'm able to control it enough to stop just short of bumping into Joe's again. To not draw any attention, I force my eyes back to my book while shifting my hand to Sadie's head. Joe shows no sign of noticing and I'm relieved.

A song comes through the speakers that I'm not in the mood to hear, so I pick up my phone to change it. After hitting the shuffle button twice, I decide to let the next song play. Before I know it, Joe snatches the phone from my hand.

"Hey!" I yell.

"I just want to see your playlists," he defends playfully.

Five seconds later his phone rings. Did he just dial his number? Reaching to grab my phone, I'm a little surprised when he jerks away.

"You didn't?"

His smile gives his intention away. "Yep."

Joe finishes punching in something as I place my book down and lunge to get my phone. He switches hands, blocking me with his right arm while using his left thumb on the screen.

"I don't want your phone number and I certainly don't want you having mine."

"Why not? You might need to get in touch with me for something," he argues.

"Why would I ever need your number?" I push his arm down out of my way to get to my phone as I'm now kneeling on the bed.

He's strong enough to keep me at bay. For some reason, I'm kind of enjoying the fight.

"I know you and Henry have each other's number."

"What does that have to do with you having mine and vice versa?"

"Emergency. And, we're friends."

"Why would I call you for an emergency?" I protest.

"The possibilities are endless. And, now you have it."

He persists to look at my phone while trying to keep me away. Frustrated and frisky, I decide to brawl. Understanding my actions, Joe shifts and pins me to his chest, my arms are now locked. I don't kick or use my legs only because Sadie would get hit and she clearly refuses to move. He's stronger than I anticipate from the other times we've spared. I lower my head to bite his forearm, but he shifts before I can clamp down enough to break free.

Joe's chest pulses behind me as he laughs. "Calm down, *Kitten*," he heartily harasses.

Did he just use Jared's pet name for me?

"Only Jared and Nathan get to call me that," I complain.

I'm able to see what he's doing with my phone since he needs his left arm to help hold me in place. He's definitely searching through my playlist. He holds me tighter each time I wiggle and secures my head with his chin since I try to thrust it back several times. He continues to laugh at me like he's enjoying the situation.

I finally stop struggling and ask, "What are you doing?"

I know what he's doing, but I'm not sure why.

"Checking out your playlist. You can tell a lot about a person from their music selection." He continues to scroll through the songs. "You've got an eclectic mix here. Don't worry, you can see mine when I'm done."

"I don't want to see yours," I dispute.

He chuckles into my ear, "Of course you do." He turns off my phone and puts it next to my book, but he doesn't release me.

"Let me go," I demand.

"Not yet," he rebuts relaxed.

"Yes!"

"No."

I growl which elicits more laughter from him.

"I'll let you go once you calm down," he informs.

"That might be a while."

"Fine by me," he says tightening his left leg around me.

As much as I hate being restrained, I know that I could break free if I made Sadie move. Ironically, she has yet to aid in my defense. Tied in his arms, the feel and smell of him starts to get the better of me, and I enjoy his body pressed against mine. Crap, now I'm really horny.

A few seconds go by before he removes his leg and a few more pass before he slowly lessens his grip on me. Before completely releasing me, he kisses the

Chapter Thirteen

back of my head. I pause for a second, in shock to his lips touching me, and to make sure I'm really free before springing over to my side of the divider pillow. I refuse to look at him as he chuckles under his breath and hands me his phone.

Ignoring him, I check my phone to see what he put in it. Under my contacts Joe added his name and wrote, *Joseph 'Blue Eyes' Covelli* and added his phone number and email. Seriously?! I don't dare delete it because I'll need to know who's if he ever does call. Damn it! Damn him!

I deny the offer of his phone by picking up my book to resume reading. I do want to see what's on his phone, but I don't want to give him the satisfaction of knowing that I do. He slides the phone down the ridge my book and I immediately toss it back to him. He gives up after one more attempt and returns to reading as well.

After some more time passes, my head jerks to the sound of Joe's voice. I must have been so focused on my book that I forgot he was even in the room. "Huh?"

Grinning, Joe repeats himself, "What are you reading?"

"Oh, sorry. *Ask and It Is Given*," I mention as I place my bookmark in the page and hand him the book.

He takes it eagerly and begins reading the description on the back. "Looks like you've read this a few times," he states, looking up after examining the book closer.

"Yeah," I reply. "It's one of my favorites."

Flipping open to a page, he begins studying it further. Realizing that I'm not going to get my book back right away, I reach to investigate what had his attention. "What are you . . . oh, never mind," I declare.

It's the book I gave him yesterday. I'm shocked to find a variety of pages already highlighted with notes in the margins. My heart melts a little when I notice that he's almost done with chapter three.

Control yourself and your thoughts, Emma.

Expecting to get my book back, I regard him as he continues reading and turns a page. I finally request with a smile, "Can I please have my book back?"

Taking a few seconds to respond he hands it to me. Sheepishly grinning Joe says, "Sure. Sorry. It just seems really interesting."

As we swap books, Joe mentions and praises the book I gave him while holding it up, "I wish I had this during the first semester. It's really insightful and helpful. I can see why you're successful with your businesses."

I blush at his compliment, "Thanks. I'm glad you like it."

We resume reading and midnight is abruptly upon us, requiring us to get some sleep. Joe slips underneath the covers as I get up to use the bathroom for a moment. When I return to the bedroom, all of the lights are off except the one on the nightstand on my side of the bed. Before turning off the light, I slide under the covers and adjust the dividing pillow and turn off the music. The condo is silent.

"Goodnight, Emma," bids Joe.

"Goodnight."

Laying, my eyes stare blankly at the ceiling. What am I doing? What was I thinking? I can't believe that I'm sharing a bed with Joe. It's not like I don't trust him or feel uncomfortable with him. I've slept in a bed with Jared, Maggie and Nathan before. So What's the big deal? It's just that I've never shared a bed with a man before. Okay, I've never shared a bed with a man who wasn't Jared or Nathan before. A man who is heterosexual. A man who I'm attracted to. A man who Maggie says likes me. Focus, Emma. Yes, there is sexual tension. Yes, there is desire. Yes, I am horny. So what? You have rules. Rules that protect you. Just go to sleep.

Fourteen

My mind stirs before I open my eyes. Laying comfortably in a foggy haze, I comprehend that there are three distinct breaths in the room. I keep my eyes closed and do not move as I relish the warmth around me. The chest that my head rests on is definitely male and the deeper tone in his throat supports the thought.

Long, steady, strong inhales and exhales gently lift my head up and down. My eyes remain sealed as I lounge quietly and motionless, listening for others noises that will give me an indication of where I am and who I'm with since I'm in no hurry to get up. Nothing.

I know Sadie's breathing without a doubt and the second one is mine. But, who is the third? Jared? No. Nathan? No.

Panic rises inside of me as I'm frozen in place and my eyes fly open. Keeping my body still, my gaze darts around to gain clues. The color of the comforter and decor of the one side of the room verifies that I'm at Nathan's. I feel my heartbeat regain its relaxed pace. Breathing in through my nose, an arousing aroma fills my nostrils and excites my lady parts. It's a familiar smell, but it takes a few extra seconds before my waking brain recognizes it — Joe.

My eyes widen as I discover that my body is pressed up against Joe's, with my head on his chest, my right arm draped over him and my right leg down the remainder of his body. Why am I sleeping with Joe? Oh yeah — I remember now. Where the hell is the divider pillow? I pull my right arm towards me a little, but am met with resistance when his left hand squeezes to keep hold. Crap. I shift backward somewhat only to find that his other arm is underneath my body and wrapped around me with his right hand cupping my waist. Joe pulls me back into him as I tug to get away. Double crap. I seriously hope that he's not awake. If he is, this will be utterly awkward and embarrassing.

Sadie shifts, revealing that she is at the lower right corner of the bed. Her location gives me enough room to wiggle my way out of this situation. I decide to go for one, full, quick roll to face the other side of the bed. As soon as I make it, I'm immediately drawn into Joe's body as his arm wraps around my upper frame and spoons me. Shit!

My brain is freaking out as my traitorous body succumbs to the sensation of his. The intoxicating scent of him only makes matters worse and my sex tingles with absolute delight. God, he feels and smells so good. Is this what it feels like to wake up next to a man? A sinfully, delicious man? Joe nuzzles his face into the crook of my neck, sending mouth-watering shivers down my spine. His hips press forward into my rear and to my surprise, my body curls into him. A craving erupts inside of me that I've never felt before and my mind surrenders to the idea that if he wants to have his way with me at this very instant, I'll let him. No. No. Focus, Emma.

Sadie nudges my leg with her head, snapping me out of my glorious moment. Okay, Emma. You can do this. I start to inch away from his embrace, but I'm met with another gentle pull and a velvet moan. His face buries into my neck more and I let out a tiny whimper when his lips and warm breath brush my skin. My heart pounds inside of me as the moisture between my legs becomes more apparent. God, I'm so turned on right now that I can smell myself. My own aroma ignites my appetite for him beyond that which I have ever felt for a man.

All of a sudden, Sadie walks over my legs and begins sniffing under my chin which brings me out of my temporary moment of defeat. I can't help but laugh at how it tickles.

My eyes shoot open at the sound of Joe moaning her name, "Saaaadieeee."

He's awake. How long has he been awake to know it's Sadie?

Curiously, Joe doesn't let go of me. "Good morning, beautiful,' he whispers.

My heart drops as the temptation returns. I can barely mutter, "Umm . . . Good morning . . . ."

He doesn't move. I don't move. Crap. What am I going to do?

Searching for something, I ask, "Where's the pillow?"

"What pillow?" he returns, still not letting go of me.

"The one I put between us last night?" I remind.

He raises his hand and pets Sadie before answering on an exhale, "I don't know. Why?"

I'm dumbfounded by his statement and actions, as well as dismayed at my own response when I roll my body into him enough to look at him. What am I doing? Focus, Emma. It takes all the energy I have not to do anything foolish with him as I stare into his hypnotizing, blue eyes.

With the best impassive look on my face I can muster, I rebut, "What do you mean you don't know? What did you do with it?"

Grinning, Joe looks like he's contemplating his reaction. "I didn't do anything. You must have done something with it," he accuses.

I'm not surprised by his playfulness and do my best to stay composed with his face a few inches from mine and complain. "Me? I'm not the one who isn't on their side of the bed."

Chapter Fourteen

He props himself up on an elbow and briefly searches the room. Joe lowers himself back down, placing his head in the palm of his hand and his left hand on my stomach. Looking at me he chuckles and gestures. "You threw it over there."

Not believing him, I sit up to see. The pillow is on the floor and on his side of the room.

While seated, I assert myself. "Seriously? It's on your side of the room. I didn't move it, you did."

With a full flirtatious tone, he replies, "You moved it . . . right before you snuggled up to me and put your head on my chest."

I swear the blood drains from my face at hearing his words. Shit! He was awake. Processing everything, I realize that that means he knew what he was doing when I rolled away.

Scooting out of the bed, I shake my head in disbelief. "No way!"

Joe is cool and calm, laughing at my reaction and my enter body ironically yearns for him.

Panicking, I question, "How long were you awake?"

With a teasing smile, he rolls onto his back putting his hands behind his head. "Long enough." He seems unfazed and almost happy to let me know.

How am I the only one embarrassed by this situation? I want to say more, but all I can do is rattle my head as I grab some clothes to change in the bathroom. When I come back out, he is still on the bed, but now sitting up and petting Sadie. I do my best to control myself, but I'm sure he sees my distress.

"Either one of us could have moved the pillow in the middle of the night. It's no big deal. I didn't mind," he comments.

I stop dead in my tracks at his admittance. I can feel his eyes watching me with precision.

"Besides . . ." he continues as he gets out of the bed. ". . . you were fun to snuggle with."

My eyes meet his for a brief moment. He slowly starts moving in my direction. Wanting to avoid Joe, I reach for the main bedroom door to open it and go feed Sadie. Keeping my gaze straight, I let out a sigh of relief when I hear a more distant door close.

I use the half bath while Sadie finishes eating to avoid going back into the bedroom. Taking a little longer than usual, I examine myself in the mirror. My hands tremble as I regain control over my breathing. What the hell was that? What the hell is wrong with me? Was I on the brink of breaking a rule with Joe?

Breathe In

Please don't be in the living room, please don't be in the living room, I repeat several times in my mind before exiting the bathroom. *Of course he's in the living room*, I exclaim to myself seeing him on the floor with Sadie. Joe looks up at me with a laid-back smile. Act normal, Emma. You can't let him know that you're flustered.

Before I can say anything, Joe asks, "Do you mind if I join you ladies?"

I try not to show my disjointed emotions. "Sure."

We head out to the beach as I debate with myself on whether or not to confront him. I find myself chewing on my bottom lip and weighing my options. I conclude that talking with him is out of the question. Let it go, Emma.

We walk peacefully and unaffected by our lack of verbal communication. I fight the urge to look at him, but sometimes I can't help it. Every time our eyes meet, he offers a sweet smile and I return a nervous grin as my body lusts after him.

My thoughts drift back to this morning. I'm confused, unnerved and still completely aroused by him. What is going on? I got comfortable, too comfortable to the point where I let my guard down. Why was I curled into him like that? Why did I let him stay that close? I fear that if he had kissed me, more would have evolved. Crap. Does he know that?

It's just after six when we get back to Nathan's and Joe and I still haven't said a word to each other. Something has to be said. I guess I should break the ice. Be friendly, not too friendly, to dispel anything from earlier while keeping him at a distance. What should I say? I scramble for something — anything.

"Do you need to shower?" Joe searches, beating me to the punch.

Be cool, Emma.

"What? . . . Oh, no . . . I um . . . I'm going to rebound," I barely mutter.

Well, that was completely ungraceful.

We awkwardly bump into each other as I turn to head into the bedroom. "I . . . I need my headphones," I stammer.

Joe smiles as he lets me into the room first. Keeping my head down, I reach for my bag that is on the dresser a few feet away. Turning, I catch the sight of Joe's almost bare back as he shrugs off his sweater and his shirt gets pulled along with it. I bit my lip as the fantasy of running my nails down his skin as he's thrusting inside of me consumes me. I tingle with delight until I find Joe staring back at me with a wicked gleam in his eye and a smirk pushed to the left side of his face.

Crap. Double Crap.

Chapter Fourteen

Holding my breath, I spin to rush out of the door. I let out a huge sigh as I close the door to the patio behind me. Sadie lays on one of the chairs with her bone in her mouth as I turn on some music. I position the rebounder and myself in the corner to hide as I start jumping, facing out towards the ocean. Peace slowly surrounds me as I bounce the built up tension loose for at least forty minutes. When I stop to stretch, I almost scream when I find Joe sitting on the same chair as Sadie. How long has he been there? I don't think I want to know.

Neither one of us say anything as I stretch and his eyes stay on his book — at least I think so. Time to shower. I hold the patio door open and wait for Sadie to follow me in, but she stays with Joe. She picks Joe over me?! Traitor.

I lock the door to the bedroom and the bathroom — I don't need Joe coming in or hearing anything. The shower is refreshing and I can no longer fight the urge to pleasure myself. Everyone will be asleep for at least another hour or two, so I savor every stroke of my fingers and the sea sponge as they fondle my skin. I begin to rub my breasts leisurely, tugging at my hard nipples a few times. The memory of Joe's warm body engulfs my mind as I carefully drag my left hand down to my folds and brush them back and forth. Thinking of him while masturbating turns me on more and I don't care. I realize that I won't be breaking any rules during this act which inflames my need. Leaning up against the tile wall, I place my left leg up on the small built-in seat. Dropping the sponge, my right hand progresses down to join my left hand. Thrusting two fingers inside myself, my left hand circles and massages my clitoris. I'm so desperate for an orgasm that I wish I had brought my vibrator in with me. As I continue to plunge my fingers inside, I do my best to curb my moaning. I have a tendency to be a little vocal. Needing more, I slide a third finger into my cave and the memory of Joe's mouth on my neck returns to my consciousness. Shoving my fingers in harder, faster, my body inches closer to orgasm.

My eyes fling open when I hear an unfamiliar sound. A naked Maggie stands before me. Keeping our eyes on each other, I resume pleasuring myself as Maggie touches herself and wades underneath the water. She moves closer, barely an inch away as she lifts her hands, needs my breasts and sucks on my right nipple. I gasp at her first touch. Sliding her hands down, she replaces my right hand with hers. Our mouths meet, grazing each other's as she sinks her fingers into me. I moan on a sharp inhale as her tongue massages mine. With my right hand now free, I fist her hair, pulling her further into my body. Vocalizing my satisfaction into her mouth and tightening my grip on her, I fiercely climax. Her fingers loiter inside of me, waiting for my last shudder of release.

Breathe In

We lick ever last drop of me off her fingers before Maggie quickly drops to her knees and returns her fingers to my sex followed by her tongue flicking across my clitoris. My fingers tangle in her hair and my hips sway with the pulsing of her fingers. It doesn't take Maggie long to return me to a point where I'm close to orgasming. A few pants later, it springs to life inside me when the though of Joe between my legs enters my thoughts.

Hungry to taste her, I spin her around to switch places. My tongue eagerly slips between her folds, catching a large gulp of her arousal and then focuses on her nub. Two of my fingers penetrate her sex, striking her in the very location that brings her to climax easily. As Maggie comes down from her release, I shift her body, making her face the wall. I creep my lips up her rear to the tops of her shoulders as my left hand reaches around to her clit and my right hand dives into her cave. Pressing my entire body against her, my hands work to make her gush a second time. Once Maggie finishes, we share the flavor of her off my fingers.

The taste of us both lingers in my mouth as we wash our bodies and hair. I ward off thoughts of who may have heard us, not wanting to relinquish this moment of satisfaction.

Dressed, Maggie and I are met by all four guys sitting quietly on Nathan's large sectional. Without a word, Maggie curls up with Henry. Jared stretches out his arms for me to join him and Nathan, so I do.

We all sit silently for several minutes until Nathan investigates, "Who's hungry?"

No one answers.

A snicker escapes Jared and I elbow him.

"Seriously? Do you guys want to eat or shower first?" Nathan inquires as the good host.

Jared immediately chuckles louder, followed by Nathan once he recognizes how Jared is twisting the meaning. I admit, it is funny, even though it is at Maggie's and my expense, and I do my best to try and come up with something to chide him, but fall short.

Maggie beats me to the punch and says innocently, "Why don't we all eat?"

Laughter erupts out of Jared and Nathan. Henry and Joe both are pursing their lips, attempting not to join in. I cover my mouth with my hand.

"What?" Maggie questions, still not getting it.

All four men are roar with laughter as I do my best to refrain my own giggles by biting one of my fingers. Joe and I catch each other's eye and we both blush. Maggie peers at us quizzically for a moment before the reason for our amusement pops into her head.

Chapter Fourteen

Trying to contain a smile, Maggie shouts, "That's not funny." She gets up to smack both Nathan and Jared, but they pull her down on top of me.

It's times like these when I wish it didn't take Maggie as long to get the joke and inadvertently extend it with her innocence.

Jumping up, Nathan yells, "Ok, we're eating."

Everybody giggles at his announcement as he moves into the kitchen. I shift to get up and help him, but Jared wraps his arms and legs around me tighter. Instead of fighting, I give into his affection — I need it. Maggie returns to Henry's lap and Joe gets up to help Nathan.

Whispering in my ear, Jared checks, "You okay?"

"Mmm hmm," I hum, curling into him more.

At first glance, if people didn't know us, they would think that Jared and I are boyfriend and girlfriend.

I continue our conversation in a low voice, "What's going on with you and Nathan?"

Jared smiles at Nathan's name and shrugs his shoulders.

"Is it serious?" I mumble.

Jared blushes but doesn't say anything.

"If it is, I'm happy for you," I convey. "If it isn't, I'm happy for you. I just want to see you both happy."

Kissing me, he breeches the topic, "I know. I love you."

Snuggling up to him, I reply, "I love you too."

I've always loved to cuddle with Jared. The weird thing is, I'm noticing a difference as well as similarities from this morning with Joe. Knowing this, I now understand that I can't let Joe in like this. It's too much. He needs to be kept at a distance.

After breakfast, Maggie and I take care of the dishes while the guys shower. Joe washes up first as Henry attempts to help with cleaning. It's clear that he's had other people take care of tasks like this for him, probably all of his life.

I read on the couch as Maggie and Henry make out once we finish tidying up. When Joe comes out, Maggie follows Henry into the bedroom. Pretending to read, I watch Joe go to back into my room and then come back with his book. We discover ourselves looking at each other a couple of times. A few minutes later, Jared and Nathan stroll out and join Joe, Sadie and me on the couch.

"What should we do today?" Nathan inquires trying to be polite.

I give him a sideways glance as I'm sandwiched in the corner of the couch by Jared and him.

"What?" he says confused by my reaction.

"This is typically the sex-capades day for you two couples," I indicate, pointing at him, Jared and then at the bedroom where Maggie and Henry are hiding.

"She's right," Jared confirms.

"Ohh, speaking of sex . . ." Nathan comments with a teasing tone. "I forgot to tell you who called for me at Nathaniel's yesterday?"

I'm not curious or excited to find out what he has to say, but ask to be polite. "Who?"

"Your friend . . . Chris . . . from Ayana's," Nathan whispers, smiling wide and giggles.

I shrug my shoulders. "So."

"Soooo . . . Denise said he seemed a little flustered when he was leaving his message. He wanted to talk about possibly wearing one of my suits for the next red carpet event, and . . ." Nathan's voice trails off looking for a reaction.

"Congrats! That could be really huge for Nathaniel's!" I comment.

I'm genuinely happy for him and the attention he could get for dressing an A-list actor.

Wise that I was avoiding that he had more to share, Nathan continues anyway, "And . . . ."

Is he actually going there?

"He told me that the next time I spoke to you that he wanted me to say hi," Nathan wickedly sings, deliberately trying to illicit a response from me.

"Ok." I shrug again, glancing at Joe with my peripheral vision.

"Ok?" Nathan questions with a little attitude. "Ok . . . not even a hi back for the guy?"

I glare at Nathan.

"Fine. Break the guy's heart."

"Stop trying to play matchmaker!" I say with a stern, low voice.

"I'm not. Just seeing . . . ."

"Don't," I caution.

He's trying to see if he can set me up with Chris again or wants to see how I handle the information in front of Joe. I'm onto his ways.

Chapter Fourteen

"Don't worry. I won't give him your number or anything," Nathan assures. "Don't get your panties all in a bunch. I know you're trying to play it cool with Joe sitting here."

I shoot Nathan a look that gets a roaring laugh from him.

"Come on," he playfully teases. "I'm just having a little fun."

"A little too much fun," I retort, eyeing him.

"Babe," Jared quietly interjects.

Leaning his head to the left, Nathan catches Joe's eyes. "She's a heartbreaker, this one! Her and her rules."

I don't give Nathan the satisfaction of a verbal response and keep my eyes on my book.

"Babe, leave her alone," Jared commands with a quiet, stern voice.

"What? Okay. Fine," Nathan replies, trying to sound innocent from his words and actions.

I continue to ignore Nathan as Jared squeezes my hand. Jared knows I'm a big girl and can take care of myself, but I appreciate the sentiment. Jared's been very protective of me, and I of him, since we met.

My attention stays on my book as Jared and Nathan whisper to each other. Jared starts playing with my hair as Nathan shifts and lays his upper body across Jared's lap.

"I love you!" Nathan professes in a cutesy voice.

I glance at him for a moment before returning to my book.

"I love you," he repeats, then bites my thigh.

"Ouch," I cry. I immediately spring up, jumping on top of him.

Screaming, Nathan calls to Jared, "Help... help!"

Nathan and I spar for four seconds until I've got him pinned to the floor.

Laughing, Jared stays where he is and insists, "Hell no. You did that yourself."

Sadie makes her way over to Nathan's face and starts licking and sniffing him.

Maggie flies through the bedroom door to see what the commotion is about. "What are you two doing?" she scolds.

"It serves him right," Jared contends. "He started it. She's going to finish it."

Everyone stares, muffling snickers.

Breaking the silence, Jared comments, "My bet is on Emma. Anyone think that Nathan has a chance?"

Breathe In

I smile when they all shake their heads. For a little fun, I decide to let Nathan think he's winning from time to time before returning him to a fully pinned status.

Maggie takes Henry back to the bedroom before Nathan and I are done. Jared turns on the television a minute before Nathan taps out of our match. When I get back to the couch, Jared gives me a high-five just before Nathan turns his playfulness on Jared. Soon after, they are heading to their room.

Before closing the door, Nathan shouts, "Everyone's on their own for lunch. We'll figure out dinner later."

Within five minutes, Joe and I hear noises coming from both rooms. Breaching the subject first, Joe inquires, "How about getting out of here?"

"Sure."

I immediately regret my agreement, but being stuck in the condo overhearing my friends having sex seems more uncomfortable than being stuck out in public with Joe.

I take Sadie with us when we take to the streets. Conversation strikes back up as we walk around and eventually sit to eat lunch. I'm glad when we're able to chat about everything and anything except what happened last night, this morning or when Nathan mentioned Chris. There comes a point where laughter floats in and out of our chatting, erasing any of the previous tension.

After lunch, Joe and I venture over to see the Santa Monica Pier. The view of the ocean is refreshing and many of the shops and restaurants are already open. As we walk, I watch women of all ages ogle Joe. It's hilarious when the women become louder because Joe's attention on Sadie and me never waivers. Does he see them, but is ignoring them, or is he really oblivious? I stop to use the restroom and when I come out, I see six teenage girls hovering around him. It's quite comical. Joe appears to be a little uncomfortable, so I stand at a distance watching for fun, but it doesn't take long for Joe to see me. He gives me a pleading look and I just smile and shake my head. It's payback time for this morning. Let's see him get out of this. All of the girls continue talking to him even as he stares at me.

Contemplating on whether to further my observation or walk away to torture him more, I'm jarred when I hear Joe say, "Sorry, ladies. My girlfriend is back."

They all turn in my direction, following his eyes and gape when they see me grinning.

"She's your girlfriend?" one of them questions with mild irritation.

Chapter Fourteen

Looks like she thought she had a chance. Joe doesn't answer her because he is in full stride towards me. Crap. What is he doing? I was enjoying the entertainment.

Wanting to avoid any awkwardness, I bend down and pet Sadie as she and Joe approach. When I stand back up, Joe puts his hands on my waist and pulls me into him. I keep my arms hanging as Joe plants a prolonged kiss on my cheek before whispering into my ear, "I know what you are doing."

Giggling I deny, "I don't know what you are talking about." I suddenly find my hands holding his arms just above his elbows and I'm also keenly aware of our bodies touching below the waist.

"Keep that up and I'll kiss you right here in front of everyone," he retorts with a devilish voice. He pulls back to examine my reaction.

Even with chaotic emotions swirling inside, I do my best to control my expression. I try to step back, but he gently draws me into him. I'm not sure what has happened to the teenager girls by this point and I don't care. His head tilts forward like he's determined to kiss me anyway.

I look away and suggest, "How about a bike ride?"

"Hmmm," he lets out in disappointment into my ear. "Sounds good, but I like what I had in mind better."

Playing dumb while still looking away, "What's that?"

"I could tell you. Or . . . I can show you." His lips fall upon my cheek again, lingering longer than usual.

You put yourself in this situation, Emma, and you need to get yourself out of it before you let it go too far. What is going to be girl? Break your rules or don't break your rules? You need to decide.

"I . . . like the idea of . . . going for a bike ride."

He moans on a large exhale into my neck and my eyelids flutter in delight. Pull yourself together, Emma. He lightly kisses my temple before slowly, hesitantly lets go of me.

I temporarily make eye contact as we turn to leave the pier. I'm grateful for Sadie's presence when she walks between Joe and me as we head back to Nathan's.

While waiting for one of the lights to change to cross the street, Joe brings up a neutral topic. "So, tell me about Nathaniel's."

"What would you like to know?"

"Anything you're willing to share," he suggests.

"Nathan started Nathaniel's a year and a half ago with only a men's line," I begin.

"And, he's starting a women's line now," he states rather than questions. "It's a little early to start a second product line."

"Normally, for any business I would agree. However, Nathaniel's is in the green," I mention.

"Wow. Really?" Joe's undoubtedly impressed. "How did he manage that? No business is ever in the green the first few years."

Contemplating how I want to explain, I hesitantly offer, "I had some assistance."

"You? Not that I'm surprised with the success of your two businesses," he shares.

His statement makes me think that Maggie and Jared may have revealed more information about me than I would like. I can address this concern later.

"Yes. Before Nathan even started talking about the idea of having his own line, I saw his ability. He's got an eye for fashion. One day when Jared, Nathan and I were hanging out, it came up in conversation. I started asking him some questions, and from his answers, I offered to be his backer right there on the spot," I explain.

"So what did he do to get in the green?" Joe searches.

"Nathan is brilliant with fabric and doesn't give himself much credit for business ability. I insisted on being a silent partner but made myself available for any questions or needs. Taking my advice, he built his company's structure and started advertising and networking before the first season's collection was complete," I openly add.

"Wow," Joe says encouraging me to continue.

Proud of Nathan, I proceeded to explain more. "He worked with Maggie on social media and Jared started wearing many of Nathan's looks on camera. Then, Naturally Me featured Nathan and some of his designs three different times before his store opened. We showcased his versatile ability to create fashion that fit the style needs of all men regardless of their sexual orientation. I also had my Naturally Me team video tape Nathan on a variety of topics, some interviews, some sewing tips and tricks that we used to promote and sell his brand before it was even available. Ultimately, we built up hype around him and the need to wear his clothing."

"Impressive," he acknowledges.

"Opening day, Nathaniel's had a line out the door that stretched around the block. Nathan sold more than half of his inventory by the end of that day," I praise. "He's had to take back orders for most products ever since."

Chapter Fourteen

"I'll have to get Jimmy out here," Joe proposes.

"Who?"

"My brother, Jimmy." Joe clarifies, "James."

"Oh. Why?"

"Aside from running his art gallery, he and his boyfriend, Allen, know a lot of people in the fashion industry. I'll have to talk to Henry too to see if he knows anyone who may be able to assist with manufacturing if he gets picked up by any stores," Joe reveals.

"You don't have to do that," I remark, grateful for his offer to help my friend.

"I know, but he's a friend," Joe insists. "Does he need additional capital for the women's line?"

"No," I report.

Smiling at me, Joe guesses but affirms, "You already took care of it."

"Yep."

"Hmm."

"What?" I inspect.

"Nothing."

We step into the elevator in Nathan's complex. I glare at him knowing something is on his mind.

"You just confirmed something for me," he shares.

"And what is that?" I pry.

"That not only are you beautiful and smart, but you're successful at a whole other level than I realized at first," he openly states.

I look away embarrassed and shocked at his words, not unsure of what to say. Fear starts to boil inside of me when he takes my hand and moves in like he's going to kiss me. Pulling away, I now know that I need to confront him.

Before opening the door to Nathan's condo, I turn to look at Joe. I hesitate for a brief moment on what or how to say it. "Nothing will ever happen between the two of us, Joe."

Confused, he searches, "What do you mean?"

Shaking my head before continuing, I sternly contend, "You know what I mean."

He pauses, scanning my eyes for something before he hints, "A man can dream, can't he?"

A tiny smile dances across his face as I get lost in his eyes, searching. Searching for what? I'm still not sure. I do know this, he just confirmed my earlier decisions about keeping him at a distance. I don't know what to say or what to do at this point. Keeping our eyes locked, I softly shake my head as I hold onto a blank, rigid expression.

His body moves closer as I stand my ground. My hands are balled into fists at my side as he brushes his right hand's knuckles over my cheek. I'm not sure how long we stand like this, but it's long enough. Neither one of us are wanting or willing to back down. His hand shifts to where his palm is cupping my chin as he leans his head forward, stopping two inches from my face. Before he can proceed any further, I cut my head to the right, away from his hand, away from his lips. He breathes a sigh of defeat out before placing his lips on my forehead. Once he backs away, I refrain from looking at him as I pivot to open the door.

The past two months with Joe have been great when it comes to hanging out. We've had all kinds of conversations; business and personal. We've joked, we've laughed and we've had fun. We've become friends, which is odd for me since I don't have any male friends who aren't gay. Now, out of nowhere he's trying to kiss me after the stunt he pulled this morning. I know we've joked around and flirted a little, but I swear I haven't lead him on to think that there's a chance of a friends with benefits possibility or a relationship.

To my relief, Jared and Nathan are finishing lunch when we enter. This is a great opportunity to either avoid going for a bike ride alone with Joe or to include my friends. I sit on Jared's lap as Nathan carries several dishes to the kitchen.

Before I even say anything, Nathan asks, "Have any plans? I'm antsy and need to get out."

"We were thinking on biking around town," Joe mentions.

"Ooo, that sounds like fun. We'll join you," Nathan returns.

"Sure," Joe and I say simultaneously.

The four of us get changed before heading out to rent bikes. We ride the streets for two hours before we get a text from Maggie wanting to know about dinner plans.

When we get back to the condo, I find out that Maggie graciously fed and walked Sadie. The boys decide to grill again, more confident in their ability since they learned how to properly use the contraption.

During dinner, Joe, Nathan, Henry and I discuss Nathaniel's current and future status. Nathan is ecstatic to get additional help and support from his two new friends. If Nathan and I were able to get the business into the green zone in just over one year, I marvel at the concept of what can take place with Joe's and Henry's connections. Everyone openly shares ideas as Nathan takes notes for later use.

Happy as I am to be with my friends, I need to distance myself physically from Joe. As we all cleanup, I check with Maggie to see when she is planning to head home. "When are you heading back tonight?"

"Henry and I were going to stay. Why?"

"I've got a lot of stuff I need to take care of," I inform her.

"It's only one extra night," she indicates.

"I know," I agree. "But, there are a lot of things I want and need to get done."

"I can take you," Joe offers. "I have a meeting tomorrow and need to head out tonight."

"Perfect!" Maggie squeaks.

I give myself a mental head slap for breeching the topic openly to her in front of everyone. I do have other options like getting a cab, but I know my friends and Joe will insist on me going with him.

I accept Joe's offer despite my contention. "Okay. When do you need to get back?"

Joe shrugs, brushing off the immediate need, "No specific time. Just enough to get sleep."

I nod my understanding.

Crap, crap, crap. I'm going to be stuck in a car with him. He better not make an issue of walking me to my door.

We all play a few board games to pass the time. Giving ourselves an easy drive on the roads and to avoid traffic, Joe and I head out with Sadie around ten. The ride is pretty quiet other than me instructing him on which roads to take to get to Pasadena.

"For someone who doesn't like to drive or be in cars, you sure know your way around," Joe teases.

"Use of public transportation," I comment.

He must have seen my leg twitching before reaching over to hold my hand. I pull away in agitation, moreover the fact that I'm in a car.

Joe reaches his hand closer to me. "Come on. I know it helps."

He's right, but it takes me a minute to take the offer. I don't want him to read into holding my hand to mean anything other than easing my anxiety.

Joe pulls up to the curb to drop me off and rushes around to help with Sadie and my bags.

"Thanks. I can take it from here," I mention.

He smiles, nods, and quickly leans in to kiss me on the cheek before I can move. His silky lips send erotic shivers over my skin. Looks like I'll be masturbating when I get upstairs.

Joe stays close with his hands in his pockets. "See you soon," he announces more than questions.

"Yep," I support. "Goodnight, Joe."

"Goodnight, beautiful."

Fifteen

The past two weeks after the snuggling incident with Joe at Nathan's are peaceful with regards to both business and personal matters. My friends and I didn't all collectively get together to hang out. Henry had to travel for business and Maggie went with him. Nathan has been spending everyday sewing and hemming, and Jared has been helping him when we aren't focused on Naturally Me. I spent this past weekend at the We Care Spa alone. Jared and Nathan watched Sadie for me since the spa doesn't allow four-legged creatures. I'm not sure what Joe had planned, but I was happy to get away.

Joe texts and calls to get my opinion for his MBA class project. He always manages to call with a few questions, but I know they aren't the real reason why he is calling. I never call him, but I'll text with an idea or two that pop into my head. The lack of physical proximity makes it much easier to focus on his questions and topics of discussion.

Nathan has been working diligently on his upcoming men's clothing line with a few items for his women's line to test the waters at how well they are received. He's been extremely focused and has taken everything that Henry, Joe or I have said into consideration. Most of our suggestions, Nathan's already implemented or is planning to in the future when the time is right. Nathan has already placed the swimsuit line out on the floor along with a few sample summer dresses for the women.

Chris has also been to Nathaniel's discussing his red carpet attire for his upcoming premier at the beginning of September. It looks like Nathan will be creating a custom piece just for Chris on top of his fall collection. Joe and Henry have also put a few of their business colleagues in contact with Nathan with regards to distribution. Nathan is so excited that he's already envisioning having a storefront in Beverly Hills on Rodeo Drive.

I've been collaborating with Nathan almost every day this week about business, and best of all, this weekend is Easter. I don't celebrate Easter, but this year is making me reconsider the holiday. Why? Joe is heading home to the East Coast to visit his family and I get a harmonious holiday with my best friends — another weekend free from awkward moments with Joe and Henry.

Everything with Naturally Me and Raven Media has been moving smoothly and profits have kicked up a little. I'm always impressed with the teams for each company. They not only work hard, but they love their jobs and offer wonderful feedback and suggestions that are regularly used. It's amazing what people will do or come up with when they are empowered and encouraged. I've been specifically working on making some updates to the software Raven Media uses to enhance my contractors' and clients' needs.

My itch for sex with a man returned over a week ago, but I've been able to suppress it with the help of increased masturbation or Maggie. I still refuse to interact with Henry, but he's been a good sport about Maggie and me having our own fun at my place or at his when he isn't around. I've thought about connecting with Chris a few times, but my body is not interested. He's a sweet guy, good looking, but he just doesn't excite me even in my heightened state of arousal. Plus, he's been asking about me every time he sees or talks to Nathan. I'm definitely not moved to have sex with a guy who clearly wants more, especially when I don't. I'm not the kind of girl who leads men on.

Every time I do orgasm, alone or with Maggie, the memory of being in the same bed with Joe at Nathan's pops up. I'm not sure what to make of it. I've never fantasized about a man before; well, not this much. I bet if I did have sex with him the fantasy would go away — but, I have my rules.

The Easter holiday weekend came and went, and in less than two weeks my friends and I will be in Hawaii for Maggie's and Henry's three month anniversary. I particularly think that it's too early to be celebrating anniversaries, but Henry continues to be just as enthusiastic about it as Maggie.

For as much time as they spend together, I'm surprised when Henry calls me a few times to ask some questions about Maggie. I'm curious as to what he has planned for the trip. Every time I ask Henry about how much I owe him for plane tickets or accommodations, he tells me it's not necessary. I'm getting suspicious of his response. Jared and Nathan have confirmed that Henry is paying for them as well, which doesn't explain anything. I should probably give Joe a call to see what I can dig up, though the idea of calling him is not appealing to me. I don't want to sound needy or desperate for information, even though I am, let alone give him any ideas about us.

As my habit, I text him. "Free for a second?"

"For you, anytime," he sends back within ten seconds.

Before I finish reading his message, my phone rings.

"Hi, Joe," I greet.

"Hey, beautiful. What's up?"

My ears never tire of hearing him call me that. He's been greeting me like that since our bed sharing encounter.

"Henry's being weird," I complain.

"How so?"

Chapter Fifteen

"He won't tell me anything about Hawaii," I assert.

"What do you want to know?"

"My part of the bill."

"Good luck with that," he chuckles.

"You know something. Don't you?" I accuse.

"Maybe," he taunts.

"Spill it," I command.

"Even if I know something, I wouldn't tell."

"Why not?"

Maybe I can persuade him.

"Why do you need to know so badly?"

"Because I don't like surprises."

I've never liked surprises.

"I am a man of my word," he goads.

"What do you want?"

Let's see what the bargaining options are with him.

"You sound a little desperate," he alleges. "Maybe I could be persuaded for a fee."

"Like I said, What do you want?"

The fish has definitely taken the bait.

"How desperate are you?"

"Depends," I begin. "What do you think is an equal exchange?"

"Hmmm . . ." he ponders.

I know he's deliberately stalling.

"A date."

"No."

He knows I don't date.

"It's just one date."

"I don't date and you know it," I softly contend.

"There's a difference between dating and a date," he points out.

"I know the difference."

"Good. Then it'll be easy for you. You. Me. Dinner. Tonight," he directs.

"This is not a fair exchange and you know it."

"Maybe it is, maybe it isn't. But you'll have what you want. Even if it's just part of the picture. I know you want it," he coaxes.

"What's expected on the date?"

I should at least know all of the terms.

He pauses, probably for some kind of dramatic effect. "Like I said, You. Me. Dinner. Tonight."

"Anything else?" I check.

A wickedly, erotic tone that I've never heard before from Joe is let out with his next statement. "What did you have in mind?"

My throat dries and my thighs moisten at his voice. "Nothing. Get your mind out of the gutter."

If he thinks this is an opportunity to making out or have sex, he's wrong. This date shouldn't be an issue. We've had meals before together, some of which he paid for and some of which I have. So what's the whole thing with calling it a date?

After mulling it over, I agree, "Fine. What time do you want to meet and where?"

"I'll pick you up at your place at six," he instructs.

"No."

"Yes," he insists. "If you want to find anything out, you won't argue with me. Besides, it's customary to pick the woman up at her place."

"Fine," I whine.

"Make sure you wear a dress."

"What? Why do I need to wear a dress?"

"Do you want the information or not?"

"Okay. I'll wear a dress."

"See you in a few hours, beautiful," he hums.

I don't answer and just hang up the phone.

What have I gotten myself into? The thought that no good will come of this is creeping into the pit of my stomach. Crap.

An hour before my meeting with Joe, Sadie is already fed and walked and I'm standing in my walk-in closet trying to decide on what to wear. What kind of dress? Causal? Dressy? Ten minutes of staring into my closet produces only more anxiety on the subject of proper attire.

Maybe I should just cancel. I don't really need to know that badly. Do I? Yes I do. I like control — I need control.

Chapter Fifteen

Not wanting to waste anymore time, I jump in the shower. I wash my hair and body and shave. Why did I just shave? I don't plan on having sex. There will be no sex happening tonight, but I do decide to pleasure myself to reduce my edginess.

I choose what to wear while putting on my makeup; something cute and comfortable. With my hair almost dry, I put on a smoked pearl colored cocktail dress that is embellished with metallic lace, has one inch straps that contour into a deep v-neck just between my breasts that hugs my upper body and loosens slightly two inches above my knees. I adorn my neck with my happiness necklace from Energy Muse that is made of a thirty inch, solid gold chain with a pendant consisting of quartz crystal, kyanite and moonstone. After giving my hair one final toss and brush, I put on solid gold earrings. To finish my outfit, I put on my light bronze, four inch strappy Jimmy Choo heels.

Just as my second shoe slips on, I get a text from Joe letting me know that he has arrived. Like clockwork, Joe is early, fifteen minutes early to be exact. Grabbing my clutch, I kiss Sadie goodnight.

Rounding the corner of the internal gate to my apartment complex, I find Joe waiting, wearing a medium grey colored suit with a crisp white dress shirt underneath that has the two top buttons undone. Joe is a man that can make any suit look good — actually, he can make any outfit look good. I feel a spark of heat and moisture between my thighs at the sight of him.

"Wow! Hello, beautiful," he greets along with his typical lean in hug and kiss on the cheek. For some reason, he lingers close, longer than usual.

"Yeah, yeah," I downplay his response and try to gain control over my raging hormones.

Joe offers me his arm as he leads me to his car waiting at the curb. A driver standing by a luxurious, black Rolls Royce Phantom opens the back right door for us both. Joe ushers me in and follows just shortly after.

I've never seen Joe drive, let alone be driven, in a Rolls Royce. I didn't know he had one. The thought that he might have rented it for the night comes to mind. Would he? I know he could. But, why?

"Where are we going to eat?" I search, wanting to keep my self focused on my mission.

"You'll see," Joe replies with a wicked grin. Knowing my car challenge, he instinctually takes my hand just before the car carries us off into the setting sun. "How's business going this week?"

"Good, thanks. You?"

"Great. Thanks." He adds, "The suggestion you made was received well by the board. They're starting to understand the requirement to shift more toward technology for many aspects of the industry as well as the economic need for a more ecological approach."

"Terrific!" I praise. "Did you mention the carbon footprint reduction concept as well?"

Joe is a very smart businessman, I can tell he's learned a lot from school as well as from his father. However, I've noticed with some of our conversations that he has a tendency to second guess himself.

"They loved it. We'll be taking action steps at the begin of the next quarter," he confesses. "My father wants to meet you, by the way."

"Me? Why?"

"He wants to meet the mind behind my brilliant consultant," he compliments. "That and I think he's considering on hiring you for specific consulting work."

"It's all you, Joe," I humbly contend. "I have nothing to do with it."

"You have more to do with it than you think," he replies honestly. "We make a great team."

"It has nothing to do with me. You are trusting your instincts and that's what gets it done," I argue.

Joe takes his free hand and tenderly caresses the back of my hand he is now holding on his lap. I feel nervous about the proximity of my hand to his groin, but his left hand is resting on his leg, just under my hand, which helps slightly.

"Have you seen the LA Philharmonic play?" he searches.

"A few times at the Walt Disney Concert Hall and Hollywood Bowl. They're phenomenal. Why?"

"Which place is better to see them?"

"Either. It just depends on the concert and the atmosphere you want. Why?"

"If I get tickets, will you go with me?"

We've done a few activities together, but the way he's asking is a little peculiar.

"Why don't I get the tickets?" I offer.

"You pick which venue you want to buy the tickets for and it's a deal."

I take the highroad not to battle this one, so I suggest, "I'll take the Hollywood Bowl. There are a lot of options other than just the LA Philharmonic that I think you'd enjoy."

Joe smiles with ease and I actually see his body relax more into the seat. "Great. Choose any event for yours. Surprise me."

Chapter Fifteen

"You sure?" I tease.

"Yep. I know we've have similar tastes based on your playlist." Joe's playful grin returns.

He clearly wants me to remember our last time at Nathan's.

When Joe helps me out of the car, I'm tremendously pleased with my attire selection for our — night out. However, I'm a little perturbed by his choice. We are dining at one of Beverly Hills' top restaurants, the Spago; one of Wolfgang Puck's locations. A wonderful, delectable choice, but a bit higher in price for a date compared to where we normally eat. The place is busy, but Joe and I are seated immediately which leads me to believe that Joe called for reservations.

Arriving at our table, Joe pulls out a chair and gestures for me to sit. As I lower down, he slides the chair under me. Joe takes his seat with calm confidence, not noticing the hostess who is practically drooling over him.

Joe looks to me and asks, "Have you eaten here before?"

"Once or twice," I comment, not revealing the truth as I study him, noting that his eyes never veer from me.

The waiter greets us with a bottle of wine in hand, which from my angle it's Dom Perignon. When the waiter offers, Joe takes a look at the bottle and nods. Next, the waiter pops the cork and fills both of our glasses. "I'll let Chef Andrews know you are here Mr. Covelli," the waiter confirms.

"What was that?" I question after the waiter leaves.

"What?"

"The bottle of Dom Perignon that we didn't order and then the whole I'll let Chef Andrews know you're here Mr. Covelli statement," I reply with a hushed, sarcastic voice. "And, where are the menus?"

Grinning, Joe answers, "I ordered the bottle of wine in advance. Chef Andrews knows my family and we don't need menus since we're having whatever the chef decides to prepare for us."

"He's deciding?" I press.

I'm not sure if I like this whole ordering my wine and food for me deal for a date.

"We have the same tastes. I told him what we do and don't like."

"How do you know my tastes?" I playfully contend.

"How many meals have we had together over the past two and a half months?"

He's right. If anyone was paying attention to what I ate and what I've talked about, my tastes would be easily identifiable. Has Joe really taken notes? If so, why? This is weirding me out a little.

Joe holds up his glass of wine and toasts, "To trusting and trying new things and being surprised."

I clink my glass with his, but I'm not in full agreement to his toast. To me, there are too many underlining messages he has buried in that statement.

Right as I'm about to begin my interrogation about Henry and the whole Hawaii trip, Chef Andrews himself is standing at our table. Joe immediately stands up to greet him. They hug and exchange pleasantries freely, proving that Joe was telling the truth and that he actually does know the chef.

"And who is this exquisitely stunning creature?" flatters Chef Andrews, delicately holding my hand and kissing it. He refrains from letting go for a few extra seconds.

"This is Emma Peterson," Joe replies.

How does he know my full name? I've never told him and for both of my businesses, my full name is not listed anywhere on the internet. In fact, my businesses and my name are not public record.

"Since when have you had a girlfriend?"

"I'm not his girlfriend," I immediately rebut.

"And, she's feisty too! I like her already. I see why you're with her," Chef Andrews adds.

"She is most certainly feisty, but unfortunately we are not dating," Joe comments with a hint of rosiness developing on his face. "But, we are on a date."

"One step closer to marriage," Chef Andrews announces.

"No," I contend. "I don't date and I especially don't plan to ever get married."

"Then why are you out on a date with him?"

"To extort information from him," I explain.

"If you hadn't seen her first, I would be chasing this one for myself. You are a lucky man, Joe," Chef Andrews admits. "Is she like this all the time?"

I instantly blush at his compliment.

"Yes," Joe confirms.

The heat in my face increases.

"I'm working on it being more than just extortion," Joe states.

Chapter Fifteen

What did Joe just say? Did he just admit that he wants more from this date than what I had intended or agreed upon? Crap. Why does he feel so comfortable being this bold — this forward? What gave him the impression that there would even be a chance for anything to happen between us? I told him nothing would at Nathan's and it's like he never even heard me.

Aware of his time, Chef Andrews redirects our conversation. "Have you ever dined here before Ms. Emma?" He takes my hand again.

"Once," I confirm the truth.

He kisses the back of my hand while eyeing Joe. "Well, I'll be sure not to disappoint!" He bows to Joe before returning to the kitchen and Joe ushers my chair in again as I sit down.

I sip on my wine a few times before I'm fully refocused back on my task at hand. "So what do you know about Hawaii?"

"Going right for the kill, huh?" Joe laughs at my blatant directness.

"It's why I'm here," I reply fully composed.

"How about I'll answer whatever you want to know when dessert is served?"

"Whatever I want to know?"

"Yes, whatever you want," he agrees.

During our first three courses, caviar, followed by stir-fried eggplant with Chinese black bean glaze and rice puff, and then a vegetable cos cos with Padron peppers, asparagus and light tomato broth, Joe and I comment loosely about the food and other general topics when he evades some of my indirect questioning that pertains to Henry and Hawaii. He doesn't comment that he notices, however, he just brings up another topic instead.

"I had an idea about how you can easily increase your profits for Raven Media without having to take on new clients or too many new staff members," Joe mentions.

I'm not surprised that our conversation is venturing back to business; it's typical for us.

"How?" I ask, full of intrigue.

"You said you created the entire software system yourself, right? From the ground up?" he searches.

"Yes, why?"

"Why not package it as a software program service for companies?"

"What do you mean?"

"There are businesses who have their own internal social media staff to handle each platform, but not a single system to access and monitor it all like

Raven Media does. So, why don't you offer it as a cloud-based system service? They pay a monthly fee and have functionality based on their needs," he explains.

Soaking in his statement, my brain factors out what could be done and what it would entail.

"That's a really great idea. I'd have to hire direct staff to handle that division and do some tweaking to the overall company structure, but I don't see why it couldn't be done," I reply.

His point makes complete sense to me.

"I'd be happy to help in any way that I can," Joe kindly offers.

"Thanks."

I sit pondering the different things I can do and almost forget where I am and who I'm with for a few minutes until our next dish arrives to the table.

Taking a second bite, I finally ask, "So, how do you know Chef Andrews?"

"My brother, John Jr., and he were good friends growing up. Our families know each other."

I nod my understanding since I have a mouthful of food. About to take another sip of wine, my hand stops just before the glass touches my lips. I see someone across the room heading in my direction. I quickly look away but not fast enough to not alert Joe.

"Everything okay?" Joe questions with a little concern in his voice.

"Yep," I agree, keeping my attention on him. I take a gulp of wine.

"You sure?" he presses.

"Mmm hmm . . ." I begin to assure until I hear my name called.

"Emma!"

Crap. This is not good.

I awkwardly stand in an effort to not encourage the person to linger or to cause the potential for Joe and him to talk. "Hi, Chris," my voice waivers a little. "What are you doing here?"

Chris places one hand on my waist and the other behind my neck, and taking me by surprise, plants a long kiss on my lips. My eyes are wide with shock and disbelief at his blatant, unwelcome show of affection in public.

Releasing my lips after I push away at his chest, Chris answers me. "I'm meeting with my agent. What are you doing here?" he asks, keeping his hands on me.

Joe clears his throat loud enough for Chris to turn his head. "Hi. I'm Joseph Covelli." After he stands, Joe reaches his hand towards Chris.

Chapter Fifteen

There is a cool, calm, distinguished manner to Joe which catches me by surprise and ironically turns me on.

"Hey man, I'm Chris Cooper."

"I know who you are," Joe states. "Seen a number of your movies. Not bad."

"Thanks," Chris replies, still hovering near me. "Apologies, I thought you were Jared or Nathan."

I don't believe Chris. He wouldn't dare act the way he did to Nathan or Jared.

"That's okay," I interject. "We should let you get to your agent."

God this is awkward.

"It's okay. I've got a minute. He's not here yet."

Chris is clearly not getting the hint.

"Caleb says you haven't been back to Ayana's since we last saw you."

"Correct," I confirm.

"I was hoping to see you again," he admits.

"I've been busy." I shift my body closer to the table, but he follows.

"Too busy to see me again?"

"I told you where things stood for me, Chris. They haven't changed."

Even if they had changed, I wouldn't let Chris know. There is no chance for a relationship between us. I'm attracted to him, but not like that.

"Then why are you on a date with him?" Chris contends.

Chris' bold question catches me off guard, leaving me temporarily speechless. The last thing I want to do is lie, but I don't owe him any explanation either. I can't believe this is happening to me right now.

Chris turns and extends his hand to Joe. "It's nice to meet you." Then, loud enough for Joe to hear him, Chris discloses to me, "I hope you'll give me a chance too." He kisses my cheek before walking away.

I take a moment to compose myself and then move to sit down.

Joe helps me into my seat without saying anything at first, but then makes it even more awkward when he rounds the table to his chair. "Nice guy."

I glare at him for a moment before taking a huge gulp of wine. "He's okay."

"Good actor," Joe adds.

"Mmm hmm," I agree, trying to maintain self control by taking another large sip of wine.

"He's the Chris who Nathan was teasing you about and the one getting the custom suit?"

"Yes," I quickly confirm, wanting to move on from the topic.

Joe nods his understanding. "Well, if you do go on a date with him, let me know."

I'm puzzled by his statement. Is he trying to torture me?

"I don't plan on it, but why?"

"So I can get the first kiss of the date." A wry smile forms on Joe's face.

He's not offended or uncomfortable by what just happened?

"I'll consider it," I reply, still in shock to his laid back manner. My body relaxes a little at his joke.

I appreciate him not taking offense to the whole situation and trying to help us both move on.

Joe and I have finished seven dishes of our nine-course meal and our conversation after the incident with Chris was a little awkward, but only for a few minutes.

When our eighth dish arrives, Joe surprises me. "So what do you want to know about Hawaii?"

"This isn't dessert."

"I know, but you've been a good sport about the whole date thing. Thought I'd show a little bit of mercy."

I pause to think about what I want to ask. "Why won't Henry let me pay for my share of the trip? I know he's said the same thing to Jared and Nathan, but I just don't understand. I can easily afford my portion of the trip."

"Well . . . Why did you give Jared, Maggie and Nathan Teslas?"

"What does that have to do with this?"

A soft chuckle escapes his mouth. "A lot."

"How?"

"Even though your friends can buy their own cars, you still went ahead and gave them as gifts anyway."

"They were business deductions."

"Yes, perhaps . . . then why haven't you purchased vehicles for the rest of your staff whether they are employees or independent contractors?" Joe doesn't give me a chance to really think about his question or answer before he continues. "Aside from the logical business side of it, you care deeply for your friends. You want them safe and happy."

"That's different," I contend.

"How so?"

Chapter Fifteen

"I didn't buy a car for any of my friends' friends. Just my friends."

"True. But, Henry believes his actions of including the three of you are an extension of his *love* for Maggie."

"Don't say the L word . . ." I request which gets Joe to laugh. "And, I don't see the connection."

I honestly don't or my subconscious is deliberately avoiding it.

Joe laughs at my contention. "You *love* Jared, right?"

There he is using the L word. Does he think that his cute smile will suffice and making up for him saying it again?

"Of course. He's my family."

"And you would do anything for him?"

"Without a doubt. There is no question," I affirm.

"And, the same is for Henry with Maggie. Money is just a resource to aid in their happiness together. The money provides choices and opportunities. It's not a matter of whether you or anyone else can afford the same things. It's a matter of enjoying life with each other."

I bob my head back and forth while trying to wrap my head around his statement. I don't agree, but I also don't disagree.

Probably seeing the debate in my face, Joe continues his explanation. "Why did you put money behind Nathaniel's?"

"Because it made sense as a business investment," I quickly admit as a knee-jerk reaction.

"Then why haven't you put money behind other fashion designers?"

I raise my brow, starting to see the connection though I don't dare admit it.

"It's not just about the investment. There are other designers with just as much potential and ability."

"True," I agree.

"It's because you *love* Nathan and would do anything to see him happy and pursuing his dream. Your money is the tool that has provided him opportunities that he might not have had otherwise."

"I guess so," I unwillingly agree, accepting his clarification.

"Does it make you happy seeing Nathan happy?"

"Yes."

"It makes Henry happy to see Maggie happy. It doesn't matter if it costs money or not to him. That's what you do when you *love* someone."

"I told you not to use the L word," I complain.

Joe just laughs.

"Besides . . . what do you know about . . . *love?*" It takes a few seconds for the last word to escape my mouth.

"Plenty. I have parents and three brothers who are happily married."

"But, have you had your own experience to validate these statements and what people do when they are in . . . ?" I can't bring myself to say the word again.

"Perhaps . . . but, it shouldn't matter."

"Perhaps yes or perhaps no?" I investigate.

"Perhaps . . ." he comments with a wicked smile.

I shake my head in disagreement over the statement about love. I still can't believe that Maggie and Henry have been saying they love each other already. The thought of love and Henry's gesture bothers me, but I refrain from asking any further questions. I got my answer even though I don't like it.

Before leaving the restaurant, Joe and I finish with a bowl of creme brûlée each as our dessert. Good thing the portion sizes have been small or else I would have had to stop when our fifth plate was served. I excuse myself to use the ladies room for a second time and am relieved when I don't see Chris sitting anywhere. Checking my phone on my way back to Joe, I'm shocked to see that it's almost ten at night. We were eating and chatting for over three hours.

"Ready to go?" Joe stands as I approach the table.

"What about the bill?"

I know he's going to insist on paying, but a girl can still try.

Offering his arm, Joe ignores my question and says, "Let's go."

Back inside the glorious Rolls Royce, Joe and I settle in quickly. The drive back to Pasadena is peaceful and relaxing. Just after the car exits onto Colorado Boulevard from the One-Thirty-Four, the driver pulls into a dark parking lot where there are only two lights nearby that are coming from a building. Joe gets out first and reaches his hand to assist me.

I know exactly where we are.

"What are we doing here?"

"A late night private viewing. You had mentioned that you've been wanting to come back." Joe takes my hand, draping it over his arm as he leads me to the front door.

Joe remembered my statement when Henry, Maggie, he and I were driving around Pasadena almost a month ago? Wow. I had said so many different things that day.

Chapter Fifteen

"You know the museum is closed, right?"

"Not for us," he insists.

An older gentleman standing just inside the large glass doors bows as we approach. "Good evening Mr. Covelli."

"Let me guess, your family knows someone," I tease into his ear.

"No. But, they're very accommodating for a more than generous benefactor of the foundation."

"Of course," I agree.

I should have known or expected this.

Mr. Brookes, the gentleman who greeted us, directs us through the exquisite Norton Simon Museum. He stays in each room with us to answer any questions we may have, but keeps his distance as not to intrude. Other than Mr. Brookes, Joe and I are alone as we soak in the marvelous masterpieces of paintings and sculptures.

The museum houses more than twelve thousand works of art, but only displays roughly a thousand between the galleries and the outdoor gardens. Other than two temporary exhibit sections, the rest of the stunning artwork ranges from Asian Art, European Art from the fourteenth through the nineteenth centuries, and modern and contemporary art from all around the world and some even from California. Many of the pieces were all original owned by Mr. Norton Simon who was an industrialist. He later joined the original museum board of directors and assisted in reshaping the structure of the company as well as donating his entire collection.

Joe follows me through the museum, always keeping one of his hands on the small of my back. The warmth of his body is invigorating and my body leans in on occasion desiring more.

Standing by Pablo Picasso's *Woman with a Book*, Joe places his hands on my waist and states, "This one reminds me of you."

I blush at the sensation of the hum of his voice in my ear. Our bodies remain more closely connected for the rest of the time at the museum, savoring the moment.

Arriving back at my apartment, Joe insists on walking me all the way up to my door. He says it's the gentlemanly thing to do on a date. I wouldn't know if he's telling the truth or not since this is technically my first date ever.

For some strange reason, right after we get to my door, I lean into him and kiss him on the cheek. I've never kissed him on the cheek let alone put my lips anywhere on his body like this.

"Thank you," I comment.

Joe's body is rigid and it takes him a moment to blink before asking, "For what?"

"For a great first date."

"So, you really have never been on a date before?"

"No."

"Well, maybe we can have many more firsts together," he presses with a widening grin.

"Don't push your luck," I contend. "If they involve breaking any more of my rules, no way."

"Which ones have we broken?" Joe takes a step closer.

Not sure if I want to answer, I hesitantly reply, "The fact that you know right where I live." I pause not wanting to admit the other one.

"And . . ." he searches, staking another step.

"I don't know if I want to tell you."

If he knows I've already let him in more than other men, this could get really weird.

"I know," he states with a twinkle in his eye.

"No, you don't," I challenge.

He moves in closer, our bodies are flush. "Tonight . . . our date," he whispers.

My body instantly tenses at his words. Suddenly, before my brain registers anything, Joe's lips press to mine with a silky, defined force. We don't move as we both breathe in and out several times through our noses. Joe pulls away, and my mouth follows his, only to be met again with more intensity this time. Everything moves in slow motion as my hands instinctually sliding up each muscular ridge of his stomach and chest. His right hand drops down my side, pulling me further into him as our lips temporarily separate. Returning his mouth to mine, Joe groans into my slightly opened mouth as he gentle presses his tongue inward. For some strange reason, my tongue reaches for his. Aware of where this is going after the third contact with his tongue, I push my hands against his chest and shake my head. His mouth hovers as his forehead rests on mine.

"Just friends, Joe," I barely sigh on an exhale.

He doesn't argue or fight — he just stays touching me, holding me.

My body craves him — it needs him — it wants him. It's demanding his body on mine. I see it and feel it when we're together, but I can't give in. I have rules, rules that protect me and keep me safe from being hurt.

Chapter Fifteen

He gently kisses me again, holding his lips to mine for as long as I let him. I finally convince my body to listen and my lips slowly peel away after about five seconds.

"Goodnight, beautiful."

His words provoke my yearning for him.

"Goodnight, Joe."

Sixteen

The past four days since my date with Joe have been normal, as normal as can be for my life. Joe texts and calls on occasion, and even tries to get me to agree to another date. I obviously decline for many reasons. I'm finding too much temptation.

I took Joe's suggestion about creating the Raven Media cloud base system software I built from he ground up into a sellable product for other companies that enable their staff the ease and flexibility my associates perform for clients. When I mention it to Maggie and Jared, they are ecstatic and excited at the potential. Two of my contractors with Raven are software developers who helped me build the initial software, so I've commissioned them to assist with the expansion and redesign. We'll test the first software version in a couple of months and we've already named it Raven 1.0. If all goes well, I'll be upgrading my server needs with my hosting company. I'm starting to consider the idea of purchasing my own servers in the future which would provide added security and profit for Raven Media.

When I told Joe about moving forward with his idea, he offered to put me in contact with a variety of businesses that would benefit from Raven 1.0 immediately. He said that his family's companies would be the first clients on the list. Joe was impressed with my idea of expanding Raven media into hosting and securities services and mentioned he knew a number of people who could supply a facility and computer hardware. I'm guessing that this might be the first area of technology that Joe wants to venture into, which makes sense. I don't have enough funding to purchase a property as well as the needed hardware and staff, but I'm sure we can work out a fair and equitable business contract once it's time to take action.

With Hawaii only a week away, my friends and I are staying local for our upcoming weekend gathering. Apparently, Joe has moved to accommodate his brother, Jimmy, and Jimmy's boyfriend Allen, who flew back with him after Easter. Joe bought or is renting a place large enough to sleep everyone and is insisting on being the host. I'm curious to see where he's living and how much he's paying to fit all of us comfortably. I never bothered to ask where he was living prior to finding out that he's moved. The few times I text him during the past few days inquiring about where his new place is located, Joe just writes back you'll see. I remind him that I'm not one who likes surprises, but he just ignores me and doesn't even offer a clue. Each time he responds I only get a LOL and smiley emoticon. When I try to find out from Jared or Maggie, they claim that they don't know either. I don't believe them and worry about my speculations.

Maggie and Henry pick Sadie and me up at my apartment Friday in the late afternoon. My knee habitually begins shaking as the car enters the streets and I look out the window to see where we're going. I don't think much about where we might be headed until Henry pulls into a building across from the Arclight Theater in Pasadena.

"Are we stopping somewhere first?" I ask as Henry pulls into a valet area.

"No. Where here," Maggie states.

"Where?" I probe.

"Joe's place. He bought the penthouse," Maggie answers, clueing me in.

Confusion and horror flood my mind as my brain tries to comprehend what Maggie just said. What? Are you serious? He bought a place here? In Pasadena? This is exactly why I don't tell men where I live. Damn it. Damn him.

I sit staring at the back of the seat in front of me as Henry and Maggie get out of the car and retrieve the bags out of the trunk. At some point, someone opens the car door to let me out, but I don't notice until Maggie interrupts my internal hysteria.

"You coming?" she checks.

I remain speechless the entire time we are greeted by the doorman and ride the elevator up to Joe's floor. Maggie and Henry don't seem to notice my irritation as they practically make out the entire time.

Why did they bother to pick me up? I could have walked since we're less than a mile from my apartment building. Why didn't Maggie say anything about Joe moving to Pasadena? I know why. They know I wouldn't have shown up or, if I did, I would be sleeping at my own place each night. They both suck right now. Wait! Jared and Nathan suck too. They are on their way and never mentioned it either. What the hell is happening?

The elevator door dings open to a small foyer that contains large, wooden double doors in front of us that are adorned with two small matching console tables and wall mirrors on either side. When the door opens, we are greeted by an older, dark-haired woman wearing a maid's uniform who recognizes Henry right away.

"Mr. Henry, come right in. Mr. Joseph said he was expecting you," she instructs with a distinct Russian accent.

"Thank you, Anna," Henry returns ushering Maggie and myself to go first. "This is Maggie and Emma."

"Pleasure to meet you, Ms. Maggie and Ms. Emma. Please, leave your bags here. I'll see that they are tended to," Anna greets warmly. "Who is this four-legged beauty?"

Chapter Sixteen

"Sadie," I offer.

"Ah, Ms. Sadie. Is there anything you might need for her while you are here?" she inquires while petting Sadie.

"No. Thank you. I have all of her stuff here," I disclose, pointing to one of my bags. "If you tell me where the kitchen is, I can put her food away."

"I'd be happy to take care of that for you," Anna insists.

"Are you sure? I don't want to impose," I reply.

"Anything for you, Ms. Emma," she states with a warm smile.

"Okay," I happily accept.

"Follow me," Ana instructs, leading the way with a brisk pace. When Anna reaches the end of the long hallway about five seconds before us, she announces, "Ms. Maggie, Ms. Emma, Ms. Sadie and Mr. Henry are here."

Catching up to her, my eyes fall upon a huge living room that has floor to ceiling windows on three of the four walls, not counting the large fireplace, is fully finished with a wet bar, three sitting areas, a large flatscreen television and a baby grand piano in the far left corner. How the hell did he buy and get this place decorated in such a short amount of time? When did he buy it? I know that this building is not for rent. I remember seeing listings for units in this place several times when I'd search where I'd like move next in Pasadena. This building was one of my top considerations. Now, I have to remove this location from my list. Damn him.

Joe is moving in our direction when I turn the corner. He must have already been heading towards us when Anna announced our arrival. Two other men are with Joe and are just getting up from the couch when Maggie, Henry and I stop behind Anna.

"Thank you, Anna," Joe replies as he moves to greet us. He hugs and kisses Maggie, hugs Henry and then hugs and pecks me on the cheek before standing close to me.

"So, which one is Emma?" One of the men questions Joe as he approaches us. "I want to meet the one who has my brother's eye."

From his statement, I know he is James. James is handsome like Joe. You can see the family resemblance, even though their body types are completely different. James has definition to his body, but it is hidden and nowhere near as pronounced as Joe's. He even has similar facial features to Joe, but James' eyes are a beautiful, emerald green.

My cheeks flush instantly at James' open statement, which gives me away.

"Ah . . . ." He inspects me from head to toe. "You're even prettier than the photo Joe showed us."

My eyes dart to Joe at the mention of a photo he has of me. I know we've all taken pictures on our phones from time to time when we all hangout, but the thought still rattles me, especially if he's talking about me to other people.

"Don't pay him any attention, Emma," the other man proclaims. "Jimmy is messing with Joe. We haven't seen a photo of you yet. Joe wouldn't share."

I can feel my face heating up more.

"She is gorgeous, though. Isn't she Allen?" Jimmy playfully questions.

"Indeed," Allen concurs.

Allen is just a handsome as Jimmy and Joe with his own striking chiseled features. He is about an inch or two taller than Jimmy, has a little more meat on his bones, and strawberry blond hair. His amber eyes sparkle in the light.

In an almost bashful tone, Joe apologies, "Please excuse Jimmy and Allen."

"We're being rude sweetie," Allen teasingly chides Jimmy.

"Where are my manners," Jimmy begins, reaching his hand forward to shake mine. "I'm Jimmy, Joe's older and better-looking brother." Before our hands meet, he catches me completely off guard and embraces me in a hug I can't escape.

"Don't mind him. He's a hugger," Allen informs me a little too late. "I'm Allen," he says as Jimmy releases me. "I'm his better half." Allen jerks his head in the direction of Jimmy and then hugs me too.

"It's a pleasure to meet you both." I reply a little shocked from their affectionate greeting.

I wasn't expecting them to be this friendly.

"And, who is this adorable four-legged creature?" Jimmy inquires, bending down towards Sadie who has been by my side the whole time.

"This is Sadie," I say, glad for the distraction.

Sadie sits waiting for my signal to greet the new strangers and I let her. She sniffs and licks both of them, but seeks Joe out for more affection.

I stare at Joe as Henry introduces Maggie to the two men. He offers me a reassuring smile, but it doesn't work. "How about a tour," Joe suggests.

"Sure," I consent, thinking Maggie will want to see the place as well.

"I'll see it later," Maggie replies as she returns her focus on the conversation between Henry, Jimmy and Allen.

Smiling, Joe acknowledges, "Looks like it's you and me, beautiful."

Unhappy with the result, I just nod in agreement as Sadie follows. There are a lot of rooms to his stunning penthouse. Aside from the living room, it has four bedrooms, four full bathrooms and one-half bath, an office, kitchen

Chapter Sixteen

with an attached breakfast room, dinning room and a den. The single floor is over four thousand square feet — I remember from the listing.

When we get to the largest bedroom, Joe mentions, "This will be your room for the weekend."

The bedroom is stunning. It's sleek, sophisticated, elegant and contemporary. The walls are painted a light bluish grey, with a similar, but slightly darker color on the fifteen foot ceiling. A king size bed, that looks like it's swimming in the room, is on the far back wall and is covered with a solid white comforter, and topped with white, blue and grey pillows, some with the hint of a golden yellow. The bed frame, nightstands, and a single dresser on the opposite wall are matching dark mahogany wood. A chaise and sitting chair with a small table and lamp sit near the french doors that lead out to a patio. Leaning on a wall next to a door that would lead to the bathroom are several pieces of art or photos most likely waiting to be hung.

"I don't need this much room," I protest, confused to why I would get the biggest room to myself. "Jared and Nathan or your brother and Allen can have it."

He chuckles, "Jimmy and Allen have their own room, and as much as I love Jared and Nathan, I'm not interested in them sleeping in my bed." I shoot him a glare, and before I can say anything, Joe insists, "Relax. It will be just you and Sadie in here. I'll be in the den."

"I'll take the den," I assert. "This is your house."

"You are my guest," he contends.

I shrug my shoulders to indicate that I don't care.

"If you don't sleep in here, the only other free bed is where I'm sleeping."

"There is the couch," I mention, turning in the direction of the hallway.

Joe takes a step closer to me, placing his left hand on my hip and spins me around to face him. "I'll carry you back to my bed if you try to sleep on the couch."

I eye him further at his threat. "Which bed?"

A devilish grin on his face implies that which bed is irrelevant and that it's the matter of being in a bed with him. My brain freaks out as my body becomes aroused by the idea.

"Fine," I unwillingly concede, not wanting to give him the hope of any possibility.

Joe leads me to his bathroom to show me where the towels and other necessities are located. The restroom is a very sleek, modern and extremely large which is pretty much the size of my bedroom. Medium grey slate tiles cascade over the entire floor, the entire walk-in shower that has a glass door and can easily fit six people, and the whole wall, where there is a solid white hot tub style bathtub. On the other side of the shower, toilet and bidet, there are porcelain white double sinks with a dark mahogany vanity.

Back in the bedroom, Joe draws my attention over to the french doors that lead out to a private patio. "Feel free to use the rebounder."

"Is this why you've gotten better when we go jumping?"

"So, you've noticed?" he smirks.

"Just a little," I dismiss while looking around the room to make note of where to snoop when I'm alone.

Heading back to the living room, we find that Jared and Nathan have arrived as well and are already making small talk with Jimmy and Allen. When I can get Jared alone, I need to remember to corner him about not telling me that Joe moved to my town.

". . . I'm so excited," Nathan shouts.

"Excited about what?" I question, coming late into the conversation.

"Jimmy and Allen are joining us in Hawaii next weekend," Jared informs me.

"Awesome," I reply.

I'm really glad to know they are joining us. It's an extra reason to avoid any awkward moments with Joe and a way to get to know him and Henry better to make sure there isn't anything that I've missed about them. Serial killers are good at hiding their true identities.

The eight of us chat like we're all old friends reuniting which is very comforting to me. Jimmy and Allen are sweet, friendly guys who easily get along with everyone. Stories are told and laughter spreads. From everything that I see and hear, Joe and Henry are exactly the type of men I concluded them to be; smart, sweet, sincere and genuine. This puts my mind at ease.

At some point during our discussions, Anna brings us tea, coffee and some hours d' oeuvres before informing us that dinner will be ready in an hour. I check the clock on my phone and am surprised when I see that it's just after five. Have we been talking for that long? I need to feed Sadie. There's no need to formally excuse myself from my friends, so I sneak out right as Maggie and Henry start sharing how they met and fell in love with Jimmy and Allen. Yes, fell in love. They both use that word freely so much now. It's been barely three months and they are talking about love. My stomach turns at the notion of them being in love.

I watch Anna bouncing between the kitchen and the dinning room before I start looking for Sadie's food.

Chapter Sixteen

"Can I help you with anything, Ms. Emma?" Anna sweetly inquires.

"I need to feed Sadie," I cordially mention, not wanting to interrupt her.

Turning to the refrigerator, Anna pulls out the cooler and offers, "I can feed her for you, Ms. Emma."

"Thank you, Anna, but I think you're busy enough getting dinner ready," I graciously decline.

"I don't mind. I'm happy to help," she respectfully insists.

I appreciate Anna's attentiveness and willingness, but there is no need. I'm under the impression that tasks as simple as feeding a dog are a part of her job description, even for guests. There's no need to expect her to take care of Sadie or me even when she seems pleased to do it.

"Thank you, but . . ." I begin.

She senses my discomfort and instead instructs, "Plates and bowls are here, silverware over here, and feel free to use any food that is in the kitchen. Mr. Joseph had me purchase a variety of items for you, Ms. Sadie and everyone else. If you need anything, don't hesitate to let me know."

"Thank you," I return, making my way to get a spoon.

Anna diligently watches me as I place the different ingredients of Sadie's food into one of the bowls I had in her cooler. Before I'm finished, Anna fills the other bowl with water. She then places a towel on the floor before putting the bowl down. As I rinse my hands in the island sink, Anna instinctually takes the food and sets it next to the water. I choose not to say anything — I don't doubt that I'm driving her crazy by doing her job.

"She's not eating," Anna voices with concern.

With a reassuring smile, I explain, "She's waiting for the command."

"She won't eat unless you tell her?" Anna affirms with amazement. "Wow."

I signal for Sadie to eat and she immediately begins. Anna stands watching Sadie the whole time. I suspect that she's planning on cleaning the dishes and not giving me the chance.

Joe enters the kitchen distracting me, which gives Anna just enough time to retrieve the food bowl. "Everything okay in here?" Joe questions.

"Just fine, Mr. Joseph," Anna replies.

I giggle at hearing her call him Mr. Joseph.

"What's so funny?" he inquires.

"Nothing, Mr. Joseph," I echo Anna's words.

This gets a laugh from Anna before she says, "I like her, Mr. Joseph."

I can't help but laugh again before pondering her chosen words.

"Me too," Joe asserts, looking right at me.

To redirect the conversation I indicate, "I need to take Sadie out."

Joe studies me for a second like he's contemplating on whether to say something or not. He silently accepts my announcement and has a look like he's deciding on whether or not to join us. A few seconds later, Joe hesitantly returns to our friends, looking over his shoulder just after he pass through the doorway.

Being outside with Sadie alone is refreshing and gives me time to think and calm down. I'm not really agitated anymore, but being alone helps me digest everything, especially the fact that Joe now lives in Pasadena. Why Pasadena? Seriously!

Once Anna lets us back inside, Sadie darts down the hallway to Joe who is hovering in a doorway.

"Where is everyone?" I ask when I get closer to him.

"Getting the tour," Joe says, pointing down the hall and then resumes petting Sadie.

Instead of joining the rest of our friends, I turn towards the living room to snoop. My attention is captured by a variety of framed pictures that sit on some built-in bookcases near the piano. I pick up one picture to examine it further. It consists of a large group of people all of different ages.

"That's my family," Joe comments, scaring me. He takes a step closer, causing his shoulder to brush slightly on my back before resting his hand on my hip.

I'm temporarily distracted by his close proximity, but I'm able to focus enough to catch the majority of the names and faces of the people in the photo. I've never been this aroused during that time of the month.

Everyone in the photo looks genuinely happy. I put the picture back and continue looking at the others as Joe stays close. My attention immediately goes to a photo of Joe sleeping while holding a resting baby girl.

"That's my niece, Lily," he indicates.

"Which one?" I tease.

He moves closer. Close enough that I feel something rub against my ass before I notice his right hand on my waist.

"What are you doing?"

He chuckles, "Nothing." His smooth cheek brushes mine.

"Joe."

"Shhh," he mumbles, squeezing me tighter.

Chapter Sixteen

I feel and hear him breathe me in and I can't move. I let him stay right where he is holding me. Why? My brain stops talking when the memories of being in bed with him at Nathan's and the kiss after our recent date come back in full force. My figure soaks up the convergence of our bodies and my mind is conflicted between my physical desire for him and my need to distance myself. I can't let him too close. I can't let him in.

"Joe."

"Mmm . . . ." His left hand is now on my waist and his mouth sweeps my skin just under my ear.

The clamor of our friends' voices in the hallway snap me back to reality. As I pull away from Joe, he does the same for me, giving us enough distance to compose ourselves. I would almost think that he doesn't want to get caught either. Joe sits on a nearby chair and pets Sadie while I continue to scan the bookcase until our friends are in view.

Before everyone gets comfortable, Anna announces that dinner is ready. We follow her to the dinning room where a table that seats eight easily and is dressed with a feast large enough for Thanksgiving dinner. Joe takes the head of the table, followed by Jimmy, Allen, Maggie and Henry to his left which leaves me to sit on Joe's right followed by Jared and Nathan. Why do I have to sit right next to Joe?

Everyone exchanges more stories and topics of discussion as we eat the mountainous meal. At some point, we all agree to stay in for the night to continue chatting and to have a mini pajama party in the living room. As everyone continues to sit and talk around the dinner table, I habitually stand up to clean.

"What are you doing?" Anna asks with surprise when I enter the kitchen.

"Cleaning up," I declare, now questioning my own actions. I place the dishes on the counter waiting for her to move.

"Go enjoy yourself, Ms. Emma. I'll clean up when everyone is finished," she instructs me.

"We are finished. And, that hardly seems fair."

"Why is that?"

She's clearly puzzled by my response.

"Because you cooked it. We should at least help clean."

Giddy from my statement, Anna reminds me, "It's my job."

"So. That doesn't mean I can't help."

"You are a guest. You are not expected to cook or clean the dishes, Ms. Emma."

"I know," I agree with her. "But, as a guest I have the right to choose to help, and, that's what I choose."

A confused and concerned expression rolls upon her face. She clearly doesn't know what to say or do. The sound of the sliding door behind me grabs our attention. Jimmy and Joe are now behind me.

"Everything okay?" Jimmy inquires.

"No," Anna declares with some trepidation.

"Yes," I assert calmly.

"Ms. Emma is trying to clean. I told her not to, but she won't listen to me." Anna rats me out.

The way she frames her words makes me think she's afraid of getting into trouble.

Joe lets out a husky laugh as Jimmy investigates, "Why are you laughing."

"It's fine, Anna," Joe assures her. "If Emma is compelled to help you, will you let her?"

"You know that I'll help despite what anyone says," I challenge, placing my hand on my hip.

Laughing more, he replies, "I know."

Unsure, Anna agrees, "Okay."

"No wonder you like her, Joe," Jimmy alleges before returning to the dining room.

"It's okay, Anna. Really," Joe consoles.

Not saying anything, Anna takes the dishes sitting on the counter in front of me.

"Hey . . ." I protest with a smile.

Joe advances towards me, pressing his chest to my back, rests his chin on my shoulder and his left hand on the counter next to my hip. Why is he so daring to touch me like this? Why am I not trying to move away?

Anna turns, catching us. She doesn't look shocked or surprised. "I like her, Mr. Joseph. She's good for you. She might even teach you a thing or two."

I can't see Joe, but I can tell by observing Anna that she's gotten to him in a playful way. Her cheerful reaction indicates that she has a long working history with him.

"I know," he admits.

Chapter Sixteen

I turn to face Joe and I find him blushing as he looks right at me. His eyes hold mine, and then, he kisses me lightly on the forehead. Why is he displaying any type of affection in front of Anna? I scrunch my nose at him in protest just before he takes my wrist and leads me back to the dining room. "Come on," he says.

To appease Anna, I internally fight with myself not to aid her with dish duty. My friends choose to joke at my expense over my eagerness to help.

"Ha ha. Very funny," I declare at one point after I'm met with a few snickers.

Jared scoots his chair closer to me and pulls me into him.

"So, Emma . . . what's wrong with my brother?" Jimmy blurts.

"Excuse me?"

I'm shocked by his statement. Did I say something offensive at some point and not realize it? My eyes dart back and forth between Joe and Jimmy.

"Leave her alone, Jimmy," Joe defends.

"It's a valid question," Jimmy contends.

Not sure exactly what is going on, I timidly comment, "Nothing is wrong with Joe. I'm sorry. Did I say something rude or offensive? I didn't mean to."

"No, you didn't," Joe reassures.

"Then, why won't you date him?" Jimmy pushes.

Where is his question coming from? Did Joe say something? Did my friends say something?

"I don't date," I present calmly.

"What gorgeous woman like you doesn't date?" he continues.

I stare blankly at his forwardness.

"Leave her alone, Jimmy," Joe says with agitation in his tone.

"Emma has never dated," Maggie chimes in. "It's nothing personal to Joe or any other guy she meets."

"Why not?" Allen searches.

"Did someone break your heart?" Jimmy investigates.

When did my dating life become the main focal point of conversation? I know Jimmy and Allen don't know me, but I'm still not comfortable discussing it with anyone.

"My dating life is not up for discussion," I state impassively.

Jared sympathetically squeezes my hand.

"Definitely heartbreak," Jimmy insists.

"Leave her alone, Jimmy," Joe asserts almost raising his voice.

I've never heard Joe get loud before with anyone.

"What?" Jimmy feigns innocence. He takes the warning look Joe gives him and backs off. "My apologies, Emma."

I silently accept his concession.

With our conversation coming to a halt by Jimmy's interrogation, everyone temporarily retires to their rooms to change for the night. Joe follows me to his room.

"I'm sorry about Jimmy . . . I . . . ."

"It's okay," I offer.

"No, it's not okay," Joe consoles, wringing the back of his neck with his hand.

"It's not a big deal. I've had it happen before. He just caught me off guard."

I have been approached a number of times by every adult member of Maggie's family as well as Nathan's. I've had random strangers, both male and female of various sexual orientations, inquire as well.

"I swear, I have never said anything that would warrant him to say anything like that," he nervously admits.

"It's okay, really." My feet take a few steps towards him for some reason.

Joe's body completely relaxes as he moves, closing the gap between us. "I just need to grab something to change into," he mentions.

"You can change in here," I offer.

A flirtatious look appears on his face.

"Down boy. I've got to take Sadie out one more time for the night."

Did he just pout?

"Are you pouting?" I question.

"No," he argues, though he doesn't change his expression until he can no longer suppress a grin. "I'll join you ladies."

"We'll be fine by ourselves."

"I know, but I wouldn't mind getting out."

We take Sadie for a walk around a few blocks and over to one of the nearby parks for her to run a little. As we take a break on the far, top left of the park while Sadie sniffs around a tree, I decide that I need to know what caused the reason for his moving.

"Why Pasadena?"

"What do you mean?" he says confused.

All I do is give him a look and I know he understands what I mean.

"I like it here."

Chapter Sixteen

"You like it here?"

"Yes," he agrees.

"And . . .?" I pry.

"And . . . what?"

He's not going to make this easy, is he?

"Any other reason?" I inspect.

"Uhhhhh . . . no." The smirk on his face indicates that he's lying.

Shaking my head, "You're kidding, right?!"

He ponders what to say, and leaves me with, "All in good time, beautiful."

When we get back to his building, Joe stands in the elevator with his shoulder touching mine. I decree not to look at him because it might encourage him to do something. From the corner of my eye, I see him staring at me until the box dings at our arrival.

Standing in the doorway to his bedroom, I offer, "Go ahead and change. I'll wait until your done."

Joe lifts his eyebrows at my words before he strides to the wall of mirrors, sliding one to the left. I didn't realize that a walk-in closet could be hidden behind it. Interestingly, Joe leaves the door propped open halfway, but I can't see it — and I don't dare to look. To be safe, I remain in the crook of the door between the bedroom and the hallway.

Two minutes later, Joe emerges from the closet with pajama bottoms on and a shirt in hand, exposing his naked torso. He deliberately waits to put the shirt on when he's standing right in front of me. Winking, he methodically shrugs on the tee as I bite my tongue. I stand rigid as he presses into me and leans in for a kiss. Pulling my head away, I shake it in opposition. His knuckles graze my cheek before his lips meet my forehead for a long embrace. He pecks the same place before he reluctantly pulls away and heads out of the room. I close and lock the door behind me for precautionary measures.

Before changing, I venture to the bathroom first. Most women would be uncomfortable sleeping in a man's bed who she isn't intimate with when she has her period, but not me. I've been using a menstrual cup for years and love it. No messy pads or tampons or the chance of leakage. I just remove the cup, clean it out in the sink and place it back inside.

Sadie watches me change as she lays on Joe's bed. I put on loose, soft pink, white and grey plaid bottoms that tighten with a drawstring, a white camisole with a built in bra and a light pink cardigan that matches the color on the pants. Choosing to take a little longer, I brush my hair before tying it up, rinse my face, and put on some lotion before snooping in his closet.

Opening the door, I discover that his closet is the same size of his bathroom. It has floor to ceiling dark mahogany wood with hints of a deep sky blue grey, like that of a summer rain storm, on the few strips of wall. The shelving is a variety of open hanging areas and different sized drawers on the two longer walls. The shortest wall is lined with nothing but a shoe rack. Everything is neatly arranged like it's a department store. Suits, dress shirts, pants, tee shirts and some sweaters hang by their garment type and then by color on one side, the other side is completely empty. The shoe's are arranged like his hanging clothes, and only fill half the space. I swear he has just as many shoes as I do. A large rectangular unit sits in the middle of the closet. Upon closer inspection, I see that it's lined with drawers on both of the long sides. The drawers that are filled with items are flawlessly folded, I know because I check. Joe is a boxer brief man — my favorite. There are drawers with ties and belts and some that have cufflinks and tie clips that are all strategically lined up. He's either one serious neat freak or Anna makes sure everything is where it should be. The thought of Anna having to do his laundry is comical and probably true.

Sliding open the last drawer, I find a collection of watches that are gold and either silver, platinum or both. A red item at the far right catches my attention and my heart flutters at the sight of the bracelet Jade bought Joe on New Year's. It's laying alone in its own little container. I know that Joe wears a watch practically every day, which means that he sees the bracelet each time. My fingers caress the beads as memories from that first day we met dance into my mind and into my gut. Pull yourself together, Emma.

Not wanting to take too long for fear of getting caught snooping, I head out to join everyone in the living room. I'm happy to find that everyone wasn't waiting for me when I arrive. Henry and Maggie have yet to emerge from their room.

Jimmy, Allen, Jared and Nathan are deciding on what movie to watch as Jimmy and Allen cuddle in one spot and Jared and Nathan are in another. Sadie curls up next to Joe with her head resting on his thigh before I sit down. Jared motions for me to visit, so I do. I slump down into his left side, placing my head on his chest next to Nathan's who is burrowed into Jared's right. Allen tosses a blanket on the three of us, then one to Joe before situating one for himself and Jimmy. Anna makes two trips out to us with drinks and four really large bowls of freshly popped popcorn.

The six of us stop waiting for Maggie and Henry after ten more minutes and commence the movie. In less than ten minutes, Jared and Nathan have eaten three-fourths of their bowl of popcorn and I only get two handfuls. I shift on the couch to where my legs rest across Jared, but my head is now on

Chapter Sixteen

Sadie's belly so I can reach the popcorn Joe has resting on his lap. Maggie and Henry finally join us just as I reach to grab another round of popcorn over my head.

At some point, I cross my cardigan and arms over my chest when I notice my protruding nipples. Seconds later, I feel something being draped over me. I look up to find Joe placing a blanket that was on the back of the couch across my upper body. We smile when our eyes meet. As I shift to cover myself better with the blanket, I feel Joe helping by pull my hair to the side when I lift my head. His fingers kiss my skin upon contact. With everyone's attention on the movie, Joe discretely glides his fingers up and down the side of my neck, causing my body to quiver in pleasure. I convince myself not to look at him, but soon I'm compelled. He returns the glance with a smile as his fingers never falter their movement, even when I look away. I notice that when someone moves or shifts, Joe's hand freezes in place like he doesn't want to be seen.

When the movie is over, the three couples rush to their rooms mumbling shouts of goodnight. Sex-capades time. I, on the other hand, take note that Anna is nowhere to be found and begin taking the glasses and bowls into the kitchen.

Joe laughs at me and comments when I pass him on my first trip to the kitchen. "You can't help yourself, can you?"

I scrunch my nose at him.

Placing the dishes down and rolling up my sleeves, I hear Joe enter the kitchen not long after me. He brings in the rest of the bowls and glasses as I combine all of the remaining popcorn into one bowl and snap on its lid before placing the empty ones in the dishwasher. I wash the glasses by hand, since I know that they are crystal and then wipe down the counter.

Just as I head towards the living room with a damp sponge in hand, Joe tenderly snags my arm. "Leave it. It'll make Anna feel needed. Important."

I nod my understanding to his statement and replace the sponge in its proper place. I turn looking for a towel and am meet with Joe standing in front of me holding one. With a smile and diligent precision, Joe proceeds to gradually dry each one of my hands before tossing the towel on the countertop.

With our eyes locked, he delicately steps forward, compressing his body into mine at the waist. With my arms already crossed in front of me, he affectionately runs his hands up and down my arms from my shoulders to my elbows. Joe lowers his forehead to mine, pressing ever so lightly. I shake my head gingerly in opposition. He cups my chin despite my protest.

"No," I whisper, placing my hands onto his forearms.

"Please," he begs, regardless of my objection.

"No," I stay firm in my conviction.

"Please," his voice cracks as he reaches for my lips.

Pulling my head away last second, I say, "I can't."

"Why," he pleads.

I wish I could tell him why, but right now I'm not even sure. How can something that feels so good, be so scary at the same time?

"We can only be friends," I tell him.

Joe groans as he places his forehead back on mine rocking it. We stand like this for several minutes before he wraps me in his arms, holding me like he never wants to let go. I lightly place my hands on his hips as we stand motionless and not talking. All I can hear is the sound of our breathing. I could fall asleep like this.

Wake up, Emma my brain shouts. Shit. I'm doing the one thing I said I can't do. I'm letting him in. This needs to stop.

Jerking away suddenly, I call to Sadie with trembling words and she follows me. I stand in Joe's bedroom contemplating what to do as I reprimand myself for allowing things to go the way they did.

"Do you need anything?" Joe questions, snapping me out of my trance.

I shudder at the sound of his voice not expecting it. "No. Thank you." I turn to face him and he's already within inches of me.

Placing his left hand on my face with his fingers wrapped behind my neck, Joe tells me, "I'll be in the den if you need me." Before I say anything, his lips fall upon my right cheek. "I won't stop wanting you, beautiful." He scans me for a reaction, and I'm not sure what I give him as he kisses my forehead again.

Joe stops in the doorway and before leaving, bids, "Goodnight, beautiful."

"Goodnight, Joe."

Seventeen

As I attempt to lift my heavy eyelids, I discover a hazy darkness surrounding me. Blinking slowly several times, my half-opened eyes won't focus to give me any clear indication of what's around me and where the blurry, flashing lights above are coming from. My body feels heavy. Still unable to open my eyes all the way, I perceive that I'm laying down somewhere. A cool dampness near my left cheek reveals itself as a slight gust of air brushes past my face. Sliding my right arm up the side of my body like a snake, my fingers creep to my lips. Drool — or, at least I hope so.

Two large and oddly shaped figures materialize in front of me. They are so close, only a foot or two away. Voices suddenly emanate from the now more defined silhouettes. Their speech sounds muffled and trails off into the distance even as I try to concentrate on their words. Who are they? What are they saying? Why can't I understand them? One of the voices almost sounds feminine.

Another indistinguishable sound gradually becomes more apparent as it grows louder and the ringing in my ears subsides. It's the engine of a car. My brain finally starts to put the fuzzy pieces of evidence together. I must have fallen asleep in the back seat. A familiar smell creeps into my nose that reassures me — my mother's perfume.

"Mom?" my throat squeezes out in a raw, breathy, hoarse tone.

Wake up, Emma." Her voice replies in a low sluggish tone.

What is she talking about? I am awake.

A sudden rush of nervousness enters my belly. The car feels as if it's flying down the road like a rocket ship as the speed of the flashing lights zooming above my head all blur into one.

"Mom," I try to shout, but not a single sound escapes my mouth this time. Confused, I try again. "Mom!"

She doesn't hear me. I don't hear me.

A single, bright white light races towards us, growing larger by the second. Mom turns her head towards me smiling. Why doesn't she hear me? How does she not see the light?

Again, with all my might. "Mom . . .!" my voice trails in my head like a deafening siren, stabbing my ears like a knife.

Time stops in this very moment. I can see everything with complete clarity as I stare in horror into my mother's eyes. No. Joe's eyes. I can't move. My mouth is left open, screaming without a sound. I can't hear anything besides a piercing ring that echoes in my brain.

My body lurches backward as I scramble to grab anything.

"Wake up, Emma!" the voice beckons.

Ignoring the command, my nails dragging over the flesh of my mother's body, reaching to yank the bloody, metal object from her stomach. Black liquid oozes from her mouth as her eyes appear lifeless.

"Mom!" I finally hear the sound of my own voice as I claw at the protrusion in her abdomen. Tears run down my face, blocking my vision as I jerk at the metal object to remove it from her cold, stiff body. "Mom . . . I can't get it out."

I'm thrown backward when the voice echoes, "Emma, wake up!"

With my mother's body no longer within reach, I scramble to get a hold of one of her legs. Using all of my strength, I pull myself over and grab onto the metal.

"I need to get it out," I cry as I'm snatched away again. "I need to . . . ."

"Wake up, Emma!" the voice orders.

My eyes fling open as I scream out in horror. Disoriented, my body shakes as tears stream down my face. "I need to get it out!"

"It's okay," a voices cracks.

I feel a tender, warmth drape itself around my shoulders.

"I need to get it out!" I sob. "I need to get it out! I need to get it out!"

"I'll be right back," the voice instructs.

"I need to get it out!" I repeat, trembling as all I can see is the image of my mother's lifeless body and the blood that is everywhere — it's all over my hands. I sit rocking with my legs curled into my chest and my hands outstretched, not wanting to get anymore blood on me. "I need to get it out," I mumble to myself. "There's so much blood. I need to get it out . . . ."

"I've got you, *Kitten*," a different voice claims as something wraps around my body. "I've got you. It's okay."

"I've got to get it out . . . There's so much blood." I inform it. "I've got to . . . ."

"I know you do. But, you can't. It's not real. Remember?" the voice reminds me gently. "Come back to me, please."

"It is real. Don't you see the blood? Look . . ." I attest.

"No, *Kitten*. It's not real," the voice declares while gripping my face. "Look at me, Emma. Come back to me. Come back to what is real."

Chapter Seventeen

I pinch my eyes shut, focusing on it's words. His words.

"It's not real?" I question, not believing him.

"No, *Kitten*. It's not real. Open your eyes and see. Come back to me," he pleas.

Choking in breathes, I open my eyes as I exhale to find Jared's face a few inches from mine. I reach to wipe the single tear that has escaped his right eye.

"There you are," he reports.

Relief consumes me as I burry my face into his chest and cling to his body with all of my strength.

"I've got you, *Kitten*. It's okay."

I overhear some commotion in the room, but deliberately choose not to listen. I don't care at this point. I've got Jared and I know I'm safe.

His chest reverberates as he pets my head and reminds me, "I'm here, *Kitten*. It's not real."

I drift back to sleep as hushed voices dance in the room

Eighteen

A murkiness in my head wakes me; a murkiness that's all too familiar. The smell of Jared relaxes me slightly as my consciousness unfolds the event that happened earlier. It wasn't just the nightmare. I haven't dreamt of my mother's body like that in years and I'm not sure why. I pray that it won't happen again.

I curl into Jared a little longer knowing that I won't be able to go back to sleep. I should probably get up to feed Sadie. Where is she?

I roll away from Jared into another body that I expect to be Nathan's. Instead, I find Joe which doesn't alarm me. I study his relaxed features and body as it's curled into mine with his hand resting on my waist. Carefully propping myself up, I glance around the room to find Nathan on the bed, but on the other side of Jared. Jimmy and Allen are on the chaise near the french door and Maggie and Henry on another chaise that was not previously in the room. My heart melts as fear swells inside. I appreciate everyone's concern, but I need to get away. I need to distance myself.

Noticing that Sadie is not in the room, I discreetly slide out of the bed and into to the hallway. Tip-toeing through the halls, I scan each room for Sadie, but she is nowhere to be found. A muted sound coming from the main entrance catches my attention and I follow it.

"There you go, Ms. Sadie," Anna whispers, unhooking her leash.

Sadie runs to me as I drop to the floor to greet her.

"She's been fed and walked, Ms. Emma."

"Thank you, Anna," I return meekly.

"Everything okay, Ms. Emma?"

"Great," I lie with a fake smile.

Anna watches me for a moment before asking, "You hungry?"

"No. I'm good. Thank you."

Ana smiles and nods before she moves on to her next task and I stay on the floor petting Sadie.

Seeing that it's after six when I enter the kitchen, I'm even more thankful of Anna for helping with Sadie. I make my morning clay as Sadie sits with her favorite stuffed sock monkey in her mouth. After using the half bath that is near the kitchen, Sadie and I play for a little while in the living room.

Breathe In

My thoughts keep drifting back to the nightmare, but I know dwelling on it doesn't allow me to move forward. I just can't shake this weird feeling that I have. I sense it trying to linger and remember that it's some of the old emotions tied to my parents' death. It's going to take a bit longer to get past all of this today.

Sadie resorts back to chewing on her bone, which indicates to me that she's done playing. I grab one of the smaller blankets from the living room, wrap it around my shoulders and head out to the patio. I'm met with a tranquil, late April, Saturday morning. I tilt forward looking over the wall out onto Colorado Boulevard as Sadie curls up at my feet. Taking in the quiet scene of Pasadena, I encourage my mind and body to unwind as I watch what little life there is occurring on the street below.

A short time later, I hear the patio door slide open and closed, but ignore who it is. A heated, firm body presses into my back, but I keep my eyes forward, looking off into the distance. No words need to be exchanged because I know who has found me. Wrapping his arms around my shoulders, I feel Joe nuzzle into my neck and breathe out a sigh of relief. Given my current state of emotions, it's hard for me to feel anything at this moment.

Joe doesn't push, poke or prod with words or his body. He just holds me attentively, as if he's afraid he might shatter me. A small part of me appreciates his sentiment, but I'm so lost in myself that he practically goes unnoticed. I'm not sure how long we stay like this, but we're here long enough for my bare feet to feel numb from the cool concrete under them.

I shift to break from Joe and go back inside. I curl into one of the corners of the couch, keeping the blanket close and rest the right side of my head on a pillow. Sadie lays on my left as I watch Joe grab another blanket before lifting my feet and sitting beneath them. He covers us both with the blanket and settles himself quickly. My blank stare meets Joe's eyes and some sensation kindles inside me as he massages my right foot. The heat from his hands quickly dismisses any remaining numbness in my foot. He meticulously rubs each of my feet, not missing a single spot. I close my eyes savoring Joe's reassuring touch.

I want to crawl into his arms. I need to crawl into his body. My heart is conflicted with craving comfort and distance at the same time. I'm so confused. Maybe I should go back to bed and lay with Jared. No. I don't want to be around a lot of people right now.

My eyes are closed as my consciousness feels Sadie now at my feet. Joe slides under the blanket cautiously like he doesn't want to disturb me. I don't need to open my eyes to know it's him. The smell and feel of his body confirms that it is.

Chapter Eighteen

Brushing my hair with his fingers, Joe searches, "You asleep."

"No," I mumble.

"Hungry?"

"A little. Why?" I turn my head to look at him.

"Here," he offers handing me a tall glass.

"Thanks." I take the smoothie from him.

"I made it just the way you like."

I pause hearing his words before taking a sip. "You made it?"

"Yes."

"You sure Anna didn't make it?"

"I wouldn't let her help me," he sheepishly grins.

My eyebrows lift in astonishment.

"You can ask her if you don't believe me."

I shake my head and gulp the rest of it down. He takes the glass from me and places it on the table before grabbing a second one.

"I'm not that hungry," I profess.

"This one is for me, silly," he chuckles.

Once he's finished, I feel Joe put the glass back as his right hand plays with my hair. He takes my left hand and holds it up to his mouth, kissing it several times before placing it back down, not letting go. I coil back into the pillow, longing to escape the drifting sadness in my chest.

Joe's body alters abruptly and I'm coherent again. I feel his body weight, but his arms are no longer around me.

"She's over here," he whispers standing up.

"Thanks. How long has she been out here?" Jared whispers with his voice getting closer.

"A while. Is this normal for her?" I hear the worry in Joe's tone.

"Not for a long time." Jared positions his arm around me.

I immediately rotate into his chest.

"I should probably wake her soon to try to get her to eat."

"She had a smoothie," Joe mentions. "I'm surprised she drank it when I gave it to her."

"Good. That's a good sign." They sit quietly for a while before Jared inquires, "How did you know she was dreaming?"

Breathe In

"Sadie came into the den and woke me up. When I saw Emma, I tried to wake her before coming to get you."

"It's usually not hard to wake her, but the way it was tonight, I'm not surprised," Jared explains.

"Can I ask you something?"

"Sure man," Jared encourages.

"What is the dream about?"

Jared takes a weighted breath in, releases it and kisses me. "You can't let her know that I told you," Jared begins.

He's going to tell him. Why? I know that I avoid talking to him about the dream reoccurring and brush it off each time. But why tell Joe? I can understand him talking to Maggie or Nathan — but Joe?

"I was the first to know," he breathes in with a shiver. "It took her almost six months after we first met for her to finally tell me what they were about," Jared informs. "Maggie and Nathan are the only other people who know." Jared squeezes me tighter in his arms. "I don't like the fact that she's been having them this much again."

I can tell that Jared is deciding on what to say.

"It's about her parents."

"What about them?" Joe timidly inquires.

"Emma was in the car when it happened . . ." he sniffs. With a horse voice, Jared continues. "She told me she doesn't remember what really happened. She woke up in the hospital three days later from this very dream. She's never been sure if the accident really happened the way the nightmare depicts," Jared painfully explains.

"Wow . . ." Joe answers in bewilderment. "That explains a lot."

"Yeah," Jared nervously chuckles.

They sit quietly as the memories of the hospital formulate in my head. Fighting off the pain, I moan and twist into Jared tighter.

"I'm here, *Kitten*," Jared assures me. "I'm here."

I arise some time later from the excruciating need to pee and the sound of laughter coming from another room. Opening my eyes, I discover that Sadie is the only one with me in the living room. After using the closest bathroom, I stagger to the dining room and prepare myself mentally and physically before rounding the corner.

"There she is!" shouts Jimmy. "We were hoping you'd make it before all the food is gone."

Chapter Eighteen

I give my best fake smile that sneaks by everyone but Jared, but I see a questioning glance from Joe.

As I sit down in the same chair I was in last night for dinner, Jared, who is to my right, asks, "Hungry?"

"Sure," I return with another smile.

Jared squeezes my hand which reinforces my speculation that I haven't fooled him. Without a word, Jared stands up, takes my plate and starts putting food on it. After placing the plate in front of me, he then proceeds to pour me a glass of orange juice. I hope he isn't planning on doting on me too much.

"We were all talking about what to do today, Emma," Maggie says. "We thought that today we could show Jimmy and Allen around town, have lunch somewhere, maybe see one of the museums or see a show at the playhouse, have dinner . . . and tomorrow we can all go trampolining."

"Sure," I agree, taking a small bit of egg.

My right hand continues to hold Jared's and from the corner of my I can see him watching me. I listen to everyone talking while I pretend to eat, only taking a few small bites here and there while keeping my eyes down most of the time. I'm grateful when no one inquires about my episode. It's nice to hear everyone joking and laughing.

"Would you like me to heat that up for you, Ms. Emma?" Anna startles me.

"What? Oh, no. I'm fine. Thank you."

Jared leans over, "Do you want something else?"

"No. I'm good."

At least he's being as discrete as he can be at the moment.

Eventually everyone gets up and heads to shower, then change for our daily excursion around Pasadena. Jared hovers, following me into Joe's bedroom and lays down on the bed with Sadie. I decide to join him rather than jump in the shower right away. I don't want to recount this morning or give him a reason to think that I'm as bad as I am, but I do feel like I need my Jared.

Joe wanders through the open door and finds us snuggling. I suggest that he showers first and he obliges without debate. While Joe's in the bathroom, Maggie pops into the room and piles into the bed with Jared, Sadie and me. She's still in her pajamas which surprises me because I would think she'd be naked and wet with Henry by now. Regardless, I can feel my mood improving with my family all around me — this is what I need.

Exiting the bathroom with nothing but a towel around his waist, Joe tries to have a silent conversation with Jared right in front of me. What the hell is going on?

Jared studies me before kissing me and then leaves. I'm left with Maggie, Sadie and a practically naked Joe.

"I'm done in there if you're ready," Joe mentions, pausing at his closet door. "It won't take me long to get dressed, so I'll be out of the room before you get out of the shower."

"Thanks."

I intended to get up right away, but my body is still a bit slow to respond. Maggie follows me into the bathroom when I finally muster the energy to get up.

"I'm good, Mags," I comment when she hovers.

"I know," she acknowledges.

Good, I'm glad that she doesn't notice.

"I just thought you might, you know, need me."

Smiling at her intention, I reveal, "Thanks, but I've . . . um."

"Ohhh, okay." She holds me tight, rubbing my back and then leaves.

I don't bother locking the door — I just don't care at this point.

When I return to the bedroom after showering, the main door is closed and no one is in the room, not even Sadie. Taking my time, I make the bed after putting on a bra and panties.

I hear a light knock on the door before it cracks open.

"You doing okay in here?" Joe questions, checking in.

Sadie wedges herself enough through the door to get in.

"Yeah, come on in," I suggest, running the towel over my long, wet hair again.

Joe halts in his tracks when he sees me and immediately looks away. Why is he uncomfortable looking at me? Inspecting my body, I don't find any bruises, cuts or abrasions. It takes my brain an extra second to understand his response. I'm still only wearing my white, lace bra and panties.

"You in or out?" I command, not caring as I hang up my towel in the bathroom. Turning around, I see that the bedroom door is closed and Joe's sitting on the bed looking at Sadie as he pets her. "Are you on Emma watch?"

"What? No," he nervously replies.

I guess my friends don't trust what I might do if I'm alone for too long.

I brush my hair with slow, robotic strokes as I look into the mirror. Taking my time, I begin applying my makeup. Halfway done, I hear mumbling coming from the other room.

"I can't hear you," I advise.

Chapter Eighteen

More mumbles, occur before I hear him clearly, "Did you make the bed?"

Stopping, I turn and see him standing in the doorway with his arms crossed and looking down. "Yes, why?"

"Just checking." His eyes stay glued to the floor.

Returning to the mirror to finish applying my mascara, I hear another voice in the distance.

"Emma, were you planning . . ." Maggie stops in the middle of her sentence.

I look over to see Joe shift out of the doorway to let her through.

"I'm sorry. I didn't mean to interrupt." She peers back and forth between me and Joe with her eyes wide and mouth open.

"You aren't interrupting anything. What's up?"

"Oh yeah, were you planning on wearing your red cardigan?" Maggie faces me, but her eyes bounce between Joe and me in the mirror.

"No. Why? Did you want to?" I nonchalantly continue as if it's just me and her in the room.

"Yeah, if you don't mind?"

"Not at all. It's in my bag," I instruct.

"Thanks, sweetie," she says leaving the bathroom.

As I put some chapstick on, I hear her shouting *thanks again* followed by a door closing.

Leaving the bathroom, I stop just before bumping into Joe. It takes him a second to realize that I'm waiting to get by him. I take my time at my suitcase to determine what to wear as I put my makeup bag away. I select a white tank top, a pair of white capris, and a thin, tan v-neck silk blouse. Grabbing my pants, I turn to find Joe sitting on the chaise reading. Bending down to place a foot into each pant leg, I look up when I hear Joe clear his voice. Gradually pulling up my pants, I stare at him. I gain his attention right as I'm rounding my hips. His eyes jump from my hands, to my breasts and then to my face before darting away, realizing he got caught. Smirking, I pick up my tank top and slip it on, keeping my back to him. I momentarily return to the bathroom to inspect myself in the mirror, put on some earrings and a necklace and run my fingers through my hair.

I set my pajamas in my clothing bag next to the dresser. Grabbing my white flats from my shoe bag, I place them next to the bed for easy access. I check my purse to make sure I have everything in there including Sadie's stuff for when we leave. My phone is still charged and there are no messages or emails that need to be tended. I slip on my blouse before sitting down on the bed to put on my shoes. Sadie rests her head on my leg, causing me to pay attention to her rather than finish dressing.

"You okay?" Joe's sweet voice asks.

Not turning to look, I answer, "Yeah, why?"

"Just checking." Standing next to me now, Joe reaches his hand towards me, "Come on."

I'm uncertain at first to take his hand, but do it anyway.

Joe pulls me into him, resting his right hand on my hip and his left on my face. He studies me carefully. Joe doesn't push like he did last night in the kitchen.

Something is different. I'm guessing that my morning incident has something to do with it. I've probably scared him off enough now where he just pities me — I hate pity from anyone. This is probably for the best — better Joe finds out now that I'm too messed up to be in any kind of relationship and why I avoid them. He can save himself from me and my demons. Yes, this is for the best.

My friends and I casually stroll the streets of Pasadena enjoying the beautiful, spring weather. Our conversations are light and airy, however, I remain less chatty. The amount of walking helps with my agitation, but it's not as impactful as rebounding or sex.

Jared stays close to me no matter where we go, holding onto my hand or draping his arm over my shoulders while keeping Nathan close as well. If at any point Jared and I break apart, Maggie connects with me, spreading her cheery, sunshine energy.

I made sure when we left Joe's, that I had Sadie wear her service dog vest. Without having to think about it, we're all able to go into any place of business. Allen and Jimmy seem fascinated by my reasoning and the use of the vest when I explained it to them during lunch at my favorite local Thai restaurant.

At some point, Jimmy and Allen ask about Nathaniel's and express their desire to see his collection. Instead of dealing with Saturday LA traffic, Nathan calls Denise to put two racks together, one men's and one women's, and to have them brought over to the penthouse for an impromptu fashion show.

After we finish lunch, we meet up with Anna just outside of Joe's penthouse building for her to take Sadie. My friends and I continue on foot to the Pasadena Playhouse for the two o'clock showing of Pygmalion. Maggie and I share a subscription which includes tickets to certain shows and a discount on any additional tickets we need. I'm actually surprised that we were able to get a few extra seats last minute for everyone to attend.

Chapter Eighteen

A few minutes into the second act, I feel something touch my left hand. Glancing down, I notice Joe's fingers inching their way up the side of the armrest and I don't pull away. In fact, I'm shocked when my hand slides closer to his. We sit for the remainder of the performance with just our pinky and ring fingers laced.

After the play, Denise arrives at Joe's penthouse at the same time we do. Joe invites her to stay for dinner as Jimmy and Allen inspect Nathan's men's line, however, Denise politely declines saying she's made dinner plans with her girlfriend.

Jimmy and Allen start picking out outfits for themselves to put on. They request Henry and Joe to try on a few items, but the sizes Denise brought are a little small for Joe's more pronounced muscular size. By the time they've seen everything on the first rack, Jimmy and Allen announce that they want every piece and get out their checkbooks.

Moving on to the second rack, Jimmy realizes that all of the clothes are for women. He adamantly encourages Maggie and I to model. I willingly try on every piece that Maggie doesn't select. Trying on new clothes always makes a girl feel better — well, at least me.

"Put this on next," Jimmy demands, shoving a tiny bikini at me.

"No," I contend with a polite smile.

"Why not? It'll look great on you."

"It's too small," I object.

He holds the bottom piece up to my backside as if he doesn't believe me. "No, it's not."

I take the small triangular piece and place it over my breasts. "See."

"It's not that bad. Put it on."

"Yeah, put it on, Emma," Nathan chimes in.

Rolling my eyes, I take the swimsuit and head into the bedroom after Maggie. Moments like these are when I'm glad that I'm completely comfortable with my own body, even when it's that time of the month. I let Maggie go out to the living room first to hide my overly exposed flesh. The room goes completely silent when I'm seen followed by several whistles.

"Damn, Emma. You are smokin'!" announces Jimmy.

Not wanting the attention and stares, I try to flee.

Allen cuts me off, "Where are you going?"

"You've seen the suit. I'm going to change."

"No way. I want to look at it," he argues.

"Fine," I whine. Standing there, I keep my eyes on the floor.

"What's this?" Jimmy questions touching my lower, back right hip, directly at the bathing suit line.

"What?" I ask, inspecting the area he's referring to, hoping I didn't snag the fabric on something.

"This," he points.

Seeing what he's talking about, I immediately slap my hand over it. "Nothing."

"That's not nothing," Jimmy contends.

"What is it?" Allen fishes.

"Nothing," I reply, covering it and stepping away from them.

"Well, I think that's it for the women's line," Jared interjects, jumping to my rescue.

"No, it's not," Jimmy defends. "There are still about ten garments."

"I can wear them all," Maggie offers.

"That'll work," Allen agrees, sensing the tension between Jared, Maggie and myself.

Maggie and I return to change. She puts on the next outfit as I put my daily attire back on. I join Jared on the couch as Jimmy and Allen ooo and ahh over the items Maggie wears until there's nothing left.

Denise leaves with one rack completely empty, making her trip down to the car easier. Jimmy and Allen actually bought the entire men's rack. However, Denise did take Joe's measurements for some options that Nathan plans on bringing to Hawaii for him to try. I assist Denise on the way down to her car since Sadie was just fed and needs to be taken out.

We sit down for dinner not long after I return to the penthouse with Sadie. The excitement and anticipation of our upcoming trip to Hawaii is the main focus for the rest of the evening.

At one point, Maggie mentions to Henry, "Honey, we should probably give everyone their plane tickets this weekend."

"We don't need plane tickets, sweetie," Jimmy answers as Henry swallows a bite of food.

"Are we taking a boat?" Maggie continues.

"No, sweetheart. We're taking the jet," Henry reassures, wiping his mouth with a cloth napkin.

Chapter Eighteen

"It can fit all of us?" she questions.

"Ours can," Jimmy mentions.

"Well, how does that work?" Jared inquires.

I'm glad Jared asks this question. I've never flown let alone have been to an airport.

"We tell our pilot where we want to go and when we want to leave. He and the crew prep the plane. We drive right up to get on it at the private airport and take off," Jimmy explains.

"No TSA or baggage check?" Nathan verifies.

"Exactly," confirms Allen.

"I could easily get spoiled flying privately," Jared adds. "Looks like I need to find myself a Sugar Daddy."

Smacking him on the arm, Nathan rebuts, "I'm your Sugar Daddy. Don't you forget it."

Everyone snickers.

"Then you need to be selling a hell of a lot more clothes to be taking me on trips with our own private plane," Jared teases.

To me, their behavior and words are indicating that their relationship has progressed significantly.

"Something you want to tell me?" I whisper in Jared's ear.

My answer is a wicked grin with the look of love in his eyes. Looks like the love bug has officially bitten both of my friends. Damn Năinai and her blessings.

Like last night, we all change into our pajamas before hoping on the couch. Everyone decides to conserve their energy for jumping tomorrow after hearing some of the stories that have been shared while a few games of pool are played before resolving to watch a movie. We all sit in the same spots as we did last night, but this time I angle my feet down the middle of the couch, resting my head on Sadie who is practically on Jared's lap. Joe grabs a blanket before sitting where my feet are which forces me to bend my knees. He places my legs over his lap before covering us both with the blanket.

After a while, I lift the blanket up to my shoulders and rest my hands on my stomach. A few minutes later, Joe walks his fingers up the side of my body and interlocks them with mine. Changing my attention from the movie to him, I watch Joe as our fingers dance around each others. Maybe I was wrong. Maybe he didn't get freaked out by this morning.

By around ten, everyone retires to their designated rooms for the night. At first, Jared and Nathan are insistent about sleeping with me in Joe's bed, but I decline. I have to reassure them several times that I am fine and will be.

Despite the emotional exhaustion from today, I can't sleep after laying under the covers for forty minutes. I try reading, but that just wakes me up more. I consider jumping on Joe's rebounder, but I don't want to get all sweaty and have to shower. The thought to snoop around his room seems like a great idea. Remembering how much clothing I saw that Joe has in his closet makes me ponder why he needs a dresser in the bedroom. My curiosity gets the better of me so I go over to check. I cautiously open and close each draw to minimize being heard. All of the drawers are empty.

With not much to go off of in his room, I creep down the hallway to see if I can find anything in the living room that I might have missed. I almost jump out of my skin when I hear a whisper halfway down the hall.

Turning, I see Joe in the doorway of the den. "Hi," I mumble softly.

"You okay?"

"Yeah . . . ." I return quietly.

Examining me, Joe prods, "What's wrong?"

"Nothing."

He gestures for me to join him in the den and for some reason I follow. Joe sits next to Sadie who is now laying on what looks like a bed.

"Is that what you are sleeping on?" I ask.

"Yes, why?"

"It looks uncomfortable."

"It's not that bad," he offers.

I sit down on his bed, using Sadie as a barrier between us. It's small and looks nice, but as soon as my butt hits the cushion, I know it's not that comfortable, not compared to his bed.

"You're sleeping on this?"

"Yes, why?"

"You've got a glorious, and probably overly priced king size bed in your room and you're sleeping on this?"

Chuckling, "You're sleeping on it."

"If I knew you were going to be on this last night, I would have insisted that you sleep in your own bed."

"So that's what this is," he says with a widening grin.

Chapter Eighteen

"What what is?"

I'm not sure what he's alluding.

"It's okay, you can say it."

"Say what? What are you talking about?"

I'm completely clueless. What are we talking about?

"If you want me to sleep with you, you just have to ask."

I shoot up to a standing position at his brazen statement.. "Sleep with you, I don't want to sleep with you."

"I don't mind. I'm actually flattered that you're admitting it and that you remember," he teases.

"What? Huh? No. No. No. No. No," I contend as he steps towards me. "I don't want to sleep with you," my voice cracks even in a whisper. "I . . ." Backing away, I shake my head as Joe approaches. My body bangs into something behind me. I'm stuck between him and the door. "Remember what?"

"You didn't have trouble sleeping that night," he calmly states as our bodies touch. "Neither did I."

What is he . . . oh! Crap. He's right. I remember now.

"No," I mutter.

My theory about scaring him away is definitely wrong.

"Do you want me in there with you? Do you need me in there with you?" His knuckles dance across my cheek and chin.

Do I? I don't want to have the dream again. He's right. I didn't have the nightmare the night we shared the bed at Nathan's. I'm so confused right now. I'm terrified. My body feels cold and clammy and I can sense that I'm shaking.

"Come on," he coaxes, taking my hand, leading me out of the den.

In fifteen seconds, we are in his bedroom with Sadie and the door is closed. Wiping a tear from my face, Joe pulls me into his body and I return the embrace for some reason. We stay connected, hugging for at least a minute.

Letting go of me, Joe takes my hand as he moves the covers, guiding me to get in first. Before I'm fully situated, he climbs in and spoons me.

Breaking the silence first, I jokingly question, "Why are you on my side of the bed again?"

A small laugh escapes his throat, "I'm not. You are on my side."

"This is my side. I slept here last night," I share.

He doesn't say anything for a moment, like he's deciding on what to say. Releasing his arm draped in front of me, Joe repositions the hair on my neck before tracing the side of my body all the way down to my exposed hip. "How about . . . you tell me about this, and I'll answer why I'm on your side of the bed." His finger circles around my right hip.

Twisting onto my back, I declare, "That's not an even trade."

Smiling he offers, "Okay. I'll answer your question plus one. Any one."

"No."

"Any two?" he returns.

I pretend that I'm weighing his offer to make him sweat. "Four questions. And they don't all have to be asked tonight."

"Three and you've got a deal," he negotiates.

"Fine," I agree.

"You forget, beautiful . . . I'm not the one who has trouble opening up," he taunts.

Ignoring his statement, I focus on getting my answer. "So? Why are you on my side of the bed?"

Playing with a lock of my hair he chuckles, "This is my side of the bed. The whole bed is my side."

I glare at him because he knows that's not a good enough of an answer for me.

"And, this is especially my side of the bed because you are in it."

My face changes to furrowed brows which elicits him to explain further.

"If, God forbid, someone broke into my home and came into this bedroom, they'd have to go through me before they can get to you."

His explanation has some logic to it.

"I have a question, but it does not count as one of my questions . . ." I begin.

Joe lifts a brow.

"This is a continuation to understand your answer and what you just said."

He nods in agreement.

"What if that person came through the window?"

Joe laughs. "We're in the penthouse. No one is coming through the window."

"Still relevant to the topic at hand . . ." I push.

"Go ahead," he muses.

To bait him further away from what he wants to know, I press, "What if, hypothetically, we weren't in a penthouse. What if we were in a one or two story home or building, that gave easy access to the window?"

Chapter Eighteen

"You're incorrigible."

"Answer the question," I urge.

"Though there is some validity to your statement, I would argue that before the person gets all the way into the room, successfully through the window, I'd already be between you and him."

With some sarcasm in my tone, "How do you or I know whether or not you are a sound sleeper and would be awake and coherent enough to do such a thing, and . . . ."

Before I can finish, Joe has his right hand clamped on my thigh just above my knee. He only knows about that ticklish spot because of Jared. I'm surprised he remembers.

"Are you sure you want to continue this conversation?" Joe maintains an even expression I've never seen before.

Smirking, I consider my choices. Not giving me long enough to make a final decision, Joe squeeze his hand on my leg and I squeal and wiggle.

"Okay," I concede.

He doesn't move his hand away from my leg, so I give him a sideways glance.

"I'm not moving until you answer my question," he asserts. His eyes stare into mine while he tries to conceal a smile. "Your turn."

With a serious expression, I inquire, "What do you want to know?"

With a worried look, Joe shifts and places his hand on my stomach. "Whatever you're willing to share."

I roll and pull my bottoms down an inch or two, far enough for him to see the scar. With his index finger, he glides over it cautiously.

"It's from the accident," I comment.

Joe traces the scar several times with his fingers. My eyes dart open when I feel his lips lightly pressing down on my hip and my body is not quick to move away from the embrace. Our gazes meet and Joe's lips return to my skin, delivering a long, gentle kiss before he slides his body closer to mine. He takes the edge of the covers and pulls them over us. Placing his hand back on my hip, he seeks more, "Will you tell me more about it? Or them?"

I run my fingers through my hair, deciding what to say. "No," I refuse.

"Please," he searches.

"Jared told you enough," I uncontrollably blurt.

I didn't want to admit to either of them that I know about their conversation about me and my parents from this morning.

"You were awake?" he verifies. "I'm sorry. I . . . ."

"It's okay," I sheepishly comfort.

Securing me tighter into his body, Joe kisses my shoulder. "Goodnight, beautiful."

"Goodnight, Joe."

Nineteen

Sultry, deep breaths on my neck and a delicate finger trailing my bare arm send delicious shivers down my spine. With darkness around me, my palm explores the iron, hot body encompassing me. The scent of him stiffens my nipples and tingles my sex. A hand caresses my jawline and I turn into it, moaning, wanting more. A single finger dances over my bottom lip and my mouth parts hungry for his taste. His lips tickle my nap once — twice — three times. What a delectable dream. I don't want it to end. I could be here like this every day for all of eternity.

"Good morning, beautiful," snaps me into consciousness.

I'm immediately met with the admiring face and twinkling eyes of Joe Covelli.

"Morning," I return groggily.

Recounting the visions in my head, I discern that it wasn't a dream.

"Told you that you sleep better with me next to you," he say with a boyish grin.

Curving away, I moan, hugging into a pillow on the other side of me. "What time is it?"

Folding into my body, he reveals, "Six-ten."

My body becomes instantly rigid. I've never slept past six, not since before the accident. "Where's Sadie?"

The answer I am looking for is confirmed by the presence of a third body on the bed that is sniffing its way over to me. Why didn't she wake me up to eat?

"I need to feed her," I remark.

Surrounding me more with his arms, Joe pleas, "Five more minutes."

'No," I object.

"Yes," he coaxes.

"Nooo," I repeat, turning to face him again since I'm now sandwiched between him and Sadie.

Kissing my nose and tugging me in, Joe restates, "Yes."

I let out an exasperated sigh which is met with laughter. "Fine," I cave.

We lay with our faces within inches of each others. Time moves exhaustingly slow, not because I'm not enjoying myself, but because of the surmounting need to pee. My left foot twitches, hoping to distract me from the increasing pressure in my belly.

"What's wrong?"

"Nothing."

"I know you're lying," he accuses.

"It's nothing really," I deflect.

"We can stop if you want. I just thought you were enjoying it from . . . ."

"No. I mean . . . umm . . . I just really need to pee," I admit foolishly.

His face relaxes, "Go pee."

"I can wait."

No, I can't, but I don't want him to know that.

He slides away from me lifting the covers. "Go."

Closing the bathroom door, I remove my menstrual cup and find that it's clean. Has it been six days already? After rinsing it, I double check my calendar in my toiletry bag. I'm ecstatic to know I don't have to wear the cup today during trampolining. After relieving myself, I put a panty liner on just in case.

Leaving the bathroom, I'm surprisingly disappointed when I don't see Joe in the bed with Sadie. The sound of a door sliding opening startles me for a second. Joe comes out of his closet and has changed. He deliberately brushes past me on his way to the restroom. I quickly shimmy out of my tank and put on a sports bra. Sliding into my running capris, I scurry to find a shirt before Joe exits the bathroom. Just as I yank a shirt out of the bag, Joe saunters over and stands, observing me. Once my top is on, he scoops me up and carries me back to the bed.

"Four minutes," he says.

All I can do is nod in agreement.

His body and smell are becoming more familiar now. I notice that his breath is steady, but I can feel his heart rapidly pounding through his chest.

"You okay?"

"Yeah, why?" he says with a shaky tone.

"Your heart his really pounding," I report.

"I'm good," he insists, drawing me in closer and moaning into my neck.

Sadie makes her way to our faces, determined and persistent to let us know she can't wait any longer. Joe finally lets go of me when he can no longer compete with Sadie's insistent playfulness.

We leave Joe's room and find Anna in the kitchen already preparing a bowl for Sadie.

Chapter Nineteen

"Good morning, Anna," I offer, without questioning her actions.

I'm suddenly acutely aware of her amazing attention to detail. Anna has the exact proportions of food in the bowl for Sadie.

"Good morning, Ms. Emma." She slides the bowl over to me. "Mr. Joseph," Anna says suggestively.

I snicker at her words.

"Why are you working on a Sunday, Anna?" I inquire after signaling Sadie to eat.

"I like my job," Anna returns, as if it is a rehearsed statement. After I give her a quizzical look, she adds, "And Mr. Joseph and Mr. Jimmy need me."

"They're big boys. I'm sure they can take care of themselves for one day."

A chuckle sneaks out of her throat. She recovers quickly by coughing and then replies, "I'd like to get a leg up on this week's chores before Hawaii. I have a lot to do before I have to pack them and myself."

Taking the glass of clay water Joe prepared for me, I verify her words, "She's packing for you?"

Joe shrugs finishing his last two gulps of his own clay drink.

Muting a laugh, I say to Ann, "I hope they pay you really well."

"Oh yes. The Covelli family takes very good care of me," Anna delightfully insists.

"Good. I'm glad to hear it." After chugging my clay, I investigate again. "So, you're joining us in Hawaii?"

"Yes, Ms. Emma."

"Anna loves Hawaii. Besides, she won't really be working," Joe adds.

"Hawaii is one of my favorite places," Anna comments with a childlike smile.

Shaking my head in disbelief and amazement to Joe's statement, I get to Sadie's empty bowl before Anna this time. My line of questioning threw her off just enough. I'll have to remember this in the future. What am I say? There will be none of this happening in the future.

After taking Sadie out for a good long walk, Joe and I have a smoothie. He insists on making it to prove that he knows how to use the blender and that he actually made the one we drank yesterday. He does pretty good, I have to say.

I purposefully keep my physical distance from Joe since we officially left the bedroom. Snooping a little in the living room, I check out more of the photos and the titles of the variety of books lining his bookshelf. I'll need to figure out how to sneak into his office to explore the wall of books that reside in there.

It's not long before Joe's close behind me. "What are you looking for?" he requests.

"Nothing," I reply putting a book back.

Enclosing my waist with his arms, he moans into my ear, "Liar."

Tempted, I resist my urges and slip away. "Do you play?"

With a devious grin, Joe answers, "I love to play." He takes a giant step towards me, drawing me into him.

"That," I turn and point.

His eyes reluctantly follow mine to the piano. He growls into my neck like a lion stalking its prey. Pressing his lips to my earlobe, "Yes. Since I was five."

"Will you play for me?"

"Now?"

I bite my lip and nod.

"I'll wake everyone."

"So," I giggle.

"So . . . I'd rather stay right here." Joe takes a few steps forward as I take a few steps back until my body is against a window.

"Just friends," I mumble into his ear.

Ignoring me, he slides his mouth along my jaw. "Just one," he pleas.

"No," I whimper.

We both know that my body is saying yes and I'm desperately fighting to keep control over myself.

"I want to hear you play. Will you?"

"When you let me kiss you right here," Joe announces in a devilish tone as he lightly grazes my lips with his finger.

"That's not fair," I scold.

"You're not the only one who can have rules," he baits.

"So that's how you want to do this?" I declare.

"You started it, beautiful," he shares.

Observing his expression, I try to determine what I want to say or do. I'm enjoying our game, but not when he pushes for another kiss — because, I foolishly want one. Knowing what a second kiss will do to me, I've got to be careful. I choose my safety net and peel away from his embrace and head to Jared's and Nathan's room.

Chapter Nineteen

Listening to make sure I don't walk in on anything, I press my ear to the door. My eyes catch Joe leaning against a wall about fifteen feet away, watching what I'm doing. Turning the knob, I give Joe a wicked grin and enter the bedroom, closing the door behind me. Safe at last. God job, Emma.

Jared wakes before I turn around. "Everything okay, *Kitten*?"

"Yeah. I just miss you," I say, buttering him up as I slip under the covers.

"Sleep okay?" He wraps his arms around me.

"Great," I say, nuzzling into his chest.

As much as I fear relationships, especially the intimacy of relationships, my body craves physical contact. I'm a tactile kind of girl who loves stimulation. When I cuddle with Jared, I feel safe and secure. There are no other expectation or obligations. There are no chances or possibilities that could arise. No secrecy, no hidden desires. Just the feeling of being safe; the feeling of being home.

Breaking my moment of bliss, Jared mentions, "You smell different."

"What do you mean?"

"I don't know, you just smell different," he repeats.

"Good different or bad different?" I search.

"Just different."

"It's probably from being in Joe's bed," I suggest.

The realization sets in. I don't smell like Joe's bed, I smell like Joe.

"That's it," he verifies.

"Why didn't you tell me?" I accuse.

"Tell you what?" he returns, clueless of my statement.

"About where Joe lives?"

"I didn't know until he texted me Friday. I thought you knew," Jared answers.

"Do you think I would have packed to stay the night if I did?" I press.

"Good point," he concurs. "Sorry."

"It's okay," I excuse.

I'm not mad at Jared, only surprised by the fact that Joe lives less than a mile away from me.

"It shouldn't matter. He's a friend," he adds.

"Yeah," I acknowledge.

breathe In

I don't really agree, but I don't want to give away that it does bother me.

We snuggle for a long time and at some point I start crying — I haven't cried in a while. I've missed him, I miss my Jared. We see each other every week, but I miss waking up and going to bed with him every day. I miss our old apartment. I miss — my parents. I remember what they look like because I have photos in my bedroom. What I really miss are their voices — their smell most of all. My heart breaks knowing that I can't remember that about them. Jared is the only smell and sound left that I have that gives me the feeling of home.

"What's wrong, *Kitten*?" Jared whispers.

"Nothing," I weep.

"Tell me," he encourages. "I can't help if you don't tell me."

"I don't remember what they sound like or how they smell. I've lost so many memories with them," I sob.

"What do you remember?" he prompts.

"You. Your eyes when we met. Your voice. Your smell. You're home," I say.

"And I always will be," he assures, squeezing me tighter. "But, you will need to find your own home with someone else. Like I have with Nathan."

His words hurt.

"So it is serious," I state.

"Yeah," he agrees. "I will never leave you. You're home to me too, but Nathan is also home now too."

"There's too much changing. I don't like it," I confess.

"Change isn't good or bad. It just depends on how you look at it."

"When did you get so philosophical?" I tease.

"Not long after I met you," he pokes.

I jab him in his ribs.

"Shhh. Quit talking. I need my beauty sleep," Nathan whines.

Jared and I both fling our bodies, dog-piling Nathan until he surrenders.

By nine, everyone is up and in the dining room having breakfast. We're out the door and piled into Maggie's and Jared's Teslas twenty minutes before our scheduled jump time. A newer trampoline facility just opened up over in Glendale off of Colorado Boulevard, so we don't have far to drive.

Jimmy and Allen groan the entire drive home and during lunch. After bellies are full from another tasty meal prepared by Anna, everyone seeks out

Chapter Nineteen

a nap in their designated rooms. Used to the rigorous workout and being well rested, I elect to grab a book and read on the couch. Sadie snuggles up in her usual position with her head on my belly.

A few more pages into reading my book and Joe comes into the living room. He positions himself down the center of the couch resting his shoulders against the same pillow as me. During the next two hours, Joe purposefully bumps into my right arm with his left as he turns a page or changes how he holds his book. He is dying for some attention and I deliberately refuse to give it — specifically to torture him. Clearly frustrated by my lack of response, Joe eventually shifts, laying next to me. I can't help but laugh at his antics.

"What's so funny?" he questions.

"Just something in my book," I fib.

Not much time passes before Joe tries another tactic to gain my attention.

"Am I distracting you?" he asks as he slides his fingers under the edge of my shirt and draws circles on my belly.

"Are you trying to distract me?" I ask, keeping my eyes on my book. Out of the corner of my eye, I can see him grinning.

"Maybe," Joe replies.

His response intrigues me, so I look at him.

Happy that he gets my attention, Joe changes his answer, "Yes. Is it working?"

I return my gaze to my book before remarking, "Yes."

"Good," Joe whispers, continuing to keep my focus off my book. He nuzzles into my shoulder and wraps his arm tighter around my waist.

"I thought we agreed to just be friends?" I remind.

"I didn't agree to anything," he defends, placing his lips on the edge of my neck. "You were the one who said just friends."

My sex salivates at the touch of his lips to my skin. My neck is my weakness — my Achille's Heel. Pull yourself together, Emma. No need for Joe to know how to get to you.

As I am about to respond to his statement, noise rises in the hallway. Joe immediately moves back to his previous spot on the couch and encourages Sadie to join him. Before I can see who is coming, Jimmy and Allen plop down on the other end of the couch. As tired as they are, their overworked muscles are probably making it hard for them to sleep.

With nothing else planned for the day, and with only four more days until our trip, those of us who do not live in this glorious penthouse elect to end the weekend early. Maggie and Henry offer first to take me home, but I politely refuse. I have about a half mile walk until I'm home. Maggie contends with my rebuttal saying I have bags to carry, but I tell her that I'll be fine and Sadie and I could use the walk. Joe announces that he will walk me home. I object, but everyone insists.

After saying farewell to Jimmy and Allen, who have trouble getting up from the couch, the rest of us leave. Before walking to my place, Joe and I bid farewell to Maggie and Henry and then Jared and Nathan as they depart from the valet area. At a relaxed pace, Joe and I take our time to my apartment. Once at the gate for my building, Joe insists on helping with the bags all the way up to the door. Not wanting to cause a scene, I agree. I try to take the bags from him when I stop in front of my door, but he won't give them to me.

"I'll carry them in," he states. "What's the big deal?"

"I like my privacy," I reply. "I don't have guys back to my apartment. You've gotten the farthest with just even knowing where I live."

"You've never had a guy in your place?" Joe sounds shocked. "What about Jared and Nathan?"

"They don't count," I argue.

"Why don't they . . . ohh." He makes the connection and a wicked grin spreads across his whole face. "You've never had a guy in your place."

"Yes," I nervously confirm, looking away.

"Would you make an exception for me?"

"It's one of my rules," I verify.

"Ah . . . then why don't you take these and Sadie inside and come back to say goodbye?"

"Why can't I say farewell now?"

He stands looking at me with his arms crossed. The look on his face confirms my speculation. He's not going to leave unless I agree.

"Fine," I sourly confirm.

He bends down and pets Sadie while I unlock the door.

I don't bother turning on a light since my apartment is fairly well lit from the late afternoon sunlight streaming in through the large windows. Five steps into my home and the sound of the light switch startles me. Dropping my bags, I turn sharply to find Joe perched in the door frame. Scared that he might try to come all the way in, I rush back over to him.

"You know, I just realized that it's almost dinner time," he states, pulling me into him.

"So?" I question, wondering where he's going with this?

Chapter Nineteen

"So, I was thinking we should have dinner."

Pulling away from his embrace, I place my hands on my hips before commenting, "We should." He takes a step in and I immediately block him with my body, "What are you doing?"

"I figured that was your way of inviting me in for dinner." Joe's eyes sparkle and the smile on his face makes it a little hard to object.

Clearly he missed my implication and I need to stand my ground. "No. I wasn't inviting you in. First of all, I have my rules. Second, what I meant was that I agree we both should have dinner, but I didn't agree that we should have it now or together."

Playing along he continues, "Fine, then you, Sadie and I will go out for dinner."

"No. Sadie and I will eat here. You can eat wherever you want."

"Well, beautiful, I choose to eat here."

"No. My place is not an option," I contend.

"You said I can eat wherever I want. So, I choose here," he goads with a smile.

A battle of wills ensues as we stare each other down for who knows how long.

Sternly I advise, "My place is not an option."

He takes a step closer, causing our noses to barely touch. "Okay, then we'll go out to eat."

"No."

With his hands on my body, Joe presses his lips to my right ear and commands, "Either we go out or we're breaking rules. You choose, beautiful."

I'm not fond of either of my two choices. Breaking any of my rules is not an option, no matter how horny I am. Fear of playing this game a second time today is also not appealing. What is a girl to do? I guess I need to choose the lesser of the two options.

Surrendering I agree, "Fine."

A victory smile emerges on Joe's face. His hands push firmly on my hips forcing me to take a step backward.

"What are you doing?" I question.

"We're eating here, right?"

Shoving him hard enough, I get him to take two steps back. "No. We're going out. Stay right here. If you move from the door, the deal is off." Before I turn, his expression softens, almost saddened by my choice, but he quietly agrees.

Breathe In

Walking back towards my purse, I check the time on the stove clock; it's almost four-thirty. Fighting the urge to be affected by Joe's disappointment, I choose to take back more control over the situation. It's time to feed Sadie. I take out the last full food containers out of the cooler. Spooning the contents into her bowl, I monitor to see where Joe is standing. He hasn't moved as far as I can see. As Sadie chows down, I inspect my purse to make sure I have everything I need. I have trouble properly keeping track of my inventory as my attention repeatedly bounces to Joe, making sure he hasn't moved. I take extra precaution and quadruple check my bag to ease my distracted mind. Sadie finishes eating and I wash her bowl.

To play Joe at his own game, the temptation to delay further greets me. Unfortunately, the thought that Joe would take more opportunity to search my apartment for clues about me enters my mind, immediately dispelling the notion.

Riding the elevator down, Joe attempts to hold my hand several times. I jerk my hand away in protest. As much as I enjoy his touch, I want him to know I was serious about being just friends. He ushers Sadie and me out first with his hand on the small of my back. I do my best not to notice. Aware that he's baiting me now, I can tell he's enjoying himself. After giving Sadie some time at the park, I start walking back to my apartment.

"Where are you going?"

"To drop Sadie off," I say.

"Why?"

"I don't have her vest," I answer.

It's not the complete answer. As much as I love having Sadie along, it's not fair to expect her to just go where ever we go for dinner, especially if it draws too much attention. Plus, I don't want to drag her into the middle of whatever this is between Joe and me.

Joe studies me for a moment, not sure what to make of my statement. "Okay," he cautiously agrees.

After dropping Sadie off, my mood changes as we enter the elevator. Did I make the right choice taking Sadie home? Should I have grabbed her vest and brought her along? Arguing with myself causes me not to notice when Joe takes my hand until the elevator door rings open and I quickly pull away.

Stopping just outside the gate, Joe turns to me and sweetly offers, "We don't have to go to dinner. It's no big deal."

"It's okay," I return with unconvincing lightheartedness.

Chapter Nineteen

"I don't want to force you to do anything you don't want to do." He tries to hide a pained expression, but his voices carries it.

"It's okay. Really. I'm sorry," I confess.

"Why are you apologizing? I shouldn't have pushed."

Joe's clearly confused by my reaction.

"It's not you . . . It's just . . ." I begin to explain.

Hearing the tension in my voice he replies, "You don't have to explain and you certainly don't have to have dinner with me, Emma."

"Yes I do," I honestly contend.

"No, you don't," he urges.

"It's just that I'm still off from this weekend . . . I mean . . ." my voice trails as I look away.

My brain and heart are still caught up and confused by the dream, the change in the dream and the intensity of it; not to mention our interactions. Our first kiss and our almost several other kisses. Our sharing the same bed again — me being able to share a bed with him a second time — having the best night's sleep when I'm with him — that my mixed emotions are getting the better of me and I don't know what to make of them let alone what do. When I'm around him, I don't feel like myself and need to get away, but the minute I'm not with him, I want him near.

A second later, Joe has me circled in his arms. I burry my face into his neck to combat the tears that are threatening my eyes. The last thing I want is to cry in front of Joe, so I work hard to control myself. Joe gently stokes one hand repeatedly over my head as he squeezes me as tight as he can. I'm able to fight off the sobs, but a few tears find their way onto my cheeks. When Joe takes my face in his hands, he kindly wipes the tears before kissing me on my forehead.

When I realize that we are back at my door, I inquire, "What are you doing?"

"Taking you home. You need to rest," he announces.

"Why? I owe you dinner," I object.

"You don't owe me anything. If anything I owe you. Three answers to three questions to be exact," he reminds.

His admittance gets a chuckle from me which in turn gets him to smile. Joe's kindness does not go unnoticed, but I do question if his actions are prompted by pity.

"I am hungry," I express as my stomach grumbles more at the thought of food.

"It's up to you. Whatever you want to do?"

I stare at him not sure what to decide as I fidget with my keys. I want both, but I can't have both. I want to move on and have dinner with him, but I also want to go inside and hide from the world, conflicted by wanting him to come inside the apartment with me and sending him home at the same time.

I'm not sure what he sees in my eyes, but Joe suggests, "We'll do dinner another time."

"You sure?" I say heart-broken.

The thought that he's avoiding me now because I'm upset concerns me.

"Yes," he states firmly as he leans and presses his lips to my forehead. His lips linger before his forehead touches mine and he gently rubs his nose with mine. Moaning I shake my head, not because I'm expecting a kiss, but for chastising myself for wanting one.

Joe moves like he's about to take my mouth with his, but then he suddenly stops. He kisses my cheek instead. "Goodnight, beautiful."

Pausing to feel his embrace a little longer, I keep my hands on his arms. "Goodnight, Joe."

Twenty

There's nothing like waking up in the morning after a night of snack indulging, sappy romance movie watching and lengthy, intense self-satisfaction to soothe an aching girl's soul. The funk has dissolved, my mood has greatly improved, however, I am just as horny as I was last night.

After taking care of Sadie, I pleasure myself again before continuing the rest of my regular daily routine. The morning flies by rapidly with a lot of work tasks and texts or phone calls with Jared and Maggie. Most of our conversations are about business, but they still manage to slip in a question or two making sure I'm doing good. After lunch, I resolve to have another self-indulging, sensual break. By two o'clock, after Sadie's and my afternoon frolic in the park, I'm on the couch working on the programing for Raven 1.0.

Being well engrossed in computer coding for who knows how long, I hear a knock at the door. I never get a knock at my door unless it's from someone I just buzzed up, and Jared and Maggie have their own keys. Looking through the peep hole, I'm surprised to see Anna standing outside. What the heck is she doing here?

As soon as I open the door, Anna offers me a friendly smile. "Hello, Ms. Emma."

"Hi, Anna. What are you doing here?"

"Mr. Joseph asked me to deliver something to you," she says.

My eyes drift down to the large, white box with a red ribbon that she's holding. What the hell is that? What would he be sending me? Why would he be sending me anything? Did I leave something over at his house? Did I leave panties there and this is his discrete way of returning them? I quickly do a mental check. No, I didn't leave anything behind.

Almost forgetting my manners, I offer, "Come in, please."

"Thank you, Ms. Emma."

"How did you get in at the gate?" I curiously question, leading her over to my couch.

"I flirted with one of the men taking care of the plants," she admits, placing the box on my coffee table.

"Smooth," I praise.

Delighted, she replies, "Thank you."

"If I left something at Joe's, I could have come to get it," I pry, wanting to know more about what is in the box without opening it.

"Mr. Joseph didn't say that it was something that you left when he instructed me to drop it off while I was running errands," she offers.

Good. Embarrassing moment averted.

Trying not to get caught up with what is in the box I ask, "Would you like something to drink or eat?"

"Yes, please, Ms. Emma. Do you have tea?"

"Of course," I reply getting up and heading for the kitchen. "I have jasmine, green tea, yerba mate, chamomile, chai or rooibos."

"The green tea would be terrific. Thank you, Ms. Emma."

Anna sits quietly as I prepare her drink. She glances around the room like she's taking notes, either for herself or Joe. "I like your home, Ms. Emma. It's nice and small. Not big like Mr. Joseph's," she comments earnestly.

"Thank you," I gratefully accept her praise. "I bet it takes a while to clean his place."

"A little. Mr. Joseph is not a messy man, thankfully, which makes everything else I need to do easier. Mr. James, on the other hand, is messy," she answers, petting Sadie. "And, it's not as big as the Covelli home in New York."

Joe said he doesn't have anything to hide, but to find out things I wouldn't normally ask him directly through Anna would definitely be helpful. I don't want to use Anna, I think she's a sweet person and I don't want to put her in a compromising position, but any additional insight to Joe or Henry that I would feel weird asking them about is a definite bonus.

"Have you worked with Joe's family for a long time?" I keep the conversation going, waiting for the water to boil.

"Oh yes. Since just before Mr. Joseph was born," she openly reveals.

"Wow, that's a long time," I comment.

"Lots of stuff I know," she replies with a telling look.

If I'm reading her right, Anna seems to be willing to share some information. What exactly and how do I ask her?

Can I ask you something, Anna," I inquire, setting down the serving tray on the coffee table.

"Sure," Anna encourages adding some honey to her tea.

"Why do you Call him Mr. Joseph?"

Seeming puzzled by my question, she asks, "What do you mean?"

Chapter Twenty

"You don't call him Joe, Joseph, Mr. Covelli or Sir," I explain.

"It's always been like that. All the staff call all the children mister followed by their first name. Mr. and Mrs. Covelli are Mr. and Mrs. Covelli," Anna clarifies, taking a sip.

"All the staff?"

I wonder how many staff members the Covelli family has.

"Yes," she asserts, but doesn't give more details.

Excited and nervous, I breech the elephant in the room and inquire, "Do you know what is in the box?"

"No," she simply states. "But, I think you should open it."

Is she suggesting that I open it now? Is she curious too? Even if Anna was Jared or Maggie, I wouldn't open it now.

She sees my hesitation and offers, "Or, when you feel it's best."

"Thanks," I return sheepishly.

We both stare at the box for a few minutes sipping our tea, like if we keep looking at the beautifully decorated box, it will open itself.

Redirecting our attention, I ask, "Do you have many more errands today?"

"No. You were the last one on the list," she reports.

A list? She was given a list?! I was on the list?!

"He told you to wait and see if I opened it, didn't he?" I press, knowing enough about Joe that he would.

Anna doesn't have to say anything, the look on her face says it all, especially her suddenly rosy cheeks.

"I won't say anything if you won't, Anna," I voice with confidence.

She proudly nods in agreement before saying, "I like you, Ms. Emma."

With a genuine smile, I share, "I like you too, Anna."

A thought pops into my head and I can't help but to blurt it out, "Why didn't Joe just deliver this himself? Did he think that I wouldn't accept it if he came?"

Anna's eyes promptly dart to me before I'm finished with my questions. The expression on her face suggests that she may have asked Joe the very same thing or Joe had commented the very idea when he asked Anna to deliver it. Anna opens her mouth briefly as if to respond, but then takes another sip of tea instead. Her omission of a verbal response answers my inquiry. Joe was afraid that I would refuse the gift. But why? Not wanting to continue the awkward silence between us, I change the topic our conversation in the hopes to get to know Anna better — where she grew up, when she moved to the States, if she has any family.

Anna and I chat for a few more minutes before she needs to leave. I mention that she is welcome anytime, whether she is sent by Joe or comes of her on accord. She comments that she would like to see me more as well, especially at Mr. Joseph's. Her words captures my attention immediately. Does she know something I don't?

I can feel the box watching me as if it has eyes. No matter what room I am in, I can feel its hot, laser beam burning a hole into my brain while it repeats, open me. The thought that Joe might have placed a recording device in or on it to spy on me comes to mind. I wouldn't put it past him. Anxiety about the possibility becomes grueling enough that I gently lift the box to inspect it. Surprisingly, the box is not very heavy. Thorough inspection reveals that there is definitely nothing on the outside. The inside is another question since I still won't open it. I elect to shake it, but that doesn't expose any clues.

By the time I take Sadie out for her after dinner ritual, I still haven't opened the box. I can feel it watching me like a hawk even as we are out at the park. Jared texts about Hawaii and I refrain from mentioning the gift. There's no hint in his words that he even knows I have it which is comforting.

Back in my apartment, I jump on the rebounder again to try to reduce the stress about Joe's gift. Thirty minutes later, I am only slightly drained and starving. I make myself a salad with some soup, and eat at the breakfast bar while glaring at the box from across the room. After two scoops of salted caramel ice cream, I opt to take a lavender and tea tree oil Epson salt bath.

Toying with the idea to just open the box, ripping it off like a bandaid, I carry it into the bedroom and place it on the edge of my bed. Once the bathtub is ready, I undress, light some candles, and put on some meditation music before slipping into the sensuous water — so much for ripping off the bandaid. The bath helps to calm me, but not as fast as I'd like. I masturbate until I have two toe curling orgasms which seem to have a marginal affect since I was thinking of Joe the whole time.

Just as my breathing normalizes, the music temporarily cuts off; I'm getting a call. Not looking at who it could be, and assuming it is either Maggie, Jared or Nathan, I immediately answer, pressing the button on the headset. "Hello," I cheerfully greet.

"Hello, beautiful," the voice rings on the other end.

Crap. It's Joe.

"Hey," I say with a shaky tone.

Chapter Twenty

"You weren't expecting it to be me, were you?"

I can hear the smile in his words.

"Yeah," I meekly reply.

"Were you expecting me to be someone else and that's why you didn't check?"

How did he know I didn't check? It is true, but still.

"Yeah," I sheepishly agree. Getting my gumption I tease, "I was expecting some other hot, rich guy to call."

"So you do think I'm hot?" he enthusiastically confirms.

Deciding to go with it, I reply, "You aren't that bad on the eyes."

A deep, hearty laugh from him immediately follows. Two seconds later, I hear a faint voice in the background saying what sounds like *Who thinks you're hot?*.

"None of your business," Joe declares to the other person.

"Who was that?"

"Jimmy," he informs.

A nervous laugh escapes my lips. Not sure how to bounce back, I stay quiet, waiting for him to talk.

"How are you feeling?"

"Good," I truthfully answer.

"You sound better."

"I feel better."

"So..." Joe begins. "I take it you haven't opened your gift yet?" he questions.

"What makes you say that?" I contend.

Maybe his response will give me an idea of what's in it.

"The way you're talking to me and haven't said anything yet," he states, sure of his speculation.

"Maybe I have," I dispute.

Laughing, he mutters, "You haven't."

Neither one of us say anything for a few beats. I'm guessing he's waiting for me, but I refuse to give in.

Finally, he starts, "So, why haven't you opened it?"

"Don't know," I say trying to brush it off. "Did you buy me something?"

"Maybe I did. Guess you'll see when you open it," he taunts.

Joe's clearly not going to give me any clues.

"Why don't you open it now?" he presses.

"Because I'm busy," I reply, trying to dissuade any notion that I'm that curious.

"Doing what? You're not too busy to be talking to me," he challenges.

"Just busy," I maintain, trying to keep my cool.

He chuckles.

"What's so funny?"

"Nothing," he expresses, followed by more laughter.

"What?" I argue. I'm not sure what I said that was at all funny.

"I just had a few possibilities of what you could be doing pop into my head," he mischievously announces.

What could he think that I am doing? My dirty mind wakes up.

"No! God, no! I've been busy since Anna dropped it off," I sternly protest while trying to cover for the fact that I have masturbated three times today, and the last time was literally just before he called.

"Then, what?" he searches. "What are you doing right now that you're too busy to open it but not too busy to talk to me?"

Choosing to lie, I reply, "Reading."

"I know you're lying," he disputes in a firm but playful manner. "You can't read and talk to me at the same time."

"Working on the new Raven software. Looks like Raven 1.0 will be finished and ready for the first round of testing in August," I lie again, trying divert our attention.

"Wonderful," he comments. "I can't wait to try it. Any more thoughts about the server and security expansion?"

"Not yet. I'm still thinking about it, weighing my options," I explain.

"Makes sense," he returns. "So what are you doing?"

Shit. Okay, Emma. Just tell him the truth. It'll just be worse if you keep trying to change the subject or lying and he keeps catching you.

Taking a deep breathe in and wincing, I reveal, "Taking a bath."

There is not a single sound coming from Joe's end of the phone. I swear it takes at least a full sixty seconds before I hear him clear his throat.

With a shaky voice, he says, "Umm . . . really?!"

I'm flattered by his response for some reason and all I can do is mumble, "Mmm hmm."

He clears his throat, but his voice trembles, "Were you thinking of me?"

My mouth becomes dry and it takes me a second to answer. "No . . ." my voice shakes.

Chapter Twenty

"I don't believe you," Joe expresses as his voice cracks.

"I wasn't . . ." I contend.

"Mmm hmm . . ." he hums into my ear. "Yeah, you were. Deny it all you want to yourself, but I can hear it in your voice."

"I don't know what you are talking about," I deny.

"Yes you do. I'm flattered. What were you doing when you were thinking about me?"

"Even if I did, I wouldn't tell you," I declare.

"Please," he sinfully begs.

Did our innocent and friendly conversation just go there? It did. I'm even more confused from the date, this past weekend and now this phone call. Yet, I'm so freaking horny. I need to redirect the topic now.

"Hold on a second. Okay?" I ask.

"Why?"

"I need to get out of the tub," I blurt.

"Should I come over?"

"Why?"

"To offer my assistance, just in case," he teases with a laugh.

"I don't need help," I jab.

"You sure?" he seeks.

"Yes." I purposefully make him wait ten extra seconds after hearing his remark. "I'm back."

"Now you can open it."

Pinching the bridge to my nose, I press, "Why did you get me something?"

"Because it made me think of you," he nonchalantly admits.

"You didn't have to get me anything," I voice, still unnerved by the idea.

"I know, but I wanted to. Not because you got me something, but because, like I said, it made me think of you," he charmingly declares.

"I didn't get you . . . oh," the realization sets in.

I did get him something.

"It was just a book."

"The sentiment is still the same," he replies. "Shoot. I'm sorry I need to go," he comments abruptly, snapping my attention back to reality.

"What? Oh, okay," I say surprised at the sudden change in his voice.

"Please open it, Emma," he timidly pleas.

"Okay," I awkwardly agree.

"Goodbye," he rushes.

"Fare . . ." I return just before the phone cuts the connection.

My heart sinks missing the term of endearment that has always ended his farewells of late.

Once off the phone with Joe, I brush my hair, rub on some organic coconut oil and put on my silk robe before returning to the gift. Sitting next to the box with one leg bent up on the bed and the other dangling off the edge, I carefully untie the ribbon and lift the lid, letting it slide off on its own. With scrupulous precision, I peel back each fold of the white tissue paper. I can see hints of blue as the last sheet of paper unfolds. Holy crap, it's one of Nathan's dresses that I wore yesterday during our little fashion show.

Luscious memories of the soft muted blue silk hugging my skin returns, taking my attention away from the note that rests on top of it. This was my favorite dress to put on. It's still as gorgeous as I remember it with it's plunging v-neck and spaghetti straps that hug and fit perfectly to my body as it accentuates every one of my curves.

My focus gets pulled to the hand written note I suddenly realize I'm holding. It reads;

Hope to see you wearing this in Hawaii.

xoxo Joe

Why did he buy this for me? How did he get it without anyone noticing? I can't accept a gift like this. It costs way too much compared to a little book.

I place the note on my dresser and hang the dress on my closet door. I put on pajamas and scoop out a few more helpings of ice cream. Turning on a movie to distract myself, my mind wanders back to the dress and the note. Mixed emotions tornado through me for the rest of the night. Laying in bed next to Sadie trying to sleep, I stare at the ceiling. My heart pounds with elation and edginess. I've never had a guy buy me something. Okay, a guy who isn't Jared or Nathan. Why did he do it? What does this mean? All I gave him was a book.

A loud, vibrating sound jolts me from my thoughts. What was that? The sound repeats itself again. Ohh, it's my phone. Picking it up off the nightstand, I check to see who would be calling me this late. Jared and Maggie never call at this hour. A picture of Joe's face consumes the entire screen from a picture I inadvertently took of him during one of our weekend trips. Shit.

Chapter Twenty

I let the phone ring another time before pressing the button to answer. Lacking a polite greeting, I blurt, "Why did you give me that?"

"Ah, so you finally opened it," he muses.

"You have to take it back," I demand.

"Why do I have to take it? It doesn't fit me," he needles.

"You know what I mean," I press.

"Aside from the fact that you looked simply radiant in it, you were positively glowing," he sensually states.

"That has nothing to do with it," I contend.

"What's the big deal," he questions.

"Why did you buy it for me?"

I'm really struggling to understand.

"Like I said, you looked beautiful in it . . . not that you don't look beautiful all the time. I wanted you to have it because of how it made you feel wearing it. I saw it in your eyes," he calmly replies.

"Ugh . . ." I let out on an exhale.

"You could just say thank you, enjoy the dress and wear it in Hawaii or whenever you feel like it."

"Fine," I whine.

"I'll take that as your thank you. You're welcome," he boasts at his victory. "At least I didn't give you that sexy bikini."

Did the thought of giving me the bikini cross his mind? A lump catches in my throat. That would have been completely embarrassing. I'm grateful that he chose the dress instead.

Not knowing what to say next, we both sit on the phone for a while just listening to each other breathing.

Unable to take the silence any further, I spout, "Why did you call me so late?"

"Because I knew you'd be up," he says.

Checking the clock on the phone, I notice he's right. It's only eleven thirty-eight.

"What are you still doing up?" I explore.

"I was debating on whether to call you back," he admits.

"Oh," I reply modestly.

How long was he thinking about calling me?

"Why?" I search.

"Because I figured you'd be mad at me once you opened your gift," he responds meekly.

"Oh."

His admittance catches me off guard. Did he really think I would be mad? I'm not really mad, just uncomfortable.

"I'm sorry," I offer.

"What are you apologizing for?"

"I don't know. I just . . . I just don't want you to think I'm mad."

"So, you aren't mad?" he checks.

"No," I assure. "I'm just really shocked at the gesture. I don't know what to make of it."

His husky chuckle returns. "You've gotten gifts before, haven't you?"

"I've given a lot, but I've never really gotten one before," I openly share.

"I'm sure Jared, Nathan, Maggie and her family have given you gifts," he urges.

"Yes, but that's different," I explain.

"How is that . . . ohh . . ." his voice trails. "So none of the guys you've been with have given you a gift?"

"I don't date remember," I remind.

"I'm sure you've seen some of the men a number of times which would have allowed for the opportunity," he mentions.

"Nope. My rules keep me at distance that don't allow for anything like that to happen," I comment.

Laughing again, he states, "You and your rules."

"Yep," I return.

"So what are they?" he pokes.

"Why do you want to know?" I peruse, confident that I won't tell him.

"Just in case I can convince you to break one or two," he goads.

"None of your business," I press back.

"That's fine," he says unfazed. "I have other sources who will tell me, if they haven't already."

Dread soars through my veins. What does he mean by other sources? I know. Maggie, Jared or Nathan. What does he mean if they haven't already? Have they shared willingly whether he's asked or not?

Changing the subject, I offer, "I should probably let you go. It's late and you have work in the morning."

Chapter Twenty

"Are you trying to get rid of me?" he confronts.

"No," I oppose.

"You remember that I'm the boss and make my own schedule, right?" he teases more than reminds.

"Yeah. I know," I affirm.

I don't know what to say and I don't necessarily want to let him go. I wonder if he's thinking the same thing.

"I'll let you go. I'll see you Thursday," he says after a while.

"Thursday," I repeat.

"Goodnight, beautiful. Sweet dreams."

"Goodnight, Joe."

Twenty One

The past few days have been met with glorious, chaotic frenzy. I haven't been tremendously busy with work tasks that need to be done, but to help pass time and take the edge off of the anticipation of Hawaii, I've invented new ones, especially by coming up with more functionality and options for the Raven 1.0 software. I went rebounding on Tuesday and Wednesday at the trampoline facility in Glendale on top of going last Sunday with my friends. Maggie and I took a trip on Monday to some of the outlet shops to do some pre-vacation wardrobe hunting. It was nice to spend half the day with Maggie without any boys tagging along. I also lined up with a lunar hair chart for her and I to get our legs and bikini area waxed and eyebrows threaded later the same day.

Last night, Maggie and Henry stayed at Joe's to make it easier to leave. I decided to sleep at home to be safe, but joined them all for dinner at Joe's. Anna cooked a wonderful meal.

Luckily, I'm a very punctual woman, so I'm ready and waiting by the time Maggie uses her key to my apartment fifteen minutes early Thursday morning. I'm greeted by Maggie, Henry and Joe, all offering to assist with my bags while Jimmy and Allen wait in the limo. I have my bags in the small foyer area which thankfully restricts how far everyone comes in. A confident smile graces Joe's face as he passes the threshold. Ignoring his blatant victory expression meant only for me, I indicate which bags are going with us and Sadie.

We pull into a private facility in Van Nuys and are dropped off right in front of a plane. Everyone follows Jimmy and Allen up the ladder and into the monstrous vehicle as I gape in wonderment. Joe pulls my arm, guiding me to the stairs. Looking back over my shoulder, I see Anna and the driver taking all of the luggage from the trunk as the crew delicately grabs each bag and places it in the undercarriage of the plane. I'm glad to know that I packed a few items in my large purse just in case.

Joe gestures for me take the steep stairway first. I contemplate on whether he's being a gentleman, wanting to get a view up my dress or both — I'm flattered either way. I signal for Sadie to head up first and I'm right behind her. At the top of the stairs, I freeze in amazement, causing Joe bump into me.

"Sorry," I offer.

"You okay?"

"Yeah, just soaking it all in."

I've seen photos of luxury, private jets, but to see it in person has a completely different effect on the mind and body. The plush, executive interior is alluring and seductive. Anyone could easily get spoiled with this kind of flying.

Walking in, I find a four person couch lining the front, left side and across from it are four reclining chairs paired on either side of a table. Behind the second set of chairs is a small counter with glasses in a cabinet above and drinks tucked inside a cubby superseding another table and chairs that seats six. I place my purse down on the counter not sure where I might sit; everyone is standing and talking.

Getting ready for take off, Maggie and Henry sit at the front table and the rest of us get situated at the rear table. Grabbing my purse, Joe hands it to me as he offers me the window seat. He sits next to me with Allen to his left, Jimmy in front of Allen, Jared across from me and Nathan in the middle of Jimmy and Jared. Sadie squirms under the table and rests between my feet with her head on my lap.

"You going to buckle up," Joe interrupts my train of panicked thought as I watch the crew outside the plane.

"What?"

"It's Emma's first time flying," Jared announces, causing my cheeks to warm.

"Here," Joe says, reaching over me to grab the strap before snapping it on the left side.

The luscious scent of Joe fills my nose, calming and exciting me all at once.

"Thanks."

"How are you holding up, Emma?" Jared inquires, reaching and offering his hand.

"I"m okay," my voice cracks.

"You'll be fine once we take off," he assures.

"You're safer in a plane than a car, you know," Joe adds.

"Mmm hmm," I hum unconvincingly.

As the plane taxis, I grip the armrests with my left hand and squeeze Jared's with my other as I watch out the window. I do my best to minimize my anxiety as the guys gab freely. As the massive contraption hurls down the runway, my heart pounds thunderously in my chest and sweat forms in the palms of my hands. At some pint, I feel a warm sensation discretely wrap around my cold left hand. My eyes dart to the all of the men around me to see if they notice Joe's hand on mine. They're thankfully distracted by their lively conversation.

Chapter Twenty One

I release the death grip my hand has on the armrest, turn it, and interlace my fingers with Joe's as he extends our hands further under the table to prevent us from being caught.

Once the plane reaches its required altitude, Jared and Joe let go of my hands. I watch Joe unbuckle his belt and then mine, promising me that it's safe. For the rest of the journey, everyone floats throughout the cabin chatting to help pass the time. I don't move other than to get up and use the restroom. I sit, read or work on my computer unless someone comes over to talk to me. Most of the time, either Jared, Nathan or Joe stay with me at the table other than Sadie who doesn't leave my side.

Lunch is served a few hours into our flight and everyone gathers around the back table so we can all dine together. Jimmy and Allen share a seat, one on top of the other's lap, to allow Maggie and Henry to join us. Anna serves a variety of bitesize sandwiches, fruit and iced tea. I make a point to try each food choice and they are all delicious.

We land in Hawaii just after two West Coast time which is eleven Hawaiian-Aleutian Standard Time. Three pearl white Teslas are waiting for us as we exit the plane. My knees tremble with excitement as the solid reassurance of land is under them again.

I enjoyed flying. It didn't remind me of anything like that of being in a car. I'll definitely have to start traveling more by plane.

Upon entering the Four Season's Resort in Maui, everyone is greeted warmly and given leis. Our bags are taken to our suites as we are checked in. Henry, Maggie, Jared and Nathan are registered to the Maile Presidential Suite while Jimmy, Allen, Joe and myself are registered for the Lokelani Presidential Suite.

Entering the suite with Joe, Jimmy and Allen, I instantly know that Henry has paid way too much for our accommodations alone. I nonchalantly check pricing with my phone as I pretend to marvel at the exquisite space — everything that my eyes fall upon is gorgeous. At a minimum of four thousand dollars a night, the Lokelani Presidential Suite can easily sleep eight adults with it's over six thousand square feet, three bedrooms, private first floor gardens, three full baths, two three-quarters baths, a kitchenette, living room, dining area, and media room. There are a variety of amenities that come with our room, but the idea of the price for two suites for five nights is astronomical. I can easily afford the trip myself, money isn't the challenge. It's the fact that Henry insisted on covering the majority of our expenses; that is the challenge for me. It makes me very uncomfortable and I need to figure out either how to accept it or how to pay my share.

Breathe In

Joe comments at some point during our tour of the suite.

"Huh?" I question since my attention has been primarily on the Four Season's website. "Oh, yeah. Thanks."

"You didn't hear a word I said, did you?" He steps closer and takes my phone, slipping it into my bag.

"This is my room. I heard you," I repeat.

The bellmen brings all of my bags right into the room and Alika, our private concierge, offers to hang all of my clothing. I politely decline. I'm a little weirded out at the idea of a stranger, let alone a straight man, riffling through my bags and handle my garments. The thought of Joe even doing it bothers me.

Alika takes Joe and me on a tour of the rest of the suite, directing our attention to a variety of indoor and outdoor options. He also mentions that he's happy to assist us with any of our needs during our entire stay. Alika shows me how to prop the sliding glass doors open from my room to allow Sadie to have access to the outdoors at any time she is in the room. He also mentions that he and several other staff will check in our suite from time to time to make sure that all of our and Sadie's needs are meet, including dog clean up.

Joe's and my rooms are side by side and each has their own full private bathroom; mine is connected to my room, but Joe's is just across the hall from his door. My room has two sliding glass doors on the far right corner, which I make note of, for when I'll need privacy for changing and for Sadie to have easy access to the private yard. Jimmy and Allen have the master bedroom which is all the way on the other side of the suite — all the better to reduce the sound of any hanky-panky. The majority of our suite's rooms have one hundred and eighty-degree ocean-front views.

Joe shouts from the living room to Jimmy and Allen, "You guys coming with us?"

"Go without us," a faint voice replies.

I'm not sure who it was, but I definitely know what they are doing.

Joe, Sadie and I head out of our suite to check in with the rest of our group who are staying in the Maile Presidential Suite which is on the top floor. Maggie is buzzing when we enter and she shows me around the suite. They have the same ocean-front view as us, but their's is from the top of the building in the penthouse. I know why Henry and Maggie gave us the lower level — to give Sadie room to run around if she's stuck in the suite for any length of time and I appreciate their consideration. The layout of the Maile Suite is very similar to ours, however, the decor is very different. A bit more modern luxury style where ours is a contemporary luxury feel.

Chapter Twenty One

Minus Jimmy and Allen, my friends and I head out to walk around the grounds of the hotel before deciding on changing into our swimsuits and lounging at the pools. Within fifteen minutes, the six of us, plus Sadie are at the Serenity Pool that has designated cabanas just for our use during our stay. The staff willingly show us the cabanas' amenities which include a television, wi-fi, mini fridge, couches and ceiling fans. Maggie and Henry are already in the water and ordering drinks from the swim-up bar with Jared and Nathan just behind them. I order a drink for myself and Sadie from our waitress before she turns and takes Joe's order.

Alika, our concierge, and Kahoni, the other suite's concierge, check on us after a while and to see if there are any services or amenities we'd like to book. We schedule a group luau dinner for tonight, and a morning of hiking at the waterfalls tomorrow. Other than dinners, I doubt that we'll all be getting together for excursions each day.

About an hour after being at the pool, Jimmy and Allen join us. With everyone a little hungry, we order some food to eat to tide us over until dinner. We drink. We eat. We swim and we laugh. Some of us nap in between in cabanas or the sun.

Knowing that we'll be hanging out together the majority of the time, Joe and I start to determine which activities we'd like to definitely do while in Maui.

"I definitely want to do a helicopter tour," Joe mentions.

"You do that," I reply, not sure about being back in the air so quickly.

"Come on . . . it won't be as fun without you," he encourages.

I mull over the thought. Once we were up in the air on the plane, I actually didn't mind it. "Okay, if you agree to go zip-lining," I add.

"Sure," he agrees. "We should see if it's still whale migration season."

"You want to go whale watching?" I muse.

No man admits that he's into whale watching openly.

"Yeah. I love sailing. It won't be as private as our family yacht or sailboat, but it's just the same."

"Okay," I agree willingly. "Wait. Your family has a yacht and a sailboat?"

"Yes. Why?"

"Could they not choose between the two so they figured they'd buy both," I mock.

"Something like that," he replies, poking me in my side.

"We all should do the couple's spa package," Maggie adds, coming over.

"Only one small challenge with that, Mags," I protest.

"What?" she innocently questions.

"Joe and I aren't a couple," I remind.

"So . . ." she pushes.

"So . . . you're completely naked during those types of massages other than a towel that gets moved around and you massage each other," I inform her.

"Oh, really?" She ponders the idea. "So. You're practically naked now. It's like the same thing."

"It's not the same thing," I argue.

"Yes it is," she rebuts. "Besides, Joe wouldn't mind. Would you Joe?"

"No comment," he says blushing.

Maggie walks away and joins Henry on a lounge chair. I watch Joe's face and I see him raise an eyebrow at me, as if hoping I will consider the option. I just shake my head in contention. Currently seeing as much naked flesh of Joe Covelli is enough of a distraction. Sunglasses easily hide any gawking I may have been doing or continue to do while lounging.

Around four, we head to our suites to start getting ready for dinner. I order some food from Alika specifically for Sadie and he is quick to appease while taking notes on what to expect for future breakfasts and dinners. After Sadie is fed, I jump into the overly large and elegant marble bathroom to shower. Since I left the bedroom door and one of the sliding glass doors open, I consciously close the bathroom door for privacy. I don't need to suddenly have a naked Joe coming to join me — I wouldn't put it past him to try.

Stepping out into the living room, I'm met by six handsome men, four wearing different styles of light grey dress suits with crisp white shirts and Jared and Nathan who are wearing khaki color suits and crisp white shirts. Maggie looks magnificent in a silk red and white floral dress. They all, gape when I come out.

"What?" I question, checking myself to make sure nothing is out of place. I instantly blush not knowing what's causing their reaction until I process what I am wearing.

Jared walks over to me first. "You look exceptionally lovely."

"I didn't know you bought the dress," Nathan remarks, jumping up and down hugging me.

"Uh, yeah. I wanted it to be a surprise," I return as my blush deepens.

I knew that if I didn't wear Nathan's dress, the one that Joe bought for me, I would never hear the end of it from Joe about why I didn't put it on, even

Chapter Twenty One

with it just being the first night. I do love the dress and the way that I feel in it. Joe shares a very pleased gleam in his eye while suppressing a smile at the fact that I'm wearing it.

We file out of the suite in pairs, with Joe and I last as we leave Sadie behind for a few hours. Piling into the Teslas that are free for our use with the suites, we drive out for dinner. It's luau time.

The setting, entertainment and food are marvelous at the luau. It's an experience that everyone should have at least once in their life. As the evening moves by and the entertainment is finished, all eight of us are up dancing and having fun. When a slow song starts playing, I rush to take my seat at the table. Five steps later, Joe is grabbing my hand and pulling me into him.

"What are you doing?"

"Dance with me," he requests.

"No."

Instead of arguing with me, Joe holds me tighter to his rock, hot body with his right hand as his left hand takes my right. "You look exquisite in that dress," he redirects.

"Thanks." I blush, enjoying the closeness of his body. "Some cute guy, I don't remember his name, bought it for me."

"Cute, huh?"

"I think so. I can't really remember," I tease.

We sway to the music effortlessly.

"I'm surprised," Joe begins.

"By what? That I'm wearing the dress?"

Chuckling, he explains, "No. But, thank you for that! You look even more beautiful under the moonlight wearing it."

After blushing more at his compliment, I'm able to ask, "Then, for what?"

"For someone who always like to have control, you're letting me lead the dance."

As I comprehend his words, my feet suddenly falter. "I'm sorry," I say after almost stepping on his toes.

"That's my fault. I shouldn't have said anything," he offers, taking the blame. He repositions us gracefully as if nothing happened.

"No, it's my fault," I disagree.

"No, no. It's mine. I shouldn't have said anything. You were doing very well," he insists, assuming responsibility. Within seconds, our step wavers again. "Now I'm distracted."

"Distracted? By what?" I ask.

He tentatively discloses into my ear, "I'm distracted by you."

Sweat gathers in my palms. Clearing my throat, I ponder what to say, but I'm left speechless. My eyes hesitantly meet his as the heat in my cheeks boils hotter.

His lips are seductively inviting, especially as he bites his lip trying to stifle a smirk. "The fact that all I want to do is kiss you right now. I'm tempted to do it, risking the chance of getting slapped," he admits freely.

My feet waver at his admission, but he flawlessly stabilizes me. I keep my head turned in the direct of our friends dancing for two reasons. One, to not give Joe the opportunity to kiss me in public, and two, to see if our friends are watching us. Thankfully, my friends are all consumed by their own partners. Relief temporarily settles in my heart, but something catches my attention just beyond the dance floor. My heart roars, my body becomes rigid, and I can feel all of the blood draining from my face.

"You okay?" Joe mutters.

I barely hear him.

"Emma? You okay?" a voice questions very slowly.

Shock engulfs me as I stand motionless. "I . . . I . . . need to use the ladies room," I fumble.

My chest aches with each shallow breath, gasping for air as I dart away from the dance floor. My vision blurs a little just before I make it to the farthest stall in the women's restroom. I'm not sure if anyone was following, but I don't care. Trembling, I press my hands to the walls to steady myself. Breathe, Emma. Breathe. My eyes were playing tricks on me. That's it. Breathe, Emma.

I hear a woman whoop, trailed by light scuffling and a man's voice. "It's okay Mama, I'm just looking for my sister, and don't worry I'm gay."

Two men's designer shoes appear at the base of the stall door, escorted by a light knock. "Emma?" Jared searches.

Sucking in some air, I confirm, "I'm . . . I'm okay."

"Will you let me in?"

"I . . . I just . . . need a minute," I claim, working on controlling my breathing.

"No one noticed, by the way," he offers sweetly. "Other than Joe, they all think you've been in here."

"Uh huh . . ." I affirm. My head is spinning and a tear or two trickle down my face.

Chapter Twenty One

"I locked the bathroom door, so no one else is coming in until we head out," he indicates. "It might not be good to let the door stay like that for too long. We wouldn't want to bring too much attention over here."

"Just a second . . ." my voice stutters. "I just . . . need . . . a second." Cautiously, I stand to make sure I'm not dizzy anymore. I take a deep breath in before unlocking the hinge.

"You okay, *Kitten*?" Jared says, studying my face.

"Mmm hmm," I testify but I still haven't convinced myself that I am.

He surrounds me with a careful bear hug. "Do you think you can make it out of here?"

"Yeah . . ." my voice shakes.

Laughing he says, "We'll you're hiding it well from your face already, but your voice says otherwise."

"Thanks," I muster.

There aren't any women waiting outside of the bathroom when we finally leave, which settles me more. Jared and I walk arm and arm over to our friends who are now sitting at the table chatting and drinking.

"Yay, you're back," Maggie beams. "Did Jared tell you?"

I bluff ignorance, "Tell me what?" I glance around the table.

The only two people who know about my lie are Joe and Jared.

Witnessing the sparkle, I know now that my eyes were not playing tricks on me.

"Henry proposed," Maggie gleams, extending her left hand over for me to see the enormous rock glistening on it as she jumps up and down.

At least ten karats, probably larger, my eyes are having trouble focusing, a rounded square, pink diamond rests in the middle of a vintage style band. Clear diamonds encompass the gem as well as the entire band wrapped around her tiny finger.

"Wow!" I gulp, keeping my eyes on the ring. "I'm so happy for you. Congratulations," I add with a forced smile, moving over to hug her and then Henry.

I immediately take my seat, feeling my legs buckling underneath me. Jared discretely takes my hand in his, dangling them between our seats. Everyone's attention goes back to Henry and Maggie as I process what happened. With my free hand, I reach for the glass of wine sitting in front of me. I chug it in two large gulps. On an exhale, I search for more. Right as he's reaching for it, I take Joe's glass and chug down the rest of his as well.

"Easy there lightweight," Joe mockingly suggests, loud enough only for me to hear as he takes the empty glass.

Our waiter brings over two bottles of champagne and new glass flutes to toast the occasion.

"To Maggie and Henry," Jared salutes, once the waiter has filled everyone's glasses.

Anxiety rises within me and my hand clenches down on Jared's.

"To Maggie and Henry," the rest of us repeat.

I down my glass of champagne discretely, only capturing Joe's attention.

"And to love," Nathan adds.

"To love," everyone repeats, except me.

I hold up my glass and pretend to drink.

"Tonight we celebrate, tomorrow I want details," Jimmy attests. "Let's get back to dancing!"

I try to sit down a few times, claiming that I'm tired, when really all I want to do is drink to numb the pain of officially losing one of my two best friends. Either Jared, Nathan or Joe drag me back out after I get a gulp or two of more wine. Joe is right, I am a light weight. I barely drink and when I do it's only a glass. The amount I'm drinking right now is a bit excessive. I'm right on the line of numbing the pain just enough, but almost too much where that line can blur and disappear, allowing the possibility of losing all of my inhibitions.

I dance with my friends but end up with Joe each time a slow song comes on. "How are you holding up?" Joe inquires holding me tight.

"Great," my mouth slurs a little. My nose takes a large whiff of him. "God, do you smell good."

A hearty laugh escapes his throat. "Careful, beautiful . . . you don't want to start anything you might regret," Joe sinfully replies.

"Mmm," I hum. "Is that a challenge?" I slide my left hand under his jacket and up his bulging chest. His right nipple hardens as my fingers graze over it several times.

Laughing again, he answers, "You have had too much."

"Maybe it's just enough," I suggest, placing my mouth closer to his bare skin.

"And, why is that?" he asks while trying to control his words.

"Enough to give you what you want." I press my hips into him.

"Now I know you definitely had too much," he whispers in my ear before kissing me on the cheek.

Chapter Twenty One

My mouth turns in the direction of his, wanting a taste. Joe keeps his mouth just far enough away as we stare into each others eyes.

"How we doing over here?" Jared questions behind my back.

"Fine," I offer, laughing into Joe's chest.

"I think it's time to go," Joe recommends.

"So, you are trying to sleep with me," I contend, snickering.

"Yep. Time to go," Jared confirms. He and Nathan dance away for a moment.

Twenty Two

"I can take her from here," Joe offers as he and Jared walk me to my room.

With a wicked grin, Jared states, "It's not her that I'm worried about."

"I'll be fine," Joe insists.

"You don't know what she's like when she's drunk," Jared argues. "She gets freakishly stronger."

"Stop talking about me like I'm not here," I slur in protest. "I'm not drunk, just a little buzzed."

The two of them stare and laugh.

Offended by their mockery of me, I demand, "Out! Out of my room!"

Jared turns and heads to my bathroom and comes back with a glass and something in his hand.

"Ooh, you're a good friend. You brought me more to drink," I confess. Taking a sip, I immediately spit it out. "What the hell is this?"

"Water," Jared comments.

"I take it back. You are not a good friend," I demand.

Joe muffles another laugh.

"Take these too," he offers, holding out his hand.

"I don't want them," I protest.

"Either you take them willingly, or . . ." he pushes.

I'm not in the mood to fight, and as much as I'll deny how drunk I am, I know that Jared would have the leg up if we did wrestle, especially with Joe to help him. I do get stronger with liquor, but not with this much in my system. Plus, I don't want to mess up my pretty dress. I like my dress and each time I remember that Joe gave it to me, I can't help but smile.

"Fine," I say, reaching out and popping the two black pills into my mouth, chasing them with the glass of water.

"She'll be fine now. If she drinks more, just feed her two more of these and extra water." He places the bottle down on the nightstand.

Jared takes the empty glass and fills it again, then hands me the glass. Despite my protest and desire for more liquor, I eagerly drink the water.

"Watch out for her," he adds. "She's sneaky."

"Got it," Joe replies.

"I love you." Jared hugs and kisses me on the cheek.

"Still not my favorite person right now," I comment with my arms crossed.

"I still love you anyway," he sweetly remarks, tugging at my heartstrings.

"Love you too," I mumble under my breath.

Joe walks Jared out while I work on unzipping my dress. Taking my shoes off, I head to the bathroom to use the mirror to see better. Yep, definitely more drunk that I thought. Eyeing my reflection, my pleased grin begins to change to a subdued sadness as the reality of tonight begins to sink into my heart. One of my two best friends is getting married. I'm happy for her, but my gut drops knowing that I've lost her. A tear runs down my cheek as I look away.

"You okay," Joe checks, walking towards me.

"Huh? Yeah. Good," I return, wiping the tear away.

"What's wrong?" he searches with concern.

"Nothing," I lie. "Umm, can you help me with the zipper?" I turn and move my hair out of the way.

"Sure." He gently lowers it with ease.

Our bodies hover close, not wanting to separate. He softly cups my chin and dries my cheeks from the tear stains. With the power of alcohol coursing through me, I kiss Joe. He returns the embrace before he unexpectedly pulls away. My eyes blink slowly as I try to comprehend what just happened.

"We should get you to bed," he directs.

"Okay," I quietly agree, pouting.

I suddenly feel frisky at the thought that he might want to fool around.

Incoherently, I take off my dress and hang it in the closet. Left with just a strapless bra and a matching lace thong, I search for pajamas. Retrieving light grey boy-shorts underwear and a matching tank top, I ungracefully change. Not caring about my hair and make-up, I turn to get under the covers. A giggle sneaks out of my mouth when I find Joe on the edge of the bed petting Sadie. I forgot he was in the room.

Amused by the thought, I tease, "Were you just watching me get dressed?"

"No," he contends, looking at me. He jerks his head away immediately.

"What's wrong?" I ask, gulping down the rest of the water in the glass on the nightstand.

Clearing his throat, he comments, "Nothing."

For some strange reason, I sit down on Joe's lap. "Are you mad at me?"

"No. God, no. Why would you think that?" he professes without hesitation. He brushes a few strands of hair off my shoulder.

Shifting, I straddle him, watching his express as he keeps his head turned to the side. I slide closer to him, but he firmly places his hands on my hips. "You look like your mad at me," I say with concern.

With a genuine smile, he looks at me. "I'm not mad at you."

My intoxication and physical desire for him urges me and my lips are suddenly embracing his. Joe doesn't fight and allows my lips and tongue to caress his. My hands slide down his shoulders to his top shirt button, and when the second button is loose, he pulls away.

"We should get you to bed," his gruff voice states.

I slide under the covers towards the middle of the bed as Sadie curls up next to me. Joe shifts the covers and then sits down. I pout when I realize that he's not joining me.

"What's wrong?"

"You aren't joining me?"

"Not tonight," he asserts.

I pout more, but it doesn't seem to phase him.

Laughing, he kisses me on the forehead. "Goodnight, beautiful."

"Goodnight, Joe."

Twenty Three

As I attempt to lift my heavy eyelids, I discover a hazy darkness surrounding me. Blinking slowly several times, my half-opened eyes won't focus to give me any clear indication of what's around me and where the blurry, flashing lights above are coming from. My body feels heavy. Still unable to open my eyes all the way, I perceive that I'm laying down somewhere. A cool dampness near my left cheek reveals itself as a slight gust of air brushes past my face. Sliding my right arm up the side of my body like a snake, my fingers creep to my lips. Drool — or, at least I hope so.

Two large and oddly shaped figures materialize in front of me. They are so close, only a foot or two away. Voices suddenly emanate from the now more defined silhouettes. Their speech sounds muffled and trails off into the distance even as I try to concentrate on their words. Who are they? What are they saying? Why can't I understand them? One of the voices almost sounds feminine.

Another indistinguishable sound gradually becomes more apparent as it grows louder and the ringing in my ears subsides. It's the engine of a car. My brain finally starts to put the fuzzy pieces of evidence together. I must have fallen asleep in the back seat. A familiar smell creeps into my nose that reassures me — my mother's perfume. When the one figure turns to look in my direction, I see Maggie staring back at me.

"Maggie?" my throat squeezes out in a raw, breathy, hoarse tone.

"Wake up, Emma." Her voice replies in a low sluggish tone.

What is she talking about? I am awake.

A sudden rush of nervousness enters my belly. The car feels like it's flying down the road like a rocket ship as the speed of the flashing lights zooming above my head all blur into one.

"Maggie," I shout, but not a single sound escapes my mouth this time.

"Wake up, Emma," she repeats, this time with a deeper tone.

Confused, I try again. "Maggie!"

She doesn't hear me. I don't hear me.

"Emma, wake up," the voice commands, getting louder.

A single, bright white light races towards us, growing larger by the second. Maggie turns her head towards me smiling, but her face is contorted. What's wrong with her face? Why doesn't she hear me? How does she not see the light?

Again, with all my might. "Maggie . . . .!" my voice trails in my head like a deafening siren, stabbing my ears like a knife.

Time stops in this very moment. I can see everything with sheer clarity as I stare in horror into Maggie's eyes. I can't move. My mouth is left open, still screaming without a sound. I can't hear anything besides a piercing ring that echoes in my brain.

My body lurches backward. "Wake up, Emma!" the voice beckons.

Gasping for air, my eyes fly open to darkness. Sadie is frantic on the bed and there is another body with us.

"Emma?"

My gaze turns in the direction of the husky sound and finds Joe.

"Emma, it's okay. It was just a dream."

Instinctually, I crawl onto his lap and wrap my arms around his neck. "Please don't tell Jared," I beg. "Please don't tell him."

Burying his face into my neck, he consoles, "No one will know."

As my nerves settle, my heart rate returns to a more natural pace. I relax my grip on his neck, but stay sitting on his lap. My fingers play with the edge of Joe's shirt as he tenderly wipes a couple of tears and kisses my cheeks. I consider a request before looking at him.

"Will you stay with me?"

"Of course, beautiful," he assures.

The immediate need to pee arises, forcing me to stagger to the bathroom, leaving Joe sitting on the bed with Sadie. When I return from the bathroom, Joe immediately picks me up, pulls down the covers, and slides us both into the bed. I lay on my back scratching Sadie's head that is now resting on my belly. Joe joins his hand with mine to comfort her and me. He gingerly kisses my temple twice. The sturdiness and heat of his body soothes the pain, beckoning sleep to fall up me quickly.

Twenty Four

The sound of sniffing in my ear wakes me from a hazy slumber. Avoiding Sadie, I curl into Joe's body and nuzzle into his neck. I'm not freaked out by his presence in the bed, but I slide my hand over our bodies to make sure we're fully clothed. I'm not sure how he ended up here with me.

"Good morning, beautiful," he hums. "What are you doing?"

My hand freezes half way down the side of his body and rests on his hip. "Good morning," I return hoarsely. "Checking to see if we're naked."

"Why would we be naked?"

"I don't know. How did you end up in my bed?"

I wrack my brain trying to figure out what happened last night. I vaguely recollect asking him to stay.

"You don't remember?" he teases.

"Kind of," I affirm.

"What do you remember?"

"Umm . . . I'm not sure."

My mouth is dry, my head is fuzzy, and I'm hoping that the image of Henry down on one knee isn't real.

"How are you feeling?" he searches.

"I feel fine. A little thirsty."

He hands me a glass of water from the nightstand and I gulp it down.

"You don't feel hungover?" his voice sounds shocked.

"Why would I be hung . . . ohh . . ." I begin to remember. "He did propose. Shit."

The memories are flooding back into my brain including the nightmare.

"How are you not hungover? I've never seen you drink that much," he admits with some concern.

The dispute with Jared over taking the pills comes to mind. "The bottle," I gesture. "One of the many benefits of activated charcoal."

"I'll have to remember that," he comments.

Wincing at not remembering much after Henry proposing until now, I question, "Did I do anything stupid while I was drinking?"

"You did a lot of things," he muses.

"Care to fill me in?"

I regret losing control over myself the way I did.

"Well . . ." he begins. "We didn't have sex, if that's what you're worried about."

Concerned, I check, "Did I have sex with anyone?"

"No," he confirms with a laugh.

I breathe a sigh of relief.

"You really don't remember."

"Bits and pieces, but I'm good not knowing anymore after finding out that I didn't have sex with anyone," I admit sheepishly.

"You hit on me," he announces.

My eyes widen as he laughs.

"And, you kissed me," he states.

"I may have hit on you, but I would remember kissing you," I argue.

"You were disappointed when I stopped the first kiss," he mentions with a grin.

"Now I know you're lying. You're the one always trying to kiss me," I contend.

"Yes, but I do have morals when it comes to kissing a woman who avoids kissing me when she's sober and plants several on me when she's as drunk as you were last night," he replies.

"I wasn't that drunk."

I know I was, but I'm trying to downplay it.

"You were drunk enough not to remember."

"Did anyone else see us kiss?"

"No."

"Then, I didn't kiss you and you have no proof," I declare.

He laughs, curling into me. "Deny it all you want, beautiful. I was sober and I know what happened."

I play with Sadie as Joe snuggles into me. Despite my sexual desire for him, my rules must not be broken. Fear of what could or may happen are just not an option, not after last night. I've got to be more careful.

My brain plays over all of the details that I can remember from yesterday. There are still too many foggy pieces. I don't trust that Joe will give me honest answers, or, he just might give me truthful answers that I don't want to hear. I'm not sure what to think.

Chapter Twenty Four

"I like this," he mentions.

"What?" I say confused by his statement since my attention has been elsewhere.

"Snuggling with you," he admits. "Can we do this every night?"

"No," I object.

As much as I enjoy snuggling with him, this cannot become a regular habit. I've been rationalizing it like I'm snuggling with Jared or Nathan, but that's not holding up well at all.

"Why not?"

"Because . . . I have rules and snuggling will just lead you on," I protest.

"Is snuggling one of your rules?"

"I thought you had sources who told you my rules," I sarcastically comment.

"I just wanted to see if you added any new ones," he teases.

His statement doesn't reveal whether or not he knows them.

"Why?"

"Because, if snuggling and kissing aren't on the list, then you shouldn't have a challenge doing either with me.

"They're definitely going on the list," I goad.

Without warning, Joe grabs my face and plants a deep, passionate kiss on my lips. I mildly protest as I secretly enjoy it. Joe breaks for a breath, giving me enough time to shift my head and stare at him in astonishment.

"What was that?" I search.

"Figured I should at least get one in if I might have to work extra hard to get them back off the list."

"I told you . . . just friends," I demand.

I'm secretly flattered by his bold move and chide myself for the dirty thoughts stirring inside.

"I would believe you, except the kiss you gave me last night says otherwise," he announces.

Sadie presses herself between us, indicating that she's getting restless and hungry. I'm able to slip out of the bed on the other side before venturing into the kitchenette to prep Sadie's food. Joe follows us and has trouble making eye contact. Looking down, I know why with my tiny pajamas. After gulping down some clay, I rinse out the glasses while Joe nuzzles into my neck.

"What are you doing?"

"Sneaking in every opportunity I can," he explains.

It takes all the control I have not to give in.

"I told you we can only be friends."

"The kiss you gave me last night suggested you want to be more than friends." Joe leans towards me like he's about to kiss me.

Pulling my head back, I state, "You mean the kiss you stopped last night?"

For the first time, Joe is rendered speechless.

"I need to take Sadie out."

Joe and I shower and change, separately of course, and then take Sadie out for a walk on the beach by six-thirty. Except for the hotel staff and a few locals, the resort and beach are empty. Everyone must still be sleeping.

By about seven, the three of us go to eat breakfast in one of the hotel restaurants. We relax in the patio dining area in the shade where there is only one other table occupied by guests, an elderly couple, who on their way out, stop to tell us that we make a lovely couple. The husband notices the lack of a ring on my finger and lectures Joe about sealing the deal when it comes to love. Yes, he uses the word love. I inform the gentleman that we are just friends and explain my lack of interest. He teases Joe that he must be doing something wrong if I'm not interested and he adds that he and his wife were friends before they got married and remain best friends. They've been happy for over forty years.

Back at our suite, I lounge in the sun while reading a book. Joe lays on the same couch in the opposite direction causing our legs to overlap. Sadie lays on the cool tile to my right and is close enough for my dropped arm to scratch her side.

Some time later, I wake in my room with Sadie on my left and Joe on my right. I must have fallen asleep in the sun and he brought me in. While scratching Sadie behind the ears, I study Joe's sleeping body. His right leg is draped over mine with his right hand cupping my waist just under the ridge of my shirt and his face is buried in the crook of my neck. It's much easier to snuggle with Joe when he's sleeping. There's a sense of innocence to him when he's resting.

I slip quietly out of the bed without disturbing Joe to use the restroom. Voices in the living room area catch my attention and I check to see who's awake.

"Good morning, sweetie," Jimmy sings.

"Good morning, sexy," Allen adds.

"Good morning." I smile sitting down. "Do we know if anyone else is up?"

"Nope," Jimmy confirms. "You hungry? We ordered plenty."

"I'm good, thanks. I ate around seven."

Chapter Twenty Four

"You are an early bird, just like Joe," Jimmy comments taking a bite of bacon. "Where is he?"

"Asleep, I think."

With a wicked grin, he harasses, "Did you have anything to do with the fact that he's sleeping?"

"What? No. We took Sadie out on the beach, had breakfast, and were reading out on the patio for a while," I explain calmly. "I'm going to get my phone and text Jared to see if anyone is awake upstairs."

"Wake Joe up before you come back, please," Jimmy directs. "I want to spend as much time as possible with my brother. He hasn't been home much," he discloses.

"You two are really close, huh?" I state more than question.

"Yes, we are," he confirms.

There's no direct line of sight from where Jimmy and Allen are sitting to my room, so I'm in the clear with needing to pretend to go to Joe's room to wake him up. I grab my phone out of my purse that sits on the dresser before heading over to Joe. He's in the same position that I left him and he looks so peaceful that I don't want to disturb him. How should I wake him? Will he wake easily?

I lightly run my hand from his should to his elbow several times and he wakes immediately.

"Hey, beautiful."

"Hey. I'm sorry to wake you."

Sitting up, he slides closer to me. "It's okay. How long have I been sleeping."

"Not long since I got up. Jimmy asked me to wake you. Says he wants to spend more time with his little brother," I explain.

He smiles at his brother's sentiment. "Is everyone up?"

"Not sure. I came to get my phone." I hold it up for him to see.

"So you weren't coming back to join me?" he pouts, moving closer.

"Joe."

"I know, just friends . . . for now." He delivers a quick kiss to my cheek, but doesn't pull away.

Not wanting to argue, I shake my head as I stand up, giving myself distance. He pulls me in for a hug before following me out to the living room.

Thirty minutes later, the eight of us and Sadie are driving to embark on an hour drive to the Northern East Coast of Maui to hike. The lengthy car ride to the national park is a little unnerving, but the breathtaking views make up for some of the agitation. We stop at one of the local shops for a few snacks and extra water to take with us. We hike on dirt, rock and wood paths and over a few bridges through a bamboo tropical forest. By the second serene waterfall, we decide to take a break and swim. Sadie jumps in and out of the water swimming with Maggie, Jimmy, Nathan and Allen, as Joe, Jared, Henry and I, the daredevils of our group, climb up the edge of the waterfall to jump in.

As the boys debate who gets to jump first, I fling my body off the rock that sits at least twenty feet above water level. I get an instant wedgie. Swimming out of the way, I join Maggie sitting on a protruding rock that is about ten feet away from the water's edge.

"Out jumped by a girl!" Jimmy shouts. "You boys should be ashamed of yourselves."

I smile at my triumph and his praise.

At some point, I slide back into the water and help Sadie up on the rock after watching her swim around it twice. Jared comes to visit and soak in the sun.

"How are you doing from last night?" Jared checks.

"Okay . . . hanging in there," I share.

"You drank a lot. You had me a little worried," he admits with concern in his tone. "You haven't drank like that in a long time."

"I know. Sorry. I'm okay. From what I remember, Joe was a gentleman. He took care of me," I offer.

"No dream?"

"Nope," I lie successfully.

"Good." he praises.

"Did I get bad?" I question tentatively.

I know he'll tell me the truth.

"No. What do you remember?"

"Not much after coming out of the bathroom with you," I admit.

"You're not losing her, you know," he encourages.

"Yeah," I disjointedly reply, not believing him.

"We're gaining a brother," he rationalizes. "And, perhaps over time, some nieces and nephews."

"Don't go there yet, please," I beg.

Laying my head on his shoulder, I search for some information that I'm not sure I want the answers to. "Can I ask you something?"

Chapter Twenty Four

"Of course, *Kitten*. What is it?"

"This stays between us," I command.

"Of course," he genuinely agrees. "Is something or did something happen between you and Joe?"

"What? No." I smoothly lie. "Why would you ask that?"

"It would be a natural, normal thing that could happen," he explains.

"Don't. Please don't," I plea.

Worry about starting this conversation has fully erupted in me.

"Okay. Sorry. What is it?"

"I don't remember anything after we toasted to Henry and Maggie other than dancing," I quietly announce scrunching my face.

"We all danced. You stayed a bit away from Maggie and Henry, but we all did for the most part. They were in their own little world by that point. When we left, you road with Nathan, Joe and me. Joe and I took you back to your room and Joe offered to assist you if you needed it. I knew you'd be fine after taking the charcoal. That shit works pretty good on you," he describes.

"So I didn't say or do anything out of the ordinary?" I check.

He thinks. "Not really. I know you and Joe joke around a lot and you did a bit before we left as well as in the car ride back."

"What made us leave?"

He laughs. "You and Joe were joking and you dogged him, claiming that he was trying to sleep with you."

"Sounds about right," I agree.

"Was he trying?"

"I don't remember, honestly."

Jared doesn't need to know the real truth behind that statement, or else I'll need to be explaining a lot of things, which I'm not interested in doing.

"Anything else you need to know, *Kitten*?"

Uncomfortably, I mutter, "Joe claims that I kissed him."

"What?!" he gasps loudly, forcing me to punch him. "Ow. Sorry. I deserved that. So, did you?"

"I don't know," I report truthfully.

"Well, he's a handsome man . . . has the hots for you, and it has been a while for you since, you know," he nonchalantly comments. "Too bad."

"Too bad, what?"

"Too bad you don't remember. Maybe you can get some action out of the situation regardless," he teases.

"No. Hell no. You know my rules," I sternly press.

"Yeah, yeah. I know." Jared wraps his arm around me, holding me tight. "That doesn't get rid of the most likely possibility that he actually does like you more than we think and that he might try at some point. What's not to like with a woman like you? You're smart, beautiful, funny . . . you love to do things and make your own money."

I shake my head, opposing his statement to end the discussion. Jared chuckles at my expense.

We continue hiking and exploring for the rest of the afternoon enjoying the sights, sounds and peace. With our bellies grumbling, we elect to find somewhere to feast. One of the locals recommends a restaurant called Mama's Fish House which is on our way back to the hotel.

Maui's first fresh fish restaurant, Mama's Fish House is nestled in a coconut grove on a secluded white beach. The building emulates old Polynesian style from the wood floor and walls as well as the original artwork that hangs inside. Jimmy's and Allen's faces beam with excitement for the art and inquire of the waitstaff for more information. Looks like they might be bringing some Hawaiian flair to their art gallery back in New York.

Everyone orders something different for appetizers and entrees so we can each have a bite of the fresh delicacies. The chef was pleasantly amenable to create a fresh, uncooked plate for Sadie.

Laughter and jokes swell from our table and out past the outdoor porch, where we're sitting in the quaint restaurant. Nothing like great food and great people to celebrate a wonderful vacation as the sun begins to set.

"So . . ." Jimmy strikes conversation back up after we've all had a few mouthfuls of our entrees. "I want to know wedding details!"

The pit of my stomach twists and my appetite vanishes instantaneously. I lower my fork to my plate and swallow a large gulp of my Ulupalakua Framboise Raspberry Wine that was made right here in Maui. The day was going so well until now.

"Yeah! Do you know who your bridesmaids will be?" Allen eagerly adds.

"Well, Emma as maid of honor, of course," Maggie immediately announces.

My eyes widen and I try to smile my excitement for being named the maid of honor and the fact that we're talking about Maggie's wedding already.

"Then Jared, Nathan, Amy and Kim," Maggie continues.

"Who's Amy and Kim," Jimmy questions.

"My cousins."

"You sure that will work?" Nathan questions.

"Why?" Maggie asks.

"Most people aren't used to seeing men as bridesmaids," explains Jared. "I'm happy to do it because I love you, but people might give some odd reactions when they see Nathan and me standing on your side."

"So. It's my wedding, not theirs. If they don't like it, then they don't have to come," Maggie asserts.

Everyone laughs at her honest declaration.

"Anything to make my sister happy!" Jared chimes in.

"Is Jared really your brother?" Allen explores.

"Emma and Jared are family. We aren't blood, but that doesn't make them any less family in my eyes. They've been my family for the last eight and a half years," Maggie explains.

Jared and I blush at her announcement. I love Maggie and the genuine relationship she's shared with Jared and me. That's what makes her getting married so hard for me.

"Who's the best man, Henry?" Jimmy pries.

"Joe, of course," he says without hesitation. "He's like a brother."

"Well, that pairing works with Emma being maid of honor," Jimmy points out. "But, you'll need to consider who the next two will be given that they'll be paired with Jared and Nathan. If they aren't gay, you'll need two heterosexual men who are completely comfortable with their own sexuality and won't mind escorting them."

"Well, since I don't have any brothers and I hardly see any of my cousins to be close to them like Maggie is with her's, I guess then next in line could be you and Allen," Henry states.

"Seriously! Oh my God!" Jimmy shouts. "This is going to be the best wedding ever!"

"Have you guys picked a location or date yet?" Allen continues.

"Shit guys, they just got engaged last night. I think they need some time to talk about it," I pronounce before taking another large sip of my wine and completely emptying the glass.

"Maggie does have her wedding binder. Remember, Emma?" Nathan reminds.

Crap. I almost forgot all about her picture binder.

Breathe In

Since she was sixteen, Maggie has had visions of grandeur when it comes to planning her wedding day. The weekend after we popped each other's cherries, she showed it to me. Then a small book, now a three ring binder full of years worth of photos and ideas of her ideal wedding with everything planned down to the last detail, minus the date and the groom. The groom changed each time she dated a guy or had a crush on a movie star. I know that Henry's face is now tapped on the shoulders of the groom's body she has next to her's in a mock wedding photo.

"A what?" Jimmy inquires.

"She's basically been planning her wedding since before Emma and I meet her," Jared informs. "The only two things that were always tentative was the wedding date and the actual groom. If she wanted too, she could have her entire wedding in two or three months given that at least one of her desired venues has an opening."

"That's a great idea!" Henry comments.

"What is, honey?" Maggie questions.

"Let's get married at the end of the summer, in the beginning of August, before my last year of MBA classes begin. We can take a short honeymoon and then an extended one during the winter season."

My eyes glaze over at Henry's words. What the hell? Is he really serious? I know he has the money to pull it off. There's no doubt there. Can Maggie handle that? Can their families handle that? Can I handle that?

"Here," Jared offers handing me his glass.

"Thanks," I mutter, then finish the last half of his Mai Tai.

Shock consumes me and lingers through the rest of dinner. I have trouble focusing on comments regarding wedding things so I simply nod in agreement to anything Maggie directs my way. Jared whispers that he's taking mental notes and will fill me in when I'm in a better state. I nod appreciatively as I stuff my face with food since there is nothing left to drink other than water.

My anxiety lessens when the waitress returns with another glass of wine for me. I instruct her to bring another one in exactly ten minutes. Without judgment, she smiles and agrees. I continue to stuff my face and drink until I literally have no room left.

On the rest of the drive back to the hotel, I'm grateful not to be in the same vehicle as Maggie and Henry. Jared and Nathan joined them to assist with my needed distance until my mind settles and can accept and move forward with the events that have taken place the past two nights.

Instinctually while driving, Joe takes my hand to comfort me.

Chapter Twenty Four

"Oh my God. I knew it," Jimmy blurts. "I knew something was going on between the two of you."

"It's not what you think," Joe firmly comments in a serious tone.

"Yes there is. Why else would you be holding her hand?" Jimmy contends.

His words snap my attention back to reality and I instantly pull my hand away.

Joe reaches over and takes my hand before replying, "Emma has trouble being in cars."

"What kind of trouble?" Jimmy gently presses.

"The bad kind," Joe informs with a stern tone.

Joe's defensiveness surprises me, especially since it's directed towards his brother. I'm surprised he has never mentioned my issue with cars to Jimmy, especially after having the nightmare at his home just before we came here.

Not liking the tension I have caused and how long it's lingering in the car, I share. "My parents died in a car accident."

"Oh my . . . I'm sorry, Emma," Jimmy apologies.

"Me too. We didn't know. Joe didn't tell us," Allen sheepishly adds.

"It's not my business to tell," Joe defends.

"It's okay," I assure all of them. "They didn't know and . . ." my voice trails off.

"It's okay, Emma. We understand," Jimmy consoles. He and Allen both reach forward and place their hands on my shoulders which helps.

Back in the suite, I opt to change into my swimsuit and head to the beach for an early evening swim. Even with all of the hiking, my body craves more strenuous activity to relax the tension and help me sleep. I plan on sleeping through the night — no more bad dreams. The guys from my suite join me, though Jimmy and Allen choose to get a few drinks at the bar first. As we settle at a casabella lounger on the beachwalk, Jared and Nathan join us too.

Peeling off my sweater and shorts, I braid my hair back and then run to the water. Sadie follows me, but quickly returns to the guys, too tired to swim out and join me. Sometime later, after enjoying the night swim alone, I head back to my friends. I curl up with Jared and Nathan on one of the extra long chairs as Joe, Jimmy and Allen sit side by side on the other facing us. We all talk and laugh as the night moves on until Jimmy and Allen turn in first. Jared and Nathan follow about twenty minutes later while Joe and I decide to wait a little before returning to our rooms. We're not interested in walk in seeing or hearing anything.

Breathe In

Once Jared and Nathan are out of sight, Joe slides over to my chair to snuggle. He claims it's to keep me warm because my hair is still wet. He adds that it's better to be sandwiched between him and Sadie than just Sadie alone. I disagree with his statement knowing his intentions, but I don't argue with him. There is a little, cool breeze and I'm grateful for the warmth of his body.

Soaking in the heat of each other's body, Joe starts to massage my shoulders. "I think we should schedule a massage after zip-lining tomorrow," he suggests.

"Why?"

"You're really tense." He presses harder on a knot and I moan out of pain and pleasure wrapped together. "See," he confirms.

"I won't need a masseuse at the rate you're going," I praise, not wanting him to stop.

"Careful, beautiful. Don't tempt me," he sinfully teases.

"What?" I innocently plea.

"You know what I mean."

Moving his hands, Joe finds another knot in my back causing me to whimper with delight.

What feels like ten minutes later, as his hands glide down to my lower back, my upper body is like putty and it curls back into his chest. Keeping my eyes shut, I relish his touch, not wanting it to end. Over time, my consciousness fades in and out as the sound and feel of his steady breathing and the ocean in my ear lulls me.

"Emma?" he whispers.

"Hmm," I breathe out.

He tilts my face closer to his. "Emma. You asleep?"

"Not yet. Soon," I mumble.

"Let's head inside."

"No," I whine.

"Why not?"

"Feels good," I acknowledge.

He chuckles lightly and wraps his arms around me tighter. "Five more minutes."

"Okay," my voice slurs.

I must have fallen asleep because my eyes fling open at the threat of being kissed again. "I'm up. I'm up," my voice retorts groggily.

Chapter Twenty Four

We return to a quiet and peaceful suite. Sadie passes out on my bed before I start getting ready to turn in for the night. My eyes flutter under the warm shower, informing me that mental and physical exhaustion are approaching. I quickly dry off, brush my teeth and dress as my body staggers to stay standing. Concern increases at the thought of repeating last night, so I get the gumption up to talk to Joe. His bedroom door is open, but I knock lightly to be sure I don't catch either of us off guard.

"It's open."

I take a reluctant step in.

"Hey," he says upon seeing me and puts his book down.

"Hey," I return.

"You okay?"

"Yeah . . ." I timidly reply.

"What's wrong?" The worry in his voice has risen. He gets up from the bed and takes a few steps towards me.

"Nothing . . . just . . . ."

How do I ask him?

"I was wondering . . . if . . ." my voice trails, searching for the right words to ask without sounding dumb. "Would you mind sleeping in there . . . or here . . . with me tonight?"

"Of course," he immediately agrees.

Leading me by the hand, Joe turns the light off in his room, closes the door and takes us both back to mine. Seeing a knocked out Sadie on my bed, Joe laughs and quietly shuts the door before turning off the lights.

We climb under the covers, snuggling right into each other.

"Thank you," I mention.

He brushes his knuckles across my cheek. "I'm here anytime you need me."

"I just don't want to lead . . ." his lips sweep across mine before I finish. My mouth seeks more of his. "Joe," I breathe in with our lips still touching.

He strokes my face again, "You don't ever have to worry about that." He lowers his mouth to mine again.

I'm too tired to fight. Mentally and physically, I'm wiped.

"Joe," I whimper again as the memory of me kissing him last night emerges.

"I know," he announces connecting his lips to mine. "Just friends."

I nod in agreement as we sweetly explore each other's mouth. Taking a breath, I repeat, "Just friends."

"Mmm hmm," he agrees, pulling me back into him.

We kiss a few more times as my body and mind are officially met with exhaustion.

Kissing my temple, he says, "Emma."

"Hmm," I mutter.

"Looks like I owe you a song on the piano."

"Mmm," I concur.

"Emma," he continues.

"Hmm . . . ."

"Goodnight, beautiful."

"Nigh' . . . " my voice trails into slumber.

Twenty Five

Waking up to a cool morning Spring breeze with the sweet scent of salt water is one of my favorite things. Rolling over, I notice that I'm completely alone in the room. Sounds coming from the patio draw my attention; I see Joe talking on the phone. I've seen Joe engage in this behavior quite a few times over the past three months, so I know it's a business call. He's had them on Saturdays and Sundays on occasion. Joe is casually pacing in the grass, stopping to pick up the ball and toss it for Sadie when she brings it over. I glance at the clock and notice it's just after six our time, which makes it nine in California and twelve on the East Coast. There are all types of possibilities to whom he's speaking with.

Joe and Sadie pop in on me in the kitchenette just as I finish preparing Sadie's breakfast and two glasses of clay. "Good morning, beautiful."

"Morning," I reply, drying my hands and then petting Sadie.

Finishing his drink first, Joe picks up Sadie's empty bowl and places it in the sink with his glass. Before I finish swallowing the last gulp, Joe sandwiches my body between his and the counter. He takes the glass from my hand, places it in the sink, and delivers a tender kiss that mirrors one we shared last night. I indulge him and reciprocate before removing my lips.

My phone chirps, interrupting Joe's attempt for a third smooch. Checking the screen, I see that Jared texted.

He wrote, "We're up . . . sort of. What time do we need to head out?"

"Within the next hour and a half. Let me know when you are ready to eat," I reply.

"Sure thing, *Kitten*," he answers, followed by a winking emoticon face and a heart.

Once in the shower, I realize that locking my bedroom door was pointless since both sliding glass doors are wide open. Good thing I at least locked the bathroom door since I decide to indulge myself with masturbation.

Joe and I meet up with Jared and Nathan by six forty-five for breakfast. By seven-twenty, we get in our designated car from the valet and head to the Northwestern shores of Maui for zip-lining. With bathing suits on and extra clothes packed, we embark on a four and a half hour long nine-line tour. We marvel at the beauty of the valleys and sugar cane fields that lead to the first line as our guides offer insight on the stunning Hawaiian landscape and culture. We travel along the double lines, racing each other as we zoom past the Pacific

Breathe In

Ocean, follow the trail to the natural pool for a zip-line splash and swim, and get to see the spectacular West Maui Mountains.

In the afternoon, Jimmy and Allen join Joe and me on a helicopter tour over the entire island. Being back in the air strangely didn't bother me when we took off. Soaring above the land, I realize that there's so much more to see and do in Maui. We only have all day tomorrow and Monday before we leave Tuesday morning, which is not enough time. I definitely need to come back again just to see the rest of this island and the rest of the land masses that make up all of Hawaii.

Getting back to the hotel, we find out that it's just the four of us for dinner. Henry scheduled a romantic dinner for him and Maggie, and Jared scheduled a couples massage and a meal for two in the suite. Since we don't need to rush and get ready, the four of us decide to take a short nap. Somehow Joe ends up in my bed with Sadie and me. He tries to kiss me again, but I skillfully avoid him. It's not that I don't want to kiss him. It's the very fact that I want to that concerns me, especially after last night and this morning.

I've kissed a lot of men, far many more than I've had sex with. None of the men I've only kissed held my interest long enough for me to want to take it any further with them. After the first kiss or two, a girl knows more about a guy than he realizes. The way he treats your mouth is a key indicator of his ability in bed. All of those whom I have had sex with were never able to satisfy me with an orgasm on their own — even the good kissers. I'd either have to rub myself with him inside of me, which many get offended by, or I'd just take care of myself at home. If Maggie was around, we'd take care of each other. I would say that there is a distinct home court advantage for women with other women.

The challenge I'm having with Joe is that I want to kiss him, which is odd because I've never wanted to keep kissing a man. Every time he kisses me, or I think about kissing him, my body wants more. I've tried going out to pick up a guy on my own since going to Ayana's with my friends, but none of the men are appealing to me. It's like my body doesn't want any other man until I test-drive Joe.

I'm not sure what I should do. I've tried to avoid him in the past and it just made it more difficult. Maybe if I give in, let him kiss me, I'll eventually get bored and my desire will go away. Fingers crossed.

The first awake from our nap out of the three bodies on the bed, and seeing the sunset on the horizon, I check the time on the clock. It's almost six. I'd get up, but my body is encased by Joe's. Rotating into him, I watch him rest for a few minutes before trailing my fingers through his hair.

Chapter Twenty Five

"Hey, beautiful," his husky voice delivers.

"Hey."

"Did we oversleep?"

"I think so," I confess. "It's almost six."

"Wow. Really?"

"Yeah," I confirm. "I need to feed Sadie. You should see if Jimmy and Allen are up."

"Five more minutes?" he charmingly requests and kisses me. His right hand pulls me in closer before it dips down to my ass and scoops my leg over his.

"What are you doing?" I slide my leg back, but he holds it in place.

"Getting more comfortable." He subdues my mouth with his. I can feel his groin against mine as my lady parts dampen.

As I draw my head away, he immediately cups my face and lures me back. I can't help but to comply with his demand. Keeping our mouths locked, he rolls on top of me placing my legs on either side of his hips. I shift, accidentally causing my crotch to grind into his. He enthusiastically moans and slides his tongue deeper into my mouth. I gasp when his hand slips under the edge of my shirt getting a hold on my waist.

"No." I demand, panting and pushing him away.

My heart jumps when I hear a knock on the door. Joe quickly and quietly exits through the sliding glass door.

"Just a second," I return, trying to sound like I just woke up.

Unlocking the door, I open it to find Jimmy. "Hey sweetie. I just woke up and didn't know if you and Joe were still sleeping. I knocked on his door, but there wasn't a response."

"Did you try using the patio door?"

"No. I didn't want to catch him naked or anything, if you know what I mean," he jokingly explains.

My dirty mind flashes to a variety of images of the things Joe could be doing in there, naked or not, which gets a giggle out of me.

"Well, we can send Sadie in there, you can try or call his phone," I suggest. A lump forms in my throat as I remember that Joe's phone might be next to mine on the nightstand.

The sound of a door opening scares me for a second until I see Joe standing behind Jimmy. "Hey," Joe says. "What's up?"

"I was checking to see who's up. Why don't you guys start getting ready and I'll wake Allen," Jimmy suggests.

"Sure," Joe and I say at the same time.

Jimmy nods and heads back to his room. I wipe my hands over my face in shock of almost being caught. Turning, I see Joe's phone next to mine. I'm glad that Jimmy didn't call it.

Handing his phone back to him, I declare, "I think it's best that you stay in your room for the rest of the trip."

With a wicked grin, Joe asks, "Will you join me?"

"No. Now get out, I need to get ready," I command calmly.

"Think about it?" he playfully pleas.

"No. Now go," I insist, taking an assertive step towards him.

Not moving, Joe admits in a tantalizing tone, "You're just as sexy when you're mad."

I glower my response as best as I can.

Chuckling, he adds, "Okay, I'm going."

Waiting to hear his door close, I lead Sadie to the kitchenette for food. After she's fed, I make sure that the one sliding door is open enough for her to get in and out. I lock both the bedroom door and the bathroom door before hopping into the shower. I rinse quickly to have enough time to masturbate. Letting my hair air dry a bit, I throw on a robe and toss the ball around for Sadie outside. She seems to have her regular energy back, so I'll need to take her for a walk on the beach tonight before bed.

With my hair almost dry from the wind, I head back to my room to finish getting ready. I put on nude lace bra and panties, style my hair up into a cute, loose bun, and put on a little bit of makeup before getting dressed. Tonight, I choose a white chiffon, dress that stops at the middle of my calf with several sheer layers that has spaghetti straps and a provocative neckline. I embellish my ears with dangling diamond and pearl earrings and my wrist with a diamond and pearl bracelet.

Just as I'm putting on my Jimmy Choo's, there is knocks on the door. "It's open," I announce.

"Allen's almost . . . damn, Emma, you look hot," Jimmy advertises. "Hey, Joe. Come check out Emma."

"He's going to see me in a . . ." my voice wanes as Joe enters the room and my eyes soak up the utterly sensual sight of him.

Did he know what I was going to wear? He couldn't have. I just put it on. He's wearing an all white suit with a white button down dress shirt and white

Chapter Twenty Five

slip-on dress shoes. His tanned skin glows underneath the elegant fabric and I have the sudden desire to lick him everywhere.

"Wow," Joe breathes.

"I know! Right?!" Jimmy agrees.

I blush at their statements and at the dirty thoughts running through my mind.

Once Allen is ready, which only takes five more minutes, we venture out to one of the restaurants at the hotel. Jimmy and Allen pick Spago. Yes. There is a Spago in Hawaii, at our hotel. Memories of my date with Joe tempt my already heightened thirst from seeing him in his suit.

Dining under the stars is breathtaking and seductive, especially with Joe sitting right next to me. Looks like my masturbation session in the shower was only foreplay given my current state of arousal. Along with the moisture that is gathering between my legs, I can feel several muscles beginning to tense in my shoulders. No drinking allowed tonight — rules would definitely be broken if I do.

I intently focus my attention on the light conversation my dining companions are having. Joe is a distraction, but it's much more tolerable than discussing Maggie, Henry, their engagement and potential wedding happening in the next few months.

"So what should we do tomorrow?" Jimmy asks. I know he's eager to spend more time with Joe.

"You boys do what you want, I've scheduled spa time," I mention.

As much as I want to explore more of this vibrant island, I need to get the kinks out of my body. Joe helped a little last night when he rubbed my shoulders and back, but the tension returned two-fold after almost getting caught by Jimmy.

"We'll join you," Allen insists.

"Sure, if you want. I just figured you two would want more guy time," I explain.

Looking at Joe, Jimmy questions, "What do you think?"

"I'm good with whatever," Joe replies. "Didn't you want to check out more local art for the gallery?"

"When are you going to the spa," Allen queries.

"The majority of the morning."

"Who are you getting all sexed up for?" Jimmy teases.

"Me," I say with half truth.

"We can easily do both," Allen suggests.

"Then, that settles it," Jimmy states. "We'll join Emma for a spa morning and then enjoy the rest of the day with other local visual delicacies."

After agreeing on our plans, I shift the conversation and start asking Jimmy and Allen how they got into the art scene and owning their own gallery. Apparently, Jimmy has been fascinated by art since a young age and was always drawing or painting. Every trip he and his family took, Jimmy would seek out the local museums and galleries. Recently, due to Allen's influence, Jimmy has been experimenting with clay sculptures. He shows me a variety of pictures on his phone of some of his original work. They're pretty impressive despite the fact that I know nothing about art.

Jimmy and Allen met in college during Jimmy's sophomore year and Allen's junior year. They were both art majors, but Allen included a minor in the theatrical arts. Interestingly, they attend Dartmouth just like Joe and Henry. Apparently Jimmy started off at Brown, but didn't like the curriculum.

I ask Jimmy if he's had a chance to visit any of the museums or galleries in the Los Angeles area. Coming to California with Joe after Easter was Jimmy's first time in LA, so I recommend a few key locations for him to visit next time he comes back. Joe mentions our recent trip to the Norton Simon and his desire to visit the Getty and the Griffith Observatory.

Finishing dinner, Jimmy and Allen choose to take another stroll throughout the hotel to look at the impressive art collection for a second time. Joe and I head back to the suite.

As we make our way back through the hotel, Joe keeps his hands to himself the whole time. He's a perfect gentleman. While walking, I vow to adhere to my earlier decision to take Sadie out for a run on the beach. I want to avoid being alone with Joe.

After getting changed, I tie my hair up and grab Sadie's ball. Just as I'm about to leave my room, Joe knocks on the door. He's changed too, and not into pajamas. Looks like he's planning on joining us on the beach. Damn it. There goes my plan of reprieve from his sexiness.

I am rather impressed at how well we run together. It feels like we complement each other each time we do. Sometimes I will push a little for a faster pace and sometimes he does. Neither one of us seem unable to keep up. I've never been able to run with Jared, Nathan or Maggie like this. Usually, my friends drop off after the second mile.

Back from our four-mile jog, I take a shower before grabbing a book and heading out to the fire pit with Sadie. To avoid temptation for when Joe comes out, because I know he'll be outside soon, I purposefully put on a pair of

Chapter Twenty Five

workout capris over my boy-shorts underwear. I don't bother with a bra, but I do grab a cardigan for additional coverage.

About ten or fifteen minutes later, like clockwork, Joe is sitting down on the same couch as me. Two seconds later, Jimmy and Allen come out as well. The three of them start chit-chatting as I read. My attention gets drawn to Joe who is suddenly massaging my left foot. I don't look up, but I'm not able to read any longer because of his touch.

"What are you reading?" Allen explores.

"Some romance novel," I whine.

"If you don't like it, then why are you reading it?" Jimmy questions.

"Maggie joined a book club at the beginning of the year and signed me up for it too," I explain. "Now, I'm stuck reading stupid, erotic, romance novels each month."

Joe chuckles under his breath.

"What's wrong with romance novels?" Jimmy contends as if he's slightly offended by my statement.

"The books that the group keeps picking are about a bunch of stupid virgins who end up having sex with brooding billionaires, who are dominant men in business and in sex," I say with mild agitation. "There's not much story and the only decent parts are the sex scenes, even though they're far fetched in how a man can please a woman. The naivety of the women is nauseating. Plus, the depictions of BDSM are weak. Not everyone who is into BDSM has a dark past."

"Wow! Either you're a virgin or you just really need to get laid," Allen announces.

"Not that it's any of your business, but I am not a virgin," I clarify.

"Someone needs to get laid then. All that angst, she must be really horny," Jimmy comments with a smile.

I don't say anything, but mentally I do agree with him. I am horny. I'm always horny. So horny that I'm masturbating practically two times a day, every day, except during the few days of my period.

"Had a boyfriend into BDSM?" Allen searches.

"I've never had a boyfriend. Remember. I don't date," I disclose.

"So you're the one into BDSM?" Jimmy presses.

"Everyone is curious and experiments in BDSM at some level. Those who deny it to themselves and their partners are either in the closet or are prudes," I point out.

Joe's hand immediately stops massaging my foot.

Breathe In

"Please, tell us how you really feel," Allen teases.

I blush a little at my rant and book bashing, but I think it's hidden behind the light of the fire.

"Sounds like she's never had a man properly satisfy her," Jimmy adds.

"When needed, I've always been able to satisfy myself," I openly share to my surprise.

At least I didn't slip about Maggie and me. No need for more people to know about how Maggie and I interact.

Joe's hand clamps down on my foot after my statement. I completely forgot that he was sitting here. He's been so quiet the whole time. Crap. I offered too much to all of them.

"So how often do you to take care of yourself?" Jimmy prods with a grin.

Did he just really go there?

"Jimmy!" Joe scolds.

This is the second time I've heard him be stern with his brother.

"How often do you?" I throw back at him.

"I don't need to with my awesome man right here," Jimmy kisses up to Allen. They exchange a few pecks and snuggle more into each other.

"Please . . . I may have never been in a relationship with a man, but I've seen and heard about enough relationships to know that everyone masturbates, at some point or another, and I'm not talking about phone sex with your partner."

The three of them stare at me blankly in complete shock to my openness.

"You know it's true. Your lack of comment right now is proof." I add, desperately trying not to gloat on the outside about my victory.

After a few minutes of silence, Jimmy inquires, "Why don't you date?"

"Choice," I coldly comment.

Making assumptions, Jimmy challenges, "Had a bad relationship at one point?"

"Nope. Never had the desire to be in one," I report calmly.

"Why not?" he presses.

"Jimmy, leave her alone," Joe defends again with less irritation this time.

"Why? I know you're dying to know," Jimmy professes.

Despite the low light of the fire, I can see Joe's face drain from all color except pure rosiness in his cheeks. I feel my own face flush a little hearing Jimmy's statement.

Chapter Twenty Five

The four of us sit quietly again. I'm searching for a topic to change to and I'm guessing that Jimmy's looking for the next question to put me or Joe on the spot.

Unable to stand the silence, Allen asks to see the book and I hand it to him. After turning a page or two, Allen comments, "She's right about the sex scenes being hot. I'm turned and it's about heterosexuals . . . ."

"Really?!" Jimmy inquires. "Let me see that."

I can't help but giggle.

Breaking the silence as he gives me the book back, Jimmy investigates, "So, Emma. When's your birthday?"

"Why?" I say rather sharply.

"I know when everyone else's birthdays are; Jared's is at the end of the month, Maggie's in July and Nathan's is in August. When I asked them about yours they wouldn't tell me."

"It's not important," I respond flatly.

"How is your birthday not important?" Joe interjects.

"It's not," I argue.

"Everyone's birthday is important," Jimmy adds.

"Not mine," I bitterly state.

"Even yours," Jimmy pushes.

Cutting Jimmy off, I launch off the couch and repeat, "Not mine." I turn and storm back to my room with Sadie following.

Aware that there's a really good chance that Joe might follow, I immediately head to the bathroom, locking the door behind Sadie. I start the faucet for the extra large bathtub and add some of the bath salts that are in my bag. I swiftly open the door and rush to get my phone for music and mediation to calm my nerves. I release a large exhale of relief seeing my room empty. Back in the bathroom, I quickly undress and climb into the exquisite marble tub that can comfortably hold two large adults. A vision of sharing it with Joe tightens my nipples and tingles my sex — the things I would do him.

After some of the tension eases, I find some porn on my phone, and listening through my headphones as I use my waterproof vibrator, give myself three glorious orgasms. By the time my hands are pruney, I exit the bath and dry off. With just a robe on, I peek out to see who could be in my room — no one. I put my tank top and boy-shorts underwear back on and then accompany Sadie on the bed. With one light still on, I lay on my back staring at the ceiling petting Sadie. Feeling relaxed but still wide awake, I check the time. It's barely midnight.

Sitting up to turn off the light, I spot Joe in the right sliding glass doorway. Sadie jumps down to greet him.

"Hey," he says timidly.

"Hey," I nervously reply.

"You okay?" He remains in the doorway.

"I'm fine." I lie.

"Jimmy was just . . ." He stands back up as Sadie jumps back on the bed.

"It's okay." I offer.

"Good . . ." he humbly accepts. "If you need me, I'm right next door. Okay?" Joe doesn't come inside my room.

Wow! Did he really listen to what I said earlier about him staying out of my room? I'm impressed.

"Yeah . . ." I agree.

He really is giving me some space.

"Emma . . . ."

"Yeah, Joe."

"Goodnight, beautiful," he states in a voice that instantly charms me.

"Goodnight, Joe," I reply softly.

Twenty Six

As I attempt to lift my heavy eyelids, I discover a hazy darkness surrounding me. Blinking slowly several times, my half-opened eyes won't focus to give me any clear indication of what's around me and where the blurry, flashing lights above are coming from. My body feels heavy. Still unable to open my eyes all the way, I perceive that I'm laying down somewhere. A cool dampness near my left cheek reveals itself as a slight gust of air brushes past my face. Sliding my right arm up the side of my body like a snake, my fingers creep to my lips. Drool — or, at least I hope so.

Two large and oddly shaped figures materialize in front of me. They are so close, only a foot or two away. Voices suddenly emanate from the now more defined silhouettes. Their speech sounds muffled and trails off into the distance even as I try to concentrate on their words. Who are they? What are they saying? Why can't I understand them? One of the voices almost sounds feminine.

Another indistinguishable sound gradually becomes more apparent as it grows louder and the ringing in my ears subsides. It's the engine of a car. My brain finally starts to put the fuzzy pieces of evidence together. I must have fallen asleep in the back seat. A familiar smell creeps into my nose that reassures me — my mother's perfume.

"Mom?" my throat squeezes out in a raw, breathy, hoarse tone.

"Wake up, Emma." Her voice replies in a low sluggish tone.

What is she talking about? I am awake.

A sudden rush of nervousness enters my belly. The car feels as if it's flying down the road like a rocket ship as the speed of the flashing lights zooming above my head all blur into one.

"Mom," I try to shout, but not a single sound escapes my mouth this time. Confused, I try again. "Mom!"

She doesn't hear me. I don't hear me.

A single, bright white light races towards us, growing larger by the second. My mother turns her head towards me smiling. Why doesn't she hear me? How does she not see the light?

"Wake up, Emma," she repeats, this time with a deeper tone.

Confused, I try again. "Mom!"

"Emma, wake up," the voice commands, getting louder.

My body hurls up as my eyes adjust to a soft light in the room. "Joe?"

"You had another dream. Sadie came to get me. I know you wanted me to stay in my room, but . . . ." his voice drops and I jump into his lap, throwing my arms around his neck gripping him tight. "It's okay. I've got you." He rocks us gently. "Do you need me to stay?"

"Can we go to your room?" I whimper into his neck.

"Of course," he replies, not letting go and carries me to his bed.

He combs his fingers through my hair as I lay facing him with our legs laced together. Seeking more comfort and contact, I inch my lips to his, grazing them on first contact. Our mouths gradually waltz together like their dancing to the beginning of The Beautiful Blue Danube by Johann Strauss II. As our kissing becomes more passionate, my left arm drifts over his hip and up his back, desperately tugging him further into me.

Suddenly alarmed by my body contradicting my brain, I jerk back. "I'm sorry. . . . . ." I blurt in an attempt to atone for my actions.

"It's okay," he soothes, coaxing my body closer.

"No, it's not," I verbally protest. "It's not fair. I say one thing and then do . . . ."

"Emma, it's okay," he sweetly assures.

I shyly kiss him again with a lingering peck. He chases mine with one of his own.

"Do you want to talk about it?"

"What?" I say confused.

Why would I want to talk about kissing him and leading him on?

"The dream," he comments softly.

"No."

"Maybe I can help if you tell me," he encourages.

"Talking about it doesn't help," I remark. "Jared's known for years and I still get them." A tear pools in the corner of my eye.

"Okay," he apologies. "I just don't like seeing you like this."

"I'll be fine," I assert with a feeling of routine that accompanies these nightmares and their aftermath. "I just need to sleep."

Moving closer, he wraps himself around me. "Goodnight, beautiful," his voice sings.

My heart bounces at his words and a smile develops on my face. "Goodnight, Joe."

Twenty Seven

The steady, warmth of Joe's breathing into my neck lures me from slumber. The combined heat from our bodies and the blankets surrounding us is causing me to sweat a little. I carefully kick the covers down, to cool my body, wanting to extend the enjoyment of being cocooned by his solid mass.

Strengthening his grip around me, he moans. "What are you doing?"

"I was hot."

"Yes, you are," he erotically states.

I poke him in his side in opposition to his meaning. Joe flinches and his lips meet my neck and my body goes instantly rigid.

"What's wrong?" he notices.

"No kissing there," I direct.

I don't really want him to stop, but my neck is one of my Achilles' heels when it comes to physical intimacy, especially if it's done just the way I like it. One or two more kisses and we will be naked.

"Why?"

"Because I said so," I inform.

He nibbles my neck this time, causing me to emphatically moan and salivate between my legs. "I will get out of the bed," I weakly threaten.

Chuckling, Joe captures my face, seducing me into an amorous kiss and embrace. I uncontrollably give in, but I haven't completely lost my wits enough to allow the breaking of my rules. As our lips stay locked, our desires heighten. His lust for me is obvious with each moan that escapes his throat. Joe breaks contact first, panting like he's trying to maintain control. Looks like I'm not the only one severely affected by all of this.

Sadie sees an opportunity and moves in for attention. She plops her head on the dip of my waist, and using her nose, prompts Joe's arm to pet her. Getting the response she wants, Sadie wedges her body between Joe's and mine. The three of us snuggle until I can no longer wait to pee. I head to the patio door to make sure no one is outside before I head to my room to use the restroom. Joe quietly makes his disappointment known.

After feeding Sadie, Joe and I take her for a walk on the beach and then have some breakfast. Our appointment for the spa is at eight, which gives us an hour and a half to eat and shower. Knowing that I'll be naked at the spa, I slip on a lace thong and go braless under my cute floral halter sundress.

The spa staff greet us warmly as we enter. Once I get undressed in a private room, a woman leads me into another room where my three companions are waiting. When I question them about why we're all in the same room, Jimmy informs me that he arranged for the four of us to have the entire spa to ourselves and any of the items I chose, they planned on doing too. Overall, I wouldn't care except for the fact that Joe is here and I'm completely naked under my robe.

Settling into the first treatment on four massage tables lined up in a row, we start off with a fifty-minute deep tissue massage. I'm delightfully pleased when I get the masseur. Hiwalani, meaning the attractive one, which fits him perfectly, effortlessly kneads the tension out of each region of my body including my rear. My boisterous moaning gets Jimmy, Allen and the other masseuses giggling. More laughter erupts from Jimmy and Allen when Joe's masseuse comments on how stiff his body becomes, making her job impossible.

"You'll have to excuse Joe," Jimmy shares loud enough for everyone to hear. "I think it's been a while since he's heard a woman moan like that, if at all."

Embarrassed, I nervously giggle, realizing that I may be the cause of Joe's tension.

Hiwalani and the other masseuses leave the room when they are finished with the treatment, allowing us to clothe ourselves. Jimmy and Allen get up first. Joe remains lying on his stomach with his face in the table cutout offering for me to get up before him. Once my robe is tied, I keep my back to Joe and let him know that it's safe to get up and put on his robe.

We're lead into another peaceful room where our E Ola Hou, the Hawaiian healing wrap, will take place. We each have our own lounge chairs that are divided by sheer curtains. As our bodies are exfoliated with ground coconut polish and noni gel, we also receive the third treatment which is a facial that cleanses, exfoliates, extracts, relaxes and massages our pores. I find the sight of three grown men and their bodies wrapped through the sheer curtains is hysterical when I look to my left.

After our body wraps and facials, we're offered some light refreshments before heading to our final treatment. I had only planned on the three services, but Joe added a fourth as a final treatment. Taken into my own private room, the specialist begins an interesting and interactive session called tapping. It focuses on meridian points throughout the body where you tap on certain locations to relieve stress. I found myself crying uncontrollably several times which at first increased my stress level. I never cry in front of people I don't know, let alone the fact that I rarely cry. The woman explains that it is a natural response the

Chapter Twenty Seven

body uses to release not only the stress, but the emotional blockages that build up. Apparently other responses like burping, yawning, laughter, scratching and even flatulence can also occur. She shows me a variety of techniques to use and recommends that I continue with other treatments either with another practitioner back home or by myself, repeating the techniques she shows me.

Once we finish our spa morning, Jimmy, Allen, Joe and I meet up with the rest of my friends for lunch in the hotel. We swap stories about what we had done the day before and this morning since we haven't seen each other since the dinner the day of our hike. I note a distinct difference with myself being around Maggie and Henry. I'm more relaxed when everyone discusses planning their wedding. The day and a half away from them, plus my exquisitely calming morning most likely had something to do with it.

After an early lunch, Jimmy, Allen, Joe, Sadie and I head out on an excursion for fine, local Hawaiian art for a few hours. Thanks to the people at the hotel and others Jimmy and Allen have spoken to the past few days, we head directly to a couple of artists' studios. Jimmy and Allen schedule a wide variety of artwork from two out of the four artists' work whom we meet to be purchased and shipped back to the East Coast. They are planning to do a show in New York before the end of the year and purchase a few of the pieces to put on display ahead of time in the gallery as well as in their own home.

Back at the hotel by three, we all opt to hang around the hotel pool for the rest of the day. Feeling overwhelmed with sudden fatigue, I head back to the suite to take a nap instead of using the cabana. Too tired to change, I flop on the bed and pass out into a deep sleep.

I wake to Joe gingerly caressing his fingers along the side of my face.

"It's time to get up, beautiful," he instructs.

Rolling over, I groggily protest, "No."

The bed shifts from his movement. "Time to get ready for dinner," he whispers.

I drag my heavy body into a seated position. 'What time is it?" My eyes flutter unable to fully open

"Almost five-thirty."

"Wow. Really?" I check the clock, not that I don't believe him, but I want to see it for myself. "Where's everyone else?"

"Getting ready. I just fed Sadie, so you're good to go." Giving me a soft peck, Joe stands and heads for the door.

I'll admit that I'm disgruntled with only one kiss.

Forcing my body up, I shower and masturbate before getting dressed. With just a little bit of makeup, I twist my hair up and put on a cute aquamarine blue cocktail dress along with a pair of open-toed, sparkling Valentino heels. For jewelry, I put on a vanilla moonstone triangle necklace with a fourteen karat gold, twenty-four inch chain and matching bracelet.

Everyone from the upstairs suite comes down to pick the rest of us up for dinner. We follow our exclusive server to our breathtaking, private, oceanfront table that overlooks the Wailea Beach. The sun slowly begins to set on the horizon, splashing beautiful blues and golds across the sky as we savor the multi-course feast that has been prepared for us and several bottles of wine.

With it being our second to last evening in Maui, we all head out to one of the popular local clubs for a night of dancing. I keep my alcohol intake to a very small minimum as does Joe and Henry. Maggie, Jared, Nathan, and Jimmy cut loose. I see Allen have a few sips of Jimmy's drinks, but doesn't order any for himself.

Taking a quick break from dancing for another drink, Maggie and Jared, in their light, intoxicated stupor, decide to single me out. "It's Emma's song!"

"This is not my song," I flatly oppose, recognizing Rihanna's *Where Have You Been* blaring over the speakers.

"Yes it is," Maggie insists. "You have yet to find a man who can satisfy you."

My eyes widen with horror. I don't like too many people knowing that much about me and my friends' openness around Henry and Joe, and now Jimmy and Allen, is starting to bug me. I get it. They're becoming friends too, but I don't need everyone we hang out with to know so much about me.

"Yep," Jared supports and proceeds to sing loudly.

Nathan and Maggie quickly chime in as I silently disagree.

"B.O.B. satisfies me just fine," I contend.

"B.O.B. does not count," Maggie opposes.

"Who's Bob?" Jimmy searches. "I thought Emma doesn't date."

Nathan fails to see my pressing look not to share. "Battery operated boyfriend," he delivers without hesitation and a huge smile on his face.

I get smug looks from Jimmy and Allen as they whisper to each other. Joe's expression I can't quite figure out. Crap. I just opened up that door.

For most of the night, Maggie and I are the ones dancing from our group. Jared and Nathan pop in from time to time, but are primarily chatting with the guys at the bar. Maggie ends up drinking a little more than usual, causing her to get more playful in public.

Chapter Twenty Seven

"Not here," I direct, gently pushing her away from me.

We dance for another song or two until she announces, "I need to pee."

In the restroom, we both enter the same stall. It's become a regular habit over the years when there's a long line or one of us has had too much to drink. We take turns with Maggie going first. As I finish fixing my dress, Maggie kisses me. We embrace each other and kiss more passionately. When Maggie dips her hand under my dress, I push her against the stall wall, pinning her.

"Not here," I command.

I'm tempted to continue, but I know that this is not the place nor the time.

"But I want it," she whines, leaning forward to catch my lips.

"Henry's right out there," I suggest.

"I want you," she begs.

"This trip is for you and Henry," I rationalize.

"I know you need it," she pokes. "I need it too."

"That's beside the point," I challenge. "You know how I am about doing things in public and having too many people know. I like my privacy."

"Back at the hotel," she entices.

I want her too. We've only interacted three times the past two month since she started having sex with Henry. The physical interactions with Joe are escalating faster than I have anticipated. If I don't sleep with Maggie, I just might end up sleeping with Joe.

"No." I object. "When we get home."

She pouts, but then has the look in her eye of a lightbulb moment. "Remember our first time?"

"Of course I do," I agree. There's no way I could ever forget it.

Maggie and I were eighteen and still virgins. Sophie, one of Jared's lesbian friends, worked at an adult shop in WeHo and helped us pick out our first sex toys. We weren't uncomfortable with Sophie, just the subject matter. I still remember the giddy, nervous feeling I had when we were in the store just looking at all of our options. The feeling heightened when Sophie was handling them and instructing us on which ones she preferred and why, as well as some great position. Sophie inquired to our sudden interest since we had always seemed embarrassed when the topic of sex came up when hanging out prior to our visit. We hesitated at first to give her our reason, but I'm pretty sure she was able to deduce our intentions from some of the questions we asked. Sophie was very thorough and informative, she even offered some insight on what to expect, but ultimately, she said, it's different for each person with regards to the level of pain in the beginning.

When Jared caught wind of what Maggie and I were planning, he bought us a few bottles of wine to help take the edge off for when we were ready. Even with someone you trust, it is nerve racking to know you are about to deflower yourself with your best friend. That night, sitting on the bed in the discrete plastic bag, hidden inside my large canvas tote bag I carried around, were three different toys along with some porn sites written on the receipt. Maggie and I sat staring at the bag in my room probably for at least an hour before either one of us said anything. Our pact and New Year's resolution needed to come to fruition, but that Friday night we just couldn't do anything but stare, laugh and even play with the toys in ways that were not how they were intended to be played with as we watched a variety of porn. We had never seen porn before, let alone what a penis really looked like. Maggie was staying the whole weekend, so it made it easier for us to get used to holding and touching the toys and the sights and sounds of sex on the laptop.

The next day, Jared went out with one of his new friends at the time, so we had the apartment to ourselves. After lunch, we resolved to meet our agreement, so we started watching more porn to help coax us into action. Hours went by and we became more comfortable with the overall concept and idea as we played at least two videos per category. Soon, we became comfortable enough to comment on what looked fun and what we might be willing to try with each other and in the future with guys. I admitted to her that I've masturbated and did regularly and was relieved when she shared that she did the same. We were at least familiar with the feeling of being aroused, touched and having an orgasm.

By early evening, we were halfway through a bottle of wine when we were starting to feel a little more adventurous. Putting on a video of three lesbians, we consented to begin touching ourselves while still clothed, and then perhaps go from there. My eyes bounced between the video and Maggie and they eventually settled on watching just Maggie. Our eyes stayed locked on each other until we both orgasmed. As I recovered, Maggie moved closer to me and brought her lips to mine. Her lips were soft, wet and gentle.

I had kissed a few of Jared's friends, mostly straight guys and some gay guys who were curious to see what it was like kissing a girl. When your eyes are closed, all you taste and feel is skin, tongue, and moisture, and the only time you notice a difference is if your eyes are open, you touch the other person in certain areas or if they make a sound.

Chapter Twenty Seven

Our mouths stayed on each other's, slowly, pleasantly poking and prodding with our tongues. One of my hands found the side of her face pulling her closer to me, causing our bodies to touch at the chest and legs. Leisurely, my hand began to caress her body and she moaned in delight. Maggie returned the exploration of my body with her tiny supple hands and then began to slide my shirt up over my chest. Our lips disengaged to allow her to take my shirt completely off as I sat up. I returned my lips to hers as my hands found the edges of her shirt and eagerly began to remove it.

I took the lead and started to direct her body backward onto the bed as I lowered myself, straddling over her as our mouths proceeded to massage each other's. On my hands and knees, I kissed her neck and her hands ruffled in my hair. I moved gradually down to her collar bone and over her chest. Sliding my hands underneath her as I kept my mouth on her warm skin, I unfastened her bra and exposed her breasts to my wet and impatient tongue. She gasped in ecstasy as I sucked on each nipple.

Working my way down her belly, I started to unbutton her pants. I could smell her before the edge of her panties were exposed. Instead of pulling her pants off right away, I returned to embrace her lips with mine as I dipped one hand along her naked body and slide it underneath the folds of her underwear. She yanked her lips away from mine when she gasped at the touch of my fingers reaching her lower lips. I fondled her with my fingers on and round her nub while licking her nipples. She panted as I circled her clitoris and she grabbed the sheets under her when I dipped one finger inside. Stroking her mounds, Maggie moaned louder and louder as her wetness spread.

Removing my finger, she whined for more. I used both hands to remove her pants and underwear, but she started kicking them off in a rush. Maggie forced her lips to mine again as she took off my bra. I positioned myself over her this time, pressing my naked chest against hers. Shifting my hips to reach, my hand brushed down her skin to find her sex again. My mouth followed as I continued to explore her wet cave. Maggie breathed in elation as my tongue slipped over her exterior and my fingers eagerly massaged her on the inside. Her sweet smell and taste in my mouth excited my desire more. Within a few more strokes, Maggie climaxed.

Before she finished convulsing from her release, I began to slide one of the smaller dildos into her soaked opening. Her own moisture would make this process easier and more pleasurable now that she was relaxed. Sliding the toy in a little, I removed it quickly when she sharply breathed in. Maggie begged for more, so I slipped the device back insider her, that time pressing a little further and didn't remove it. She groaned, throwing her head back. I paused momentarily waiting to see her eyes again before continuing with my next thrust. Her moaning grew louder as she bit her lip and nodded for more. Again, I pulled out slightly and then plunged in one fluid movement. I paused waiting for Maggie to catch her breath when I saw the look of both pain and pleasure sweep across her face.

"Again," she cried out after several breaths.

Following her direction, I repeated the thrust and this time her face showed a little less pain.

"Again," she demanded.

That time, I returned my mouth to her nub and kept my eyes on her as I glided the dildo into her body with more ease.

"Don't stop," Maggie exclaimed.

I continued licking and pulsing repeatedly until she finally orgasmed and was shaking from the sensations.

I left the toy inside of her as I slide back up her body, kissing lightly from just above her lower lips all the way up to her neck, waiting for her instructions. She embraced my naked torso with one arm while placing her other hand along side of my face. We rolled together until I was underneath of her. After a few more kisses, she quickly went to the bathroom and removed and cleaned the dildo before returning.

Maggie kneeled on the bed over me, eager to return the favor. With most of her weight on top, our mouths met again as she caressed my jaw, neck and down to my breasts, and I moaned in satisfaction. Taking the lead, she moved down my body kissing a pathway to the edge of my bottoms. In one fluid movement, she unbuttoned my shorts and had them halfway down my legs.

We were both completely naked and exhilarated at the site of our unclothed bodies. She mounted me as I had her, pressing her entire hot, naked body onto mine. My skin was on fire and I could feel every little sensation, even her rock hard nipples brushing over me. I felt moisture dripping from my loins as our mouths wildly explored each others. Her mound was fondling mine as she moved her hips back and forth and I moaned loudly from the stimulation.

Pulling her mouth from mine, she began her adventurous exploration of my breasts and nipples as she carefully manipulated them with her hands and tongue. I groaned in disappointment when she drew away and headed south to my womanhood. As her lips pressed against my sex, my displeasure melted away. I could feel her warm breath sweeping across my skin as her tongue erotically investigated my folds. My hands found their way to my breasts, my eyes rolled in the back of my head, and my senses heightened as she slid a finger inside my cavern. I lost my breath as her mouth and fingers proceeded their slow, tantalizingly delicious rubbing between my legs.

Chapter Twenty Seven

Moan after moan escaped my throat, getting louder and louder with each passing of her fingers, until the sudden rush of relief filled my entire body and poured out stronger than I had ever felt, even during masturbation. My eyes swelled with moisture, but not near as much as there was between my thighs that Maggie was lapping up. She crawled over me, sucking my skin as I yearned to taste myself on her lips. More. My body craved more and instinctually I began thrusting and rubbing my groin against her leg. We stroked ourselves against each other's thigh until we reached climax together.

Slinking back down my body as I tried to regain steady breathing, Maggie waited for my command to enter me with the foreign object. Unable to speak, I nodded with desire, a fervent need. A wicked grin spread across her face as she slowly began to fill me. She pushed gently and steadily as she watched my response. My hands grabbed my nipples, tightening with each passing stroke she nudged in. My insides yearned for more, more throbbing, more thrusting, more of this object inside me. I could feel everything.

"More," I cried out in jubilation, "More!"

Suddenly there was a sensation that was a mixture of pain and pleasure that throbbed, ached inside of me. Maggie started to withdrawal the apparatus from me. Unable to speak, I ferociously shook my head, indicated my wants. Swiftly, she thrusted into me again and I howled at the repeated feeling of titillating torment. My arousal slowly overtook my body as my panting grew with each plunge of her delightful assault on my sex. A feeling of peaceful contentedness rose inside of me as each thrust brought me to a glorious orgasm.

My eyes were immediately heavy from the exhaustion and my body was triumphantly satisfied from what had just taken place. Maggie joined me, laying on the bed as our body lightly touched. We looked into each others eyes and had a giggling fit for several minutes. Our bodies were pleased, very pleased, but also sore.

The rest of that weekend, Maggie and I explored each other several more times as we experimented with different positions and ideas we wanted to try from the videos. Our bond as friends was forged into a tie that words cannot explain. I felt safe. I felt free. I felt reborn.

"I haven't forgotten either," Maggie comments. She must have seen me drift off remembering it. "Henry's never been with two women at the same time."

"I'm not sleeping with Henry," I firmly snap. "We've never been with one of your boyfriends. Why would I with your fiancé?" I almost throw up in my mouth after uttering the word fiancé.

"It's not like we haven't shared a guy before," she gently presses.

"This is different. You know that," I explain.

Breathe In

"You promise that we will when we get back?"

She's finally giving up on her quest.

"Yes," I agree.

We head back to the guys at the bar after washing our hands and primping in the mirror. Maggie curls into Henry as I'm left standing by myself.

"What took you two so long?" Nathan needles.

"Nothing," I reply.

"You two were getting it on," he claims.

All of the tension Hiwalani massaged out of me this morning is starting to return.

"No." I sharply retort.

"Leave her alone, babe," Jared defends.

"Who was getting it on?" Jimmy questions after sipping his drink.

"Maggie and Emma in the bathroom," Nathan giggles.

"No, we didn't," Maggie interjects. "We just kissed."

"Wait. I thought you were into men," Allen inquires.

"She is . . but, when she can't find a man to satisfy her needs, she and Maggie hook up. They've been dong it since . . ."

I punch Nathan in the arm, cutting him off.

"Ow," he whimpers. "What the hell."

Pissed, I walk away not sticking around to hear the rest of the conversation. Not sure where to go, I make my way out to the parking lot. As I lean my back on the car and cross my arms, I see Joe following after me.

"Leave me alone," I demand.

"Jared didn't want you by yourself."

"Well, then he should have joined me," I say with agitation. "Besides, I'm a big girl and I know how to take care of myself."

"Jared didn't send me. I offered when I saw him going after you, but he was trying to keep Nathan from coming too," Joe admits.

We stand without saying a word for a few minutes. Joe keeps his distance, but I can see the concern on his face. He wants to comfort me, but he's not sure how.

"Want to talk about it?" Joe suggests rather than questions.

"About what? What do you want to know?" I heatedly throw back at him.

Chapter Twenty Seven

"I don't need to know anything. I just thought you might want to talk," he defends.

"Emma!" Maggie shouts from a distance. She continues shouting my name until she's a few feet away. "Emma. The others want to stay, but Henry's coming so we can head back. "

"Sounds good," I deliver with some irritation.

Maggie doesn't seem to notice or realize that my anger wasn't meant for her. She and I stand holding each other until Henry arrives.

Joe opens the front passenger door and waits for Maggie to get in.

"I'm sitting in the back with Emma," she announces.

"You should sit with Henry," I encourage, cognizant to what most likely will happen on the drive back to the hotel if we sit together and I'm not in the mood right now.

"No. I'm riding with you," she insists.

Pulling her away from the car, away from earshot of Joe, I explain, "Maggie, I appreciate everything you're doing, but I'm not in the mood and the last thing I need is . . . ."

"Okay. I understand," she assures, a little disappointed by being turned down.

"Why don't we see if Joe doesn't mind driving," I suggest. "That way you and Henry can relax and enjoy the back seats."

"Yeah," she cheerfully agrees.

Joe agrees to drive and gets the keys from Henry after closing the door behind me. Maggie and Henry enter the car on the same side as Joe. Within twenty seconds, we're pulling out of the parking lot and Maggie's climbing onto Henry's lap. I do my best to tune them out while I sit in the front seat with my arms crossed, still fuming from Nathan's sharing episode.

About twenty minutes later, the four of us are entering the lobby of the Four Season's. I bid Maggie and Henry goodnight before rushing back to Sadie and my room.

"How's my girl doing?" I ask Sadie as I step into the foyer of the suite.

She follows me all the way to our room eager for my attention. I avoid talking and making any kind of contact with Joe as I slam and lock my door closed. I then proceed to close and lock each of the two sliding glass doors and glide the wooden privacy shutters to block anyone from being able to look in while the lights are on. Flopping down on the bed, I cuddle with Sadie for a few minutes. She always knows how to calm me.

Breathe In

Restless and sweaty from dancing, I head into the bathroom for a shower. I purposefully grab my vibrator and pleasure myself — stopping after two intense orgasms. Once my pajamas are on and I finish getting ready for bed, I slip under the covers, turn off the lights, and focus on Sadie until my brain and body turn off for the night.

Twenty Eight

Pain and tension in my neck and shoulders pull me from a somewhat restful night's sleep. I stretch a little on the floor before opening one of the sliding doors open wide enough to let Sadie out. Unfortunately, Sadie forces me out to the patio after her when she decides to enter Joe's room. I can't see anything, but Sadie comes immediately when I quietly call her name.

After Sadie runs around the yard for a few minutes, the two of us head back inside for her breakfast. Without realizing it, I make two glasses of clay along with Sadie's food. The thought to just drink both glasses comes to mind, but suddenly Joe appears.

"Good morning, beautiful," he says pleasantly.

I nod indifferently.

"Still up for scuba?"

I almost forgot that we scheduled to go over to Molokini Crater today.

"Mmm hmm," I reply as I gulp down the last of my drink.

Joe and I barely talk from our morning greeting until finally boarding the boat. When we arrive at the dock, I notice that Joe commissioned a private charter boat for our excursion instead of the group tour I had booked. I'm all about privacy, but the whole concept of paying a lot more for certain private access to things is weird to me.

I overhear him using boat lingo with the captain and crew just before the boat launches out into the water. With a beautiful interior living room, and one hundred and eighty degrees of view, Joe, Sadie and I have privacy and a spectacular display of the ocean.

Poking and jabbing at me a few times with words and his body, Joe threatens to spar with me if I don't lighten up.

"Go ahead and try," I encouragingly nudge. "You won't win."

"Ahh, there's the Emma I'm looking for," he playfully responds.

"What is it with guys like you and the need to have private jets or private this or private that?" I pick.

"What's that supposed to mean?" he chuckles.

"You know what I mean. We could have done the group tour I booked for where we're headed." I mention.

"This coming from a woman who loves her privacy," he taunts, wrapping his arms around me.

Breathe In

"Ohh no you don't," I protest as I slip away from his embrace. "Yes. I like my privacy, but this is a little overboard, don't you think?"

"No," he argues, moving closer to me.

Shaking my head, I turn and look out the window.

He doesn't force physical contact, but Joe stands close enough that when the boat sways, our shoulders bump into each other.

At some point, he places his hand on the small of my back and I allow it. "Thought you might like to know that the boat runs off of all electric motors," he comments.

"Really?"

He's piqued my interest.

"Yes. I know how important that is to you and I've been exploring more stuff about greener technologies across all industries since all of our business conversations," he states.

I think he's trying to impress me. I'm flattered and think it's cute.

Extending our witty banter from before, I reply, "So, you were listening?"

"I always listen," he informs.

The boat sways again, knocking me more off balance this time. My body lunges towards Joe, but he catches me effortlessly. Wrapping his arm around my waist, Joe steadies the two of us. I don't try to get away from his embrace and we end up staying connected until the boat gets closer to our diving destination.

Once we're close enough to the reef, Joe and I start stripping down to our bathing suits. Joe's bare chest is an added view of beauty aside from the crystal water. Our captain and the crew instruct us on how to use the Snuba gear, but I get distracted on occasion when I look at Joe's half naked body.

Snuba is different from snorkeling and is more closely related to scuba diving. Instead of carrying the oxygen tanks on our backs, they are attached to a raft that floats on the surface of the water. We're able to go as far as fifteen feet deep below water level.

Strapped into our harness and with flippers on our feet, Joe and I head into the water. Sadie joins us for a few minutes, but I signal for her to stay on the boat until Joe and I return. While using the gear, we're monitored the entire time we're under water, but Joe and I are the only ones entering. As we begin swimming around, I see why Joe ordered the private charter, other than to impress me and be mindful of the environment with the electric motor, we are free to swim around and there isn't a crowd of people near us, allowing for more of the marine life to swim closer.

Chapter Twenty Eight

I've seen pictures of aquatic life, but seeing it up close and in person is a completely different feeling. It's otherworldly. The variety of colors and species is astounding. At some point, a bale of turtles come near us, close enough for us to reach out and touch their shells and bellies. Watching the animals dance around in the current is relaxing and peaceful. I feel the tension from last night and this morning melting away.

Fifteen minutes left on our tanks, we turn around to head to the boat. Surprisingly, several whale sharks head straight for us. As they approach, I notice that they circle around Joe and me. Staying close together, we watch the gentle giants. Even though I know that they're vegetarians, the idea of being this close to a shark is still a little unnerving. One circles close enough, allowing Joe and I to reach out and touch it. I'm definitely glad that I didn't cancel this morning's adventure.

Sadie jumps into the water to greet us when Joe and I resurface from our excursion, getting a good laugh from us and the crew. Once we're back on the boat, Joe, Sadie and I are offered a private lunch off of the bow of the boat. I should have seen this coming. A private boat. A private tour. Of course, we would have a private lunch. I'm starting to wonder if Joe planned this whole thing to be like a second date.

"So, what's this all about?" I explore.

"What are you talking about?"

"A private boat. A private tour and now a private lunch. I'm starting to think that you are trying to sneak in a second date," I state the obvious.

"No," he bashfully disagrees. "We're two friends hanging out."

"Would you have planned all this with your brother?"

"Probably," he answers slyly.

"Right . . ." I sarcastically reply.

He tries to hide a smile that forms in the left corner of his mouth. He's definitely lying.

"Do you want to stay out here a little longer? Or, did you want to head back?"

"Now I know you're lying," I heckle.

We decide to jump in the water to cool off before heading back to Maui. Sadie joins us again, happy for the swim.

Once the boat starts moving back to land, Joe takes me on a little tour, answering my questions about sailing and boats. Several times, Joe tries to get close and kiss me, but I amusingly avoid. A girl needs to make the guy work for it sometimes; we can't always be that easy.

Breathe In

While we are in a small, shallow hallway, the boat rocks hard enough, forcing us to collide. Joe steadies us up against the wall, pressing himself into me. We stay connected, drinking in the sight, smell and contact of our bodies. Seeing a chance, Joe kisses me and I willingly accept. As if we have all of the time in the world, our mouths leisurely dance on and around each other's. Softly, carefully, tenderly, we explore with our lips and tongues. His right hand sturdies us while his left caresses my cheek, chin and neck. Altering his feet, Joe pulls away and rests his body against the other wall. We exchange a glance or two before he cajoles me to move closer with his hands on my hips. Missing the closeness, I press myself against him as I run my hands up his chest and around his neck, returning my lips to his. Joe's hands slide around my waist, drawing me closer.

"Excuse me, Mr. Covelli," a voice uncomfortably mutters from my left.

I immediately break physical contact with Joe.

"My apologies. I need to get into that room," one of the boat crew members informs, pointing to a door on the other side of us.

Shock and surprise swell inside of me like a swarm of bees. I completely forgot where we were. Embarrassed, I rush past the crew member and up a flight of stairs to the deck with Sadie on my heels. Joe finds me a minute later standing on one side of the boat. The soothing touch of his hand up and down my back titillates me at my very core, but does little to relax my stiffness. He sense my uneasiness and settles his hands on my shoulders, massaging them same way he did the other night on the beach.

Once the boat docks in Maui, we head back to the suite to wash up and change. I hang out with Sadie on the patio under the porch and Joe joins us on the other lounge chair as the three of us wait for our friends. We've scheduled a private dinner in the suit for our last night, so we read, talk and play with Sadie to pass the time.

Just as the sun starts to set, all eight of us are relaxing on the patio while the chef and his staff prepare the meal in the kitchenette. We laugh. We joke. We play card games as we eat and drink into the night.

Nathan purposefully sits next to me the majority of the time, trying to make amends for last night. He repeatedly apologizes, feeling bad at not remember what had all happened since he had so much to drink. I know Nathan loves me and was just kidding around, that's what he, Jared, Maggie and I do, which is why I can't stay mad at him for very long. The challenging part for me is when there are other people around. Usually he's good about it in public, but I can sense that he sees Joe and Henry as part of our circle already, and Jimmy and Allen seem to be adding to the mix as well. I'm not fond of this group getting bigger.

Nathan knows a good deal about me and my past from Jared; how much from my past, I'm not entirely sure. Jared and him didn't meet until just before the night Maggie and I lost our virginity, and it took a while before Jared included him in our outings. Nathan wasn't there for the brunt of my first few years in California like Maggie and Jared, and over time he learned more about me. Nathan is family now, but it took a lot of time. It takes a lot of time for me to let anyone in.

I head inside to grab more drinks and snacks for everyone and Nathan follows me to assist.

Almost finished with the drinks, Nathan comments, "You know, you are going to need to open up more for these guys like you did with me."

"Why? What are you talking about?"

I'm not sure where he's going with that statement.

"They're family now, especially with Maggie and Henry getting . . . ."

Hurt and scared by his words, my voice cracks as I cut him off. "They are not family. You, Jared and Maggie are family. Maggie's family is family. That's it. That's my family. The rest of them are not my family and never will be." I turn to get away and find Joe entering the dining room. My eyes immediately dart away, not wanting to explain myself. As I circle all the way around to head to my room, I see Maggie already out of the restroom. My heart stops as a knot forms in my throat. I know that Maggie heard me by the look on her face.

I dash past Maggie slamming my bedroom door behind me. Like last night, I close my room off, not letting anyone in. I'm ashamed that Maggie now knows how I feel. I'm embarrassed by my outburst. I'm humiliated that I just ruined Maggie's celebration weekend. I'm mortified by it all. Panic, fear and sadness surround my heart and soul. Why did you have to say anything, Emma? Why couldn't you just not say anything?

A light knock on the door snaps me from my self-bashing.

"Emma? Emma, please let me in," Maggie calmly pleas.

I can't face her. I know I can't face her. Not now.

"Please, Emma. It's just me," she mentions. "I'm going to stand here until you let me in," she sternly commands.

She knows how to get to me. I carefully unlock the door and crack it open an inch or two.

"There you are," comments a smiling Maggie.

I look away as a tear falls down my face.

"Come on. Let me in," she directs politely.

Looking beyond her, I check to make sure no one else is lurking. I take a step back, let her enter and lock the door. Before I turn all the way around to face her. Maggie throws her arms around me which catches me off guard.

"I'm sorry, Emma. I didn't realize how this would affect you," she announces.

"I'm fine. I over reacted and I'm sorry I'm ruining your vacation," I reply, fighting back tears.

"You're not fine. My vacation is not ruined. You didn't overreact, you've kept things bottled up inside, not wanting to hurt me. I know that," she replies softly in a motherly tone. "I should have known this wouldn't be easy for you."

"I've just gotten good hiding it from you," I openly admit

Crap. Did I just say that?

She leads me over to the bed and we lay down facing each other.

"What else are you hiding from me?"

"Nothing," I honestly admit when it comes to the topic of her and me.

We don't need to venture into the other topics I'm hiding from her and Jared right now.

"Do you think Henry and I are moving too fast," she asks with concern.

"No. You are moving at your own pace, which suits you and Henry," I offer honestly.

This puts a smile back on her face.

"I know he loves you and he wouldn't have proposed if he didn't. You two fit each other perfectly. It's just a lot and all at once for me," I share.

A tear falls from the corner of her eye. "Are you afraid that you are losing me?"

"A little," I honestly answer.

I'm actually surprised that she's talking to me right now. How can she not be mad at me? I feel like I'm being selfish.

"Ohh, Emma," she cries, moving closer to me. "I'm never leaving you. You're my sister. I love you."

"I love you too," I weep.

She moves closer and we mold into each other's body.

Time passes and my tears eventually subside.

"Give me a minute. I'll be right back, Okay?" Maggie announces.

I nod, not sure what she's doing.

Chapter Twenty Eight

Maggie opens one of the sliding glass doors just over a foot and Sadie pops through. Maggie heads outside as Sadie and I snuggle on the bed. A minute or two later, Maggie comes back.

"I'm back," she announces.

Maggie leaves the door open slightly before returning to the bed and climbs over me. She lowers, placing her body on top of mine. Stroking my face, Maggie leans in and kisses me. I can immediately feel that she needs this just as much as I do. I should have believed her last night.

With the lights off and a small breeze flowing in, Maggie and I satisfy each other. After oral and finger stimulation, we both take turns using my dildo and vibrator on the other. After four intense and long overdue orgasms given by someone other than myself, my body becomes lethargic and drunk on well-achieved physical satisfaction. The glorious smell of sex permeates the air. I barely remember Maggie draping the sheets over my naked body as my mind drifts to a deep sleep.

Twenty Nine

I wake to sniffing in my ear; Sadie's hungry. Sitting up, I quickly cover my naked torso when a pair of legs to my left are seen out of the corner of my eye. My heart leaps at the thought of Joe coming into the room at some point last night. Gradually turning my head, I discover that there are actually two bodies, Jared's and Nathan's. A sigh of relief escapes my lips. I'm safe.

The next few hours, I eat, take Sadie for a walk, shower and pack. Jared and Nathan went back to their room sometime while I was not in the suite.

By about nine in the morning, we are standing outside the stairs of the plane to head home. Losing about three hours of time with our flight, we're schedule to get back to California between six or seven in the evening.

The flight back home is long, but peaceful. Everyone bounces around chatting, except me. I'm still a bit quiet after last nights debacle, but I'm more willing to sit and listen to everyone talking. No one asks about what happened after I left the patio, nor do Maggie or I share.

Jimmy and Allen stay on the plane when we land in Van Nuys. They're waiting for the plane to refuel before heading all the way back to the East Coast. Jared and Nathan return to Nathan's in Santa Monica and Maggie, Henry, Joe, Sadie and I head back to Pasadena. After saying farewell to Maggie and Henry, Joe entices me up to the penthouse with the mention that a song is owed to me on the piano.

"What would you like me to play?" he asks sweetly.

"What do you know?"

"A lot," he says. "I can play an eclectic mix, just like your playlist."

His devilish grin makes me laugh. "Play whatever you feel like playing," I suggest.

Joe motions for me to sit with him on the piano bench before he begins. Barely taking his eyes off of me, Joe starts with the beautiful Prelude in C Major by J.S. Bach. I watch his fingers dance along the keys. His movements are so graceful like he doesn't have to think about what he's doing.

"I love this song," I say as I hum along.

Joe plays several more songs, many that I'm familiar with. There's even one from the newer Pride and Prejudice movie. Some of them, I can't name off the top of my head, but their melodies are easily recognized. I lean my head back, close my eyes, and sway to the music.

Breathe In

Before my eyes open after he finishes the last song, Joe nuzzles into my neck and requests, "Stay tonight."

"What?" I return, surprised at his request.

"Stay with me tonight," he tempts.

"I need to get home," I suggest more than state.

My body is shouting yes, but my brain is screaming no.

"Please." He uses his lips to persuade me. "Please," he begs again.

"I can't," I decree.

"Not even just to snuggle," he coaxes.

"No," I return sternly.

Joe accepts my refusal, but continues to keep our bodies in close proximity.

Five minutes later, Joe, Sadie and I are in his car. Since he already knows where my apartment is, I direct him to park in the underground lot. There's an elevator in my building that makes it easier with bags.

The gentleman that he is, Joe insists on helping Sadie and me all the way up to my door. I have reservations when he crosses the doorstep with two bags in his hands, but I fight the urge to complain. He made it this far when he, Henry and Maggie came to pick me up.

Placing my bags down in the corner by the door, Joe pulls me into him. He delivers a sex-tingling kiss that makes me melt on impact.

"Can I come in? Stay for a little?" He playfully nips at my bottom lip.

"No. I'd be breaking my rules," I remind.

Wanting more, he consumes my mouth and I completely give in.

"We should probably break them one at a time then," he suggests.

"I can't break them. Not anymore," I comment before squeezing my mouth on his.

His hand slips up my back, grazing my bare skin that isn't covered by my dress followed by another thrust of his lips. My sex instantly dances with desire.

"So we are only breaking one right now by kissing?"

Moaning, I release to answer, "No. I haven't added kissing."

"So none are broken . . ." his voice trails exploring my mouth more. "I can live with that for now."

Catching my breath momentarily, I report, "Two."

Breaking our connection for a split second he contends, "Two?"

"Mmm hmm," I mumble locking my lips with his. "Possibly three if I let you stay," I confirm as he buries his face into my neck, growling.

Chapter Twenty Nine

"What are your rules?"

"I think we should say goodnight," I suggest.

"Is that what you want?"

"Joe," I plea.

I honestly don't know what I want at this point. My kissing theory does not seem to be working out right now. I know that I want him more than ever, but I know that I don't want to break any more of my rules. I'm afraid of what will happen if I do.

He gives me one long kiss that mirrors our first followed by a peck before saying, "Goodnight, beautiful. Sweet dreams."

"Goodnight, Joe."

Thirty

Now home from an eventful vacation, the last three days of the work week find me catching up with my business teams regarding current statuses and needs throughout each day and night. I'm able to avoid seeing Joe in person, but we do talk and text on occasion.

Joe heads back to the East Coast Friday afternoon to visit his mother for Mother's Day. I visit with Maggie and her family along with Henry and his parents, who finally find out about the engagement as part of their Mother's Day gift. Jared goes with Nathan to his parent's house to see Nathan's mom.

Monday morning starts a whirlwind of frenzy for me beyond work and my overzealous itch for sex. As Maggie's maid of honor, I'm subject to a bunch of unruly tasks I wasn't aware of or prepared to handle. I've never gone to been apart of a wedding, let alone gone to one before, and all of my maid of honor duties are surprising, to say the least. I love Maggie, don't get me wrong, but having to help plan her wedding before the end of summer is a daunting task, even with a bride who has every last detail planned and a maid of honor, like myself, who knows how to structure, organize and plan. If we can't find a suitable venue that can accommodate over four hundred people as well as provide privacy, all the remaining arrangements we need to make will be for nothing.

I've created two to-do lists, both with their own hierarchy of priorities that need to work side by side. My fist list is planning and scheduling all tasks pertaining to business, primarily for Naturally Me with Jared, and asking him to take on more responsibility. Maggie's able to oversee Raven Media while planning her wedding is easy and not as time consuming; there's a lot less involved and she doesn't need to oversee the programming that is required for the new software since she doesn't know coding. For me, with the added work to complete the new Raven software in time for beta testing prior to tweaking and then marketing and advertising, my free time is cut drastically. My second list is all the things that are required to do, organize and get done for Maggie's wedding.

Mŭqīn and Henry's mom, Mrs. Wú, are assisting — well, trying to assist. They both mean well when they keep making suggestions or recommendations, but their added options leave Maggie questioning all of her previous ideas, leaving her indecisive. As long as Maggie makes a decision and sticks with it, my job is much easier.

On top of work and Maggie's wedding, there is also the added fact that Jared, Nathan and Maggie have birthdays coming up in May, July and August which just add to the party planning and attending to-do list chaos.

"I don't know where to start, Emma," Maggie says, walking into my apartment.

"What are you talking about?" I ask, not sure of what topic has captivated her mind.

"The wedding . . . I thought I knew what I wanted, but now I'm not sure," she explains.

"It's your day, no one else's. Do what you and Henry want to do. If other's don't like it then tough," I encourage. "What happened to the Maggie from Hawaii who said she doesn't care what people say about having two out of the five bridesmaids being men?"

You're right," she agrees with some conviction.

"I love Mŭqīn, you know I do, but this wedding is about you and Henry. That's it," I remind.

"I know. I know," she acknowledges.

"First things first, have you and Henry set an engagement party day and time with Mŭqīn and Mrs. Wú?" I direct to get her focused and on track.

"My head is spinning from them both talking to me this past weekend that I'm not even sure," she discloses. "Is that one of the first things I need to do? How do you know that?"

"You're looking at the queen of research, Mags," I point out sarcastically.

"How could I forget a thing like that?!" teases Maggie. "Okay. Give it to me straight. What needs to be done between now and the wedding and can this be done?"

"It will be very time-consuming and stressful at times, but the key is to stay focused and decided on what you want. It can be done. Others have done it," I assure.

"Okay," she says chugging the rest of my tea. "Let's do this!"

Maggie and I go over the different tasks and events that typically make up a twelve month wedding planning time frame that she needs to have completed by the day of her wedding which has yet to be set within the next three months. I instruct her to get on the phone with Mŭqīn and Mrs. Wú to pick a day and location for the engagement party, that needed to happen yesterday, then I start making phone calls to all of the wedding venues she has listed in her binder.

Chapter Thirty

By the time Maggie gets off the phone, she has success with setting the engagement party to the following Saturday at the Wú Family house in San Marino. I, on the other hand, had to scratch every venue off of her list of options. Six of the eight were too small for a four hundred plus wedding guest list and the other two were booked solid. The two that could fit Maggie's wedding size did put her on a wait list if there are any last minute cancelations. Maggie was sad to hear about the venues, but is eager to search for other options while waiting to see what Mŭqīn and Mrs. Wú find as well.

Before dinner time, Maggie and I are able to order her engagement party invitations with all of the necessary details Mrs. Wú gave us which includes additional information about local hotel accommodations for any out of town guests who will be able to attend. The invitations are set to be finished by mid-day tomorrow. For the engagement party alone, one hundred and fifty immediate family members and friends are being invited compared to the four hundred and forty-six who will be invited to the wedding.

The next day, Maggie and I pick up the engagement party invitations before connecting up with Mŭqīn, Năinai, Mrs. Wú and Amy for lunch at the Peking Wok. While we eat, the six of us discuss the save-the-date announcements options that I have on my iPad. We can't order the cards until we have a date, but we have the design chosen which will correspond with the official wedding invitations and all of the necessary information aside from a few minor details. We also create the list of five different stores for the wedding registry before we all begin prepping the engagement party invitations to be sent out today. Amy and I both suggest sending out an email invite to everyone about the party just in case of timing issues with mail delivery. Mŭqīn and Mrs. Wú mention that they already called and sent notification to family in China.

Before Maggie and I head out to drop off the invitations at the post office, Mrs. Wú and Mŭqīn have three people joining us to be interviewed for the job of wedding planner. After some reservations, Maggie chooses a sweet woman named Amelia for the job. On the way to the post office, I mention that having an extra person to help with tasks and phone calls for the venue would be beneficial, which turns Maggie's anxiety into excitement. I selfishly love the idea of a wedding planner. She's another person to assist Maggie and me and can help take the burden off of both of us. Plus, I don't really know the first thing about planning a wedding, so having someone who does this for a living will help make things go smoothly.

Wednesday, I'm temporarily free from any wedding planning needs since I have a full, pre-scheduled day of filming for Naturally Me with Jared and the crew. After the crew sets up in their usual location, we map out the needed

Breathe In

footage that is required to be taken. I head to my bedroom to change for any shots that will include me. When I return to the living room, I find an extra person joining us.

"Hey, Jared," I call.

"Yeah, *Kitten*?"

"I need you for a second," I comment.

Jared joins me in the bedroom.

"What is he doing here?" I ask.

"Who? Joe?"

"Yeah, Joe." I establish.

What the hell is Joe doing in my apartment?!

"He's here to watch and see how we do things," Jared explains nonchalantly. "He's curious about the behind-the-scenes and all. Why?"

"I've got rules about guys being in my apartment," I remind him.

"Joe's a friend, he's one of the group. What's the big deal? Besides, Ian's been here since day one," Jared comments.

"Ian doesn't count, he's happily married with a baby on the way. Having Ian here is like having you or Nathan over," I express maintaining my cool. "Next you're going to tell me that you invited Chris too."

"No. No," he reassures. "I would never invite Chris. I know where things are with him. Is it really a big deal with Joe here? If it makes you uncomfortable, I'll ask Joe to leave."

"No. It's fine. He's here and I don't want to make a scene," I reply.

I guess this was going to happen at some point. I was just hoping that it would be way off in the distant future.

"Is it because he likes you that makes it weird?" Jared checks.

"What?! No," I quickly respond. "Does he really like me?"

I know Joe likes me, but I'm trying to downplay my awareness of it. No need to lead on to anything.

"Not to make it more uncomfortable, but yeah, he likes you. A lot," Jared verifies. "I'm surprised he hasn't made a move yet, especially after claiming you kissed him that one night in Hawaii."

"Thanks," I sarcastically say.

If Jared only knew. I'm extremely happy to know that Jared doesn't seem to know what's been going on. I don't want to lie, but I don't want to tell. This is just so weird and strange for me.

Chapter Thirty

Back to the group, Jared rounds up the team to start the first video and Joe walks over to greet me. "Hey beautiful," he says with a hug and a kiss on the cheek.

"Hey," I return.

"Is it okay that I'm here? Jared said it wouldn't be an issue, but if it is I can leave," he offers politely as if he heard what Jared and I were just talking about.

"No, it's fine," I encourage. "Just as long as I don't find you snooping in my underwear drawer, you're good."

With a wicked smile, he asks, "What about other drawers?"

I punch him in the arm. "Very funny."

The rest of the day moves fast with shot after shot of video episodes and topics. At one point, I'm able to let the team do their thing and I show Joe the current standings of the new software program for Raven. He seems pretty impressed at the speed with which it's all moving along and is eager to help in any way he can.

By five-thirty, our day is finished and we head out to dinner. I always treat the team to a celebration meal after a long day of hard work. Just sitting down at the table, I get a phone call from Maggie freaking out over still not finding a wedding venue even with Amelia's help. Excusing myself, I head out to the street to calm her. I encourage Maggie to stay focused on the positive and that the engagement party is already planned and everything is going to work out just fine. Reminding her about tomorrow helps too — when we're to start the adventure of wedding dress hunting.

For the next few hours, I dine with my crew, a few of their spouses and my friends at the Parkway Grill. Conversations are light and friendly as everyone celebrates a successful day and toast early to Jared's upcoming birthday which is in just two weeks. My mind gets distracted from some of the conversation by thinking about the to-do lists, but I force myself to stay in the present. Once we have full bellies and there's less traffic outside, everyone heads home for the night.

Joe walks me home from dinner and asks, "How's the wedding planning going?"

My eyes widen and dart to him, suggesting many different meanings.

Laughing, Joe replies, "That bad?"

"Only when you've never been to a wedding or been a part of one, have roughly three months to plan what usually is done in twelve months and a date and venue have yet to appear. Yesterday, we just sent out the one hundred and fifty invitations for the engagement party that is taking place next weekend and I've got a bride who is getting opinions from everyone on what she should do, causing her to question everything . . . I have three friends with birthdays that will be occurring the entire time on top of my businesses . . ." I answer in one long breath.

"Wow," he reflects. "Well, if you need any help, don't hesitate to let me know."

"What do you know about weddings and planning them?" I contend with amusement.

"Enough. To start, I have three married brothers, remember?!"

"Touché," I admit.

"Sounds like you need some down time already," he suggests.

"Yeah right. That won't happen until Maggie and Henry are on the plane for their honeymoon," I retort.

"I can help a little tonight if you'd let me," he mentions.

Flattered, I remark, "I'm not sleeping with you. I'm not that desperate to just throw my rules out the window, but thanks for the offer."

"I wasn't offering sex, but it's good to know you were considering it," he teases. "I was going to suggest that we get Sadie and head back to my place for a movie and maybe some snuggling."

His recommendation gets a smile from me which in turn gets him to do the same. I definitely need a break and Joe could be a really good distraction.

Twenty minutes later, Sadie, Joe and I are at Joe's penthouse. "Where's Anna?" I search.

"She's off for the rest of the night. Why?" he questions.

"Is it just us?"

"Yes," he confirms with a boyish grin. "Is that okay?"

"Yeah," I say tentatively.

What have I gotten myself into? Was this a good idea?

"I promise to behave," he offers.

"Yeah . . . that was really convincing and reassuring," I present in a mocking tone.

The thought of being alone with Joe makes me edgy. There's no one here to interrupt or catch us snuggling, but there isn't anyone her to caution other things from possibly happening.

Chapter Thirty

Just snuggling, Emma. That's what he said. Joe said he'd behave. You can just snuggle. You can. Can you?

After scooping some ice cream for dessert, Joe and I settle in the left corner of his couch. He sits down first and guides me to sit between his legs with my head against his chest. Once Sadie gets settled, Joe covers us with a blanket before handing me the bowl of salted caramel yumminess.

"This is good, but not as good as my homemade recipe," I comment.

"You make your own ice cream?"

"Mmm hmm," I return with a third mouthful.

"Do you plan on sharing? You know I made that big bowl for us to share?"

"And here I thought you were just trying to give me a sugar rush," I say sarcastically.

In less than ten minutes, Joe and I finish the huge bowl of ice cream. We play fight over the last few spoonfuls, accusing the other of sneaking some extra bites.

Joe sweetly caresses his fingers over my bare forearm as I try to watch the movie. My brain bounces between everything that's going on and the insatiable itch this Sex Kitten has and is having bad for the man behind her. Periodically, Joe kisses me on the top of my head and I'm left wondering if this was a good idea. My kissing theory is a dud so far. All I want to do is to continue kissing him and there are other lustful vision of desire dancing in my head.

At some point during the movie, I shift to reposition my body and end up looking at Joe. Why am I compelled to look at him?! I have no idea. He immediately makes eye contact before lowering his lips to mine. Joe's hand leaves my arm to find and hold my neck as he continues to ardently kiss me with only a little tongue on occasion. Joe breaks the embrace each time, but a couple of times he initiates first by repositioning my head for easier access to my lips.

As the movie comes to an end, Joe squeezes me tight. "Will you stay tonight?"

"No," I politely refuse, looking deep into his eyes. Leaning forward, I kiss him fervently.

"No one is here," he coaxes before returning the passionate embrace and pulling me onto his lap.

"All the more reason for me to leave," I let out in a breathy voice.

Joe moans his disappointment but doesn't push.

Fifteen minutes later, after making out, Joe walks Sadie and me home before we partake in our regular departure ritual.

After delicately mauling each other's mouths, Joe bids, "Goodnight, beautiful."

"Goodnight Joe," I return with a smile.

Thirty One

Over the course of the rest of the work week and into the weekend, when I'm not tied up with working or personal items, my time is dedicated to Maggie and assisting her with wedding choices and planning. My schedule is booked from sunup to well past sundown.

Come Friday afternoon, there still isn't an official wedding date or venue. However, we do have Maggie's custom wedding dress, a mother of the bride, a mother of the groom, a grandmother of the bride and three bridesmaids' dresses being created all thanks to one of Jimmy Covelli's designer friends, Ali Jacobs. Maggie, Amy, Kim, Mŭqīn, Năinai, Mrs. Wú and I were measured on Thursday, and hopefully within a month, the dresses will be at a point for us to do the first fitting.

To help take the edge off of Maggie's anxiety, I arrange for us to visit a baker with all the girls who were fitted along with Henry, Jared and Amelia to taste wedding cakes and desserts. Maggie and Henry didn't select what they wanted, but they did enjoy the sugar high before Henry has to leave for a business trip.

Certain things like flower arrangements, a photographer, a band or DJ, place settings and other things can't be finalized due to not having the venue yet, but Maggie and Henry have half of their gift registry completed as well as all the details for the engagement party. In the meantime, I have Kim, Amy and Jared assisting with the bridal shower. We're scheduling to have the shower sometime in June at Kim's house in San Marino.

Nathan, as busy as he is, graciously takes the lead on finalizing Jared's birthday party that is scheduled this Wednesday, three days before the engagement party. I instruct Nathan to oversee the final arrangements since the bills have already been handled.

With Henry away for business this weekend and into next week, Maggie plans to stay with me. She voices that she loves and appreciates everything that Mŭqīn and Mrs. Wú are doing, but needs a break from all of their help and opinions. Aside from a much quieter environment as a de-stressor, I'm also able to provide Maggie with some much-needed physical relief and satisfaction which I selfishly enjoy.

"Do you think we'll find a venue soon?" Maggie asks with concern.

"Of course, Mags," I assure.

It's just a matter of which one and when.

breathe In

"Good. Oh, Henry and I decided last night that if we are going to have bachelor and bachelorette party, that we want it a few days or a week before the wedding and we don't want anything big . . . just a few friends," she presents. "We'd don't mind having the parties become one party either."

"Really?! That could make some things easier. I'll contact Joe to make plans," I reply. "Have you and Henry picked the rings yet?"

"No, but we narrowed it down to three each. We might need your help when he gets back," she states.

"Sure," I confirm. "I've already started to look into getting the marriage certificate and license."

"Thanks so much, Emma. I really appreciate all of your help. You don't know how much having you help with all of this means to me," she says.

"Of course, Mags. Anything for my sister," I encourage.

"Does Jared know about the birthday party or is he still in the dark?"

"Still in the dark from what Nathan tells me," I reinforce.

"Awesome. I can't wait for Wednesday. I think it will be a great to get Henry's and my attention off of the wedding for a little bit," she admits.

"I bet," I console. "I know how Mŭqīn and Năinai can be, even with the best of intentions."

"I know, right?!" she agrees.

An hour after dinner and a session of sex, Maggie and I are curled up on my bed watching a movie with Sadie. My phone chirps halfway through and I discretely check to see who's calling.

I don't answer, but text Joe back. "Maggie's over."

"Is she missing Henry?" he writes.

"And, avoiding family regarding wedding opinions." I return.

"How long is she staying?"

"Not sure. Most likely the whole weekend. Why?" I answer.

"Curious. Thought I might be able to convince you for another snuggle night," he texts. "What are you ladies up to?"

"Movie," I answer.

"Where?"

"My bed."

It takes him a few extra seconds to reply. "Naked?"

"No."

"Too bad." He added a winking emoticon.

Chapter Thirty One

"We were earlier," I jab.

Let's see him respond to this.

"Any photos or video?" he texts after at least twenty seconds.

"Nope. Jealous?" I poke.

"A little," he professes. "Was really hoping to get to see you."

"See me or see me naked?" I pry.

Why not have a little fun? I'm safe texting.

"Both," he returns.

I smile ironically at his admission.

"Henry tell you about the laid back bachelor and bachelorette party they want to do? They wouldn't mind combining them into one?" I reply, skillfully moving the conversation off of me being naked and the idea of him being on top of me and naked out of my head.

"No. Good to know, though," he confirms. "Looks like we get to spend some extra time together. For planning purposes, of course."

"Right . . ." I sarcastically respond.

"Who are you talking to?" Maggie interrupts.

Before I can answer, her phone rings.

"It's Henry," she squeals.

I pause the movie as she leaves the bedroom for some private time. "Henry just called," I inform Joe.

Why did I just tell him?

"Alone at last," he muses. "So, who's better to snuggle with?"

"Up for debate," I taunt.

"If you'd stay the night I could sway you or change your mind," he writes.

"Just friends," I assert.

"For now . . . ." He kindly changes the subject, "Talked with Jared earlier."

"About what?"

"General stuff. Looks like he still doesn't know about Wednesday," he confirms.

"Good. Nathan will be happy to hear that," I reply.

"How long do Maggie and Henry usually talk?"

"Not sure. Why?"

"The more they talk, the more time I get with you," he comments. "Will you switch to the phone?"

"Why?"

"So I can hear you."

"Why do you need to hear me?" I write.

"It's easier to know and understand your reaction," he states. "And, I like hearing your voice."

"No," I object.

I want to hear his voice too, but I like the advantage texting provides, ensuring the mystery of what I say and what I mean.

"Why not?"

Maggie bounces back in the room with an improved mood.

"Maggie's back. Starting movie," I inform him.

"Text me later," he writes.

"Maybe," I contend.

"Please."

"Can't guarantee anything," I say.

"I'll be hoping you do. Goodnight, beautiful," he texts.

My fingers stutter across the phone screen to write, "Goodnight, Joe."

Maggie and I finish the movie and then have another round of sex before succumbing to the late evening for rest. After using the bathroom for the last time tonight, I find a passed out Maggie on the bed with Sadie curled up next to her.

I send one final text just after midnight to Joe. "Sweet dreams."

I hear my phone buzz and I check Joe's response.

"With you in them, I will." Joe adds a winking emoticon. "Goodnight, beautiful."

"Goodnight, Joe," I write.

Thirty Two

Just as I finish cleaning up breakfast Saturday morning, I get a text message from Amelia to call her. I return the call immediately after drying my hands.

"What's up Amelia?"

"I can't get a hold of Maggie. Where is she?" she says frantically.

"She's here and in the shower. Why?"

"I need to talk to her right now. This is time sensitive. I've got the St. Regis on the other line," she exclaims.

"Hold on. Maggie!" I yell running into the bathroom. "Maggie!"

"What?" Maggie answers.

"Get out of the shower. Amelia needs to talk to you. She has the St. Regis on the other line," I explain.

"What?!" she shouts. "Holy crap!" She jumps out of the shower and grabs the phone from me as I wrap her in a towel. "Hi, Amelia!"

Following Maggie out to the bedroom, I listen and watch. I pace the room with Sadie on my heels waiting for more information. I should have pressed the button for speakerphone to know what's being said.

"Okay, hold on. Emma, can you get my phone and call Henry?"

"Why?"

"I need to know if likes the date," she explains.

"Maggie, you don't need to talk to Henry. He told you that any date would be fine. You need to trust you gut and make a decision," I instruct.

Processing my words, Maggie answers Amelia about ten seconds later. "We'll take it!" Maggie beams the minute the words come out of her mouth.

"So?" I inspect as she hands back my phone.

"So, we've got the St. Regis for the Saturday before my birthday!" she squeals with complete elation. Jumping up and down, Maggie continues with more details. "Apparently a celebrity just canceled. The hotel didn't say why, but we've got the entire hotel. It's going to be only us for the whole weekend!"

My heart settles and tension releases from my body that I didn't know I had. It's all coming together. Maggie's going to have her dream wedding.

"Get dressed and call Henry. I'll call Mǔqīn and Jared. We've got a lot of things to do," I direct.

The timeline for the wedding has just been bumped by approximately a whole month. Maggie and Henry were shooting for late August but now the wedding is set for the end of July, just three days before Maggie's twenty-fifth birthday. I'm grateful that we've got Amelia to help as well as the rest of the family. Everyone is going to need to pull together if it's all going to happen and happen successfully.

Maggie, Mŭqīn, Năinai, Mrs. Wú, Amy and I drive down to the St. Regis in Dana Point, California to meet up with the head manager of the hotel. Amelia arrives at the same time as the rest of us while Jared and Nathan show up about ten minutes later. Formal introductions, arrangements and instructions on the variety of services the hotel can provide are the priority of this initial meeting. Maggie, Amelia and I will be back several more times with Henry to determine food and wine selection for the rehearsal dinner and wedding reception along with other meetings for table arrangements and other necessary incidentals. We are given a brief tour before we are provided a complimentary lunch for our small group. As my companions finish eating, I'm able to collect the remaining needed information to complete both the save-the-date announcements and the wedding invitations. I order a proof of each of the few designs that Maggie had chosen which should be ready by Monday.

By the time we leave the hotel, everyone has agreed to their assigned tasks to move the wedding planning forward. Jared and Nathan follow Maggie and me back to my place. As I cook dinner, Maggie fills Nathan and Jared in on all of the details they may have missed, on what needs to be done, as well as checking in with Henry.

Jared and Nathan leave around ten, and after getting changed into my pajamas, I find Maggie asleep in my bed. Not wanting to disturb her, I grab a book and head to the living room.

My phone suddenly vibrates, scaring me enough to cause me to jump a little.

"Heard you ladies got good news today," streams across the screen as a text message from Joe.

"Yes," I confirm. "Henry tell you?"

"Yes. You ladies celebrating?" he continues.

"No. Did earlier. Maggie is passed out," I respond.

"What are you doing?"

"Reading. You?" I inquire.

"Was trying to do the same," he writes.

"Trying?" I text.

Chapter Thirty Two

The phone buzzes at me. Joe's calling.

"Hey," I greet in a hushed tone.

"Hey, beautiful," he returns.

"Why were you *trying* to read," I investigate.

"I was distracted . . . kept thinking of you," he admits.

"Joe," I mildly protest.

I secretly enjoy hearing his confession.

"It's the truth," he admits. "Any chance I can see you before Wednesday?"

"No," I argue.

"We do have a bachelor-bachelorette party to plan," he reminds.

"That can wait until after Saturday," I claim.

"You avoiding me?" he teases.

"Maybe," I nudge back.

"Mmm," he hums. "You have an interesting way of engaging in foreplay."

"This is not foreplay," I appeal.

Definitely flirting, but this is not foreplay.

We sit quietly on the phone for a few minutes of relaxed silence. It's funny how it never feels awkward. I enjoy listening to him breathe on the other end. It makes me think of the second time we shared a bed together. The first time was a little stressful, but the second time was thoroughly enjoyable.

"Did you fall asleep on me?" he checks.

"No," I laugh. I watch Sadie suddenly get up and head to the front door.

I'm not sure what she's doing.

"Where are you?" he asks.

"In my apartment. Remember?" I remind.

"I know that. Where in your apartment?" his voice is quieter.

"Why? Are you trying to have phone sex with me while Maggie's asleep?" I accuse playfully.

"No, but we could if you're up for it," he wickedly returns.

My sex tingles at the idea. It technically wouldn't be breaking a rule. Why am I even considering the notion?

"I don't think so," I reply in the best resolute tone I can muster.

Ten seconds later, I hear a strange noise.

"Knock knock," he whispers.

Sadie starts whimpering.

"What do you mean . . ." my voice trails as my brain processes the noise and his words. "Where are you?"

"Knock knock," he repeats.

The noise happens again and Sadie's whimpering gets louder.

Jumping up, I rush to the door. I look out the peephole to find Joe standing outside. Shit. Crap. My heart rate increases as a weird mix of emotions run through me.

Instead of opening the door, I question in a loud whisper, "What are you doing here?"

"Wanted to see you . . . and Sadie," he confidently replies.

Without thinking, I open the door. "Go . . ." I begin to order, but he cuts me off with a sultry kiss. My brain fights to gain control of my body that has already wrapped my arms around his neck.

Chuckling, Joe announces with his lips still against mine, "See. I knew you missed me too."

I bashfully peel myself off of him, but he keeps a firm grip and doesn't let me go right away. When Joe bends down to pet Sadie, I check to make sure the door is unlocked before I close it behind me.

"What are you doing here?" I express with agitated shock.

"I told you. I wanted to see you." He sandwiches my body between his and the hallway wall, nuzzling me.

My hands instinctually slide up his arms and I cuddle into him. Joe's mouth sweeps up my neck towards my ear, shooting exquisite electric shocks throughout my body. Filled with desire, my lips seize his. I reluctantly pull away once I recognize my blatant need and embarrassing actions. He guides my attention back to his face as he gently nudges my cheek with his palm. Before either of us say anything, his mouth is seducing mine. He releases my lips as I try to reconnect, wanting more.

"You can't be here," I caution.

"No one can see us. No one will know. I promise." He reassuringly kisses me several time.

"Maggie's inside," I remind.

"She's asleep," he replies calmly, followed by his mouth returning to mine. "It's okay."

We stay connected and stand in silence for a while as our bodies have their own conversation. Joe caresses my cheek each time our mouths unite.

Chapter Thirty Two

"What are your rules?" he mumbles.

"Huh? Why?"

"I want to understand them," he admits.

"Why?"

"You have them for a reason, and I want to understand them. I want to understand you."

Contention forms in my stomach over telling him. Part of me wants to throw my rules out the window, but at the same time, I need them more than ever. I know that things are changing and that scares me even more.

Considering what to say, I embarrassingly admit twisting his shirt in my fingers, "Umm . . . It's complicated . . . especially with you . . . I . . . ."

"Will you tell me?" he requests politely, trying to get me to look at him.

I don't need to let him know about the internal struggle that I'm having. He just wants me to tell him what they are. It's not his fault that I'm confused by my wants and desires. I don't understand them which frightens me.

Sucking in a deep breath and avoiding eye contact, I reveal them. "No dates, before or after meeting. Never sleep over at their place after sex. Never let a guy know where I live. Never have a guy back to my place. Always us protection. Never sleep with a guy who I could or do see regularly and always have more than one exit strategy."

Joe doesn't say anything for a minute and I start to panic. I can feel my body fidgeting.

"So we've broken just a few," he states matter-of-factly with a hint of consoling.

"You're not some random guy. Your a friend of Henry's. Breaking them was never a consideration with any of Maggie's ex-boyfriends' friends," I blurt.

Chuckling under his breathe, he comments, "Well, at least kissing and snuggling aren't rules. I'm glad you didn't add them."

"Yeah," I timidly laugh.

I can't believe I told him. What was I thinking?

"I should let you go," he advises.

"Okay," I agree.

"See you Wednesday," he proclaims more than asks.

"Wednesday," I repeat.

"Goodnight, beautiful," he delivers delightfully, sealed with a kiss.

"Goodnight, Joe," I express after seeking another kiss.

Breathe In

Joe walks away backward with a grin on his face until he hits the corner for the elevators. Once he's out of sight, I sneak back inside without a sound. I grab my vibrator and take care of myself in the office as to not draw any unwanted attention or wake Maggie. She is sound asleep and doesn't even flinch when I get into bed.

Sunday meets Maggie and me with reviewing the proofs for the save-the-date cards. The gold embossed cards with an adorable photo of Maggie and Henry are ordered and expected to be ready by Wednesday morning the latest. We have a lunch meeting with Amelia, that lasts several hours, to choose which of the services the St. Regis offers that Maggie and Henry will be using. As Maggie and Amelia talk with Henry on the phone regarding other arrangements, I check in with Nathan about Jared's party that is happening in a couple of days. Nathan's excited to hear that Jared still doesn't know about the party and that Joe confirmed Jared's present will be arriving Tuesday.

Early evening and dinner finds Maggie, Jared and me using my iPad to select more items for the wedding gift registry while Henry is on speaker phone. Henry sweetly delegates all decisions to Maggie, but he happily offers his opinion and desires. I keep to myself and only direct them back to the task at hand when their chatting gets too far off topic. Maggie and Henry talk into the evening as Jared, Sadie and I curl up on the couch.

Monday morning, I wake my best friends up to join me at the local trampoline place for an early morning, hour long intense workout to begin our day and planned, hectic week. Maggie's grateful for the distraction and the physical exertion. After showering and breakfast, the three of us take care of business needs. With a short nap and lunch in our bellies, we then journey with Sadie out to our next round of wedding appointments. Time to meet up with Amelia to pick out a band or a DJ for the ceremony and the reception.

Maggie successfully chooses a harpist for the ceremony and decides on a DJ for the reception. Jared parts ways with us to help Nathan at Nathaniel's. With Jared gone, Maggie and I stop at the Mondrian Hotel where we're hosting Jared's private birthday party up in their infamous Skybar. I check in with the management team on any last minute details that need to be addressed that Nathan couldn't take care of over the phone. Maggie and I then proceed to the private airport to pick up Henry and make our way to the Li family house in Chinatown for dinner.

Waking alone to peace in my apartment Tuesday, I quickly jump into my regular routine and prep for the Naturally Me crew for another day of filming. Jared and I decided to get ahead of schedule with the filming side of things prior to our days being bombarded with last minute errands and details for Maggie's wedding. With extra filming complete, we can stay ahead of schedule

Chapter Thirty Two

and have a backlog of video that only need to be edited and posted. During our lunch break, Jared has an awesome idea for Maggie's wedding. Before the end of the day, Henry and Maggie hire Ian's and his wife's company for video and photography.

With everyone gone, I jump on the phone with Nathan making sure that everything is lined up for Jared's birthday party tomorrow. "As far as I can tell, Jared doesn't know," I mention.

"Good. I hate to keep Maggie in the dark about the added surprise, but I know she'd slip," Nathan adds.

"I know. At least Joe has been a big help," I console.

We don't like keeping secrets from Maggie, but with all of her wedding planning, she can easily get distracted and say something by mistake to Jared.

"Thanks for footing most of the bill, *Kitten*."

"I'm happy to since you've been handling most of the arrangements for me on top of being so busy with Nathaniel's. There's no way I'd be able to plan it with the wedding and Maggie's and your birthdays coming up," I express.

"Did Joe say if Jimmy and Allen are going to making it?"

"They were ninety percent sure last time I talked to Joe, but I'll double check since I've got to call him anyway about the gift. I'll text you," I say.

"Great. I've got to go. I need to finish a few things before Jared gets here," he indicates.

"Sure. See you tomorrow, babe."

"Love you," Nathan declares.

"Love you too," I add.

Not wanting to call or text Joe right away, and avoid any chance of him trying to come over, I take Sadie out for a long, peaceful stroll. An hour later, I change and rebound before hopping into the bathtub.

Twenty minutes into my relaxing bath, my phone chirps.

"Hey, beautiful," Joe writes.

I dry off my hands and pick up the phone to respond. "Hey."

"Jimmy and Allen just arrived," he offers.

"Awesome."

"What are you up to?"

With a grin, I admit the truth, "In the tub."

There's no way he's coming over if Jimmy and Allen are with him and a girl can have a little fun.

"Mmm . . ." he texts. "I'd be there in less than five minutes if my brother wasn't here."

"What makes you think I'd open the door?"

"Don't know. But, that doesn't mean I wouldn't beg to be let in," he muses. "How did your day go?"

"Good. Got a lot more filming done. Maggie and Henry have a photographer and videographer. How was your day?"

"Long, but good. Would have been better if you were around. Who'd they get?"

He sure knows how to make a woman feel special.

"Hired Ian from the Naturally Me crew. How's the birthday gift?" I redirect our attention.

"Good. You sure Jared's going to like it?"

"If not, he'll hate me for a while," I explain.

"I don't think he'll hate you," Joe consoles.

"Thanks."

"Want to sneak over to cuddle?"

Laughing, I write back, "No."

I do want to feel his body on mine, but the idea of getting caught is not appealing to me. I'm not sure what we are doing, but I like it.

"Please," he begs.

"Use your pillow," I suggest.

"I am. It's not the same, especially when it doesn't smell or feel like you," he writes. "When can I see you again?"

"You're going to see me tomorrow," I remind.

"Not like that," he texts.

"Like how?" I question, feigning ignorance.

"Just you and me," he explains. "Alone. Snuggling."

"Not sure," I answer.

I want to see him sooner than later, but I'm getting nervous. I'm not sure where things are going with him. I like the flirting. It's fun. However, I do know that I'm tempted to break more of my rules.

"Why?"

"Because."

"Because?" he searches.

Chapter Thirty Two

I don't write back.

"Tomorrow, then," he confirms.

"Tomorrow," I agree.

"I'll pick you up at three," he instructs.

"Sounds good," I write with eager anticipation.

"Goodnight, beautiful."

"Goodnight, Joe."

Thirty Three

Wednesday morning I pick up Maggie's save-the-date cards and hop on the train with Sadie to meet up with her and the rest of the family at the Li home. In less than two hours, Mǔqīn, Nǎinai, Amy, Jade and I have the announcements sealed and ready to be sent out in the mail. Amelia, Henry and Mrs. Wú join us shortly after and we go over more details for the engagement party. Normally, I would invite Jared along, but with his party tonight, I don't want the cat getting out of the bag.

I excuse myself from the group of women around one-thirty to head home and start preparing for Jared's party. Before leaving, I give Henry the green light to fill everyone in on the plan and the secrecy. We should be safe from Jared knowing, but I remind Henry not to let Maggie talk to Jared until tonight.

Once home, I rebound for a few minutes before getting into the shower. As I finish getting my dress on, Joe texts that he's coming up. Fifteen minutes early as always. I rush to double check Sadie's bag and finish transferring items to my gold clutch. There's a knock on my door just as I'm about to put my shoes on.

Wearing an elegant navy blue pinstriped suit and crisp, light blue dress shirt, Joe greets me with a passionate kiss before the door is opened all the way. "Hey, beautiful," he says in his sexy voice.

"Hey," I reply in a similar tone. I'm immediately lost in his ocean blue eyes that shine with his suit.

"Looks like we're matching," he says.

Glancing down at our clothes, because I temporarily forgot what I put on, I notice what he's talking about. I'm wearing a navy blue dress that has a squared-off scoop neckline that boasts a chic notch that accentuates my cleavage with puffed cap sleeves. I've accented my outfit with a curved double gold bar necklace and the gold bracelet Jared gave me for my twenty-first birthday that is engraved with the words of a Chinese proverb, Where there is life, there is hope.

"You better put your shoes on or else we aren't leaving this apartment," he confesses his internal thoughts.

Clearing my throat, I reluctantly slide away from his body. "Maybe I should change," I comment.

"If you take that dress off you won't be putting anything else back on," he declares, sliding his right hand on my hip.

I flush at his forwardness. Joe's getting more daring — a little too daring perhaps. Determined to stay clothed and to adhere to my rules, I put aside my concern of our matching outfits. I'm not ready to humor the idea of us doing anything sexual, let alone give him any indication that there's any chance for something to happen.

Once my shoes are on, Joe escorts me down to his black Rolls Royce Phantom. We slide into the back seats with Sadie first, followed by me and then Joe. Joe's driver temporarily pulls into his building for us to drop off Sadie; Anna is watching her for the night.

Walking into the Mondrian lobby, Joe and I are greeted by the manager immediately. Before following the manager to Skybar that is located on the roof, I inform him that I need to take care of something first and I'll meet him there in approximately twenty minutes.

Getting into the elevator, Joe steadies me as we rise to the sixth floor. I'm excited and nervous at what is about to happen.

"You ready?" Joe breathes into my ear.

"Mmm hmm," I return as my heart beats faster.

This is it. Hesitating for a moment, I breathe in deeply to relax my jitters. Joe's hand raises slowly and knocks.

"Coming," is faintly said on the other side of the door. The door opens and we're greeted by a smiling, older gentleman with salt and pepper hair and dark amber eyes. "You must be Emma," his raspy, sweet voice announces. He delicately takes my right hand in his and kisses my knuckles. "You're more beautiful than I expected from the photos on your website."

"Thanks," I accept as he steps in to hug me. I return the sentiment to easy both our nerves.

"You must be Joseph," he adds extending his hand forward. "Emma's boyfriend, I presume."

"Just friends," Joe corrects with a grin.

"Looks like you're working on fixing that from the looks of it," the older gentleman replies.

I nudge Joe at his open response that is smeared all over his face. "May we come in," I ask, trying to change the subject.

"Yes, yes. Please come in. Where are my manners?!"

Joe remains standing as I sit in one of the small chairs by a round table.

"Mr. Frasier . . ." I begin.

"Please, call me Aaron," he insists.

Chapter Thirty Three

"Mr. . . . Aaron. It's so nice to finally meet you," I continue.

"Likewise, Emma. You don't know what this all means to me," his voice cracks as he sits on the edge of the bed.

"I just hope that our efforts aren't for nothing," I admit sheepishly.

"Just to be able to see him again will bring peace to my heart, even if he wants nothing to do with me," the older man sitting in front of me reveals. "If Jared is the person you say he has become, all we can do is believe in him."

"I agree." Checking the clock on my phone, I explain, "Everyone is scheduled to be here within the next half hour. I have to meet with the manager upstairs to review a few things, but you are more than welcome to join Joe and me instead of staying here, if you'd like."

"Sure, that would be lovely. What time is Jared supposed to get here?"

"Not until around five," I report.

The three of us head up to Skybar and I'm very pleased to find that the staff has provided everything that was requested and the decor is more beautiful than I expected. As the manager and I wrap up our conversation, Maggie, Henry and the rest of the Li family are ushered in minus the children. Jimmy and Allen arrive five minutes later along with Mr. and Mrs. Wú.

Joe and I make introductions with our friends and family to Mr. Aaron Frasier before the rest of the invited guests are allowed to join us. Maggie immediately cries when she meets Mr. Frasier and the entire family openly accepts him. I only hope that Jared does the same.

By the time all of the guests have arrived, I get a text from Nathan that he and Jared are just five minutes away. I instruct everyone to take their seats at the dining tables around the room. Maggie, Joe, Henry, Jimmy, Allen, the Li family and I hover near the main entrance before all the lights, but a few hanging Christmas style lights, are turned off.

As the door is held open for Nathan and Jared to enter, the main lights are switched on and everyone shouts "Happy Birthday!"

With tears forming in his eyes, Jared greets everyone who comes up to him.

We've finally surprised him for his birthday. Aside from our immediate family, I've invited a large group of friends and acquaintances Jared has made over the years. Molly, Garrett, Sophie, Ian and his wife, Vanessa and her boyfriend, and Connor and his boyfriend are with us just to name a few of the hundred people we invited.

As cocktails and hors d'oeuvres begin to be served, I lead Mr. Frasier over to Jared. The look of shock consumes Jared's face as the awareness of whom

I'm with sets in. To preface everything before anything happens, I address Jared and take full responsibility. "Jared if you're going to be mad at anyone, please only be mad at me."

"Jared," Mr. Frasier musters, holding back sobs.

"Pop-Pop?!" Jared mumbles. "Is it really you?"

"Yes, my dear boy. I've missed you so much," Mr. Frasier confirms, reaching forward to Jared.

Within a blink of an eye, Jared rushes towards his grandfather and hugs him. My anxiety dissipates at seeing the warm and happy reunion, and I fight the urge to cry myself. Maggie wraps her arms around me as we stand and watch our best friend reunite with a long lost family member.

Jared's Pop-Pop, Mr. Aaron Frasier reached out to me online in March through Naturally Me. It took me two weeks before I sent a reply because I was nervous and not sure what to do. I initially avoided telling Nathan and Maggie because I wasn't sure if Mr. Frasier was telling the truth.

Over time, Mr. Frasier explained to me and shared stories that he was Jared's grandfather. I confided in Joe and he helped me hire a private investigator to validate my suspicions and Mr. Frasier's claims before telling anyone else. Once I had proof beyond some of the pictures Mr. Frasier shared over time, I spoke to Nathan during one of our business meetings when Jared wasn't around. Nathan and I debated back and forth about our apprehension before ultimately deciding on reacquainting them. The question no longer became should we, it was then a matter of how and when.

Mr. Frasier is Jared's mother's father. Not long after losing his wife to illness, Mr. Frasier had also lost his only grandson after the incident with Jared and Jared's father. Apparently, Mr. Frasier had known that Jared was different at an early age despite his daughter's and son-in-law's denial. When he found out that Jared had left, Mr. Frasier has been searching for Jared ever since. Mr. Frasier didn't want Jared to think he felt the same way as Jared's parents.

Leaving Jared and Mr. Frasier alone, the rest of my friends and family mingle with our guests. The two men have a lot of catching up to do and I've got plenty of time to hear all about it. I'm just happy that the reunion is a positive one.

Sometime later, I feel familiar arms wrap around me from behind.

"Thank you," Jared cries into my neck.

Spinning to see him, I return the gesture. "You're welcome."

Not wanting to let go, Jared and I stay locked for a long while.

"I love you," he professes.

Chapter Thirty Three

"I love you too," I genuinely remark.

"You don't know how much this means to me . . ." he begins before tears take over again.

"We've got plenty of time for you to tell me all about it," I encourage.

"Yeah," Jared sobs. "I wish I could do the same for you."

"Tonight isn't about me," I scold gently. "I've given Mr. Frasier accommodations until Sunday here at the hotel and I also got you and Nathan a room for tonight."

"Yeah, they told me. He insists you call him *Pop-Pop*," Jared affirms, nuzzling more into my neck.

"*Pop-Pop* it is." After a few minutes of our embrace, I pull back a little and wipe the tears from Jared's face. "This is supposed to be a happy day," I tease.

"It is. These are happy tears," he explains.

"Good," I say. "Today is your birthday. Go visit with your grandfather. I'm not going anywhere."

"You better not," he taunts, kissing me on the nose.

The rest of the night, the air is filled with love, laughter and happiness and the man of the hour is Jared. The DJ plays wicked music for dancing, we have half naked men as servers who also put on a burlesque show for the birthday boy, all courtesy of Nathan, and the drinks and food are endless.

I finally sneak out to use the restroom and to take a breather. As I step through the doors to head back into the party, I hear Jared getting on the microphone.

"Excuse me everyone," Jared begins.

A hush gradually drapes the crowd.

"Excuse me. I just wanted to say thank you to all of you for coming tonight. It means so much to me."

A few people whistle and yell Jared's name.

"There are a few people here that I want to acknowledge and thank. Emma, Maggie and Nathan. I love you! Thank you for making tonight happen." Jared clears his throat before continuing. "If you haven't met him already, please make sure you meet Pop-Pop." Jared pulls Pop-Pop up on stage. "I haven't seen my grandfather for ten years . . . ."

The crowd erupts with cheers and whistles.

"And . . . he wouldn't be here today if it wasn't for someone else in this room . . . someone very special to me," he pauses to hold back tears. "Emma . . . where are you, *Kitten*?"

Breathe In

Dread consumes me. Jared knows I hate being the center of attention, especially with large crowds. I duck into a corner to hide.

"I know you're out there. Stop hiding and get your ass up here, Kitten," Jared requests with an assertive but loving tone.

Joe snatches my hand and drags me to the stage as I shake my head profusely. Crap. How did he find me? Maggie pushes me from behind.

"No, no, no . . ." I mutter.

A few people meow as I'm pulled closer to the stage.

"Here she is . . ." Jared announces as he helps me up the stairs. "You're going to need to get used to this for Maggie's wedding," he broadcasts over the microphone.

I wince at the truth as everyone politely laughs. See a chance, I try to flee.

"Ohh no you don't . . ." Jared stresses. "You're staying right here." He wraps his left arm around me holding me tight. "Words can not express my deepest gratitude to my girl . . . my sister . . . my Kitten . . . my Emma . . . for making tonight even better, by helping bring my Pop-Pop back to me. I love you, Emma." Jared squeezes me and kisses my cheek.

The crowd cheers and applauds as the discomfort settles into my bones.

"So with that said . . . thank you everyone, again, and enjoy the rest of the evening!"

I'm grateful for Jared's short speech and know that I'll get over it after another drink or two.

Later in the night, Pop-Pop and I share with Jared and the rest of the family the whole story of how Pop-Pop came to be here at the party. Jared apologized to Joe for not including him when thanking Nathan, Maggie and me, but Joe was a gentleman about it.

Everyone stays until the place closes, except Maggie's family. Thankfully, all of our guests graciously leave as the staff politely leads the way out.

Pop-Pop is a trooper and stays up until our time in the restaurant comes to a close. Joe and I walk Pop-Pop back to his room, and when we get there, Nathan comes out the room across the hall and reveals that the hotel arranged for him and Jared to be near Pop-Pop, allowing their conversations to easily continue into the night.

Joe takes me home, but we stop by his place first to get Sadie. We find Sadie and Anna asleep on the couch when we get in. Jimmy and Allen aren't back yet, which means they're still out partying or with my friends.

Chapter Thirty Three

Sweeping me into him for a kiss after Anna leaves, Joe requests, "Stay the night."

"No," I hesitantly disagree.

"Why not?" he questions, kissing me before I can answer.

"Jimmy and Allen are here," I present.

"Not yet," he disputes, then tries to seduce me more with his tongue.

"Soon enough," I battle in between breaths from our mouths being connected. "Beside, even if I considered it, they'd see me in the morning and I have nothing to wear."

"You won't need clothes," he states, barely letting go of my lips.

"Exactly. Which supports my refusal."

"I'll lend you a shirt," he offers.

Pecking him on the lips, I repeat myself. "No."

"Then, can I come over to your place?" he questions with the sexy voice.

Joe is starting to become more forward which is turning me on and also heightening my resolve to follow my rules. I can't break my rules — not any more.

"No," I say a few seconds later after saying it in my head first.

"What if I promise to behave?" he searches.

"Definitely not," I reply.

Joe huffs into my neck and groans at his failure to sway me.

Dropping Sadie and me off at the apartment, Joe tries to persuade me into letting him come inside. I contend with the notion that if he did stay that our friends would assume we are sleeping together. After some time kissing in the doorway, Joe reluctantly heads home.

"Goodnight, beautiful," he sings, rounding the corner to the elevators.

"Goodnight, Joe."

Thirty Four

Thursday and Friday, I close myself off from distractions to focus on business. I spend the majority of the days working on the new Raven software and some Naturally Me content. I'm glad I chose to stay away from people to work because half of the time I am inundated with phone calls or text messages for both personal and business reasons.

Maggie is mostly calling about wedding stuff and asks me to tell Jared that Pop-Pop is invited to the engagement party. I only get to speak with Jared briefly, but I don't mind, knowing he's with his grandfather. Amy is calling to give me updates on the information gathering she was doing for me about Maggie's bridal party. Nathan is calling about Nathaniel's. Henry is beginning to panic a little between Maggie, her family and his family and I think he is seeking calm reassurance from me that everything is being taken care of. Joe — well, let's just say that Joe is Joe.

Early Saturday afternoon, I'm finishing getting ready for the engagement party as my phone chirps from a text message.

"Here," Joe writes.

Like clockwork, Joe is fifteen minutes early.

"It's open," I text back before heading into my closest to get my earrings and shoes.

In many traditions, it's not customary for anyone else to wear white other than the bride-to-be, but this is a Chinese wedding mixed with many Western traditions. I'm wearing a pure white silk, gently ruched sheath dress that stops at my knees with angular, abbreviated cap sleeves. To wear a hint of red for good luck, I'm wearing my ruby earrings and shimmering red Valentino heels.

"Emma," Joe's faint voice calls from the doorway.

"In here," I shout, holding the molding between my bedroom and walk-in closet, slipping on my right shoe. Just as I'm getting my left foot into its shoe, I see Joe standing in the doorway of my bedroom.

"Wow!" he exclaims with wide eyes and a dropped jaw.

My gaze gradually trails up and down Joe's body two times while I remain slightly bent. I've never seen Joe wear a suit minus the jacket and have a vest on instead. Boy does he look scrumptious. Visions of ripping off his clothes seduce my mind and I gladly let them delight my sex until I realize that Joe is standing a foot away from me. What is he doing in my bedroom?

Joe carefully slides each of his hands onto my waist, but doesn't move to kiss me. He just stands watching me, like he's waiting for something.

"What are you doing in my bedroom?" I search.

"You said you were in here," he answers with a provocative smile.

"That wasn't an invitation," I explain in a flirtatious tone.

Why am I trying to be sexy?

"My mistake," he seduces, tightening his grip and pulling me closer.

I find my hands sliding up his hot, muscular chest and my fingers lock behind his neck. Unable to control my urges, I deliver my lips to his. Joe molds his mouth to mine, following my lead as our lips and tongues unite to dance as one. We both refrain from allowing our true needs to surface; our need for more.

Joe breaks contact first and I desperately seek more, chasing his mouth. Like an unspoken knowing, we remain touching, not wanting to let go.

Trying to redirect our attention, Joe says, "So this is your bedroom, huh?"

"Yeah," I confirm with my voice a little shaky. "You shouldn't be in here."

"Why not?" he teases.

"Another step closer to breaking a rule," I blurt.

Shit. I can't believe I just said that.

After a breathy chuckle, Joe continues, "Another step closer, huh? We've already broken a few."

"Exactly," I concur, hinting that I don't want to check anymore off the list.

"We'll, we better leave, or else we'll never get out of this room," he suggestively infers.

"Only in your dreams," I goad.

I can't help but be flattered by his forwardness. It's strangely not bothering me as much.

I've never had a man pursue me this intensely before without it feeling creepy, and I've never desired a man with such severity. I'm enjoying this game of chase we've started and I'm guessing he does too. It has come to light in this very moment, that it's not simply the matter of will I surrender to the temptation of the forbidden fruit, but a matter of when. Does Joe know? Has he known this all along? Have I?

"Already have, beautiful," he entices. "If you only knew."

Chapter Thirty Four

Heat engulfs my cheeks and spreads throughout my body like a wildfire. I turn my face away trying to hide. Joe laughs heartily before kissing me on my temple and then leads me out into the living room.

Joe, Sadie and I head down to the garage where he parked.

"Since when did you get a Tesla?" I inquire as Joe opens the door.

"Since recently," he admits. "I liked Jared's and Nathan's since meeting you guys at the beach."

I roll my eyes and shake my head as I get in. "What happened to the Audi and Phantom?" I ask as Joe climbs behind the driver seat.

With a wicked smile, he confirms, "I still have the Phantom, but I got rid of the Audi."

"Boys and their toys," I muse.

"My parents are excited to meet you today." Joe changes the subject abruptly as his eyes shift from a strange glare at my legs and sprint to my face.

I can feel all of the color drain from my entire body.

"What's wrong?" he inquires with concern in his voice.

"Huh? Nothing," I lie. "I didn't realize that they would come all the way out here just for an engagement party."

"Our families have been doing business together the last few years aside from the fact that Henry is like another brother to me," he explains.

"I know," I mention, fidgeting with my purse.

I wasn't expecting to meet them this soon. I thought I'd meet them briefly at the wedding. This is all weird and awkward for me.

Anna greets Joe, Sadie and me in the middle of the hallway when we arrive. She takes Sadie's bag of food and toys from Joe and informs us that Mr. and Mrs. Covelli are finishing getting ready while Jimmy and Allen are waiting in the living room.

"Emma, you're here!" Jimmy shouts full of excitement, jumping up from his chair. "I've missed you, sweetie!"

Both Jimmy and Allen lightly encase me in a joint hug.

"Don't get her dress all messed up, babe," Allen scolds.

"I'm not," Jimmy rebuts.

"We just saw each other at Jared's birthday party," I remind.

"A lot can happen in just two days," Jimmy instructs. "And, I must commend you. That was a fabulous party!"

Breathe In

"Thanks," I accept graciously. "But, Nathan helped a lot since I've been busy with wedding duties."

"Is Pop-Pop coming today?" Allen asks while greeting Sadie.

"Yes," I confirm.

"Great. It'll be so nice to see him again," he replies with enthusiasm.

"What took you so long to get here? What were you two doing?" Jimmy presses, insinuating more than I would be willing to explain, even if something did happen. He bends down, taking his turn to greet Sadie.

"What are you talking about?" I calmly feign ignorance to his stipulations.

"Joe left like a half hour ago. It doesn't take thirty minutes to drive a half mile and back," Jimmy continues.

"Now James, leave the lovely lady alone," a charismatic woman's voice chides from behind me. "It's none of your business of what she and your brother may be doing."

"Yes, Mom," Jimmy concedes without hesitation.

Spinning around, my eyes fall upon a stunning, dark-haired woman who makes me feel like I'm meeting an older Audrey Hepburn, if Audrey Hepburn was still alive. Her striking resemblance to Audrey is uncanny and wasn't noticed in the photos I've seen around Joe's penthouse.

"Emma, this is my mother Elaine Covelli," Joe introduces.

Adorned with a Manhattanite presence and charm, Mrs. Covelli glides towards me, reaching her hand out. "Emma," her voice flows like silk. "It's a pleasure to finally meet you. My boys can't stop talking about you."

Taking her hand, I blush at her greeting. I'm temporarily speechless by her presence.

"What a strong handshake. Far better than those weak ones most of the women I know give," she defines.

"Thank you," I utter.

What an interesting comment to make; one that I was not expecting.

Before I can mutter an appropriate greeting, Mrs. Covelli releases my hand, steps in and gives me a hug. "Mrs. Covelli," I nervously reply while trying to regain my composure after her warm embrace. "It's nice to meet you as well."

"Have we meet before?" she questions, taking another step back, looking me up and down. "I swear we've met before."

"No, Mrs. Covelli," I answer politely.

"Please, Emma, call me Elaine," she insists with kind eyes and a flawless smile.

Chapter Thirty Four

"Sure," I accept, even though I don't feel comfortable calling her by her first name.

"Maybe you just remind me of an old friend," Mrs. Covelli says, rationalizing her feeling of familiarity.

"Perhaps," I agree.

"I finally get to put a face to the name," an unfamiliar deep voice declares from my back left.

"Emma, this is my father, John Covelli," Joe introduces.

Mr. Covelli is a strikingly handsome, older gentleman. I immediately see the family resemblance between Jimmy and Joe and their father. Joe is almost a younger version of his father, but has his mother's radiant blue eyes. Mr. Covelli has a chiseled jawline slightly more pronounced than Joe and his demeanor exudes a regal confidence paired with humble sweetness and a depth of wisdom.

"Father, I would like you to meet Emma. Emma Peterson," Joe adds.

Mr. Covelli holds out his hand. Taking mine, Mr. Covelli raises it to his lips and he bows a little before kissing it. "Emma, it's so wonderful to finally meet you . . . meet the woman who my sons have been raving about and who has been aiding our business."

"I haven't done anything Mr. Covelli," I humbly reply.

"Nonsense. You've had a lot of great suggestions that we are incorporating into our business and it looks like we're changing standards thanks to your input," he explains. "And please, call me John."

"Honestly, I haven't done anything. Joe's the person taking action. We've just talked," I object.

"Don't be modest, Emma," Jimmy contends. "It's not every day a woman with your brains and beauty, like Mom's, is found in the business realm."

"You've done more than you realize," Joe includes with a smile.

I immediately blush hearing their words. I've never been praised for what I've been able to do with regards to business. Okay, maybe a little from Jared, Maggie and Nathan, but it's different when it's not my friends.

"She is definitely stunning," Mr. Covelli chimes. "I see what lured you, Joseph."

"Indeed," Mrs. Covelli graciously agrees.

My cheeks burn hotter as the temperature in the room kicks up a few degrees. I hope I'm not sweating.

"She does look familiar Elaine. I can't place it either. We'll remember who she reminds us of," Mr. Covelli agrees.

"Do you have family in New York?" Mrs. Covelli seeks.

"No ma'am," I offer, keeping it simple.

"Oh well, it'll come to me sooner or later," Mrs. Covelli insists.

"If you're free this week, Emma, I'd love to get together with you to discuss business," Mr. Covelli adds.

"Me? Why?"

"I'd love to hear more about what you do and the potential company our family may have as our first technology investment," he explains.

"Sure. If you'd like to," I reply, accepting his invitation.

"Of course," he confirms. "Let Joseph know when you're free and the four of us will chat. Our schedule is flexible while we're here."

"Okay," I consent.

What is this fascination with me that Joe's parents have? I'm no one special. I have had success; I've made millions each year for the last four years between my two companies, but that's pocket change when it comes to a family who makes billions and most likely trillions by now.

"Yes! You must come over, and not only to talk business," Mrs. Covelli insists. "It'll be nice to have another woman around. No offense gentlemen."

The men lightheartedly laugh at Mrs. Covelli's jab. Joe and I make introductions between his parents and Sadie after Sadie whimpered several times to be noticed. Our conversations remain light and friendly until Anna leads us towards the door to leave.

A few minutes later, the six of us are down at the valet, ready for our journey to San Marino. To my surprise, there is a stretch limo waiting. Mrs. Covelli and I are ushered in first followed by the men. I sit facing Mrs. Covelli, Mr. Covelli is next to her followed by Jimmy. Joe is inadvertently next to me preceded by Allen.

As the vehicle takes off, I do my best to suppress any outward signs of agitation for being in a car. I don't want to draw any unnecessary attention to myself with Mr. and Mrs. Covelli. Jimmy and Allen direct most of the conversation while I sit quietly, twitching the fingers of my right hand under my purse. I'm conflicted with odd emotions when Joe doesn't take my hand — I've become so accustomed to it.

Chapter Thirty Four

"How are you holding up, Emma?" Jimmy inquires, snapping my attention away from the window.

"I'm fine. Thank you," I return with a smile.

"Why would you ask such a question, James?" Mrs. Covelli explores.

Why did he have to make a comment? I appreciate what he's trying to do, but I don't want to have to explain myself to his parents. I don't need any more focus on me.

"Emma doesn't like being in cars," Jimmy notifies.

I do my best to hide my discomfort.

"How else do you get around, darling?" Mrs. Covelli inspects rather than explore the reason why.

"I walk or bike mostly, but I also take the local train or bus," I explain.

"There's a train in California?" Mrs. Covelli says with a little surprise in her tone.

"The majority of the train here in LA is underground, which is why you probably haven't noticed it," I explain.

"It's actually very efficient and effective," Joe adds openly.

"You've taken public transportation?" Mrs. Covelli lightheartedly mocks. "It takes you getting out to California to try public transportation?"

"It's because of Emma," Jimmy accuses, throwing a jab at Joe.

"I like her even more," Mr. Covelli comments with a smile. He winks at Joe and laughs when I catch him.

"Me too," replies Mrs. Covelli.

Joe blushes and hangs his head for a few moments, obviously taking the good-natured fun his family is having at his expense. I lower my eyes and watch my twitching fingers before returning my gaze out the window.

Guests aren't scheduled to arrive until three in the afternoon, but the six of us arrive just after two for the party. The Wú house is exquisite to say the least. I would suggest that it's almost a mega-mansion. With an authentic French Country Manor exterior and a modern Chinese zen flair interior, which gives the home an interesting and appeasing French-Asian fusion style, the Wú estate sits on at least an two or three of land and will easily entertain the one hundred and six guests who responded their attendance. The house is formally decorated for today with a beautiful, large white tent pitched in the backyard to keep out the hot Summer sun. A variety of traditional Chinese wedding decorations and flower bouquets, with the colors of red, white and gold, are intricately placed throughout the interior of the house, the tent and

Breathe In

the back yard. Buffet tables of endless food are already being stocked and there are two open bars on either end of the Olympic-sized pool. There are ceiling fans and chandeliers hanging in the tent as well, keeping the interior lit and cool at the same time. Amelia worked with Mrs. Wú on all of the decorations and party arrangements; they did a wonderful job. I'm glad I didn't have to take care of all of this in such a short amount of time.

I don't have time to explore the Wú mansion due to meeting all of the guests and Henry's entire immediate family, who flew in from China this past week. Maggie seems more nervous than I would have expected her to be — she's a little excited, but really more nervous. Then again, Henry has a very large and affluent family. I bet I know what's going through her mind. All Maggie wants is for them to like her.

Maggie's wearing a gorgeous red silk strapless dress that ends at her knees with a simple, white silk sash around heir waist paired with sparkling red Jimmy Choo heels. Henry is wearing a solid light grey vest and pants with a white dress shirt that has thin red pinned stripes and a solid red tie.

I'm excited to see that Jared, Nathan and Pop-Pop have already arrived and rush over to them. I know I need to be polite and finish meeting the guests and all of Henry's family who are already here, but I need to see how things have been going since Jared's birthday party Wednesday night; Jared and I have only spoken once since then. Jared explains that the past two days have been exceptionally well for him and there's talk about Pop-Pop officially moving out to California from Arkansas. Pop-Pop's been retired for a number of years and said that he would much rather be around happy, loving family members aside from catching up more with Jared for all of the missed years.

On top of meeting Henry's grandparents on both sides, I also meet his mother's brother and wife, their two sons who are married, one of which who has a baby on the way, and Henry's father's brother and sister and their spouses, who each have a son and daughter Maggie's age, but who are not yet married. Everyone seems extremely friendly, especially once they know that I speak fluent Mandarin.

I'm excited to meet old friends of the Li family who live in China. Many of them know who I am from pictures and stories Năinai or Mŭqīn have shared with them over the years as well as when some of them visited a few years back. The last time Maggie and her family went home to China, they invited me to join them. I hesitated for many reasons, but I'm now considering and understanding the need to open myself more to Maggie's family. They've given me so much and I need to honor their kindness and generosity.

Chapter Thirty Four

The rest of the engagement party is a blur. There are so many people to meet that I've already forgotten most of their names. If I had the choice, I would stay in a corner, but being the maid of honor puts you out in the open almost as much as the bride and groom for most of the party. There are a number of times I'm able to hide out in the kitchen; I'm able to give my feet a rest as the maids and catering staff bounce in and out serving food and drinks.

As the sun begins to set, I start to hover around Jared since a few of Henry's friends and some of the other single men haven been trying to strike up conversation and blatantly pick me up. Jared immediately knows what I'm doing and places his arms around me. I stand quietly as Pop-Pop shares story after story about Jared from before Jared and I met. I haven't seen Maggie much other than her off in the distance, chatting away with all of the guests.

At one point, Joe, Jimmy, Allen, Jared, Nathan, Pop-Pop and myself are sitting around a single table and Jade is on my lap — she plays with a lock of my hair as she swings her feet on either side. A few other men and women our age hang around too. Everyone is chatting freely as I watch filled with contentment. Half of the guests have left and it's still a little early for the rest of us to head home. Joe's parents are still catching up with many people they know.

"Hey Jade," Joe calls. "Did you see what I've been wearing today?" Joe holds up his right wrist and shifts his cuff.

I notice what he's showing her, but my attention is captivated by the ruby cufflinks.

Jade beams with excitement when she sees the bracelet she bought Joe at New Year's. "You still have it?!"

"Of course I do," he replies. "I'll keep it forever."

Jade is now bouncing a little on my lap full of happiness.

Joe gets up and returns a minute later with an extra plate of dessert. "Want one?" he asks Jade.

"Mommy said I can't have anymore," Jade pouts.

"I don't see Mommy around. Do you?" he returns.

"No . . ." she confirms, shaking her head.

"Then, this is just between you, me and Emma," he sweetly states.

"Don't bring me into this," I tease.

Jade laughs taking a small cupcake for her first round of over indulgence. After Jade's first bite, Joe takes her off my lap, suggesting it's better to get his suit dirty than my dress. I sit watching the two of them, quietly giggling at their secrecy. Joe reaches towards me offering a bit and I gladly take one, leaning

breathe In

in with my mouth without thinking. The fire in my body roars when my lips make contact with one of Joe's fingers. I wasn't paying complete attention, nor was Joe, because our eyes have been locked the entire time. As I whip my lips with a finger, I check to make sure no one saw our exchange — looks like we're in the clear.

About an hour later, Jade is asleep on my lap and the crowd of guests has diminished. Kim and Peter come over to say goodnight and carry Jade home. Not much later, Joe, Jimmy, Allen, Mr. and Mrs. Covelli and I are back in the limo on our way to Pasadena.

Joe drives Sadie and me home after saying goodnight to his family. When we get to my apartment, without thinking, I unlock the door and proceed in. Sadie stays nearby laying on the floor as I put her bags on the counter. Before I turn around, Joe's hands are on my waist pulling me into him as he kisses my shoulder. He tickles the base of my neck with his lips, gradually moving up all the way to where he grabs the bottom of my earlobe with his teeth.

I emphatically moan louder under his seduction and my hand reaches up, seizing his hair. "What are you doing?" I manage to utter when his lips temporarily move to their next target.

"Having a little fun before I have to go," he teases into my ear as he spins me around to face him. "Unless you let me stay."

"You can't stay. You know that," I comment after our lips lock several times.

"Why not?" he whines a little, enticing me to reconsider.

"To start, people know you are here," I contend, taking his mouth with mine.

"Mmmm." Joe keeps himself locked to me. "Then I better make this count."

Within seconds, I find myself pressed up against something, probably a wall, but I'm too distracted to really care by his tongue swirling with mine. My hands grip onto his shirt, pulling him closer. One of Joe's hands slides up over my ribs and I gasp in ecstasy as he cups my breast. He pulls away from my wanting mouth and resumes his previous lure on my Achilles' heel.

"Not . . . the . . . neck," I whimper, rilled with pleasure.

He chuckles lightly as he continues his pursuit. My fingers tighten in his hair and my eyes flutter as the desire to rip our clothes off rises inside of me.

"Joe . . ." I plea.

"Not yet," he taunts while adding his tongue into his persuasion.

"Mmmmm . . . Joe . . . nooooo . . ." I beg, unable to stop moaning.

He temporarily relieves me of his fiery torture by returning to my mouth. I grab the back of his neck, yanking him into me, needing more. Joe tightens

Chapter Thirty Four

his grip around my waist before sliding one of his hands up my back and the other over my ass. Pulling him into me further, I feel his hot, swollen erection twitch on my lower belly.

Knowing, no, feeling his desire for me, entices my itch. He wants me. I want him.

"No . . ." I weakly command, pushing him away.

My brain hasn't completely failed me yet.

We both pant, trying to regain our composure which is not so easy when you're still locked in a steamy embrace.

"Sorry," he stammers, shifting slightly back, but continues to hold onto me.

I step into him seeking his lips. I'm not sure if I am trying to console him, myself, or both of us from our heated outburst.

"If I'm going to go . . ." he states, keeping his lips to mine. "We need stop."

"Mmm hmm," I agree, continuing my embrace.

"Emma . . ." he hums.

"Mmm . . ." I take another kiss before he pulls away.

"Do you want me to stay?" he questions, keeping his mouth an inch away.

My body wants him to stay. I can't take it anymore, but my brain is still a contender on the debate — a weakening contender — and I'm not sure for how much longer. Rules, Emma. You have rules and now is not the time, especially if we factor in his family. They know he drove me home and the longer he stays the easier suspicion arises even if Joe hides the truth.

"My rules . . ." I weakly answer.

"We've broken a few already," he reminds.

"Your family . . ." I add.

Joe and I kiss a few times with slow, lingering pecks.

"Can I see you tomorrow?" he searches with longing in his voice.

"I'll be tied up with Jared and Nathan for business," I affirm.

"All day?" he slightly huffs disappointment.

"And night," I announce.

"Monday?"

"I'll still be with Nathan and Jared," I explain.

"Tuesday?"

"I'll see you in the morning for the meeting with your dad, but then I have wedding things to attend to with Maggie and Amelia," I explain.

Without saying another word, Joe sweetly kisses me, keeping his hands only on my face. He groans as he reluctantly peels away. I don't make it easier when my mouth chases his. My body instinctually follows him and Joe doesn't seem to mind as his hands return to my hips and our lips reach for contact. Holding on to each other, we gradually move towards the door.

"Goodnight, beautiful," he lulls, creeping away from my body, opening the door behind him.

"Goodnight Joe," I reply as he closes the door between us.

Thirty Five

After a restless night's sleep, mostly waking up with the insatiable need to pleasure myself, even after having three intense orgasms courtesy of B.O.B. before bed, I leave Pasadena to visit with Jared, Nathan and Pop-Pop, taking Sadie with me. We meet up in WeHo at Nathaniel's late in the morning so Nathan can check in on the store before we have a day of just the five of us. Sales have been doing really well and Nathan eagerly shares with me three different sketches he has for Chris' custom suit along with sample fabrics. Whichever ones Chris doesn't choose, Nathan will just put them out as one of a kind items. We're apparently waiting for Chris to arrive to decided which suit he wants before we go to lunch.

Just as Chris literally walks into the store, he's followed by Jimmy, Allen, Mr. and Mrs. Covelli and Joe.

What is everyone doing here? I wasn't excited about the fact that I would be seeing Chris today and now with all of them here, who knows what might happen. I can handle Chris or Joe alone, but having them both here — shit! This is not good.

We all begin to greet each other and exchange introductions. I immediately feel awkward when Chris moves in to greet me with Joe standing by, waiting to do the same. Chris tries to kiss me on the lips, but I'm able to deflect his attempt. After Chris kisses me on the cheek, he maintains a lingering hug. I feel awkward with Chris touching me — he's not the one my body craves. Chris stays next to me with his hand on my hip as I try to pull away when I greet Joe.

There's definitely some peacocking going on by Chris. He better not be trying to claim me like Caleb did the last time I was at Ayana's. Jared sees my signals and swoops in flawlessly to get distance between Chris and me.

After a few minutes of pleasantries, everyone gathers around as Nathan show's Chris the three suit options. Nathan has outdone himself again. He has created three distinct outfits that alter the style of a customary suit just enough for it to stand out. There are three specific suits with flecks of color to pop and accentuate a mood, as well as define a particular statement that go with the color scheme of the sci-fi action movie. Chris' reaction gives it away that he's not much of a fashion guy despite his interest and awe for what Nathan has designed. Jimmy and Allen offer their comments, as well as Mrs. Covelli, on which outfit would be the most stylish for Chris' body type.

Breathe In

"This one. Don't you agree, Emma?" Mrs. Covelli addresses, snapping my attention away from my thoughts of Joe and me together last night.

I was picturing Joe naked from the waist up since I know what that looks like.

"I"m sorry. What?" I return hoping not to sound flustered.

"This one," she points at the charcoal grey design that has gold pieces for the vest, tie and handkerchief. She takes the fabric pieces and holds them just under Chris' chin. "See. This is the one would be the most dashing on Chris."

"Yes," I force out quickly, tightening my grip around Jared's waist.

I'd much rather see Joe wear it — and then not, with it ending up on my bedroom floor. Mrs. Covelli could have held up a photo of Chris, naked, and I wouldn't have even noticed. Joe naked, on the other hand — I feel my mounds tingle at the idea — ow that would be dashing. Joe naked with me on top of him. Yes. That would be —

"Oh my God, Emma! You have to!"

Jimmy's declaration snaps me back to the conversation.

"Have to do what?" I ask.

I hope no one noticed my daydreaming.

"Be Chris' date for the premier so pieces from Nathan's men's and women's lines are on the red carpet," Allen states with jubilation.

"Nathan should create a custom matching piece for Emma," Jimmy announces.

"Oooo, yes!" Allen cheers.

"Wait?! What?" I return, clueless about what everyone else is talking about.

"We should totally wear the other two suits Nathan makes and attend the event too," adds Jimmy.

"Oh my goodness, baby. You are a genius," Allen praises with his voice up a whole octave.

"I can get enough tickets for us all to go. Just tell me how many and it's done," Chris cordially offers.

I glance around the room staring into the faces of everyone waiting for my answer. Everyone seems excited by the idea and are encouraging me to agree with their eyes — everyone but Joe. Joe's eyes look blank, like he's trying to hide any emotion while his jaw is clenched. Chris is emphatically smiling at me, coaxing me with his grin while Nathan begs with his hands clasped together as he mouths please, please, please.

The room feels hotter and I swear it's starting to spin.

"Please, Emma," Nathan begs, taking my hands in his. "It would mean so much to me!"

Chapter Thirty Five

Not wanting to disappoint Nathan, and because I know that it would make the most sense, strictly from a business standpoint to have more items on the red carpet, I calmly agree shrugging my shoulders. "Sure."

Cheers erupt from my friends except for Joe and me. I smile and play along in the moment, but I'm not really happy to be doing it. I think I catch a temporary expression of disappointment on Joe's face. If I was going to be caught out in public on anyone's arm other than Jared or Nathan, a man who was not gay, I would much rather it be Joe.

Chris comes close and hugs me. "That settles it. We'll all go," he comments, keeping his arms around me and kisses me on the cheek.

After some decisions are made about who's wearing which suit and who can and wants to attend the event, Nathan takes Jimmy's and Allen's measurements while Mrs. Covelli shops the racks and buys a few pieces. As Nathan and Denise finish taking my measurements, Mr. Covelli insists on taking all of us out to eat to celebrate.

Nathan, Jimmy and Allen encourage that Sadie and I ride with Chris and I politely don't argue with them in front of everyone. With four cars, our large group of ten adults plus a dog hit the road following Mr. and Mrs. Covelli in Joe's Phantom.

My heart sinks in my chest when we pull up to the valet of Spago. Yes. Spago. The very restaurant Joe took me to for our date where we ran into Chris. God, can this day get any more unnerving?!

The staff is very amenable to Sadie being a part of our dining crowd as they take us to a very large, round table that easily seats everyone comfortably. Chef Andrews comes out to great us and exchanges pleasantries with Joe, Jimmy and Mr. and Mrs. Covelli. The chef also makes his way over to me, singling me out, but graciously doesn't mention how we know each other or the night of Joe's and my date. Jared gives me a questioning glance and I whisper that I'll fill him in on the whole thing later. I'll be sure to tell him we stopped in for lunch during an outing to figure out what to do for Henry's and Maggie's joint bachelor-bachelorette party.

As we dine, Joe is practically sitting across from me as Chris, who has deliberately moved his chair several inches closer to mine, is to my right and Jared is to my left. Conversations are light and friendly as usual and my amount of commenting and interaction is limited. I can't help but glance at Joe on occasion. Every time I look at him, he's staring right back at me. There are a few times, as Chris leans in and whispers in my ear, I see Joe look away. My eyes have to focus on a spot on the table to make sure I actually hear at least some of what Chris is saying.

Breathe In

Chris tries to take my hand in his several times, but I'm able to reach for my glass to take a sip at each attempt. Nathan and Jared fill everyone in on how we meet Chris first at Ayana's opening almost a year ago, and then several more times with the most recent being about three months ago. I'm very grateful when my friends leave out the fact that the second time we saw Chris that he and I had sex — no need for Joe to know that right now.

After several failed attempts to hold my hand, Chris places his arm along the back of my chair, placing his hand on my left shoulder. It's confirmed that he's definitely peacocking right now and I'm starting to get mad.

"I think your phone is buzzing," Jared says, leaning towards me.

I look down at my purse that is sitting on the floor in between our chairs, next to Sadie. The phone is not lit up.

"Looks like Amy is calling you," Jared continues with a wink. "She probably has some bridal shower questions for you. You should talk to her." Jared says his last statement loud enough for everyone at the table to hear.

"Yes," I reply, getting the hint that he's saving me from Chris. "Thank you."

I grab my purse after tucking the phone back into its pocket so no one sees the truth. As I stand, Mr. Covelli, Joe, Jimmy and Allen all rise as well. "Please excuse me for a moment," I request.

A few feet away from the table, I take out the phone and raise it to my ear as I walk to the front of the restaurant. Aware that I'm not as skillful at pretending to be a person talking on the phone, just in case anyone follows me, I press the button to call my most recent contact. Please pick up, please pick up I coax as I turn the corner just beyond the front doors.

"Amy here," Joe's voice sings with a wicked grin hanging in his tone.

He's playing along. Good.

"Hey," I eke, feeling embarrassed.

"So what kind of questions should I be asking you about the bridal shower?" he continues with a hint of amusement.

"Where are you?" I question, panicked to who might hear him.

"By the bar. Don't worry. You secret is safe with me," he teases.

"Thanks," I greet.

"So, why did you call me?"

"You were the last person on my most recent," I admit.

It's true. He had texted me earlier in the day.

"I'm flattered," he says.

I don't say anything for a moment, not sure what to say.

Chapter Thirty Five

"You okay?" he searches.

"I'll be all right," I offer, trying to sound confident.

"You're a good friend," he mentions.

"What do you mean?" I reply confused.

How am I a good friend by calling him?

"To do what you are doing for Nathan," his voice falters a little, implying his true feelings.

"I'm doing it for Nathan . . . because he's family. It's just a business transaction," I assure.

I think I'm trying to console both of us. I didn't realize he'd be affected by this, let alone myself.

"I know," Joe agrees without judgment. "I would have done the same if I was in your position."

He's clearly not happy with the idea of me going on a date with Chris and neither am I.

"Chris can consider it our first and last date . . . not that it will even be a date," I blurt.

Joe laughs a little which eases my nerves. With a lightness in his words, he asks, "Can I get the first kiss of the night, then?"

"Sure," I agree a little too quickly.

Joe laughs again at my directness.

"I might even let you take me home," I bait, wanting to continue our playfulness.

I'm so glad that he's not making this awkward.

"You have yourself a deal," he consents.

"Will that be a challenge for *your* date?" I press, flirting a little.

"Won't have one," he admits.

Flattered by his words, my curiosity gets to me and I'm compelled to ask, "Why not?"

"Never bothered with dates to big events, actually to any event . . . and the one who I'd want as my date is already taken," he sensually confesses.

"Joe . . ." I plea.

I know he's referring to me.

"It's the truth," he affirms.

I can't help but smile as I bite my lip to curb any outward expression.

"How will your date handle another man taking you home?"

"Don't know. Don't care," I say without thinking.

Joe does his best to suppress a laugh.

"Besides, he's not going to be picking me up at my place. We'll meet at Nathaniel's."

"This is a time I'm grateful for your rules," he openly declares.

I blush at his forwardness. I'm grateful for my rules too. It'll make that night be less complicated, stressful and easier to cope — well, at least with Chris.

"We should head back to the table," I suggest.

"You first," he offers. "I'll arrive a few minutes later."

"Okay," I agree.

"Thanks, beautiful," he sweetly states.

"For what?"

"Calling me."

"See you in a minute," I disclose.

"See you in a minute, beautiful," he hums.

Jared helps make things more bearable when I return to the table by placing his arm along the back of my seat before Chris. When he needs a bite of food or a drink, Jared awkwardly reaches with his non-dominate hand. Something he's had to do a few times in the past for me.

When lunch concludes, our group bids farewell and Chris gives me a lengthy goodbye, which entails one of his hands on the small of my back while the other holds my face so he can kiss me on the lips. From this action, I have decided that Chris must be put in his place, letting him know exactly how things stand, but in a less public manner — no need to embarrass the man. Chris is a very good looking guy, don't get me wrong, but I'm not turned on by him anymore. When he kisses me, it's like I'm kissing Jared. I guess this is what women equate to as kissing their brother.

I elect to stay with Jared, Nathan and Pop-Pop at Nathan's in the spare bedroom. I've always left a few items at Jared's for when I do stay because it's like my second home, so we stop at his place for me to grab a few things before going straight to Nathan's.

Around ten-thirty at night, Sadie and I are on the bed while I work on my iPad. I try to busy myself with work as a distraction from thinking about Chris peacocking and what's happening with Joe. I wish Joe was with me right now. I need someone to snuggle with.

"You okay, *Kitten?*" Jared asks, walking into the room.

Chapter Thirty Five

"Yeah. Why?" I reply, trying to brush off where my thoughts might have been.

"The whole Chris thing. I know it's not what you really would want to do and I know that you are just being really cool about it for Nathan, which he and I really appreciate," he consoles while sliding onto the bed, snuggling up next to me.

"I'll be fine. Anything to help Nathaniel's," I assure unconvincingly.

"Emma?" he questions with worry.

"Everything's fine," I lie.

"Emma . . ." he pushes, not believing me.

"What?"

"You know you can talk to me," he offers, taking my iPad from me.

"I know," I confirm.

"What's really bothering you?" he searches, wrapping his arms around me as I curl into his chest.

"What are you talking about?" I deny while searching to see what he may have seen.

"He clearly likes you," he mentions calmly.

"Who? Chris? I know that. I'll deal with him the night of the event. I couldn't put the man in his place in front of everyone today," I concur.

"I know. Chris clearly isn't taking the hint, but I was referring to Joe."

"What about Joe?"

"You didn't see his reaction when you agreed to go to the premier with Chris, at lunch, and then when Chris planted a kiss on you to say goodbye?" Jared says with a little shock in his voice.

"What are you talking about?"

I know what he's talking about, but I've got to deny anything and everything, even to my best friend.

"Nothing . . ." he says, trying to end it.

"What?" I press.

I need to know what he knows or at least know what he thinks.

"Nothing . . ." he repeats.

I drop pushing the subject, though I'm not sure why Jared brought up the topic of Joe's reaction. What has he seen? What does he know? I might need to back off from being around Joe as much just to throw off my friends. I might have to pretend to want to go out to satisfy my itch. Damn it.

"I know Nathan might have said a few things that may be leading Chris to believe you're interested or there's a chance with you," Jared comments, changing back to the main topic of discussion.

I outwardly wince.

"Nathan means well. He just wants everything to . . ." Jared continues before I cut him off.

"I know. Nathan's worried that if Chris doesn't think there's a chance with me that he might not wear the suit and then there goes the opportunity of Nathaniel's getting noticed on the red carpet," I confirm Nathan's intentions.

"Yeah . . . ." Jared confirms.

"Where's my favorite person in the world?" Nathan's voice sings from the living room.

"In here," Jared replies.

"Okay, my second favorite person . . ." Nathan corrects himself as he appears in the doorway.

Jared and I just glance at him. "Uhh . . . here," I comment, suspecting he's referring to me.

"There you are," he beams with excitement. "I love you!"

"I know. I love you too."

"No. I really love you. I know how hard this is and will be with Chris and Joe . . . I mean . . ." he adjusts his words.

I see a look from Jared after Nathan says Joe's name as he slides onto the bed on his belly.

"What about Joe . . ." I seek.

I know there's something that they aren't telling me.

"Nothing . . . I just meant Chris. I know you don't like him like that and I really appreciate your willingness to . . ." his stops, searching for the right words.

"Lead Chris on so he won't back out of the agreement," I answer for him bluntly.

"Something like that," he confirms.

"I'm doing it for you . . . because I love you and you are family. Plus, it's a needed business transaction," I comment.

"I know, and that's why I love you," Nathan repeats, hugging me. Nathan asks, "Please don't be mad at me for . . . ."

"For what?"

"Continuing to lead Chris on," he admits sheepishly.

Chapter Thirty Five

"It's okay . . ." my voice trails a little. "I'll do my best to play along and say nothing until that night."

Nathan and I don't really say anything else after our quick verbal airing of the life-size elephant challenge that will be occurring until the premier is over. He stays with Jared and me, petting and playing with Sadie on occasion before giving Jared and I some much-needed friend time.

Jared hands me back my iPad, but stays with me for a long while. We don't talk. We just fall back into our old habits of when we used to live together, sitting quietly just being there for the other. Jared runs his fingers through my hair; one of my favorite things he's always done.

Needing some fresh air before bed, and still unable to fall asleep at eleven-thirty at night, I take Sadie out for a walk on Ocean Drive. Almost back to Nathan's, my phone buzzes.

"Hi," I answer, trying not to sound too excited.

"Hey, beautiful," he returns with his low, husky voice.

"What's with the sexy voice?" I ask.

"What sex voice?" he chuckles.

"You know what I'm talking about . . . you know what you're doing." I reply.

He laughs. "Do you like it?"

"No comment . . ." I return playfully.

"So you do," he accuses. "I'll have to make a point to do it again in the future."

"How was the rest of your day?" I redirect our conversation.

"Good. Yours?"

"Good."

We don't say anything. Well, I don't say anything as I enter Nathan's condo and head back to my room.

"What are you up to?" he inquires.

"Just getting back into Nathan's," I whisper, not wanting to be overheard.

"Took Sadie out?"

"Yeah. What are you still doing up?" I close the door to the bedroom.

"Wanted to hear you voice before I fall asleep," he sweetly admits.

A weird feeling surfaces in my belly. I'm not sure what it equate it to. Maybe, it's like the feeling I got as a kid the night before Christmas when my parents were still alive. I'm not sure why, but I like it. It reminds me of happy times and happy feelings that have been long lost.

"What are you up to?" I peruse.

"Laying in bed. Thinking of you," he says, using the sexy voice again.

"Mmmm," I hum.

"Is that for what I said or how I said it . . . or both," he questions.

"Hmmm . . . I think I'll keep that to myself for now," I taunt.

"So that's how you want to be?" he quips.

"A girl can't share all her secrets," I muse.

He chuckles. "No. I guess not . . . but you are giving me enough."

"Enough?"

"Yeah, enough to work with," he devilishly stabs.

"What do you mean?"

"A guy can't share all his secrets," he returns with his husky voice.

"I see how it is," I reply with my own provocative tone.

I'm thoroughly enjoying the banter. It's turning me on.

"Keep that up and I'll be driving over to Nathan's," he directs.

"What?" I feign my actions and words.

"You're tempting me to come over and show you, not caring who's there," he shares.

I redden at the thought. Would he really do that? Would I mind? No. Not Really. Okay, maybe part of me for letting people know, but I'm so horny right now that I'm so tempted to provoke him to see if he really does it. Besides, even if he did come over, that doesn't mean I'd let him in.

"We need to start using FaceTime," he declares.

"Why?"

I know why, but I just want to hear him say it.

"So I can see your reaction. It's killing me when you don't say anything," he explains.

"Why? What do you mean?" My brow furrows a little at his statement.

"I can guess easier at what you're thinking when I see you compared to this. This is torture, but texting is even worse," he admits.

Biting my lip, I can't help but laugh out loud a little at his words.

"You know what I'm talking about, and don't say that you need to have some secrets," he insists with a hint of defeat.

Chapter Thirty Five

"You don't seem like a man to give up let alone be defeated so easily," I bait.

"I'm not giving up . . . especially after seeing your reaction to agreeing to be Chris' date," he recalls.

"Please don't remind me," I whine. "Shit. Now the moment is ruined. Why did you have to mention him?"

"Damn. Sorry," he quickly apologizes.

"Now you've got to make it up to me," I entice to get our focus back on our playful banter.

"Anything . . . name it!" he says, practically jumping through the phone.

"Hmmm . . ." I try to think about what he could say or do right now. "Say something with your sexy voice," I direct.

"For you, beautiful, anything," his voice delivers perfectly, echoing through my ear and erotically teasing my whole body.

"Mmmm . . ." I return as my right hand uncontrollably dips down between my legs. I can't will it to stop. My breathing heightens as my fingers glide up and down my mounds over my underwear. Control yourself, Emma.

Joe clears his throat before investigating, "What was that?"

"Hmmm . . . nothing," I contend, regaining self-control. Funny thing is that I don't sound flustered.

"That didn't sound like nothing," he retorts a little shaky. "Do you . . . uhhh . . . need some assistance?"

"No," I deliver as my hand slides up and over my nipple.

"Sounds like you do," he asserts clearing his throat again.

"Mmmm . . . no."

I feel like I should be alarmed or embarrassed at what is happening, but I'm not. This is so weird.

"I should let you go," I say, wanting to continue to pleasure myself without him hearing me.

What the hell am I doing?

"I think I should stay on. Make sure you're good," his voice cracks as he disagrees.

"I'm good . . ." I report.

"I"m not so sure," he suggests.

"Jared and Nathan are nearby if . . ." I begin to say before he cuts me off.

"I doubt that they'll be able to assist you properly," he advises.

I laugh a little which gets him to laugh too.

"I should get to bed. I've got a long day tomorrow," I mention.

I don't really want to rush him off the phone, but I'm so horny and I don't want to masturbate with him on the phone. He already suspects enough.

Joe groans his disappointment into my ear. "Is that want you want?"

"I want a lot of things, but that doesn't mean I should," I profess with hidden undertones.

Clearing his throat first, Joe asks, "What do you want?"

My smile widens as my hand dips down to my lips again. "Bed. I . . ." my voice trails as I bite my lip to stifle any noises from coming out as my traitorous fingers gloriously torment me. "Goodnight, Joe," I manage to mutter.

After an outward breath into the phone, Joe returns with his sexy voice, "Goodnight, beautiful. Sweet dreams."

"You too," I mumble as my fingers slide below my underwear before I hit the red, end button.

Thirty Six

I wake rested, but my mood is a little funky even after masturbating from the borderline phone sex Joe and I almost had. When I relieve myself, I realize why I'm not so chipper, that time of the month has arrived. I must not have been paying attention to my calendar. My period starting will help me adhere to my rules — at least for another few days.

I still can't wrap my head around what's going on with me and my blatant forwardness with Joe last night, but I must move forward and not let it distract me while I conduct business. I can't loose focus. There are too many things that need to be taken care of that are important, including Maggie's wedding. I may not still be one hundred percent elated about how quickly Maggie and Henry are getting married, but my feelings will not hinder me from doing my maid of honor duties or make sure that Maggie's wedding is flawlessly joyful.

Jared and Nathan are still sleeping, but Pop-Pop is out in the living room reading a newspaper when Sadie and I exit the bedroom. We exchange pleasantries before Pop-Pop joins us on our morning walk.

Back at the condo, I fall right into the rest of my morning routine of rebounding, stretching, showering and then start preparing a hearty breakfast for my companions and myself. While I work on my computer in the living room, Nathan and Jared finish getting ready for the day as Pop-Pop putters. The four of us, plus Sadie, hop into Nathan's Tesla and head on over to Nathaniel's.

After Nathan double checks my measurements for the one-of-a-kind dress he's making for the September movie premier with Chris, I hide in his back office to work on the computer, bouncing from tasks for Nathaniel's and Naturally Me, but mostly on the software for Raven Media. I slip out of the office from time to time, needing a stretch or a drink, but I work straight through lunch. Jared brings some food, but I barely taste it because I'm so focused. I'm not even sure what I had to eat.

Jared's been doing a great job taking on extra tasks for Naturally Me as I work with Hannah and Brandon on the coding for the first round of the Raven 1.0 software. If things go smoothly and there is an immediate demand for our new service, moving forward on the business investment deal with Joe and his father will come much quicker, leaving me with less time for Naturally Me. I'm considering on speaking with Jared about taking over, giving him a percentage of Naturally me, but I'm not sure how receptive he'll be or if I'm willing to let go of it. I trust Jared completely there's no challenge there. It's just that for me,

Breathe In

things are changing all across the board in all aspects of my life; Maggie and Henry getting married, Jared and Nathan being in a committed relationship, Pop-Pop joining the family, Naturally Me, Raven Media and Joe. Chris — he's a temporary state that will be finalized the night of the premier.

Pop-Pop is an adorable man. During one of my breaks, I watch him without hesitation walk around checking the store and fixing little things that need to be fixed. The front door hinge squeaked each time someone came in; not anymore. When Jared and I discuss Naturally Me, Pop-Pop listens quietly and asks questions once Jared and I are finished. I think I'm going to have to talk to Jared about finding a permanent position, full or part-time, for Pop-Pop. He's eager and happy to help so we might as well add him to the roaster based off of what he feels most comfortable doing.

With headphones in my ears streaming classical music, Jared practically scares me to death when he taps me on the shoulder. I almost scream — I am that focused.

"Come on, we're leaving for dinner," Jared announces.

"I have to feed Sadie. Where are we going?" I ask, checking the time — it's almost five.

"Pop-Pop and I took care of her already knowing you were working. Joe's parents invited us over. Didn't I tell you?"

"No," I contend, squinting my eyes in an as playful manner as I can.

"Sorry," Jared sheepishly states.

"Yeah, yeah," I tease. "You owe me."

"Sure do, *Kitten*," he replies, helping me pack up.

Jared, Nathan, Pop-Pop, Sadie and I pile into the car and make our way over to Joe's penthouse. We thankfully make it in just about an hour — got to love the HOV lane. After friendly greetings in the living room with Mr. and Mrs. Covelli, Jimmy, Allen and Joe, we are ushered into the dining room by Anna.

As dinner is served, conversations are light and fun. I see a distinct difference with Mr. and Mrs. Covelli and how they speak. They are less formal and even more friendly. Mrs. Covelli and Pop-Pop swap stories about their families for most of the meal which keeps everyone easily entertained.

"So, Emma," Mr. Covelli begins. "Which of your two businesses did you start first?"

"No business talk during dinner, John," Mrs. Covelli reminds playfully.

"My apologies, my love. I'm just trying to get to know Emma better. I have no intention of actually talking business," he sweetly announces.

Chapter Thirty Six

"Your intention is never to talk about business, but your habit always ends up there, sweetheart," she reveals teasingly.

"You are right as always, my love. My apologies," Mr. Covelli answers sweetly, taking her hand in his and kissing the back of it.

I can easily see the love and playfulness of their relationship. It appears as if they are restraining their banter as to not draw too much attention away from their guests, but enough to show their personalities more to make us feel more comfortable. I admire them and feel more comfortable than I usually do with most people I meet.

"Emma, my dear, have you always lived in California?" Mr. Covelli proceeds.

"No," I reply keeping things simple.

"Where else have you lived?" he continues.

"Jersey," I offer taking a sip of wine.

Mr. Covelli chuckles, "You're a very to the point kind of woman."

"My apologies. Yes, sir."

"There's no need to apologize. I admire that," he flatters.

"Thank you," I graciously accept.

"I take it that you grew up in New Jersey?" he investigates further.

"Yes sir," I answer with a softer smile.

"Where are your parents? It would have been nice to have them here tonight as well," Mrs. Covelli politely interjects.

Not wanting to be rude, but wanting to answer her question, I inform, "They're back in Jersey."

"Do you get to visit them often?" Mrs. Covelli continues.

"When I can."

"Do they come out here more to visit you then . . . since you're so busy with your businesses?" she pushes, wanting to know more.

"Now, my love, you are starting to talk about business," Mr. Covelli muses.

"Oh John, don't you start," she baits with a twinkle in her eye.

As much as I hate being the topic of discussion, I am enjoying Mr. and Mrs. Covelli. Ironically, some of their playfulness reminds me of how Joe and I are together. I can't help but smile a little watching them.

Everyone sits quietly looking to me. Crap. Do I really have to answer?

"It's a little hard for my parents to visit," I reply, hoping my answer will suffice her curiosity.

"Why is that, my dear?" Mrs. Covelli presses.

Breathe In

Jared squeezes my right hand that is resting on my lap. I take a sip of water and clear my throat trying to avoid the awkward silence. Unfortunately, I know I need to answer.

"My parents are . . ." I begin, but fall short of saying more.

"They are no longer with us," Jared offers on my behalf.

I see the shock on Jimmy's and Allen's faces first. Joe didn't tell them?! As my gaze sweeps across the table to Mr. and Mrs. Covelli, I see Anna gently touch her heart before making the sign of the cross. Mr. and Mrs. Covelli's reactions do not match the others who did not know. Their eyes soften as they offer a reassuring smile in consolation.

"My apologies, Emma. I'm so sorry," Mrs. Covelli warmly states.

I nod acceptance, though I sense a hint of pity behind her words. I appreciate her kind gesture, but I hate receiving pity from people.

"That explains a lot," Jimmy randomly blurts.

Joe punches him in the arm, hard enough that I could practically feel it on the other side of the table.

"Ouch," Jimmy mumbles.

An uncomfortable mood permeates the room.

"Excuse me for a moment, please," I proclaim, quickly standing up from my seat. Jared lets go of my hand and doesn't follow, giving me the needed space he knows I require. Joe, Jimmy, Allen and Mr. Covelli all stand up when I do.

Not sure where to go and not wanting to be completely rude, I swiftly exit the dining room. Without thinking, my body takes me through the halls and I find myself in Joe's bedroom of all places. What am I doing in here? I don't really care. I just need a moment.

Sitting on the edge of his bed, I close my eyes and focus on my breathing. Breathe, Emma. Just Breathe. My mind starts to wander as I feel the need to be consoled. One would think that my best friend, my brother, who has loved and helped me all these years, would be the one to come to mind. Not at all. Not him. The person I want to enter the door is the man who my body desperately craves. I want Joe Covelli.

The uncontrollable urge to pee rises to the point where I can no longer hold it while waiting for Joe to find me. I hurry with the hopes of him standing in his room waiting for me. Regrettably, no one is there, not even Sadie. Where is she? She followed me into the bedroom.

I tentatively make my way back to the dining room and find everyone talking freely. Sitting back down, I smile and make eye contact with everyone

Chapter Thirty Six

as I listen in on the new topic at hand. To show my respect and that there are no hard feelings, I do add a comment or question from time to time on the various subjects.

We all continue to talk late into the evening, eventually moving from the dining room to the living room. Joe graciously plays the piano on occasion, even when smaller conversations take place. Seeing Pop-Pop yawn a few times, Jared suggests we make our way home. Jared, Nathan and Pop-Pop drive Sadie and I home since it's already well after ten. The three of them join Sadie and me up in my apartment, giving Pop-Pop a quick tour of the place as well as use of the restroom.

After saying farewell to my family, I strip down and hop into the tub for a relaxing bath. Roughly ten minutes later — I know because of the three songs that just finished playing, my phone chirps.

"Hi," I greet in a relaxed tone.

"Hi, beautiful," he soothingly returns. "I'm just checking in."

"About what?"

"Earlier, at dinner," he admits.

"Ohh. Yeah. I'm fine. Thanks," I offer.

"Really?" he searches.

"Yeah," I let out on a sigh.

"Jared and them still there?" he investigates.

"No, they left a few minutes ago," I reply.

"What are you doing?" he seeks.

"What am I usually doing this time of night when you call?"

I can feel him smile as silence falls upon our conversation as usual. Neither one of us really needing to talk at the moment; just enjoying hearing the other one breathe. By now a few thoughts of Joe joining me are entertained, but with it being that time of the month, I have trouble envisioning it fully.

"I'll let you go," he surprisingly states.

"Oh, okay," I reply, trying to curb my shock.

"I just wanted to make sure you are okay," he kindly enforces.

"Yeah," I say, not knowing what else to utter.

"Goodnight, beautiful," his voice sings, resonating throughout my entire body. "See you tomorrow."

"Yes. See you tomorrow. Goodnight, Joe."

Thirty Seven

The next morning I jump right into my regular morning routine. By eight-forty-five, I am walking up to Joe's penthouse, without Sadie. He insisted on picking me up, but I refused. I need the movement after plugging away half of the early morning on the computer for Raven Media and finalizing things for our meeting — working out got pushed to the side for later today.

With the warm weather, having this somewhat of a business meeting with Joe and his father and knowing that I'll be with Maggie for the rest of the day taking care of wedding things, I put on a cute floral dress that fits my body and flairs out slightly just below my hips to the tops of my knees. I opted out for jewelry other than my moonstone necklace and I've got a simple, white Coach bag and silver strappy Jimmy Choo heels on.

After Anna greets Sadie and me at the door, she leads me into the living room to wait for Joe and Mr. and Mrs. Covelli.

In less than a minute, Joe is walking briskly to greet me. "Why didn't you let me come and get you?" Joe comments, moving closer.

"I told you that I needed the walk," I reply impassively.

"You shouldn't have walked dressed like that," he contends with a hint of concern. He leans in for a kiss on the cheek while placing his right hand on my hip.

"This is Pasadena and it's broad daylight, Joe. I'm not going to get mugged or anything. Besides, even if someone tried, you know . . ." I begin before he cuts me off.

"You know what I'm talking about," he presses.

"I'll consider it for the future," I announce, wanting to change the subject and taking a step back, hearing footsteps in the hallway.

"You look lovely, by the way," he adds sweetly in a low voice.

"Thanks."

It's hard to stay miffed with those gorgeous blue eyes staring back at me.

"Don't you look stunning," Mrs. Covelli reports with a smile. She continues moving towards me.

This time, ready for a friendly greeting, I initiate a hug first. "Mrs. Covelli, it's a pleasure to see you again."

"Please, Emma, call me Elaine," she reminds.

"My apologies. I'll do my best to remember Mrs., I mean Elaine," I return.

Breathe In

"There. See. That's better," she generously announces.

"You look lovely as well," I praise.

She's wearing a stunning pearl white business suit like dress, golden heels and accented the outfit with a thick gold necklace and matching earrings and bracelet.

"Why, thank you. You're too kind," she accepts graciously. "John will be out in just a moment. He had a quick call he needed to take." Gesturing towards the couches, "Please sit. Would you like anything to drink?"

"No. I'm fine. Thank you."

"Very well, then. I'll leave Joe to entertain you while I go check on John and let him know that you've arrived." She glides away in a relaxed, prompt manner.

"Hi," Joe nervously says, taking a step closer.

"Hi," I return, doing the same.

A laid-back smile appears on his face. Neither one of us talk. We just stand, staring into each other's eyes. The silence is not awkward, but the sexual tension is at its peak, even for me with my period.

A man clearing his throat suddenly catches Joe's and my attention. My head snaps around to see where the sound is coming from. Mr. Covelli is patiently waiting with a grin on his face and his hands clasped in front of him.

"Mr. Covelli," I address, turning toward him.

"Emma, please call me John," he corrects cordially.

"Yes. Mr., I mean John," I reply, taking a few steps towards him to greet him properly. "Thank you for having me back so soon."

"You are quite welcome. However, this is not my home," he reminds sweetly.

"Yes. Of course," I nervously answer while chiding myself. "Where would you like to have our meeting?"

"She cuts right to the chase, Joseph," Mr. Covelli states.

Joe smirks and I lower my eyes to the floor bashfully for a moment.. "My apologies."

"No need to apologize, dear," he reassures. "Besides, Joseph probably has told me more about you than he has of me to you."

"I know a bit," I slip.

That's not what I wanted to say.

Laughing, Mr. Covelli continues, "Good. Hopefully, he's only shared my good moments."

Chapter Thirty Seven

"Of course," I declare.

"Good. Good," he states. "He's done the same for you."

I smile at his comment. "Thank you."

Mr. Covelli leads the way into the dining room where place settings for four have already been put out. Anna offers us some drinks as small talk erupts while we wait for Mrs. Covelli to join us.

"If you don't mind me asking, how long have you had your two businesses?" Mr. Covelli investigates.

Pleased with any easy question that I'm willing to answer openly, I explain, "I started Naturally Me, my online wellness blog website, when I was eighteen and my social media management company, Raven Media, when I was twenty."

"Impressive," he commends. "How old are you now . . . If you don't mind me asking?"

"Thank you. I'm twenty-four."

"Ahh, the same age as Joseph," Mr. Covelli states openly. "From what Joseph tells me, you never went to college."

"No sir," I affirm. "I was homeschooled by my mother until . . ." my voice trails a little.

"I'm sure she'd be very proud of you," Mrs. Covelli adds, entering the dining room.

"Thank you. I would hope so," I reply, struggling to maintain a professional demeanor.

This is not the time or place to allow memories of my parents to hinder me.

"How did you get into starting Naturally Me?" Mrs. Covelli inquires.

"I became interested in alternative healing methods from Maggie and her family which spear-launched my desire to learn as much as I could."

"Wonderful," Mrs. Covelli comments.

"And, then your second business?" Mr. Covelli reminds me.

"A few years into Naturally Me, I started using social media to promote the website. When my staff and I were bogged down on time, jumping from one platform to another, I created the software to connect all of the accounts and maintain them in a centralized location," I describe.

Anna starts serving each of us, offering plates of breakfast foods to choose from as our conversation moves forward. I nod my desire or offer no *thank you* to Anna as she offers each choice.

"You created the software?" Mr. Covelli checks.

"Yes sir. With the help of two of Jared's friends who are also programers and who currently work for Raven. Once the system was in place, we used it to easily promote both Naturally Me and Raven Media."

"How many clients do you provide services for now?" Mr. Covelli seeks more.

"We have fifteen clients for the social media management services alone, not counting Naturally Me as a client."

"What other services do you provide?" Mrs. Covelli questions.

"Social media marketing and strategic planning, media development and other advertising and marketing consulting services."

"Maggie is her COO for Raven and Jared is the same for Naturally Me," Joe adds.

"Yes," I agree.

"What are you looking to change with your company?" Mrs. Covelli peruses.

"Joe had the idea that I should rework the current software to offer it as a cloud packaged based service for companies who already have their own social media staff. This way I can offer the same managing benefits to more companies minus the overhaul of directly handling their online marketing platforms and communication. Ultimately, I would like to switch to that service completely."

"How do Joe, Elaine and I come into play?" Mr. Covelli asks.

I'm sure that Joe has filled his father in on a lot of this information, but perhaps he's seeking to hear it directly from me.

"The challenge is if there is a demand for the use of the software, and it increases beyond a certain point, which could happen rather quickly, the hosting company's servers will be bogged down, causing them to run slowly; not to mention the potential security concerns. It would be better to create my own hosting company with my own servers and implement my own security software. That also makes the possibility to provide hosting and additional services as new streams of revenue, if I choose."

I give Mr. and Mrs. Covelli a moment to process what I've said.

"My hesitancy to move forward is that I don't have the funding to jump right into the ideal situation of having my own servers. I'm not interested in tying up a large portion of my cashflow. Raven Media has enough liquid cash to purchase either a building or the hardware needed outright as well as at least the first year's worth of salaries, but not both and I'd like to minimize the use of a bank loan to do it."

I wait a minute or two for Mr. or Mrs. Covelli's response, but they just sit and nod their heads.

Chapter Thirty Seven

"My apologies. Did I offer too much information?"

"No, no, my dear," Mr. Covelli sweetly returns. "I'm just factoring certain pieces in my head."

Mrs. Covelli smiles as if she is doing the same.

"Oh, okay."

"She literally knows every step that is required to move forward on this pretty quickly. She's ahead of schedule already on the preliminary software," Joe praises.

"It sounds like it," Mr. Covelli concurs, looking pleased.

"Why don't you just use the current server company and switch once you're close to that point?" Mrs. Covelli investigates.

"To switch over to a whole new system can take from twenty-four to forty-eight hours to occur, leaving our company and our clients without any services or functionality during that time."

"That's a long time to not to conduct proper business," Mr. Covelli states, showing his comprehension to the potential dilemma.

"Precisely," I acknowledge.

"If you had the proper funding, how long would this all take to set up?" Mrs. Covelli inquires.

"Since the product is digital, it would all depend on how long it takes to close on a property, deliver the needed hardware, set it up and hire additional staff. My current team and I should have the software finished before the end of the year . . . after testing and retesting, that is. The first round of testing will start just after Maggie's and Henry's wedding."

"That quick?" Mr. Covelli says with a little surprise.

"They already have the basis for the software. They are just building out the functionality to make it more appealing as well as secure," Joe includes.

"Interesting," Mr. Covelli comments while Mrs. Covelli nods in agreement.

"Costs can be offset by placing the servers underground to help with the cooling along with adding or refurbishing the facility to be as green as possible," Joe adds.

"They'll be even lower with the new hardware company I have discovered. They use vacuum tubes which reduce the computing temperature significantly while simultaneously increase network speeds," I mention.

"You didn't tell me about that," Joe teasingly stipulates.

"I know," I playful contend. "I can't share all of my secrets."

383

Joe gives me a look from my statement which forces me to bite the inside of my lip to refrain from our little inside joke.

"Looks like another potential power couple," Mrs. Covelli muses.

"Indeed," Mr. Covelli agrees with a widening smile as he looks back and forth to Joe and me.

What does Mrs. Covelli mean by a power couple? Joe and I aren't a couple.

"Do we have specs and numbers?" Mr. Covelli checks.

"Of course," Joe returns with a smile. "And, I don't doubt that they've improved with Emma's discover of the new hardware."

"I have them right here if you'd like to see them," I offer, reaching into my purse, grab my attache and handing all three of them a copy.

After a few minutes of silence as they turn the pages to the five-page document, Joe announces with surprise, "You've reduced the initial cost by a quarter?"

Smiling, I nod and verify, "The initial investment in a green facility will pay for itself in less than a year, each of the states with properties you are considering offer tax incentives for green technology, and if my calculations are correct, we'll be over producing power, allowing us to sell the additional energy back to the utility companies."

"Wow!" Joe exclaims.

"Exciting," Mrs. Covelli comments. She exchanges a few silent glances with her husband as if they are speaking some kind of code. I can't make out what they may be saying and watching them is extremely fascinating.

'Well . . ." Mr. Covelli begins. "Draw up the paperwork, Joseph, and we'll get started immediately. Whatever is needed, we'll make it happen. This will definitely be a beneficial investment. Congratulations to you both!"

A little nervous because I wasn't expecting the Covellis to agree so quickly, my eyes dart back and forth to the three faces smiling at me. "Wait. What?" I stutter, revealing my shock.

Is this really happening?

"Don't you need more time to consider? I mean . . ." my voice trails.

"We've heard plenty of information. Between what Joe told and showed us earlier, Elaine and I were already convinced. Hearing it directly from you solidified the deal," Mr. Covelli admits, taking his wife's hand.

"But we need to go over particulars, like percentages and how much and . . ." I anxiously blurt.

Chapter Thirty Seven

"Emma, dear, those are all incidentals. I'm sure we'll all come to an agreement on those pieces. For now, let's just celebrate this joint venture. I'm sure we'll figure out how to make it mutually beneficial," Mr. Covelli diplomatically commands, dismissing the importance of the details.

"Umm . . . okay," I stammer, confused by the whirlwind of emotions bouncing inside of me.

"Emma, are you excited about the premier?" Mr. Covelli inquires.

"Yes, but the premier can't be determined until we establish a facility," I mention courteously.

"No," Mr. Covelli chuckles. "I'm referring to the movie premier, with Chris."

I preform a mental head slap, not catching Mr. Covelli's redirection of our conversation to another topic. My eyes expand when my brain fully processes what Mr. Covelli meant. "Sure," I offer a little too impassively.

"You don't sound too excited," Mrs. Covelli states. "He seems like a very nice young man."

"Yes, he's very nice. It's just . . . the premier is a business transaction for me," I explain my apprehension.

"How is it a business transaction for you?" Mr. Covelli searches.

"I'm a partial owner of Nathaniel's," I disclose.

"She's being modest. She's more than just a partial owner," Joe interjects.

"Ahh," Mr. Covelli says.

"Did you two date at one point? That would explain his affection towards you and yours to him. I'm guessing you broke it off," Mrs. Covelli specifies more than questions.

Joe appears calm at his mother's prying, but he does slightly shift in his seat.

"I don't date, but something along those lines," I explain.

"Ahh . . . well, regardless, make sure you allow yourself to have some fun. The boys will be there along with your friends, so you'll have plenty of pleasant distractions," Mrs. Covelli presents kindly.

"I will. Thank you," I reply.

It takes a minute or two for our conversation to strike back up again. Mrs. Covelli keeps things light by asking me questions about our recent rip to Hawaii and any details about Maggie's and Henry's wedding I can share.

By ten minutes after eleven, I excuse myself from our meeting. I have to get home and change before meeting up with Maggie at the Li family home for more wedding preparations. Just as Joe is escorting me down to his car, because he insists on driving me the half mile home and not taking no for an answer, we see Jimmy and Allen when the elevator doors open. They're happy to see that I haven't left and assert that they will join Joe and me. Jimmy and Allen say that they have yet to see my home and felt left out since everyone else — everyone but Chris — know where I live.

I was a little disappointed that it wouldn't be just Joe and myself. For some reason, I was hoping to have some time with him. I need to explain that we need to back off or because of what Jared and Nathan were hinting towards the other night. At the same time, I was happy to have Jimmy and Allen to tag along. They are really fun to hang out with, and given the fact that I have my period, having them around makes it less awkward, preventing the chance for things to evolve further with Joe. I've heard of some women having and enjoying sex when it's that time of the month, but the whole idea bugs me out. I don't think I'll ever be that comfortable with someone to even consider it.

Jimmy, Allen and Joe join me in taking Sadie to the park after we get to my door. Once we're back to my apartment, they peer around, commenting on a variety of things before I rush them out with Sadie and me. They try to get me to agree to have them drive me down to the Li home, but I politely refuse, explaining that it will only take me about ten to fifteen minutes to get to Maggie by train. If we drive, it would talk more like forty minutes or longer with LA traffic.

The rest of the day, I'm with Maggie until she drops Sadie and me off at home just after eleven at night. Still processing the verbal agreement Joe, Mr. and Mrs. Covelli and I have pertaining to business, I refrain from telling Maggie anything. I don't want to jinks the good news and want to wait until I'm with her and Jared at the same time. I need to make sure that Joe doesn't say anything either. I text him and he graciously obliges. He asks if he can stop by, but I decline. I'm mentally and physically tired and the last thing I want to explain to him about putting the breaks on any physical interaction is all due to Jared acting weird and my menstrual cycle.

Thirty Eight

The next morning, as I'm returning from taking Sadie out for an early, peaceful, morning jog, I stop in my tracks as she bolts towards our door. Sadie never leaves my side until we're in the hall, but today is different. She's in a full run. Why? There are only one of four reasons she would do it — she sees Maggie, Jared, Nathan, or — Joe.

"Are you stalking me?" I allude, squinting my eyes at him as I approach.

"No . . . not unless you'd like me to," Joe counters in his delectable sexy voice.

"The sexy voice won't help you," I sass with a smirk.

"You sure?" he surveys, pulling me into him.

I easily submit to his mouth.

"Nor will a kiss," I tease, staying close and just barely letting go of his lips. "This is the reason why I don't let men know where I live. They think they can just stop by anytime they want."

Joe takes the keys from my hand and unlocks the door without saying a word. We stay close until the door is open enough for me to squirm out of his reach.

"So why are you here, especially this early in the morning?" I pry, heading towards the kitchen.

"I didn't get to properly say goodbye yesterday after our meeting since Jimmy and Allen tagged along," he reveals, closing in on me while I gulp down some water.

"You've gone days before . . ." I begin.

"Exactly," he interrupts, erotically hijacking my mouth for several beats. "I couldn't wait days to feel you again."

Not caring about the sweaty mess I am from running, I surrender to him. I'm not sure what exactly happens until I feel him lowering me onto my bed. The weight of him pinning me down ignites my itch and I moan, wanting more. Why now? Why couldn't he wait a few more days? I want this — but not like this, not with two more days to go with my period.

Barely shifting his body or removing his lips from mine, Joe manages to shrug out of his shirt. His skin feels like hot stones that have been sitting in the sun. Not too hot to touch — just hot enough.

Shaking my head, I mildly protest even though I continue to kiss him back. Joe grabs my hips and rolls us to where he is under me and I'm straddling him. In one swift movement, he glides us to a seated position and has my shirt tugging away from the top of my head. Great — not my other Achilles' Heel which is being on top! Damn it!

My arms tighten around his shoulders until his mouth moves to my chin and begins sweeping down my neck. I feel my thighs squeeze around his legs as my hips starts to lightly grind him. Joe's hands grip my ass like he's encouraging me to keep rocking.

"No . . ." I pant, pushing him away with my hands on his chest.

"Why?" he groans, but doesn't stop his pursuit on my neck as he heads down to my collar bone.

"Because . . ." I try to rationalize it out loud.

It makes sense in my head why, but I don't want to explain the real reason to him, let alone the fact that I need to leave soon.

"Because, why?" he seeks, slowing his pace.

The only thing I can come up with other than, I have my period, is, "Because I don't want to break two rules at the same time."

With a smile returning, Joe investigates. "So you do want to . . . ."

Before I'm required to give any kind of an answer, my head jerks towards the kitchen when I hear the buzzer. "I need to get that," I announce still sitting on his lap. "I'm waiting for a package to be delivered."

Joe chuckles. "I'm right here." His lips continue their track up and down my neck.

I purse my lips at his cute response. I totally set myself up for that. Joe holds onto my waist as I try to dismount him. The buzzer goes off again. My eyebrows lift as I give him a glare. With a smile, he tugs at the nape of my neck, seeking a kiss before letting me go.

As I get out to the kitchen area, my phone chirps and the buzzer sounds a third time. I yank my phone out of my purse as I head to the door. Maggie's calling. I can call her back in a second once I check who's trying to come up.

"Hello?" I greet a little out of breath, pressing the buzzer button.

"Hey! I forgot my key and I really need to pee," Maggie answers.

Shit! Shit, shit, shit, shit, shit!

"Okay," I mutter while pressing the button to have the outer gate unlock for her.

"Thanks," she offers.

I bolt back into my bedroom, almost colliding into a topless Joe. "You need to go! Now!"

Chapter Thirty Eight

"Why?" he nonchalantly inquires as I toss him his shirt and start to push him to the door. Joe pushes his weight back into me, slowing us down.

"Maggie is on the way up! You need to go!" I shout.

"What's the big deal? She knows we hang out," he rebuts.

"Because you're topless, have a raging hard-on, I'm a sweaty mess and I'm not about to . . . " I pause not wanting to finish the sentence.

I don't want my friends to know that there's the potential of anything happening between Joe and me. Why? I'm not quite sure and now is not the time to speculate.

Joe laughs at the start of my answer. "About to what?" he presses, more from amusement at me panicking rather than really needing to know, as if he already knows what I would say.

Finally at the door, I open it and check the hallway. It's clear. Shit. No, it's not. I hear the elevator ding open. I shut the door but leave it unlocked.

"I thought you wanted me to leave," Joe sarcastically states.

"Not funny," I announce, grabbing him by the hand and pulling him towards the office through the hall that leads to the second bath and bedroom.

He moves a little lighter this time, but not as fast as I would like.

"Stay here! Do not say a word or come out. If you do, I will kill you. When I get Maggie to follow me into the bathroom, then you will quietly exit my apartment. Got it?" I order.

Joe grabs my face and plants a sensual kiss on my lips. It takes me a few seconds to pull away.

"I'm here," Maggie shouts, opening the door.

"Stay and hide," I mouth to Joe.

Running down the short hall, I almost collide into Maggie as she heads toward the guest bathroom. Shit! What the hell?!

"Hey," I greet. "Why don't you use the master?" I direct.

"This one is closer," she replies, yanking her dress up and her underwear down, leaving the door wide open. "What took you so long?"

"Sorry. I was in the bathroom when you buzzed," I lie convincingly.

"Ohh, sorry."

"It's okay," I remark. "Why are you here so early?"

Maggie finishes relieving herself before answering, "Henry left early this morning for some business back in China. He's going to be there for at least a week, maybe longer, and I figured since I was up, knew you are always up early and I'm starting to freak out about all of this while he's gone, and that I need my best girlfriend."

"There's no need to freak out," I console as we head out to the kitchen. "Everything is getting done. Having Amelia is a godsend."

"I know, right?!" she agrees with a sigh. "It's just my family and Henry's family. It's getting to be a little too much for me. I need a break from it all or else I'm going to snap."

"Don't know why . . ." I sarcastically reply which gets her to smile.

"So . . . before we get into wedding stuff, I want to know about the premier!" she discloses.

I internally cringe before passively asking, "What about it?"

"Nathan told me, but I want to hear it directly from you! Are you excited?" She bounces up and down on the bar stool.

"Ahhh, sure," I proclaim.

"Why aren't you excited?" she asks with a disappointed pucker. "You've got a hunky guy taking you out for a night in the spotlight."

"All of that," I contend, taking out some fruit from the fridge for us to eat.

"So, you really are just doing it to help Nathan?!" Maggie double checks, not that she didn't believe Nathan when he told her.

"Yes. It's just a business transaction to get Nathan and his designs noticed," I reinforce.

"So you really aren't into him anymore?"

"Who? Chris?"

"Yeah, Chris."

"No. And, I was never interested in the first place," I disclose.

"You were interested in him enough to have sex with him," she reminds.

I wince but fail to hide it.

"Why don't you sleep with him again," Maggie suggests.

"No! Hell no," I rebut.

"Was it that bad?" she searches.

Maggie and I never actually talked about it that night after Ayana's beyond the few details I disclosed at Nathan's the next day. We were too busy getting each other off. I don't want to say too much. God only knows Joe is enjoying overhearing this conversation. I know he is. I would be eagerly listening in if I was him right now.

Chapter Thirty Eight

"He finished before me and it was Molly who got me off, remember," I blurt loudly.

Shit. I meant for that to be more of a whisper.

"Well, thank God for Molly," Maggie chuckles. "And, then me later that night!"

I can't help but join her in the amusement. "Yeah . . . ."

"What's up with you?" she accuses.

"What?" I deny.

"Don't what me," she declares. "You've been weird lately."

"No, I haven't," I try to deflect her statement.

"Yes, you have and you are right now," she stands her ground.

I don't say anything and we stare at each other for what feels like a minute in silence.

"You need to get laid. When was the last time you had sex?"

"I don't need to get laid," I proclaim, not wanting to talk about it.

"Bullshit," she yells and immediately clasps her hands over her mouth.

We both giggle. Maggie never swears.

"When was the last time you got laid?" she presses.

"The other day," I answer.

"With who?" she pries, not believing me.

We openly talk about sex, so she knows that something is up since I'm trying to avoid the whole thing.

"B.O.B."

"Battery operated boyfriends don't count," she declares.

"B.O.B. counts," I retort, defending my statement. "I can always count on B.O.B. to do his job."

"Self-satisfaction never counts." Maggie studies me for a moment. "Oh my God!"

"What?" I reply with a mouth fully of strawberry.

"Oh my God!"

"What!" I repeat.

She's starting to freak me out.

"Did you? Yep! You totally did!" she shouts.

"What the hell are you talking about?" I search.

I'm so confused by what she's implying.

"You slept with Joe!"

"What?! No! No, no, no, no, no!" I rebut.

"Yes, you did," she continues. "Jared said . . . ."

"What did Jared say?" I explore trying to keep calm.

"Nothing," Maggie denies.

"What did Jared say," I enunciate each word.

"Jared said you two were acting weird the other day when you agreed to be Chris' date."

"How were we acting?"

"Okay, it was more Joe than you," she express.

"I did not have sex with Joe," I stand firm.

I haven't. A few minutes ago, I might have, but I'm telling the truth; at least about the sex topic.

She watches me closely. "Okay. I believe you," Maggie says with conviction. "Then with who?"

"You are the last person I've slept with," I announce.

"Seriously?!"

"Yes, seriously."

"We definitely need to get you laid. Why not Joe. He's available and you're . . . ."

I quickly cut her off, "No!"

"Why not? He's totally into you. Nathan said that he looked heartbroken when you agreed to do the premier with Chris," she continues.

"I'm not talking about this with you again . . ." I declare shaking my head.

"Why not?" she pushes.

I glare at her because she knows why. Plus, I don't want to talk about it with Joe in the other room.

"It might do you good," she expresses.

"What?"

"To sleep with Joe."

"Why is that?" I giggle nervously.

"You clearly haven't been with a guy since Chris, which was . . . back in February, and you've never gone this long . . . ."

I jump on her train of thought, "We've trolled and I've trolled since then."

Chapter Thirty Eight

"That may be true, but you've obviously been picky . . . picky enough not to sleep with anyone other than me." After a moment of silence, she asks, "Why don't we go trolling tonight?"

"I don't think so."

"Why not?"

"Because . . ." I return, trying to avoid the reason.

She studies me again before taking out her phone.

"What are you doing?"

"Checking."

"Checking what?"

"That explains it," she affirms.

"What?"

"You. Your mood. Aside from not getting laid in a while you're menstruating."

I don't freak out when Maggie announces it because we're practically on the same schedule. Then I remember that Joe is in the other room. Crap.

"You know what . . ." she begins.

"What?" I place the forks and empty fruit bowl in the dishwasher.

"I'm a day or two late . . . must be the stress of the wedding," she speculates.

"Probably," I agree.

"You don't mind if I crash here until Henry gets back, do you?"

"Not at all," I confirm.

"Okay. After we're done menstruating, we're going trolling . . . for you, of course," she asserts.

"Don't have time," I contend.

"There's always time to get my best friend laid. You know you should seriously reconsider being with a guy more than just a few times . . ." she suggests.

"Why is that?"

"Because by the third time Henry and I . . . ."

"Ahhhhhh! La la la la la! I don't want to hear about you and Henry," I scream plugging my ears. "It's bad enough that you already tried to talk me into having a three-way with you two. La la la la la la."

Maggie's mouth finally stops moving and I take my fingers out of my ears.

Maggie grabs my hands and holds them down while she blurts, "By the third time we got into really knowing each other. I orgasm a minimum of two or three times each time . . . ."

Breathe In

I fight her to get my arms back. Maggie can be really strong when she wants to, but I break free a little too late. I quickly plug my ears and scream again. "Ahhhhhh!"

I watch her face to make sure she's done. Maggie laughs at me and after a minute of making sure she won't continue, I drop my hands from my ears and begin to laugh as well.

"We still need to find you a man who can really satisfy you," she insists.

"Drop it," I urge.

"I can't believe with all the men you've slept with that not one of them has been able to get you to orgasm without you having to . . . ."

"Drop it," I repeat a little more sternly.

A thud sound comes from the floor by Sadie. Maggie and I laugh. "It's okay Sadie. I wasn't talking to you," I inform, picking up her bone and giving it back to her. "I was talking to Aunt Maggie."

"Now you know why Jared, Nathan and I say that song is your theme song," Maggie throws in and sticks out her tongue when she's finished.

Maggie is right. I have yet to find a man who can satisfy my sexual needs, a real man, that is, who isn't named B.O.B..

"If we're going to get out of here anytime soon, I need to shower," I announce.

"We should hit the spa sometime this week," she says graciously dropping my sex life from the current topic list. "I think we could both use it."

"Definitely!" I agree.

"Oooh, do you mind if I borrow some jewelry?"

"No, not at all," I offer, heading towards my bedroom with Maggie close behind. "You know where they are."

When Maggie and I get back to the kitchen for a small bite before continuing with the rest of our day, I notice writing on the notepad attached to the side of my fridge. It says;

Glad to know you talk about me. See you soon, beautiful!
xoxo Joe

It quickly rip it off before Maggie can see it and shove it into my wallet.

The rest of the day, it's just Maggie, Sadie and me until we head over to Nathan's for dinner with him, Jared and Pop-Pop. I decide that it's time to fill them in on the business deal that I'm working on with Joe and his parents.

Chapter Thirty Eight

"So, that's why you two have been spending so much extra time together," Nathan states.

"Yes. For business and planning the joint bachelor-bachelorette weekend."

"And, getting Pop-Pop here for Jared's party," adds Maggie.

"Well, that explains a lot," Nathan confesses. "And, here we thought you two were having sex."

So the truth comes out. That's what they've been talking about.

"Makes sense," Jared adds with an expression like he's still not completely convinced.

I don't want to lie to my friends, but I don't want to admit to them either that there is something, what I'm not exactly sure, happening with Joe. I'd rather use him for his body to satisfy my itch and once I'm ready to move on, like I do with all men, I'll eventually admit to it — maybe. All I know is that Joe and I want to fuck each other, and I desperately need to fuck him so I can get back into my regular trolling routine.

"So what does this all mean for us?" Maggie searches.

"It means that you'll still be COO, you'll have more staff to run everything and you'll be making a lot more money . . . that is, if you still want the job."

"Of course I do. Wow! I'm so excited. This is so much fun," she beams.

I smile at Maggie, happy and relieved to hear that she's still on board. Turning my attention to Jared, I continue with more explanation. "Jared."

"Yeah, Kitten," he says.

"Because this expansion is going to take up more of my time . . ." I start.

"Yeah?" he replies.

"That means I'll have less time to work and focus on Naturally Me," I explain.

"What do you need from me? I can easily do more if you need. I'd be happy to," he eagerly supports.

I take a moment to think about how I want to phrase my next statement. "I was thinking about more than that."

Jared cocks his head to the side, showing that his interest is piqued.

"I was thinking of turning over fifty percent of the company's ownerships over to you. You ultimately do what I do, but we can . . . ."

"Oh my God! Are you serious?!" he shouts, almost on the verge of tears.

Nodding, I continue, "We can hire some more staff, maybe even find a place for Pop-Pop if he'd like."

"Of course!" Jared shouts, jumping up and hugging me. "Thank you for believing that I can . . . I love you!"

"I wouldn't trust anyone else," I return, fighting back tears. "I love you too!"

"Looks like you're going to be my sugar daddy!" Nathan teases.

"Hell yeah!" Jared confirms. "I don't mind being one."

Pop-Pop is emotional too, especially after hearing how determined Jared and I are to find a place for him as well.

Once we get settled with our emotions, Nathan grabs two bottles of wine and we pop them open to celebrate. Our conversation for the rest of the night turns into questions and ideas for both companies and eventually over to incidentals where we are laughing into the night.

Back at my apartment and laying in bed with Maggie, who is already asleep next to me, I stare at the ceiling with contentedness surrounding my heart. I knew my friends would be excited and happy for me, but I didn't expect them to be this enamored with how things are changing, let alone myself. This is one point in my life where I don't mind the change. The pride and love I have for Maggie and Jared is at a level I can't even describe. I'm even more thankful and grateful for them being in my life.

Thirty Nine

Come Monday night, Maggie is still sleeping over, working and conducting wedding stuff as Henry has yet to return from China. She's needing more down time in between being around family and checks with Amelia for wedding needs and details. Maggie reports that business is going very well for Henry, he's just really busy. I don't doubt that he's trying to get additional things done prior to the wedding.

Jared joins Maggie and me for the night so all three of us can discuss and schedule needed steps for both businesses this week. With tomorrow being the start of June, the three of us have a lot of things to take care of regarding business and Maggie's wedding. The wedding is less than two months away and almost every weekend is booked with some kind of event — Father's Day with Fùqīn and Pop-Pop, the bridal shower, 4th of July, the bachelor-bachelorette weekend Joe and I have to finish planning and then the rehearsal dinner and wedding. There are only one or two weekends that have yet to be booked for some kind of a party or gathering.

Just after dinner, Maggie inquires, "Who are you texting?"

"No one," I reply, focused on the conversation.

"Is it a man?" she playfully pries.

"How long have you known me to know that I wouldn't give my phone number out to a man, let alone any straight man," I remind.

She pauses for a moment. "Well, Joe is a man and I know he has your number."

Jared and her snicker.

"If you must know, I'm talking with Amy and Kim." I show her my phone's screen just long enough for her to see who's in the conversation.

"Why?" she searches.

I look up at Maggie to answer. "I talk to them regularly, not just when the family is together."

"And, she's finalizing bridal shower arrangements," Jared interjects.

"Thanks," I sarcastically reply.

"What?! It's not like she doesn't know when it is," he shrugs.

Maggie and Jared let me be for the next few minutes as I continue texting with Amy and Kim. Joe texts again for the third time today, asking the same question he's been asking every day since our heated interaction where we almost got caught by Maggie. He keeps sending, When can I see you?. I've been purposefully ignoring him.

"We need to finish planning the bachelor-bachelorette party," he writes.

Wow! It took him four days to send a different message.

"And, we need to go over the paperwork I have for Raven Media," he includes.

My conversation with Amy and Kim just wrapped up, so texting Joe a response won't be noticed by my two friends sharing the couch with me. I guess ignoring him for four days is enough time.

"I know," I write back.

"Are you avoiding me?" he inquires.

"No. Why would I do that?" I text.

"You've ignored my texts and calls the past few days," he states.

"Maggie and Jared have been here. I've been busy taking care of business and wedding stuff," I reply.

"What we need to take care of falls under the same categories," he writes.

"Yes," I agree. "But, not me needing to respond to you asking when you'll see me again."

"Those two things were implied in the question," he texts.

"Didn't hear it implied," I write.

I hope he catches my sarcasm.

"What did you hear?" he searches.

I send back a winking emoticon.

"I'm not sure what you are implying," he texts back.

"You know what I mean," I stipulate.

"If we were talking in person, I would know," he writes.

"Knowing you, we wouldn't be talking," I comment back.

Joe sends back a winking, kissing face emoticon.

I can't help but smile.

"That's not a bad thing, is it?" he checks to validate my statement about us not talking if we were together.

"Maybe," I reply.

"Are they staying the night again?"

"Yes."

"Can you sneak out?"

Chapter Thirty Nine

"And, go where? Your family is at your place," I answer.

"Wherever you want," he writes. "I just need to see you."

"Why?" I press back.

Let's see what he'll admit.

"I miss the taste of your lips on mine," Joe texts.

My heart skips a beat and I'm unable to respond.

"Please," he begs.

I don't write anything because I'm not quite sure what to say. This is torture for me too. I should have slept with him sooner, like I do with other men — but, Joe isn't like other men.

By the end of the week, Joe schedules another meeting between his parents, himself and me. The preliminary paperwork that he had done for the first round of negotiations went faster than I had expected. Joe said that he's trying to help facilitate a number of key pieces prior to the wedding so that way, once the wedding is over, we'll have more time to take action for purchasing and refurbishing a property, loading in and setting up hardware and the necessary staff.

I have to say, I am very impressed with the amount of detail and thoroughness Joe put into the contract. There are only a few minor tweaks we all agree upon during the meeting which, once corrected, I'll review with my lawyer before we have another official meeting to sign the documents.

With fifteen clients paying for social media management, and most of them paying for premium services, Raven Media is grossing just shy of two point eight million dollars a year. What we make for media management does not including the additional services we supply, which gives us a grand total of four point seven million dollars, which is approximately half a million more than last year. After salaries and expenses are paid, Raven Media nets two point six million; I pay my staff very well. After taxes, the company only has to pay federal taxes because of where it's incorporated, and with the previous years' earnings, Raven Media officially has eight point seven million in liquid cash. The cost for the servers and staff for the first year shouldn't drain all of the capital.

Because I've already established a high value for the company from its inception, the Covelli family is offering a very interesting deal that I can not resist, which is one of the tweaks we agree to make during the meeting. The Covellis are taking a smaller percentage of ownership of Raven. Instead, they are purchasing the property that will house the physical location of the servers and will be charging Raven Media a monthly lease to rent most of the building.

They've got their eye on several properties that can allow for other businesses to rent space as well, which expands their profit potential with refurbishing it as a green building. The Covellis are using their purchase of the property as the test pilot for greening any existing properties they own. If all goes well, this property will be the litmus test for redefining corporate and hospitality facilities and industries.

After the meeting, which took place at his penthouse, Joe takes me home. Suddenly, Joe hits the stop button on the elevator before pinning me to the side wall. Expecting a heated embrace, I'm surprised when Joe takes his time, trailing his fingers down my cheek, over my neck and back up as he delivers a sensually slow kiss. As I slide my hands up his chest, Joe creeps his tongue into my waiting, open mouth. It's like he's purposefully controlling himself as he relishes in every single sensation. My mouth seeks more when he pulls away just far enough out of reach.

"So, you've talked to Maggie about me?" he inquires.

"What are you talking about?" I check.

"The other day, when she came over and you hid me in the closet. You said *I'm not talking about this with you again*, meaning me," he reminds.

"Did I?"

"You did," he affirms. "How often do you talk about me?"

"I don't," I argue.

"Sounds like you do," he challenges with a wicked grin.

"No," I purposefully disagree.

"Hmmmm," his throat groans.

Joe's lips move in, seeking more of mine. There's more force and desire behind each kiss.

"I want you," he says in his low, sexy voice.

All I can do is nod my understanding. He's completely seduced me with his mouth.

Anticipating another kiss, I'm sourly disappointed when Joe turns his head and seconds later the elevator resumes its ascent. He stays pressed against me, staring into my eyes, but doesn't kiss me. I lean to capture a kiss, but he wickedly denies me of the pleasure. A devilish smirk emerges in the corner of his mouth when I moan my dissatisfaction. It's like he's taunting me, wanting me to tell him that I want him too and that I won't get to taste his lips until I do. I try again, but he pulls away just as our lips are about to connect. I groan louder which gets a chuckle out of him. Reaching my hands up, I clasp the back of his neck and pull him towards me. Just as our lips brush, Joe suddenly

Chapter Thirty Nine

has my wrists pressed against the wall and our lips are now inches apart. I whine my protest when he hits to button to make the elevator move again.

The door dings, and just before it opens, Joe shifts away from me, facing the entrance. He seems as cool as a cucumber; like nothing has happened and he's completely unaffected by it. I know he is, though. I felt his erection pressing against me. I can see it bulging slightly through his dress pants when my eyes drift down to double check.

As the door opens, Joe takes my hand and leads us out of the box. My body jerks to the left as I had already started to go right to the main hallway. Seconds later, Joe has managed to direct us both beyond the stairway door and has me with my back to the cool concrete wall. He presses himself against me, and the rigidness of his penis is there from before. Cupping my face in his hands, Joe proceeds to tease and torture me with his mouth, barely making contact the first few times.

"Please," I beg, unable to wait any longer. My hands grip his forearms out of desperation as I press my ass against the wall to help me reach is lips. I feel his erection stiffen.

I've never begged for a man to kiss me — but, I like begging him for some reason.

"Say it again . . ." he whispers.

"Please," I force before he's done directing me. "Please." My chest heaves from the pent-up need and desire.

Our mouths converge as we both moan with satisfaction. We stay glued to each other for several minutes until we hear the ricochet of another door opening in the stairway below. We don't move as we listen and watch each other's eyes.

"My Dad, Mom and I have to head back to New York for some business."

"When?"

"Tonight," he says with frustration in his voice.

"Okay," I barely mutter.

I wasn't expecting news like this.

"I don't know when I'll be back," he informs me with pain in his face. "At least a week . . . until just after Father's Day weekend, but maybe longer."

"Ohhh." My stomach drops.

"Do you think . . ." he starts, but stops himself.

"What?" I search.

"Nothing," he contends.

"What?" I press.

He doesn't say another word. Joe wraps his arms around me, hugging me, holding me — like he doesn't want to let go. I consciously take in the feel and scent of him.

"Promise me you won't not talk to me," he pleas after several lengthy kisses.

"Sure," I reply.

"Promise?" he checks.

"Yes," I confirm to assure him, sealing the agreement with a kiss.

A weak smile dances briefly across his face. "Good." He takes another long look at me before saying, "See you soon, beautiful."

"See you soon, Joe."

I watching him swiftly pull away and head down the stairs. As he rounds the next flight, our eyes meet and Joe takes a deep breath in before continuing down. My eyes follow him, trying to catch a glimpse, even when he's officially out of sight.

Forty

As the second week of June begins, I'm home alone with Sadie as Maggie heads back to Henry. Maggie and I had sex a few times after our cycles stopped, but it was never enough for me. I've never had that challenge before with her. If anyone can help with the itch, Maggie can, especially after a few intense sessions. Masturbation is not helping either; it only makes me hornier. I need to fuck a man — not just any man. I need to fuck Joe Covelli.

By the end of the week, I've been able to get a lot done with work and the wedding for Maggie, despite the distraction of my itch. I've had to masturbate at least two times a day, every day, especially after talking to Joe at night. We talk and text every day since he left, but it's not enough. Joe's still in New York and has been bouncing around the country for a few meetings. He tries to coax me into joining him on one of his trips, but I can't take the risk. The risk of my friends knowing, let alone the risk of being completely and utterly pleasantly distracted by him and his body, not to mention all of the time and attention I have to give to the businesses and the wedding. Having sex with Joe is definitely going to happen. It's just a matter of when our schedules line up and when we will not be interrupted. Strike another rule off the list.

It's now halfway through the third week in June and I'm going crazy. This weekend is Maggie's bridal shower and Joe has yet to come back. One would think that we've already had sex with the way my body is reacting to him not being around. Why didn't I sleep with him already? I would be on to the next toy by now.

Jared's been doing a great job taking over a lot more responsibilities for Naturally Me and he's hired Pop-Pop as his assistant, teaching him the ropes. They were over yesterday to squeeze in some additional filming so Pop-Pop can see how the show runs and operates. We've already had a steady increase in numbers in gross income from the initial launch of the pet division with Sadie. All of the preliminary social media advertising completely paid off. The first month when the soft launch for the pet division occurred back in May boosted our monthly profits by ten percent and they are now up almost fifteen percent for June.

Maggie's being doing an awesome job juggling things between Raven Media and her wedding. I keep her up to date on what Brandon, Hannah and I have been doing with the software and what the next steps are once I meet up with the Covellis to sign the paperwork. Maggie has reported that many of the independent contractors were excited to hear the changes that will be made, especially since they will not be losing their jobs. They all will be shifted around to assimilate to new positions that Maggie's already been training them on as well as being informed that they have an increase in pay coming once the switch occurs. Until the paperwork is officially signed, and the wedding is over, the Covellis and I can't move forward with moving into a property, however, the Covellis have already begun negotiations with one particular property.

Nathan has been feverishly working on Chris', Jimmy's and Allen's suits and my dress for the premier. Once Chris heads back to Nathaniel's for the first official fitting, the Raven Media team assigned to Nathaniel's can start promoting in advance that Chris will be wearing a custom piece designed by Nathan. Most movie stars don't advertise in advance who they might be wearing, so I'm a little concerned that Nathan may have promised something to Chris on my behalf. When I ask Nathan about when he needs me for my first fitting he just tells me not yet. I'm not sure what to make of his response, but I'm glad that he isn't needing me to be there with him right now. I don't want to run into Chris. The less, I see Chris the better.

Saturday early morning, Sadie and I are already in San Marino at Kim's house making sure things are ready for the bridal shower. Henry gladly keeps Maggie occupied since he's still making up time from not seeing her much even with him being back. Jared and Nathan are already on their way. The caterers are scheduled to arrive within the next thirty minutes to start prepping in the kitchen. Amelia joins us and is a great asset to the team, making sure everything is taken care of and ready.

Kim has a beautiful home, a house I wouldn't mind living in. Being a successful naturopath married to a just as successful Chinese medical doctor, with a joint practice, Kim and the Chang family is in want for nothing. There are five bedrooms, four full baths, and two half baths laid out in a spacious rancher style home. Since the weather isn't supposed to be too hot today, we're able to have the tables set up on her back patio to entertain and host the bridal shower. With the slightly higher ceiling, adorned with several ceiling fans, she's able to accommodate the seventy-five guests who are schedule to attend which includes us, Maggie's family and many of Henry's family who have stayed since the engagement party or who have recently arrived.

As the party begins at eleven and doesn't conclude until almost five, I'm finally able to relax, knocking another maid of honor task off the list. Jared and Nathan help me pack Henry's car when he arrives to pick up Maggie. Once the caterers are gone and Kim's maids are halfway done with clean-up, Jared, Nathan, Henry, Maggie and I drop Sadie home and then head out to meet up with Pop-Pop at Katana's on Sunset for some sushi and sashimi.

Chapter Forty

Just as we are seated, my attention is pulled away from Maggie telling me something when Jared shouts out to someone. "Hey man! Welcome back."

I do my best to focus on Maggie, but she turns with a perky smile to greet the person who I only see in my peripheral vision. Without needing all the details, I know exactly who it is when my body shivers.

"We've been wondering if we'd lost you to the East Coast," Jared teases.

"No, at all," Joe's voice announces with a husky tone. "Happy to be back."

I rise slowly to greet Joe last out of everyone. "Hey," I offer casually.

I'm miffed that Joe's back, well, just by his impeccable timing. It's that time of the month — again.

"Hey yourself," he returns.

I can see the restraint in his eyes. It's taking a lot of willpower for him not to kiss me right now.

Once everyone settles into their seats, Henry and Joe allow the rest of us to order a spread for everyone to share while we wait for Pop-Pop. Small talk erupts quickly as if no one has been gone.

"Pop-Pop," Nathan yells.

Everyone greets Pop-Pop, and after several hours of dining and conversations, Nathan decides to be funny. "Why don't we hit up Ayana's for the night? Huh?"

"Not funny, Nathan," I retort.

"Come on . . ." he presses back.

"Babe, leave her alone," Jared jumps to my defense.

"What's Ayana's?" Pop-Pop inquires.

"A nightclub," Maggie informs.

"Ohhh, I'm too old for a night club," Pop-Pop replies with a chuckle. "But, thanks for asking."

"You keep that up and you'll have to find Chris another date," I announce sternly.

"Okay, okay," Nathan concedes. "I'm sorry."

"You'll have to do better than that," Jared instructs.

"I love you, *Kitten*," Nathan presents, batting his eyes.

"That's nice," I return coldly.

"Ouch! I feel the ice all the way over here," Nathan dramatically declares.

"Serves you right," Maggie digs.

Breathe In

"I've been meaning to ask you, why do you call Emma, *Kitten*?" Pop-Pop investigates.

"Because she looked like a cute, little, lost kitten when we first met," Jared half lies.

I watch Maggie and Nathan snicker a little.

"That's sweet," Pop-Pop replies.

The other half of the truth of why Jared calls me *Kitten* is because I'm like a cat when it comes to men. I only want to be touched when I want to be touched. I like affection, but only from certain people. I'm picky, like a cat, in the sense of who I'm willing to talk to and sleep with. I get the itch to be touched and when I've had enough, I just walk away without a care in the world.

Once we're ready to go home, Jared, Nathan and Pop-Pop leave in one car, Maggie and Henry in another and Joe and myself in the last one. Once on the road, Joe takes my hand as we head back to Pasadena. I lay my head back on the seat and close my eyes to rest for a few minutes, tired from the long day.

I wake to Joe's warm hand stroking my face.

"Emma," he whispers.

"Hmmm?" I reply before opening my eyes.

"We're back," he informs me.

My eyes open and I don't recognize where we are for a minute. "Where are we?"

"The parking lot in my building."

"Why?"

"No one is here. Just you and me," he reveals.

"I need to get home to Sadie," I admonish.

A noise comes from the back seat and I feel and hear a dog sniffing my left ear.

"I picked her up. You were out cold," he chuckles.

We both scratch Sadie's head.

"How did you get into my place," I ask eyeing him.

With a sex tingling smile, Joe explains, "I used your key." He gestures to my purse.

At a loss for words, I just nod my understanding.

Joe is a perfect gentleman. He helps Sadie and me out of the car and he doesn't touch me other than to place his hand on the small of my back as

Chapter Forty

we ride up the elevator to his door. As soon as his front door is closed, Joe's demeanor changes. Taking his time, like he's plotting every next step, he holds me against his body as he places his keys, money clip and loose change in the large bowl that sits on the table by the door. He switches hands on my back, not letting go, before checking the pockets on his other side. Instead of waiting for him to finish, I rush, grabbing the back of Joe's head and plant my lips onto his. Joe doesn't move anything except his lips. His manhood twitches, but other than those two organs, Joe is motionless until I gradually pull my mouth away.

"Mmmmmm," he groans in protest. "God, I've missed the taste of you."

I don't return the sentiment, not that I don't feel the same. It's just that I've never said anything like that to any guy before, and I'm not about to start. It's too foreign and I don't want to give him the impression that I want a relationship.

"You've got very bad timing," I whine after he pushes my body against the wall and squeezes my ass.

"What do you mean?" he questions, not wanting to let go of my mouth.

I pull away and offer a look. A please don't make me say it out loud look.

"You're kidding me?" he replies, catching the hint. "It hasn't been that long . . . has it?"

"Unfortunately . . . yes," I regrettably confirm.

He kisses me again before saying, "I don't care if you don't."

"I do," I profess, stopping a kiss.

We don't say anything for a minute as we hold each other.

"I could help . . . ."

"No! Out of the question," he protests before I finish.

His response is definitely not what I was expecting. My brows furrowing at him and are my only best reply.

I've never offered or thought about helping a man get off before, especially since every man I've been with has left me high and dry, having to finish the job myself. There were one or two guys I hooked up with in the beginning where I did, but then I would be left unsatisfied. I'm not sure why I'm offering now, but I do feel a little bad.

"What?" he asks seeing my express.

"Nothing . . . I've just never had or heard of a guy refuse to at least get his own needs taken care of . . ." I explain.

"I'm not getting any until you are, which will be at the same time," he sternly declares.

I wince and he notices.

"What?"

"Does masturbation count?" I shyly question.

"No," he chuckles. "I'd have some serious cases of blue balls if I wasn't."

I sigh with relief and giggle at him for actually saying blue balls.

"We're on the same page about that, beautiful. Don't you worry," he sweetly comments.

"I guess you should just take me home then," I mention.

"Why? Do you want to go home?" he says full of concern.

"No . . . I . . . um," I giggle nervously, not sure what to say.

"I want you to stay regardless," he states, sealing his words with a steamy kiss.

"No one is here?" I check.

"Just you, me and Sadie," he confirms.

"Not even Anna?"

"Not even Anna."

"Good," I exhale returning my lips to his.

Joe offers me a tee shirt to sleep in and he and I snuggle into his bed with Sadie while we watch a movie. Joe ends up falling asleep before the movie is finished. I can't sleep since it's still early for me, so I get up to snoop around a little. Sadie stays with Joe, too tired to get up and join me.

"What are you looking for?" Joe says, startling me as I slip a book back into its spot on the bookcase in his office.

I find him leaning in the doorway. "Nothing? What are you doing awake?" I inquire, turning and propping my ass on the shallow edge of the bookcase.

Joe takes a few steps closer. "You weren't there to keep me warm, so I woke up." Joe catches a piece of his shirt I'm wearing and tugs at it for me to move closer.

"I'm not there with you any nights," I rebut, sliding my hands onto his shoulders.

"Exactly . . . so I notice when you get up," he informs before seeking a kiss. "How long have you been out here?"

"Probably . . . ten . . . fifteen . . . minutes," I suggest in-between slow, erotic kisses.

Chapter Forty

"Mmmm . . . too long then," he moans, scooping me up.

"I need a book," I profess just as he turns to leave the office.

"You sure I can't distract you with something else?"

"Yes," I whine, not liking my own answer.

He gently lowers me to the ground and I hop over to find a book.

"I might be able to find one faster if you help me," I tease.

"As tempting as that is, I'm enjoying the view from here," he says with his sexy voice.

I bite my lip when I turn on my tip-toes to look at him.

"Keep that up and it will be my activity of choice as your only option," he devilishly threatens.

I deliberately reach a little higher to the top shelf for a book to cause Joe's shirt to slide up higher and just barely expose the bottom of my ass cheeks. I can hear Joe growl his disapproval of my actions.

"Found one," I announce, slowly turning towards him. As I approach him, I deliberately brush my hand across his stomach.

"You're asking for it," Joe announces as he scoops me into his arms.

Back in his room, Joe settles us into his bed. Between Sadie and Joe's hot body, it doesn't take more than ten pages for my eyes to droop. At some point, I feel a shift in the bed and wake just enough to feel Joe sliding the book from my hands and covering me with the blanket.

"Emma?"

"Hmmm."

"Goodnight, beautiful." I feel his lips on my temple.

I can't help but smile at his comment. "Goodnight, Joe," I breathe out.

Forty One

Three days after the bridal shower and the interesting night with Joe, I've been intensely focused on work when I'm not helping Maggie with wedding matters. My excitement about seeing Joe tonight, since all we've been able to do is talk and text, is quickly squashed before noon. I just found out that he is going back to New York for business and his date of return is unknown.

I'm starting to wonder if my decision to sleep with him is a good idea. I want him. There's no doubt about that. However, at every turn, the chance of me allowing myself to give in, break a rule, there seems to be either a warning sign or an obstacle hindering it from occurring. Maybe I'm not supposed to sleep with him. Maybe I need to hold fast to my rules and do my best to satisfy my itch some other way. I'm so confused and don't know what to do.

The Fourth of July is just two days away and the days seem to be moving extremely slow, even with the mountain of work for business and the wedding. My attention is easily pulled away from work by my sexual need and I find myself masturbating at least three times a day. I feel like I have A.D.D.. Last night when I was with Maggie and Henry, I was seriously contemplating the idea of just having a three-way with them. Okay, I'd most likely would have just fucked Maggie and let Henry watch. It scares me that I would even consider the option because I'm so horny and can't seem to be satisfied by B.O.B.. B.O.B. always satisfies me, even if there is the assistance of Master P.

Yesterday, I went with Maggie and the rest of the bridal party for our second to last fitting for the dresses. We all look gorgeous! I think I'm actually starting to get excited about all of this.

Today, Jared, Pop-Pop and I are preparing food for the Fourth of July picnic tomorrow. Since Amy and Eric got their new home a few years ago, they've allowed Jared and I to host our traditional Fourth of July picnic at their house. There's more room and a lot less people than the park where we used to have it and you can't have a picnic inside an apartment. Since our second Independence Day together, Jared and I have deemed this our holiday with our own traditions. We celebrate more than the birth of America. We celebrate the rebirth of our new found life together after our hardships.

With Pop-Pop as an extra set of hands, Jared and I put him on non-cooking prep duty. Ultimately, Pop-Pop is in charge of making sure all of the coolers and bags are washed and prepped, grilling utensils are cleaned

Breathe In

and accounted for and all games and sports related objects are organized and packed. Knowing that Pop-Pop is wicked on a grill, Jared and I ask if he'd honor us as being head chef. Pop-Pop beams with delight and enthusiastically accepts.

"How do you buy all this food without a car sweetie?" Pop-Pop investigates.

"She has it delivered," Jared answers for me since my mouth is full of food.

"Wow! Really?"

"I belong to two different farming co-ops that have about twenty different organic and biodynamic farms who sell directly to the public. I order weekly, bi-weekly or monthly and they deliver what I request," I explain.

"Even the meats?"

"Most of them. There are several different businesses I buy from online for most of my needs. For smaller sizes of fresh meats for Sadie, I sometimes walk down to the Whole Foods."

"How far is that?"

"Just down the block."

"We need to get some more quinoa, so we'll walk down later so you can see how close it is," Jared instructs.

"Okay!" replies Pop-Pop. "Ohh, Emma. You should see the dress Nathan is creating for you."

"Pop-Pop!" Jared yells with shock. "She's not supposed to know anything."

"I know that. I just wanted to get her excited about it," Pop-Pop confirms his intentions.

"What am I not supposed to know?"

"Anything about the dress. Nathan wants it to be a secret until the night of the premier," Jared answers.

"Great . . ." I announce sarcastically.

"I know you aren't excited about going with Chris, but if you knew what the dress looked like, you'd feel different," Pop-Pop sweetly states.

"Come on, *Kitten*, think about the amount of money that will be pouring in from your investment," Jared coaxes.

"I could work with that," I comment.

"That's the spirit!" Pop-Pop cheers.

By late morning on the Fourth of July, Nathan, Jared and Pop-Pop pick Sadie and me up, along with all of the food we've got prepared, and head down to Amy's house in Arcadia. Just after twelve, Pop-Pop has the grill to full

412

Chapter Forty One

temperature and is starting to cook the burgers and chicken. Our usual group has grown a little this year with many of the Wú family members. The kids and Sadie are playing in the pool most of the day and by the time the sun starts to set, Jared and I get the sparklers out for the kids. Amy's and Eric's house is not far from the park where the community fireworks are set off, which works perfectly for us. No need to drive and find parking. Just before it's fireworks time, we turn off all of the lights inside the house and in the backyard. Jade joins Jared and me on a blanket that we are laying on. Not long after all of the kids have fallen asleep, I head home with the same group that brought me down for the barbecue.

The two-week countdown to the wedding has begun and Maggie is outwardly excited and nervous beyond her usual habit from the years I've known her. She's starting to sweat over all of the little details. Amelia and I are both having to continually remind Maggie to breathe and relax. Good thing this weekend is the joint bachelor-bachelorette party weekend. With what Joe and I have planned, Maggie and Henry should be ready for the big day.

Joe arrived back in California early this morning. I have mixed emotions, but the predominant feeling is elation and relief. Four days and counting until we whisk our friends away for, well what I hope is, an enjoyable weekend before their wedding. No one other than Joe and I know where we are headed.

After some really busy and hectic days, I eagerly greet my friends as we board Joe's private jet, or at least I think it's Joe's, to embark on the bachelor-bachelorette party weekend. The plane is much bigger than the last one we used for Hawaii. I guess when you're making billions and most likely trillions, having two planes is kind of like having two or three cars. Jimmy, Allen, Jared, Nathan, Henry, Maggie, Amy, Eric, Kim, Peter, Joe, Sadie and myself along with Henry's other two groomsmen, Lee and Richard climb aboard the massive plane.

Maggie squeals with excitement when we land in Sedona, Arizona. She, Jared and I took a road trip here a few years back and I know she's been dying to visit again. Joe and I knew that Henry and Maggie would need some time to relax and decompress before the wedding, so we figured Sedona was the best place to go. Two limos are waiting at the airport for our arrival and we all pile in to head to our accommodations.

Joe and I booked L'Auberge de Sedona for the extended weekend. We have an early check-in for today, Friday and we don't check out until Monday morning. Maggie and Henry, Amy and Eric, and Kim and Peter are booked in the Spa Suite Cottages as the rest of us are rooming in our own Garden Cottages.

After we all check in, we're picked up for the first of two scheduled group adventures. Joe and I booked a private Grand Canyon tour that will show us Oak Creek Canyon, Ponderosa Pine Forest, lush meadows and then on to the awe inspiring Grand Canyon before we head to the El Tovar Lodge along the South Rim of the Canyon for lunch.

Once our bellies are full, we head back to L'Auberge for individual journeys to begin. Maggie and Henry opt to have some of the spa packages in their room that Joe and I purchased in advanced for them. I call the lobby to make sure some champagne and strawberries are delivered as well. Kim and Peter and Amy and Eric elect to do the same thing. I decide to go for a hike, wanting to get Sadie outdoors since she was cooped up a little between the plane and then while we were gone for a few hours on the tour. Jared, Nathan, Jimmy, Allen, Joe, Lee and Richard all tag along.

The seven of us plus Sadie, load into two of the three Teslas Joe and I rented and head over to The Hike House for our first stop. We schedule a two-hour hike, grab some extra gear and food and drive over to Red Rock. Red Rock is one of my favorite places since the last time I was here with Maggie and Jared. There's an energy vortex there that is peaceful and relaxing and I plan on putting in some good intentions for the wedding to go smoothly.

Joe busts on Jimmy and Allen a few times when they whine about our pace or complain about being tired and needing a break. Lee and Richard resume their blatant hitting on me from this morning. There's no way Jared can save me since they know that he's with Nathan, so I figured, why not have a little fun anyway and flirt back.

"Looks like you've got two new admirers," Jared teases as I gulp some water.

"I'm not minding the attention," I admit.

"Obviously," Nathan jabs.

Shrugging my shoulders, I retort, "What? Like a girl can't have a little fun flirting back?"

"Not at all," Jared assures.

"I think Joe's feeling a little left out, though," Nathan says, loud enough for Joe to overhear.

"Left out about what?" Joe searches.

"The flirting Emma's doing with Lee and Richard, but not with you," Nathan states, deliberately seeking to get a response from both of us.

Lee and Richard seem pleased. Joe just chuckles and shakes his head.

Wanting to play a little, I goad him. "Aww, Joe . . . are you feeling left out?" I slowly take a few steps towards him before I lunge to spar with him on the path.

Chapter Forty One

"Knock it off you two," scolds Nathan.

"You encouraged it," Jared comments.

"They can go for as long as they like," Jimmy adds. "I don't mind the extended break."

"I've never seen a man be able to keep up with you like that, Emma," remarks Jared.

"I'm just toying with him," I reply with a wicked grin before I move in with another move landing me on Joe's back.

"Or is he toying with you?" Nathan questions.

"A little of both," Joe baits.

After a few minutes, Nathan announces, "Okay. Okay. Break it up you two."

"Like I said, you started it, babe," Jared enforces.

"And, now I'm regretting it," Nathan states. "Damn straight people and their weird ways of flirting."

Releasing Joe, I swerve and set my target on Nathan.

"Ahhhh," Nathan yells, ducking behind Jared.

Jared steps to the side, but Nathan quickly follows him to block me.

"Now you know to keep you big mouth shut," Jared roasts.

"What a great boyfriend you are," Nathan complains as I get a hold of him and Jared does nothing to stop me.

"Don't start something you can't finish, especially when it comes to sparing with Emma," Jared mocks as I take Nathan to the ground.

It takes Joe sneaking up from behind to get me off of Nathan.

"Thanks, man. I owe you one," Nathan says, catching his breath while Joe holds me tight.

I do my best to keep a playful expression as my insides are electrified by the sensation of Joe's body against mine. His manly musk is arousing. The warm smell of sweat dances in my nose and shoots down into my sex causing moisture to form.

"Okay, I think we need to start to head back if we're going to make it for dinner," Jared informs us.

"Fine," I whine. "Ruin the fun."

"You'll only entice them more," Jared whispers in my ear, pointing to Lee and Richard.

Jared's right. I don't mind encouraging Joe because I know where things would go and Jared has seen Joe and I spar several times. With Lee and

Breathe In

Richard, on the other hand, I'm not sure what to expect with them, especially to go from just verbally greeting them, like I did with Joe and Henry when I first met them, to now where I'm openly flirting. I'm not interested in them, just having a little fun as well as doing whatever it takes to dissuade my friends from thinking something is going on between Joe and me.

Back at the resort, we shower and change and meet up with everyone else for dinner at L'Auberge's Oak Creek Restaurant. Everyone is dressed up and having fun as we eat. I'm even enjoying seeing Joe squirm a little when I flirt back with Lee and Richard more than him.

Joe and I announce before we finish dessert that he and I have planned a particular adventure for all of the couples early tomorrow morning. We don't tell them what, but we do inform them to dress warm and to be up before the sun rises. We stay in the restaurant eating, drinking and swapping stories until it closes at nine.

Jared and Nathan walk me back to my cottage to hang out for a bit.

"So what is planned for us?" Nathan inquires.

"I'm not telling."

"Come on . . . just a little hint," he presses.

"Nope."

"So, what was with all the flirting earlier?" Jared investigates as I change into pajamas.

"What?" I deny.

"You know what," Nathan adds with a wicked smirk.

"Emma's got the itch!" Jared announces.

"Shut up!" I yell, not liking to be reminded about how horny I am.

"Emma's horny, Emma's horny," Nathan sings and dances around the room, then dry humps Jared.

"Yes I am. So, why don't you two go back to your own cottage and leave me alone with B.O.B.?"

"Why don't you just pop on over to Joe's . . ." Nathan blurts.

"What's that supposed to mean?" I address with my hands on my hips.

"Nothing . . ." he rebuts.

I eye the two of them as they snicker. Neither say a word.

They hug and kiss Sadie and me goodnight, and before I have the door closed all the way, Nathan shouts, "Have a great night with B.O.B.!"

Chapter Forty One

"I will," I blurt. I clasp my hand over my mouth once I realize how loud I was and hear Jared and Nathan laugh all the way to their cottage two buildings down.

I lace on my shoes and take Sadie out for a walk around the resort before we turn in for bed and I intentionally use B.O.B. until he's doesn't have a single bit of juice left in him.

Back inside the cottage, I close all the blinds, turn on the television, and have a little talk with B.O.B. about my expectations for the night before we get started. B.O.B. gloriously provides two wickedly awesome orgasms as our warmup before I decide to take a quick break and hop into the tub.

Just as B.O.B. is rounding the corner of my third orgasm with the assistance of Master P, my phone chirps. I close my eyes so I won't get distracted by who it is. Unfortunately, as my mind beings to recollect what time it is and who could be calling, B.O.B. and Master P start to loose their appeal until one particular person comes to mind. I orgasm instantaneously with fierce voracity that brings a smile to my face as my body convulses its release.

I let the euphoric feeling linger for a few extra minutes before my eyes flutter open to see who was calling. My grin widens when I note that it was the very person I had envisioned with me in the tub. My finger presses the callback button as I continue to bask in the glow of satisfaction.

"Hey, beautiful," he hums with his sexy voice.

"Hey . . ." I answer with my own sexiness that is a little more provocative than I had desired.

Joe chuckles before asking, "So I can guess how you are doing . . . should I ask about B.O.B.?"

I wince full of embarrassment. "You heard that?"

"Yes . . ." he laughs. "That and you've never answered the phone quite like that before."

"Yeah . . ." I say shamefaced.

"Is there any chance I can give B.O.B. a break for the rest of the night and take over?" Joe nervously questions.

"Umm . . ." I hesitate.

I definitely want him, but with our friends so close, anyone could knock on the door and hear things, and then how would that help dissuade them?

"I don't think that's a good idea . . ." I regretfully turn him down.

"Had to ask," he tries to shrug off his disappointment.

"If the sleeping arrangements were a little different . . ." I begin to blurt.

Breathe In

His voices perks up on his next questions. "Were you thinking of me at any point?"

I deliberately bit my lip from blabbing that I was — but then thought that not saying anything might confirm that I was and I'm too embarrassed and caught off guard to be able to come up with a good comment. Shit!

I hear Joe laugh a little on the other end of the phone. "I'm flattered."

"I didn't say . . . ."

"You don't have to," he interjects before I can deny anything.

"I wasn't," I try to lie.

"Sure," he contends.

"I'm serious."

Joe just laughs. "I'll let you go so you can finish . . . thinking of me . . . before you go to bed," he offers with the sexy voice again.

The kitten inside me stirs. She wants to play.

"Goodnight, beautiful," he bids.

"Goodnight, Joe."

"I'll be thinking of you too," he shares before hanging up the phone.

I stare at the phone in absolute shock. Did he just admit that he'll be thinking of me while he masturbates? He did. He totally did. The kitten inside paces with eager anticipation at the gate being unlocked. It's a good thing that I brought some extra juice for B.O.B..

At four in the morning, there's a knock on my cottage door. I'm up and already dressed for the surprise, so I'm not shocked or concerned with who it is. Sadie darts out the door before it's open all the way, finding a place to pee since I just finished feeding her, Joe quickly closes the door behind him and presses me against the wall as he delivers a steaming hot kiss. Joe keeps our lips linked as he reaches back to open the door when Sadie whimpers to be let back in. He uses his foot to close the door as our mouths desperately explore each other's. I moan with every breath as I try to control the kitten's itch.

"Good morning, beautiful," he purrs.

"Morning," I return.

"How's B.O.B.?" he explores.

"Let's just say that he's still sleeping . . ." I reveal.

"Nice," he replies, taking my mouth with his again.

I reluctantly peel away. "We've got to make sure everyone is getting up."

"Five more minutes?" he begs, pressing harder against me.

Chapter Forty One

"One." I peck him on the lips.

"Four." He devours my mouth.

"Two," I breathe in before seeking his mouth.

"Three."

My agreement is confirmed by my lack of words and the continuation of my lips tasting his.

By four-twenty, Joe and I have our friends rounded up and inside the large van that was sent for us. Everyone remembered to dress warm and I hand out thermoses of coffee and tea to help wake them up.

"Why do we need to be up so early," Jared whines, stretching his legs across mine.

"You'll see," Joe returns.

"You are too chipper in the morning," Nathan retorts with grumpiness in his voice.

"He's an early bird like Emma," Jared groans, curling into Nathan who is sitting in the corner where the seat ends at the side of the van.

I laugh outwardly at my friends. Had they just been paying attention when they were getting into the vehicle, they would have seen where we were all going based on the company logo and description on the side of the van.

As we round the last turn of the driveway for our destination, I hear Maggie squeal with excitement while the rest of the men groan. Amy and Kim perk up as well when they realize what Maggie is shouting about in a voice probably two octaves higher than her usual vocal range.

"Ohhh my God, ohhh my God, ohhh my God," she finally says more audibly. "I love you, Emma!" Maggie bounces up and down in her seat.

In the main building, my friends are greeted and debriefed by the staff of Red Rock Balloon Adventures. Joe and I give Maggie and Henry, Jimmy and Allen, Jared and Nathan, Kim and Peter and Amy and Eric each a picnic basket that has fresh fruit, croissants, wine and cheeses along with an additional thermos of either coffee or tea.

"You aren't going?" Maggie asks.

"No."

"Why not?"

"This is for couples and I'm not going up there by myself," I explain.

"Joe can go with you," she mentions, glancing at Joe.

"Joe and I aren't a . . . ."

"I'm game if you are," Joe interrupts.

I narrow my eyes at him as Maggie runs away shouting to one of the staff members to see if they can prep a balloon for us.

"Seriously?"

"It makes it easier to keep Lee and Richard away from you," he declares, revealing his true intentions.

"So, you are jealous."

"No," he denies.

"Right . . ." I offer sarcastically.

"It'll be fun," he coaxes.

"I wouldn't know," I return as my eyes drift up the side of the massive balloon that is closest to us.

"You've never been up before?" he says, sounding a little surprised.

"Never been in a relationship, remember."

"You don't need to be in a relationship in order to take a balloon ride," he informs.

"I'm not dressed for it," I counter.

"Dressed for what?" Nathan jumps in.

I didn't see him approaching Joe and me.

"Maggie's trying to see if there's a way for Emma and I to go. Emma's never been. She's using the excuse that she isn't dressed for it," Joe announces, catching Jared up on our debate.

"You should go, Emma," Nathan insists with a devious smile and a sparkle in his eyes. "Joe will keep you plenty warm. I'm sure the balloon operator will even turn his head if it comes to drastic measures for Joe to keep you warm enough."

I punch Nathan in the arm as the heat in my face spreads through my entire body. Joe laughs and the closest balloon operator mentions, "That wouldn't be the first-time something like that happening up there."

"What are we talking about over here?" Jared checks running over after using the bathroom a second time.

"Nothing!" I sternly reply.

"Maggie and Joe are trying to get Emma to go up if there's another balloon," Nathan informs.

"So, why don't you. You've never been," Jared remarks.

Chapter Forty One

"We don't know if there is another balloon and operator, and I'm not dressed for it," I repeat, a little irritated that this topic is still continuing.

Shrugging his shoulders, Jared rebuts, "So. Joe can keep you warm."

"That's what I said," Nathan snickers.

Jared quickly catches the hint and joins in the laughter.

"You should give B.O.B. a rest. Let Joe take over," Nathan comments.

My mouth drops at his words and I'm absolutely mortified. The heat in my face is scorching hot like the sun. My only option — walk away.

"Come on, Emma," Jared yells.

"We're just having a little fun," Nathan protests.

I head toward the main building to get away to wait until everyone is up in the air and it's time for Joe and me to head back.

Maggie sees me heading toward her and confirms, "They don't have another operator today."

"That's fine," I snap at her, wincing immediately after the fact. "I'm sorry, Maggie."

"What's wrong? What happened?"

"I don't want to talk about it," I avoid the topic.

"What did Jared or Nathan do? Say?" she checks.

"Go ask them. They'll be lucky if I talk to them for the rest of the weekend," I say through gritted teeth.

Shit. Fuck me. There goes any chance of hooking up with Joe anytime soon. Looks like I'm going to be celibate for a while. God damn it! I need to go get more batteries for B.O.B. now. Maybe I should look into rechargeable ones.

Jared and Nathan try to smooth things over with me before they take off in their balloon, but I hold onto the grudge. I normally brush things off, but their blatant teasing right in front of Joe really bothers me. What would cause them to be so bold?

I don't talk to Joe the entire ride back to the resort. He doesn't try to have a conversation, but he does sit next to me. At one point, Joe stretches his arm across the back of the seat and starts brushing his fingers along the nape of my neck. My brain tells my body to move, but I don't. I'm not really mad at him. I know that. I know that this is just a knee-jerk reaction to distance myself and I hate it.

By the time the couples are schedule to be dropped off after landing and having a picnic lunch, I'm already in the spa. It's the best place for me to avoid anyone right now. The pool — I can't go there. They'll find me and the last

Breathe In

people I want to find me practically naked are Joe, Lee and Richard. I could have gone on a hike with Sadie, but I'm not familiar enough with Sedona to feel comfortable doing it; plus, I don't drive which makes it hard to get anywhere off the resort unless I ask Joe, Lee or Richard to drive me, and that's not happening.

I successfully make it back to my cottage without being seen until my foot hits the first step. "Emma." Jared's voice sounds apologetic. "*Kitten?*"

My eyes dart to him, narrowing at the use of my pet name. I quickly look away as I search for the key to let myself in.

"Come on, Emma! I'm sorry," he pleas as I slam the door behind me and lock it. "I'm going to stay out here the whole time. I'll know when you leave."

I close the blinds and curtains and then plop on the bed. Sadie joins me, sensing that my uneasiness has yet to completely dissolve. Jared knocks on the front door several times as well as the sliding glass one off the porch; reminding me he's still out there.

I'm not really mad at him. How can I be? He's my brother and I know it's just good natured fun. All the teasing, especially right in front of Joe, concerns me though. They have been doing it more frequently. I doubt that I'd be acting like this if I wasn't so horny.

The girls come and get me for dinner. We chat freely and no one brings up the fight with Jared and Nathan, so I know that Maggie hasn't said anything to Amy or Kim. At dinner, I sit between Maggie and Amy and completely avoid Jared and Nathan.

"How long are you going to be mad at us?" asks Nathan right in front of everyone a few bites into our entrees.

I refrain from making eye contact with him. Everyone at the table goes silent.

"They know I'm talking to you, Emma," Nathan announces.

I lean over and whisper something to Maggie.

She gasps, "I'm not saying that."

I give her a stern, pleading look.

"I can't, Emma," she says, fidgeting.

"What?" Henry asks. He leans over to hear Maggie. Henry's eyes dart to me and then Nathan before he looks back at Maggie.

I tap Maggie's leg.

"I'm not addressing that matter now. Later, between just the two of you, I will. Now, both of you stop fighting and let's have a wonderful night," she sweetly commands.

Chapter Forty One

It takes a few minutes before conversations strike back up again. Thankfully, Jimmy and Allen always know how to do it gracefully until they bring up the topic of the premier.

"That is not a topic for tonight," Maggie instructs everyone at the table.

A hush falls across the table.

"Shit, Emma. I'm sorry. I really am sorry," Nathan honestly apologizes.

He clearly knows what I said to Maggie by her remark.

My eye catches something across the room behind Nathan and Jared after I make eye contact with Nathan — something cute — something yummy. The kitten and the itch have returned. I quickly look away not wanting anyone to see. Both Jared and Nathan look over their shoulders and return with smirks.

I continue eating, but my eyes continue to glance beyond Jared and Nathan on occasion.

"I dare you to go talk to him," Nathan jabs.

A smirk curls in the corner of my mouth. I say nothing.

"Who?" Maggie inspects.

"I double dog dare you," Nathan presses. "And if you do, I'll never tease you again. Ever."

My smirk creeps over to the other side of my mouth as I consider the challenge. It's not really a challenge at all, but I could use this to my benefit. My eyebrow lifts to Nathan's statement to bait him. This just might be the opportunity to get both him and Jared off my back about Joe.

"I triple dog dare you," Nathan adds with a gloating smile.

You won't be the one gloating for much longer Nathan.

"What's happening?" Jimmy inquires.

"What are you daring her to do?" Maggie searches.

"She knows what he's daring her to do," Jared replies, watching me intently.

I look to all of the faces at my table staring back at me. The majority of them don't have a clue. This is going to be good. I lower my fork. Gulp down the rest of my wine. Wipe my mouth and kiss Maggie on the cheek before I stand up. "Ever?" I state more than really question.

"Ever!" Nathan repeats.

"Where are you going?" Maggie asks as I start to walk away.

I kiss Amy and Kim on the cheek as well and I head off without a word. I don't look back. I continue forward in my pursuit.

Breathe In

"Hi," I offer with a dazzling smile to a handsome man sitting at the far end of the bar.

"Hello, gorgeous," he returns.

His mocha latte skin shimmers in the light, accenting his pearl white teeth and chocolate brown eyes. He closely resembles the television star Michael Trevino who would make any woman's panties drop.

"Is this seat taken?" I ask in a flirtatious tone.

"Not at all, my dear," he says, standing up to pull the seat out for me.

"Is this your first time here?" I inquire.

"Sedona, no. At this resort, yes," he replies with a gleam in his eye, returning to his seat. "I'm Javier." He extends his hand forward.

Placing my hand in his, I offer, "Emma."

"It's a pleasure to meet you, Emma." Javier lifts my hand to his mouth and kisses it.

"The pleasure is all mine." I take out a pen from my purse and jot down a little note for Javier on a napkin. Once he's finished reading it, we exchange a few glances. I place my hand on his knee to finalize what's about to happen.

Javier covers my hand with his and slides it up a few inches. His eyes scan the room behind me and I know he sees my friends watching.

"Would you like to go somewhere a little more quiet," I say seductively followed by a wink. "To chat, of course."

Javier eagerly jumps to his feet and assists me off of my chair. "Shall I order us a bottle for the room?"

"Why not," I giggle, stepping into him.

Javier instantly places his hand on my hip and dips it just a little low where his fingers extend to the top of my ass. I press my body into him as I glance over my shoulder with a wicked grin to see who of my friends are watching. The entire table are watching me, especially Joe.

When the bottle of wine is delivered to his room, Javier answers the door with his shirt off, his belt undone and barefoot. "There were a couple of men out there snooping," he informs me after closing the door.

I can't help but gloat with a wicked grin as I unzip my dress and it drops to the floor.

Two hours later, Javier and I exchange a heated kiss just outside his room, just in case anyone is watching. I make my way to my cottage, doubting that any of my friends are still in the dining room or lobby waiting for me.

Chapter Forty One

Just before I take my keys out to let myself in, I text Javier. "Thanks for a hot night!"

"Thank you! Anytime baby!" he writes. "Call me next time you're in Vegas."

Sunday, I decide to do an early morning yoga class and then hang out by the pool. Just after a quick dip in the refreshing water, as I get my sunglasses on and lay down on the lounge chair, I hear Jared and Nathan approaching. Sadie rushes over to them and I pretend to not notice.

I'm not mad anymore by their good natured fun from yesterday, but that doesn't mean I still can't have a little fun.

"Hey, *Kitten*," Jared greets, sitting down on my chair.

"You're blocking the sun," I state flatly.

He shifts. "Is that any better?"

To comment, or not to comment on his blatant attempt to block more of the sun?

"Wonderful," I retort.

"Come on, *Kitten*. You can't be mad at us anymore," Jared groans.

"Yes I can," I rebut, lifting my sunglasses up.

"No, you can't," Maggie's voice calls from a few feet away. "This is my weekend and everyone needs to be talking, having fun and being happy. Including you!"

"Next weekend is your weekend. I'll be all of that then," I playfully contend with her as I close my eyes and lower my sunglasses back down. The stinging of a towel being whipped on my leg jolts me up. "Hey!"

Maggie winds up for another blow. "What was that?" she threatens with a wicked grin.

"Okay. Okay. I'll be nice. I'll be happy," I confront with a fake smile.

"Smile like you mean it," she commands.

"That's kind of hard with the pain in my leg," I rebut, but still try to comply to prevent another attack.

"That's better," she accepts. "You two shoo. We've got some girl talk to do."

Maggie delivers a stern look that she learned from Mǔqīn. A look they won't dare to battle. Jared and Nathan retreat to join the men of our group as Amy and Kim hop over. Now I know what Maggie meant by girl talk.

"Did you really sleep with him?" Amy blurts.

I blush with embarrassment since all the guys from our group turn to look in our direction. I'm grateful when I notice that no one else is around the pool area.

"Why is my sex life the topic of discussion?" I ask, deliberately lowering my voice to give them all the hint to do the same.

"Maggie's told us about, you know . . ." Amy says.

"No . . . I don't," I return, narrowing my eyes.

"About how you are with men," Maggie explains.

"It's perfectly natural for women of any age," Kim interjects to my defense.

Kim knows more than Amy because if and when I do need to consult with a doctor, I make appointments with her.

"I know that. I wish I had the balls to do it before I was married. I did have a three-way with my roommate and a guy back in college one night . . ." Amy's voice trails off.

"You never told us that," Maggie expresses.

"I've never told Eric and I wasn't sure we could share that kind of stuff. Besides, Mǔqīn or Nǎinai are always around," Amy adds. "I like this. We should have a girls' only weekend again."

"Definitely." I concur.

"Emma and I deflowered each other," Maggie offers.

My hand instinctually launches in Maggie's directions, clipping her in the shoulder.

"I did the same with a girl in college," Kim admits.

The four of us giggle at our openness and I feel much better overall.

"So do you two still, yah know?" Amy searches.

"Sometimes," Maggie discloses. "Emma's not into as much because of Henry."

"Why not? You're into men, obviously," Amy investigates.

"We've shared a man or two, but she would never with any of my past boyfriends, let alone Henry," she reveals.

"And, I don't plan to," I inform them. "It's just too weird."

They all nod their understanding.

"So how was he last night?" Maggie presses.

"Javier?"

"Ohhh . . . even his name is sexy," Amy comments.

At this moment, I have the desire to tell the three of them what really happened. I want to tell them, but something is telling me to hold off even though I'm really enjoying our current girls' moment we're having.

"Better than the majority," I offer with a wicked smile.

Chapter Forty One

The three of them squeal loudly which causes all of the men to turn in our direction. Jimmy and Allen come running over, jumping in to find out what's being shared. The four of us refrain from anything other than giggles.

By late afternoon, our whole group decides to go on another hike, wanting to catch the beautiful sunset off of the mountains before returning back for dinner. The four of us girls gravitate towards each other more during the hike. I think we feel more connected after our poolside gossip session. The boys try to listen or join in, but we're able to keep our voices low for just the ladies.

After dinner at a little local restaurant that we find on the way back from the hike, Maggie walks me to my cottage. Our conversation is light as she joins me, lounging on my bed. We don't have sex, we just sit and talk like we used to.

"I have a confession," I begin.

"You did sleep with Joe," she yells.

"What?! No!" I return with shock.

"Ohh. Sorry," she apologies.

"Why does everyone think that something is going on with Joe and me?"

"Do you really want to know the answer to that?"

"Yes!"

"Because of how you two are together."

"What does that mean?" I say confused.

"You've never gotten along with a man before. A non-gay man," she offers.

"So."

"You two have very similar personalities. He's clearly into you and you do flirt back," she explains.

"Why would that lead my friends to thinking that Joe and I are sleeping together?"

"We've never seen you this comfortable with a man . . . especially, a man who you know has the hots for you," she reports.

I'm rendered speechless for a moment. "It's nice to be pursued . . . especially in a non-weird way. I swear. We haven't had sex. Joe and I are just friends."

"I believe you. Honestly, I do. It would make the most sense, though."

"What would?"

"You and Joe hooking up."

"Why is that?"

"Because, like I said, you two get along. You're compatible. The logical conclusion would be that you two would have or eventually would have sex."

breathe In

Seeing my lack of response, Maggie continues. "The ease in which you and Joe are friends is like Jared and Nathan . . . or Henry and Me."

"What does that mean?"

"It means that the two of you are a perfect match for each other . . . if you would only get out of your own way and date, that is."

I sit stunned for another minute. "Shit. And here I was just going to tell you that I didn't sleep with Javier."

"What?!" Maggie's jaw drops. "What? He's so hot. Why didn't you sleep with him?"

All I do is give her a look.

"What?! Seriously? He's gay?" Maggie responds with absolute astonishment.

"You can't tell Jared or Nathan!" I disclose.

"Crap! I would never have guessed . . . when did you know?"

"Right when I saw him. He flirted with the bartender. I knew it was the prime opportunity to bait Nathan and Jared to get them off my back."

"So, are you still going with Chris to the premier?"

"Of course. Regardless of the shit Nathan pulls, it's a business transaction that I want to happen. I'm an investor in his company. Remember?" I explain.

"Damn, you're good!"

"Thanks!"

We giggle a little.

"I swear I will take that to the grave," Maggie confirms.

"Thanks. You know you can't tell Henry."

"Why not?"

"He'll just tell Joe who will tell Jared."

"No, he won't," she defends.

"There's a guy code just like there's a girl code."

"But, there's a code between husbands and wives too," she stipulates.

"True," I agree. "But, you're not married yet!"

"So, I'll tell him on our wedding night."

"How about after the night of the premier. I don't want Jared and Nathan to find out before then," I suggest.

"Good idea! I know nothing."

After Maggie leaves, I snuggle into bed with Sadie and a book. Jared and Nathan come knocking on the door — actually doors. They each take

428

Chapter Forty One

a door and keep knocking until I finally let them in after five minutes of the irritating sound.

"What?" I whine, opening the door.

Jared tackles me, wrapping himself around my body. "I love you!" he shouts, kissing me all over my face.

"We both love you!" Nathan says, adding himself to the human pile of bodies.

"I love you two too . . ." I mutter, barely able to breathe from them squishing me. They continue to shout several more times, "We love you, we love you . . . !"

"So, you aren't mad anymore?" Nathan seeks.

"Javier took care of that," I offer with a smile. "I just wanted to make you two sweat a little."

"I want details . . ." Nathan shouts.

"You are excluded from details," I object.

"Why? You always give details," quips Jared.

"You two don't deserve them. Not right now, anyway," I counter.

"Awww . . . come on," Nathan whines.

"No."

"Maggie will tell us," Nathan protests.

"No, she won't. I didn't tell her anything either because I know you two will try to get it from her," I oppose.

"Damn," Jared exclaims.

"Seriously?!" Nathan pouts.

"Well, we all need to go," Jared instructs.

"What do you mean?"

"I got a text from Maggie summoning all of us to her and Henry's suite. She said to make amends and pick you up on they way."

"Why do they need us?"

"I don't know." Jared shrugs.

Jared, Nathan and I are the last to show up at Maggie's and Henry's cottage around nine forty-five. Everyone is sitting around the room either on a bench, chair or the floor surrounding a blanket that has some food and beverages on it. I'm relieved when I see everyone else dressed more relaxed or in their pajamas too.

"Yay, you made it!" Maggie beams.

"Hey, what's going on?" I question, hugging her.

"Henry and I wanted to toast to all of you," she explains, handing me a wine flute.

"Joe and I should be the ones toasting," I politely object.

"Not tonight," she declares.

Henry waits for Maggie to get settled on his lap. "Maggie and I would like to thank all of you for your love and support. It means a lot to us and it has helped greatly with the short time frame we've imposed on everyone to help make the wedding happen so quickly," Henry starts.

"Joe. Emma," he pauses for a few seconds. "Maggie and I are beyond appreciative for this weekend you gave us here in Sedona. It's been a gloriously relaxing and fun celebration which is exactly what we needed. Thank you."

My heart melts a little at his gratitude and sincerity. I'm actually starting to like Henry. Not that he's a bad guy or I didn't like him before, it's just that I'm actually starting to see him as an extension of Maggie, another member of our family.

Everyone raises their glasses, expecting Henry to signal the end of his toast, but he continues. "I toast to all of you who are not just friends, but who are our family."

"To our family," Maggie excitedly repeats.

"Family," we all cheer before taking a sip of our wine.

All fourteen of us and Sadie hang out, eat and drink as we swap stories. Henry explains how he met Lee and Richard during college, and like Joe, they became like brothers. There are a lot of similarities between the four men. They are all good looking, confident, but not cocky, successful and easy to get along with guys. I learn that Lee is a lawyer and Richard works on Wall Street.

At some point, Jimmy and Allen convince everyone to play some kind of question game. The questions are rather funny as well as some of the answers until they become a little more bold and daring.

"Who's most likely to get hitched next?" Allen inquires.

"Jared and Nathan," I shout before anyone else comments.

Jared and Nathan both blush at the prediction. Score one for Emma on the roasting.

"Okay. Okay," Jimmy starts. "Who after them?"

"Emma!" Maggie cheers.

My eyes narrow at her statement. "Not happening."

"You can't denounce Năinai's blessing," she retorts.

"What's Năinai's blessing?" Jimmy searches.

Chapter Forty One

"Every New Year's Nǎinai blesses the family and each family member . . ." Maggie grins.

"What did she bless?" Allen inquires, seeking clarification.

"Long story short, Nǎinai blessed Emma with a husband and children," Amy explains, excited to share.

"Nǎinai's never wrong," Kim validates.

"Just because she was accurate with you two," I point to Maggie and Jared. "Doesn't mean that the same will happen with me. I'm not in a relationship, therefore, there's no chance of me being the next one after you two to get hitched."

"Yes, it will," Jared interjects. "Deny or fight it all you want . . . but you will."

"Nope! If anything, Jimmy and Allen are next in line," I contest. "Remember, you're still on thin ice." My eyes fall upon Joe, catching him with a smirk.

"Maybe it's Javier," Maggie says with a wink.

I roar with laughter. "Maybe."

"Who?" Jimmy searches.

"Emma's hot hook up from last night," Amy explains.

"He was hot," Maggie adds.

"Details, Emma," Allen yells.

I see curiosity building in the faces of all of the men, including Eric, Peter, Lee and Richard.

"Nope," I object.

"Why not?" Jimmy pleas.

"Those two can tell you why," I voice, pointing at Nathan and Jared.

Everyone looks at Jared and Nathan. Silence falls upon the room.

"Just give us a little," Jimmy begs.

"He's hot," I share.

"That's obvious," Allen argues.

"Definitely hot," Jimmy adds.

I snicker at Jimmy's comment. If he and the rest of them only knew.

"Let's just say . . ." I pause for effect. "I'd repeat last night with him again. Anytime. Anywhere."

"So, who's next to get into a relationship?" Amy continues with the next question a few seconds later after letting my statement sink in as if she was having visions of a night with Javier herself.

"Joe," Jimmy answers rather quickly.

All eyes bounce between Jimmy and Joe.

"Why do you say Joe?" Nathan investigates.

"I've heard him on the phone at night with a girl . . ." Jimmy teases. "It's been going on for like a month now."

Joe doesn't say anything.

"How do you know it's a girl?" Lee jabs.

"Joe is not gay. He's definitely talking to a girl," Jimmy defends.

"Who are you talking to?" Lee questions.

"No one," Joe states, clearing his throat.

"She isn't no one . . ." Jimmy disputes.

"Drop it," Joe says with a stern, calm voice.

"You've never talked to a girl on the phone, ever, so . . ." Jimmy continues before Joe cuts him off.

"Drop it," he repeats in the same tone, but louder this time.

A thud is heard in the room. Everyone looks around, but I know what happened. Maggie, Joe and I start laughing.

"It's okay, Sadie. He wasn't talking to you," I comment, returning her bone.

Once everyone realizes what happened, they start laughing uncontrollably.

Other questions come up that are less intrusive and less personal until, over time, everyone starts to leave for the night. By midnight, I've got Jared, Nathan, Jimmy, Allen, Lee, Richard and Joe all walking me back to my cottage since it's the first one we get to on the way back to our corner of the resort.

Laying in bed, all I can think about is how gentlemanly Joe was when he was being pestered. He didn't confirm or deny who he was talking to on the phone. He didn't say anything. He didn't rat us out. In this moment of realization, I become extremely horny. Before I know it, I have my phone in my hand and I'm texting Joe. "Thanks," I write.

"For what?" he replies instantly.

"Not saying anything tonight . . . sharing our late night conversations."

"It's none of their business."

"I know."

"And, thanks for talking to me."

"Why wouldn't I talk to you?"

"Because . . ." I'm not sure what to write back.

Chapter Forty One

"Because why?"

"Never mind," I say.

I'm not sure I want to have that conversation with him.

"Having trouble sleeping?" he redirects.

"A little." I look at the clock and see that it's almost one. "Shit. Sorry. Did I wake you?"

"No, not at all. Need some company?"

"I don't think that's a good idea."

I want to see him. I need to see him, but I'm afraid of what might happen or be said since last night with Javier.

"Why not?"

Before I'm able to come up with a reason and type it into my phone, Joe calls using FaceTime. "Hi," he greets.

"Hi," I utter.

"That's better," he claims.

"What is?"

"Seeing you . . . I love it when you bite your lip like that," his sexy voice replies.

I pull the top of the covers over my face so only my eyes are showing. I'm flattered by what he said — a little too much.

"Don't hide your face . . . please," he begs.

Sadie suddenly shifts in the bed and is sniffing my ear, causing the blanket to fall down below my chin. "Hey!" I proclaim, pushing her face away.

"That's better . . . now I can see you. Hi Sadie!"

Sadie perks up hearing Joe's voice, scanning the room for him. "He's right here Sadie," I direct her to the phone screen. "Ewww . . . gross!" I exclaim.

I hear Joe laughing as I get up to wipe off her slobber. She literally licked the phone and my hand.

Once I'm back in bed, Joe comments, "Javier is a nice guy."

"Uhhh . . . yeah." I watch the corner of his mouth curl up.

"It's okay. I know."

"Know what?"

"You're secret."

"What secret?"

"You're secret about Javier," he chuckles.

"What are you talking about?" I deny.

433

"I know he's gay."

"What are you talking about?" I respond, trying to deny, but my voice is a little shakier.

"I saw him leave the lobby this morning after breakfast holding hands with his boyfriend," he shares.

"Ohhh . . . ."

"Don't worry, no one else saw them," he confirms.

"Good. I don't want Jared and Nathan to know."

"Why?"

"They'll stay off my back about stuff until I tell them," I share.

"Nice. When did you know?"

"What?"

"That he was gay."

"I saw how he smiled at the male bartender when I first noticed him," I reveal.

"So you knew the whole time? You were purposefully baiting Jared and Nathan?" he says not really shocked.

"Yep."

"Nice."

"Thanks." I mentally pat myself on the back.

"So what did you two do up there for two hours?"

"How do you know I was up there that long? Were you out in the lobby waiting?"

"No," he replies, trying to remain calm.

"Really . . . ?" I muse.

"I heard Jared and Nathan talking on their porch. Jared was shocked that you didn't talk to him when you got back to your cottage," he reveals.

"Good."

"Do you plan on telling them?"

"After the premier," I admit.

"I'm curious to see how they react."

"Me too. Maggie knows," I confess.

"She might tell them," he confronts.

"No. She won't. I didn't give her any information. She just knows he's gay," I say confidently.

Chapter Forty One

"They might try to get it out of Henry."

"She's not allowed to tell Henry."

"How did you manage that? I know they tell each other everything."

"She tried using the husband and wife code of trust thing . . . I told her they aren't married yet. Besides, by the time they are, she won't remember to tell him. She'll be so wrapped up with the honeymoon and everything," I explain.

"True."

Neither of us say anything for a moment and I catch him yawning. "I should let you sleep," I suggest.

"No. No. I'm fine," he contends. "So how is B.O.B. doing?"

"Don't know. I haven't revived him from the other night," I giggle.

"I can take over duties if B.O.B doesn't mind . . ." he delivers devilishly in the sexy voice I enjoy so much.

My vagina tingles at the thought. I feel my face reddening and I'm not sure what to say.

Joe laughs. It must be at my expression.

"Even if I did agree, I would say you look too tired," I tease.

"Not for that," he opposes.

I can't help but laugh. I think that's a knee-jerk reaction for men. I've heard Jared and Nathan say it a few times.

"We should get some sleep," I suggest.

"Yeah . . . ."

"Goodnight, Joe," I bid.

"Goodnight, beautiful. Sweet dreams."

Forty Two

Back in Pasadena, I'm busy from sunup to well past sundown every day through Wednesday with business and final wedding preparations. Wednesday afternoon finds me down at the St. Regis with most of the main wedding party, even though the wedding isn't scheduled until early Saturday afternoon.

Thursday morning, we're greeting friends and family of both the bride and groom as they start to filter into the hotel. Amelia and I are going over last minute details with Maggie and Amelia's assistant, Barbara, before we attend several meals and activities that are scheduled with some of the key guests whom Mrs. Wú wants to introduce to Henry and Maggie. I'm not really required to speak, but I'm there for moral support and assistance if needed. As best man, Joe attends as well, but we hardly get a chance to speak with each other, even during dinner and late into the evening.

By the time we are no longer needed, Joe and I head back to our suites by around eleven. Oddly enough, Joe's room is right across from mine. I take a long bath, and for as horny as I am, I'm unable to muster the energy to masturbate. I'm mentally and physically tired and hope that the bath will encourage sleep to come quickly.

My heart saddens when I remember that Sadie is not with me when I get out of the tub. There's no way I'd be able to take care of her and all of my responsibilities with the wedding. I've spent a night or two away from her in the past, but this weekend is different. The stress of being perfect, saying the right things and acting perfect has my body wound like a top. Anna agreed to take care of her for the long weekend, so knowing that Sadie is in good hands takes a small bit of stress away.

Unable to fall asleep, I tiptoe across the hotel hall with my phone and room key in hand. Within five seconds of tapping on the door, it swings open. I see a tired, half naked Joe standing in front of me. Joe takes me by the hand and leads me into his room without a word. He puts on a shirt before joining me in his bed. We lay silently as Joe spoons me and lightly brushes his fingers up and down my left arm that rests above the covers. Even in the dark, my eyes stay open, barely blinking as I miss Sadie and go over in my head what to say for my toast for Saturday.

"Hmmm?" I inquire, realizing Joe said something in my ear, but my thoughts were too hectic and drowned him out.

"Missing Sadie?"

"Yeah . . . ."

He tightens his arms around me and my body softens when his lips caress my neck. My mind calms while his sweet breath dances over my shoulder several times. Suddenly, my eyes feel heavy like they are being pulled down by weights.

"Goodnight, beautiful."

"Goodnight, Joe," I purr.

Forty Three

I wake to Joe's fingers gently stroking my face. "Emma . . . ."

"Hmmmm?" I keep my eyes closed.

"I know you're tired . . ." he comments.

"Then, stop trying to wake me," I complain in a groggy voice.

Joe's lips sweetly taste mine, like he's carefully licking every drop of ice cream before it runs down a cone. "It's time to get up," he instructs.

I groan my protest as I roll more into his hot body and take his mouth with mine like I'm devouring the rest of the ice cream.

He chuckles as he pulls away from me. "If you want to make it to your room safely, without being noticed, you'll need to get up."

My eyes bolt open and my head darts around the room as I launch to a sitting position. Shit. I completely forgot where we were. My racing heart slows a few beats as I enjoy the sensation of Joe's lips softly pecking my exposed shoulder. I turn my head in the direction of his face and our gazes lock instantly, sending sparks into my veins. Two seconds later, I find myself laying on top of Joe with our mouths hooked together. I groan disappointment when I unwillingly pull away. Joe laughs while his mouth strives to stay connected to mine as we come to a sitting position. My arms tighten around his neck and his around my back.

Releasing me first, he unconvincingly says, "Go."

I don't move to get off his lap. My fingers twist into his shirt.

Gently cupping my face, Joe repeats, "Go."

My eyes find his. I don't move.

With a wicked grin, he teasingly threatens, "I don't want you to . . . but . . . ."

Nodding, I lean in for one last, long kiss before I slowly slide backward to the end of the bed. We watch each other as I gradually move to the dresser where my phone and room key wait.

Back in my room, I take a longer than usual shower to wake up and my brain starts to go over the schedule for the day. By eight-thirty, I meet everyone for breakfast in the main restaurant. The rest of the morning is spa time as all bridesmaids get waxed, eyebrows threaded, manicures, pedicures, facials and have our hair twisted up into three different styles.

Breathe In

Maggie never made a final decision on hairstyles for herself and us. Normally, I would enjoy the spa, but my brain is distracted by the ever increasing pressure of my toast.

I've never given a toast. I hate talking in or to large crowds, let alone being singled out in one like Jared did at his birthday party. I don't know what to say. I know that I don't want it to be a cliche, boring, impersonal or contrived. How do I make it from the heart when I'm not good at expressing my feelings, even to my two best friends? The very idea of getting up in front of over four hundred people makes my stomach churn.

By mid afternoon, Amelia and I are rounding up the wedding party for the official dress rehearsal that is taking place outdoors on The Pacific Lawn. The official numbers for attendees has increased over the past month with a final headcount for everyone are, including the bride and groom, at a total of four hundred and eighty-six people.

Standing next to Maggie at the alter is surreal. It's not the big day and I'm having wedding day jitters. I feel like I need to pee and I just went before we got outside. The thought of having to walk down one side of the semi-circle staircase all by myself is daunting. To distract myself, I glance around the beautiful private, oval-shaped setting that has a trellised gazebo with rose bushes and jacaranda trees. My eyes sweep across to the groomsmen and I find Lee and Richard smiling back at me with the look guys give women when they're interested and hoping to talk, or something else, later. I quickly look away and find Jimmy and Allen teary-eyed which makes me laugh. If they're this emotional now, how bad will they be tomorrow? A smirk flits across my face at the thought just before my gaze hits the stunning blue eyes of Joe Covelli who is looking back at me. My smile curls just before my eyes dart to the ground and then trail up to Maggie and Henry who are intently listening to the priest. I survey across the setting behind us, to see where all of the guests will be sitting tomorrow and a lump catches in my throat. There are already a lot of chairs out in the grass, but the staff are adding more. Nausea returns.

Once we finish at the gazebo, Amelia walks us to where our precession should go after we climb up the stairs back into the hotel. She points out several locations where pictures will be taken and then leads the way to a hidden room where we will all wait to be announced for our entry into the reception that will be occurring in The Pacific Ballroom. We proceed into the ballroom where the final touches are taking place and we're shown where to go when we are announced. I'm hoping that Joe is paying attention because I'm busy checking out the decadent, all white and crystal decor that the room is covered in. The only things missing are the red floral arrangements that are schedule to be delivered early tomorrow.

Chapter Forty Three

By the time we sit to eat for the rehearsal dinner, my brain has fogged over and I'm not registering anything. Food. My body needs food if I'm going to be required to function any further. After eating my salad, relaxation washes over me when I realize that I don't need to give a toast tonight. I kick my heels off under the table to give me feet a break.

As we're sitting around chatting, Jared sweetly massages my feet and calves as discretely as he can under the table. I pretend to listen to everyone chatting, but my brain is on overdrive trying to think about what to say tomorrow. I do try to focus on what people are talking about to see if that might help spark and idea or two. So far, nothing has helped.

Leaving the private room of the restaurant once we're all finished, Jared, Nathan, Amy and Kim follow me back to my room and I barely notice them.

"You okay, *Kitten*?" Jared checks.

"Huh? . . . yeah . . . why?" I mutter.

"You don't look like you're here," he informs me.

"She hasn't looked like she's been here since this morning," Amy comments.

"Huh?!"

"What's wrong?" Jared sweetly presses.

"Nothing . . . I'm sorry. Here." I hand them each a schedule for tomorrow, the big day. "I have backups, but try not to loose these."

"What's bugging you?" Jared searches, looking at the paper I give him, then takes a photo with his phone and pockets it.

"Ohhh, great idea!" Amy comments. She and everyone else takes a picture with their phones.

"Nothing, I'm fine," I lie.

Amy and Kim head back to the family once we've finish, but Jared and Nathan stay.

"I think we should stay the night," Jared announces.

"Why?"

"You're clearly having a challenge with the wedding," Nathan states.

"No, I'm not. I'm just freaking out about what to say for my toast!" I share.

They both stare at me for a moment.

"Is there anything we can do to help?" Jared searches.

"No . . ." I whine.

"You sure?" Nathan double checks.

"Yeah . . . I . . . I just need . . . ."

Breathe In

Jared places his hands on either of my arms just below my shoulders. "You know whatever you say will be perfect, right?"

My head slowly lowers down. I can feel the tears swarming in my eyes and blurring my vision.

"*Kitten* . . ." Jared calls, prompting me by the chin to look up at him.

I let me head lift, but I keep my gaze down.

"*Kitten* . . ." he sweetly lures.

Two tears tumble down my cheeks. Jared wraps his arms around me and I instantly curl into him. I feel Nathan do the same behind me.

"I'll be right there with you," Jared states.

Nathan runs his fingers through my hair. "Do you want us to stay the night?"

I shake my head.

"Do you want us to stay for a while until you calm down?" Nathan inspects.

I shake my head again as I sniffle. "I just need a bath and some rest," I announce.

"You sure?" Jared probes.

"Yeah . . . I just need to be alone for a while."

"Okay, Kitten," Jared confirms with heartfelt understanding. He hugs me tighter for a few more minutes, kissing me on the side of my head on occasion.

The three of us finally say goodnight and I move to the bathroom to start the water. Just as I'm lowering my body into the steaming, hot water, my phone chirps.

"Hey . . ." I greet with a tired voice.

"Hey, beautiful. You okay?" Joe queries with concern in his voice.

"Yeah . . . ."

"You don't sound like you are. What's up?"

"Just tired and I'm freaking out about my toast for tomorrow," I explain.

There's no need to hide the truth from him.

"Can I help?" he sweetly offers.

"Yeah . . ." I perk up a little. "Write it for me."

Joe laughs at my forwardness. "That I can't do . . . but I can help."

"What did you write down?" I investigate.

"I don't have anything written."

"Then, you don't have anything either?"

Chapter Forty Three

"I have the gist of what I'm going to say. I'll let the moment pull it all together," he comments.

"Great..." I sarcastically reply.

"You'll do great," he encourages.

"If you haven't noticed, I'm not one for talking, let alone expressing my emotions to even the people closest to me," I remind.

"That doesn't mean that you will have a challenge tomorrow," he cheers.

"You're too..." I pause trying to find the right word.

He's too chipper, enthusiastic and calm which is a little sickening. How can he be so calm?

"What?"

"I don't know... but it's not helping," I inform.

"Well, how can I help? Do you want me to come over?"

"That would be nice..." I begin to admit.

I hear a knock on my suite's door a few seconds later.

"I didn't say right now."

"Why not right now?"

"Because I'm in the tub," I notify him.

Joe clears his throat, but doesn't say anything for a minute. "How long have you been in?"

"Just got in. Why?" I explain.

I hear him groan and I find myself giggling.

"What's so funny?"

"You," I confess.

"How about you text me when you're done and you can come over like last night," he sinfully suggests. Before I get a chance to say anything, he ensures, "Just snuggling. I promise."

"Okay..." I quickly agree, perking up.

"Yeah?" Joe sounds a little shocked.

"Yeah."

"You done yet?" he playfully examines.

"No..." I giggle.

"How about now?"

"You're incorrigible. Give me about fifteen more minutes," I request.

"Sure. I'll leave the door propped open. Just come on in," he discloses.

"Okay."

Neither of us say anything for a minute. I don't want to hang up and from the sound of it, or the lack thereof, neither does Joe.

"I'm hanging up now," I announce with a smile.

"Okay."

I turn on some music and let four songs play before I hop out of the tub. My feet still ache, but they're much better between Jared rubbing them earlier and now the bath. Not wanting to dress too cute or sexy, I put on a light grey fitted v-neck, a pair of underwear and three-quarter length black, cotton sweats. I curl my hair into a bun and wrap my hair tie around it twice. I brush my teeth, use my mineral salt deodorant, and add some coconut oil to all my exposed skin.

Even though I know he's leaving the door propped open with the security bar, I text Joe as a heads up. I don't know what I could walk in on and want to make sure no one else is in there before I just pop over. Once I know the hallway is clear, I tap on his door before pushing it open.

"Come on in," he says in a loud whisper.

Closing the door behind me, I turn to see Joe sitting on his bed with a book. "Hey," I greet.

"Hey," he returns, putting his book down on the nightstand. He stands up when I get close to the bed and pulls me into him. He doesn't kiss me right away, he just looks at me.

"What?"

"Nothing," he assures grazing his fingers along my cheek before they slide to the nape of my neck as his mouth moves in to welcome me.

I eagerly accept his lips, sliding my hands to his waist and pulling him further into my body. I moan with each slow, seductive kiss. Some of the tension in my body relaxes, stirring the kitten inside from slumber. I growl when he takes his lips away from mine.

With a chuckle, Joe says, "Come on."

He takes my hand and leads me to the bed. We curl up before looking for something to distract us on the television. Once we settle on an action movie, Joe's strong hands tenderly massage my neck and shoulders. My body instantly surrenders to his touch. After some time, long enough for me to drift in and out of consciousness, I wake to his hands stopping. Joe laughs when I moan my objection. I groan louder when he gets out of the bed.

"I'll be right back," he comforts. He disappears into the bathroom for a minute.

Chapter Forty Three

When I hear the door open, I jump up to take my turn. Joe delivers a glorious kiss before letting me pass. Returning to the bed after relieving myself, I give Joe a quizzical look when he's not in the same spot as before. Without a word, Joe taps a spot behind him on the bed. I place my hands on his shoulders as I tuck my feet under me, slipping in behind him.

"What are you doing?" he questions when I start to rub his shoulders.

"I thought you wanted a turn," I confess.

Laughing, Joe instructs me to lean back. As I shift, I feel his hands reach back and pull my legs out from under me. He moves closer to me where my sex is literally against his lower back. My hands slide up his arms, ready for their task, thinking he's now ready. After the first squeeze, my hands stop when I feel Joe's hands firmly begin to work their magic on my left foot. I let out a whimper from the pain and pleasure. Joe leans back into me where his back is against my chest and our heads are practically even. I slide my hands down onto his chest, resting them as he continues to relieve all the aches from the muscles in my feet.

At some point, I feel Joe tuck his arms under my waist and shift me on the bed before I'm covered with the blankets.

"Goodnight, beautiful," Joe hums quietly in my ear.

"Nigh," my voice breathes out as a smile curls on my face.

Once his body settles, I curl into his delectable form before sleep takes me over again.

Forty Four

As I attempt to lift my heavy eyelids, I discover a hazy darkness surrounding me. Blinking slowly several times, my half-opened eyes won't focus to give me any clear indication of what's around me and where the blurry, flashing lights above are coming from. My body feels heavy. Still unable to open my eyes all the way, I perceive that I'm laying down somewhere. A cool dampness near my left cheek reveals itself as a slight gust of air brushes past my face. Sliding my right arm up the side of my body like a snake, my fingers creep to my lips. Drool — or, at least I hope so.

Two large and oddly shaped figures materialize in front of me. They are so close, only a foot or two away. Voices suddenly emanate from the now more defined silhouettes. Their speech sounds muffled and trails off into the distance even as I try to concentrate on their words. Who are they? What are they saying? Why can't I understand them? One of the voices almost sounds feminine.

Another mumbled sound gradually becomes more apparent as it grows louder and the ringing in my ears subsides. It's the engine of a car. My brain starts to put the fuzzy pieces of evidence together. I must have fallen asleep in the back seat. The front right figure turns to face me, but the face is blurry at first until my eyes adjust to the odd lighting.

"Maggie?" my throat squeezes out in a raw, breathy, hoarse tone.

"It's your turn," her voice replies in a low sluggish tone.

A sudden rush of nervousness enters my belly. The car feels as if it's flying down the road like a rocket ship as the speed of the flashing lights zooming above my head all blur into one.

"Maggie," I shout, but not a single sound escapes my mouth this time. Confused, I try again. "Maggie!"

She doesn't hear me. I don't hear me.

A single, bright white light races towards us, growing larger by the second. Maggie turns her head towards me smiling. Why doesn't she hear me? How does she not see the light?

"It's your turn . . ." her voice says deeper and slower than before.

My body lurches backward as I scramble to grab for Maggie. Suddenly, my arms and legs are tied to the hood of a car. Stark white lights blind me as I yank at my hands to get free. I feel the rope burn into my flesh as the blood starts to drip, staining the car red.

Breathe In

"Maggie!" I yell again without a sound coming from my mouth. My head jerks back as I see Maggie behind the steering wheel. "Maggie?!" my throat shrieks with emptiness.

The sound of the car engine reviving reverberates through my body before Maggie steps on the pedal, sending us flying into the air.

"Maggie . . . no!" I howl as the vehicle launches towards what I can now see are hundreds if not thousands of other cars in front of us. My heart is filled with horror and fear as I desperately scream out one more time, "No!"

I gasp for air as my chest heaves from fright.

"Emma?! What's wrong?" Joe says with grogginess in his voice.

"Nothing . . ." I evade.

His hands are on either side of my face. "Emma," he pleas.

"Nothing . . ." I repeat a little more calmly.

"You had the dream again," he states with concern.

"Yes . . . No . . . kind of," I answer, confused by the vivid images rattling in my brain.

"What do you mean kind of?"

"It was different," I admit.

"How was it different?" he searches.

"I don't want to talk about it," I declare, throwing my arms around his neck.

Joe tightly wraps his arms around me as he lowers us back down on the bed. The sound of his breathing and heartbeat pull me back to reality. I press my lips to his, seeking distraction from the images of the nightmare. Joe returns my heated embrace until my hands slide to the bottom of his shirt trying to desperately remove it. My brain and body are willing to do anything to get those pictures out of my head.

"What?" I question confused by his sudden rejection. Not wanting to hear his answer, I seize his mouth again, this time trying to remove my own shirt.

"Not like this," he contends, blocking my arms from rising higher.

"Why?" I ask, seeking his mouth.

Joe kisses me back, but I can sense his restraint. "You know why," he points out.

He's right, but there's still a small part of my ego that is hurt by the rejection. I turn away from him embarrassed.

"Hey," he calls, pulling me into him. "It's okay."

"No . . ." I object.

Chapter Forty Four

"Yes, it is," he confirms.

"I should go," I announce pulling away.

"No..." Joe tightens his grip around my waist. "Stay... please," he begs in a softer tone, kissing me sweetly.

It takes a few more times of Joe requesting for me to stay before I sheepishly agree. Joe holds me firmly to his body, and after a few minutes, he relaxes and his fingers are running through my hair. It doesn't take long for me to fall back to sleep with him comforting me.

Forty Five

By six forty-five, I wake from the alarm I set on my phone. The alarm is still chiming as Joe tries to keep me in bed with him a little longer. "I need to turn it off," I whine, slipping from his grip.

As soon as I turn off the sound, Joe scoops me up and carries me back to bed. He plants himself on top of my body as his lips greedily take mine, barely letting me breathe for several minutes.

"I need to go," I state in-between kisses, finally getting the chance to get some air.

"What time do you need to meet up with them?"

"Eight," I laugh as I can hardly free my lips to answer.

Joe turns his head for a second before immediately returning his mouth to mine. "You've got plenty of time to stay for a while."

As I slide my hands down his chest, Joe growls with delight until I wiggle my fingers to tickle him. "Hey!" he objects, squirming to get me to stop.

"I need to get up."

"You don't need an hour to get ready," he reports. "You're already beautiful."

My heart flutters like a baby bird learning to flap its wings. Panic at the feelings stirring inside me alter my mood abruptly. "I need to go," I say in a more serious tone.

Joe lets me up, but he follows me like a puppy to the door. Not waiting for me turn, Joe spins me into him before my hand reaches the door knob. His sturdy, morning wood presses into my belly as my ass hits the door. My left leg lifts up, wrapping itself around his waist. Hot moisture releases from my cave as my lips part and come into contact with Joe's erection with only a few layers of clothing in between. My sex can feel the heat coming from his throbbing penis as she rocks into him. Joe yanks his lips from mine and our lungs pant from lust and need.

"I should go," I restate the obvious, knowing that it's just a matter of seconds before I'm naked, whether my nakedness is done by me or him is unknown and doesn't really matter.

Joe doesn't say anything. He just stares into my eyes, holding me, but keeping himself just far enough away.

Breathe In

Once the hallway is clear and I'm able to get back to my room, I quickly swap out the batteries for B.O.B. and have a three-way with him and Master P. The boys do their job, curtailing the kitten's itch for the time being with two intense orgasms.

Good thing I was already packed and prepped to head to Maggie's suite last night, or else for the first time in my life I would have been late. All I needed to do was shower and grab my bag.

By the time all the bridesmaids are in the suite, the breakfast I scheduled to be delivered arrives. In the living room, we sit for a few minutes eating and chatting before Amelia and Barbara go over details with all of us and make sure everyone has their copy of the schedule I handed them last night. Jimmy and Allen pop in to say hello and see what we're all doing — the men aren't getting ready quite yet.

Jared and Nathan are wearing black tuxedos with red bow ties and handkerchiefs that match the red floral lace in the bridesmaids' dresses. The groom and groomsmen have the same style tuxes.

The dresses are delivered by ten and the seamstresses are checking our fits one final time before they are steamed in the bathroom. Mǔqīn and Nǎinai are wearing matching gold qipaos with a lucky dragon pattern that have three-quarter length sleeves and trail all the way down to their ankles. For the bridesmaids' dress, we also are wearing qipaos, but ours are red, with a lace collar and shoulder area. The lace drapes over the tight fitting solid red silk gown down to our ankles as well. The bridesmaids' dresses have an open back that is elegantly draped with the red lace.

Maggie's dress is the most exquisite of all of the custom pieces. Ali Jacobs created a mermaid style silk white dress with cap sleeves that round Maggie's arms just below her shoulders. A see-through white chiffon circles around Maggie's neck, down to her sleeves and flows out and over the edge of the poof bottom with a ten foot train in the back. Hand sewn into the chiffon are red floral lace and dragon designs that leave enough space to see Maggie's collar bone area and half of the white silk fabric underneath. When Maggie turns, she has a more pronounced open back dress that starts from the base of the lace collar, stretches out towards her cap sleeves and ends at the small of her back.

All female bridesmaids and the bride are set to wear matching diamond strappy Jimmy Choo four inch heels, ruby stud earrings and ruby and diamond bracelets. Maggie gave us the bracelets last night at the rehearsal dinner.

Chapter Forty Five

Our nails and eyebrows are checked before we start to get hair and makeup done. Maggie is just getting to have her hair done when all of the bridal party flowers are delivered to Maggie's suite. Once I'm dressed and finish pinning a red rose on Jared and Nathan I head over to Henry's suite to pin the groom and groomsmen since I have a few minutes of time before Maggie will be getting dressed.

"Sexy!" Jimmy shouts when I enter the door after knocking.

I ignore his comment since I'm pressed for time. "I need all of you to line up with your jackets on."

"What's up?" Henry inquires.

"I need to pin you," I explain, holding up the box of roses.

I watch the men gather together and I struggle to keep my eyes off of Joe. I purposefully dart my eyes around watching them, but my body's response to seeing him dressed up is making it challenging to focus. Henry's up first and seems calm considering how edgy Maggie was when I left her a few minutes ago. Next is Jimmy and then Allen who, once I'm finished with them, hover and verbally make comments about my dress and how I look. It takes everything I have not to show my nervousness as I pin Lee and Richard next. Fùqīn follows with tears collecting in his eyes.

"You okay?"

"If you look this beautiful, I can only image how beautiful my daughter is right now," Fùqīn's voice shakes.

With a smile and a tear threatening me, I confirm, "Definitely!"

Fùqīn kisses me on either cheek. I know he wants to hug me, but is refraining from the outward gesture as to not mess up my dress.

"Mǔqīn and Nǎinai look lovely as well," I add sweetly.

"I don't doubt it for a second," he returns with a tear escaping from the corner of his eye.

I lift my hand to wipe his face and Fùqīn gently captures my wrist, kissing my palm. "Do you want me to come and get you when she's dress?"

"No. I want to see her just as I'm about to take her to Henry."

I nod my understanding.

Joe steps up for his turn as I clear my throat to evade getting choked up. Just as I'm about to push the pin in, Joe yells, "Ow!"

Joe and the rest of the guys chuckle as I punch him in the arm. "Not funny," I remark with a lump in my throat.

Breathe In

Joe leans in to apologize as I finish putting the rose on. His scent alone sends my hormones into a frenzy and I feel the heat in my cheeks elevating. My gaze bounces back and forth from my hands and his eyes. The kitten purrs as she rubs up against the cage door inside. Focus, Emma.

Back at Maggie's suite, a few tears break free from my eyes at the sight of Maggie in her dress. None of us have seen her in the dress, she wouldn't let us see it other than on the hanger. She looks — like a queen. There are no other words to describe her. She is a queen.

When I'm not needed, I sit, frantically shaking my leg, still trying to decide on what to say.

Valerie, Ian's wife, and her photographers request a few posed pictures before it's time to head out to the room to wait for the wedding to commence. They've been taking photos the entire time since we got into the suite and a one of them followed me to Henry's suite. I need to make sure that I don't always look like a deer in headlights.

With a red rose bouquet in hand, I start off the precession with Joe. He models my steps down the curved staircase until we meet in the center. My body shakes from nerves, but Joe's sweet smile eases some of the tension before we start walking arm in arm.

"You look beyond beautiful," he whispers before we get to the first row of guests.

"You don't look too bad either," I playfully respond. Our eyes meet briefly before I quickly return my focus on where I'm walking in order to not to fall. We successful manage to make it to the alter without a step out of place.

Now the hard part, stand while the rest of the group makes their way down. They aren't supposed to start until the pair in front of them have made it to their positions by the alter. Jared and Jimmy are next and they beam from ear to ear. A few gasps escape guests' mouths when they see two men walking together and again when Jared stands behind me. Kim and Richard are the last two to come down before the parents. Mŭqīn is being escorted by Eric followed by Năinai being escorted by Peter. When the harpist changes her song, Fŭqīn appears at the top center of the stairway. Five seconds later, I know because I counted, Maggie emerges. A light buzz of chatter floats in the air as Fŭqīn and Maggie walk down on the same side together all the way to the edge of the first row of guests. Henry steps down to take Maggie's arm from Fŭqīn and Joe helps Fŭqīn to his seat next to Mŭqīn.

As Maggie climbs the three steps, our eyes lock and it takes everything I have to fight back tears. I feel Jared's loving hand rest on my left hip as if he already knows what I need. All I can do is look down at the ground to prevent

Chapter Forty Five

the water from dripping. I want to see Maggie, but I know that I'll lose control if I do. I feel Jared take a step closer, sliding his left hand over my forearm and clasping the top of my hand. He holds me softly but firmly as my ears listen to the priest's words.

When the time comes for me to take Maggie's bouquet, I muster a quick glance at her face with a smile before lowering my eyes. That split second is all I need for her to know how I feel and for me her. Upon the priest's cue, I turn and hand Jared Maggie's bouquet before he hands me the box that contains Henry's wedding ring. Once Maggie takes it, Jared and I swap again.

I'm able to finally peek up when the priest announce that Henry may kiss his bride. Just like in a fairy tale, Henry dips Maggie backward a little when their lips join for a second time. I find myself chewing on the inside of my lip as my gaze lifts and connects with Joe. I can't help but smile when I see him, especially when he's staring back at me.

Once Maggie and Henry make their way inside, the rest of us follow, awaiting instructions for photos. By the second photo area out of three, I manage to get Amelia and Barbara to get some of the waiters to sneak some food out to everyone in the bridal party. With a bottle of champagne, we have a mini toast at the third and final photo-op location.

In the reception, Mŭqīn and Fŭqīn are announced first, followed Mr. and Mrs. Wú, Kim and Richard, Amy and Lee, Nathan and Allen, and then Jared and Jimmy before Joe and myself. Once we are standing by our seats at the table, Maggie and Henry are introduced and the entire room cheers. Maggie and Henry start going around the room to greet and thank everyone for coming. Everyone mingles and enjoys hours d' oeuvres for the next half hour until dinner is served.

Some soft music comes over the speakers signaling Joe and I that it's time to toast now that dinner is finished. Once the song finishes, Joe stands tapping his fork on his glass. Amelia hands Joe the microphone.

"Good evening," Joe greets the room in Mandarin. "Henry. Maggie. It is my utmost honor and privilege to share this day, your day, with you. The love you have for each other is an old love that has cycled back around to find itself once again here in this present moment, and will continue to do so, growing and inspiring with each lifetime you two share together. Your love is endless and I hope to share the same kind of love with someone, someday. Live each day with love in your heart, no matter what the circumstances are, and you will be forever rewarded with love around you and within you. Love will test you. Love will guide you. But most importantly, love will make you stronger, so long as you let it. Lead with love in your heart every morning you wake and end with love in your heart every night before you go to sleep. To my seventh brother and my fourth sister, Henry and Maggie!"

My eye catches Joe as I do my best to stop the few tears that have rolled down my face. How am I to follow that?

After everyone takes a sip from their glass, Jared nudges me to stand. My lips purse as I watch the room's attention turn to me. Jared kindly takes my hand. I look to him and he nods. "You got this," he mouths.

My eyes circle back around through the crowd, but I force myself to only focus on Maggie and Henry. They are the only important people in the room right now. Envision that they are the only two people in the room right now, Emma. What would you say to them?

"Hi," I begin in Mandarin. I take a deep breath, trying to figure out how to start. "I'm not one for words, especially when it comes to expressing my emotions. I've had a lot of them since you two met . . . and some . . . not so good."

I hear people laugh. Maggie and Henry both smile and laugh a little too. Jared squeezes my hand encouragingly.

"I've already lost one family and I wasn't interested in losing another. I'm still not." I look to Jared pulling him closer, and then back to Maggie. "But . . . even in this short time of getting to know you Henry . . . I've realized some things. To me . . . Maggie was already a perfect. The perfect friend, aside from Jared . . . ."

Laughs erupt.

"She's the perfect sister . . . who I almost might not have ever known. But, seeing her with you . . . she is even more perfect than I had ever imagined she could be. Seeing Maggie light up when she's with you . . . I now know that she can only burn brighter with each passing day. I haven't lost Maggie. I have gained a brother. Thank you," I pause, barely able to continue. "May you both shine bright together, forever. To my sister and to my new brother. I love you both."

I try to sit down since it took all my energy to stand without falling. Just as my butt hits the seat, Maggie and Henry come over, hugging and kissing me. Maggie is a mess crying, causing a few tears to drop from my eyes as well. Jared wraps his arm around my shoulders commending me on my efforts when we sit back down. I hope I didn't sound like a bumbling idiot.

Maggie and Henry immediately go right into their first dance as Mr. and Mrs. Henry Wú, which doesn't give me more than five seconds of freedom from attention. Joe tugs at my hand, reminding me that we're supposed to join them along with the rest of the bridal party.

Chapter Forty Five

"You did a wonderful job, beautiful," Joe sweetly praises.

"Yours was better," I claim.

"I think we both did great," he assures.

"You did better, but thank you," I graciously accept.

Joe helps to continue to distract me from worrying about tripping and falling on the dance floor by talking about incidentals. We mostly talk about who we caught gasping when Jared and Jimmy came down the stairs after us and then again when Nathan and Allen did. He's able to get me to relax for a few minutes, forgetting where we are and what we're supposed to be doing.

"You look devastatingly sexy in that dress," he professes in his sexy voice — my favorite of his voices.

My face heats up, but thankfully my feet don't falter. "Stop distracting me," I playful chide.

"How is the truth distracting you?" he teases back.

"The sexy voice," I remind.

Joe laughs. "I was just whispering."

"No, you weren't. You knew what you were doing when you said it."

"I'll do my best not to distract you then, not at least while we're dancing."

"Too late," I claim.

"Really? How is that?"

I offer a wicked grin, but say nothing.

"Now you're distracting me," he delivers seductively. Joe's hand tightens on my waist, forcing my body into his a little more.

"Careful. You're going to make Lee and Richard jealous," I goad.

"Hopefully I'm making every man in this room jealous," he devilishly admits.

I bite my lip trying to prevent too much of a smile on my face.

"You definitely have all the single women jealous," he informs me.

"And, probably most of the married ones too," I add sinfully.

"I don't mind if you don't," he suggestively infers.

The next song comes on and Jared is suddenly whisking me away from Joe. "I'm stealing Jimmy's turn to dance with you," Jared confesses.

"What are you talking about?"

"You're supposed to dance with all of the groomsmen."

"Since when?"

Breathe In

"It's a tradition and Amelia mentioned it yesterday. I'm supposed to dance with all of them too, but I knew Jimmy wouldn't mind and you'd be willing to dance with him later."

From one song to the next, I dance with Allen, then Lee and Richard. The DJ starts to play music for everyone to dance to which is my cue to get off the dance floor. Jared, Nathan and the rest of my friends yank me back onto the floor. I willingly dance for a few songs and end up dancing with Jade and Rey a little too. I make a break for the bathroom and make it without any distractions.

Back in the ballroom, Jimmy takes me for the next slow song to dance followed by Henry, Nathan and Pop-Pop. The DJ feels frisky enough to play another slow song which gets three good looking men, whom I don't know, asking me to dance.

"Thank you, but I have to decline. I don't dance with anyone I don't know," I graciously decline.

"What about with an old man such as myself?"

I turn to find Mr. Covelli behind me.

"Mr. . . . I mean John. I was wondering if I'd get a chance to say hello to you and Mrs., I mean Elaine," I greet, happy for the excuse to not talk to the men whose names I have already forgotten.

Mr. Covelli leads me out to the dance floor with regal grace. Our conversation is light because Mr. Covelli informs me that Mrs. Covelli told him not to discuss business with me until after tomorrow. Once we finish, Mr. Covelli hands me off to Jared for safe keeping which I greatly appreciate.

Later in the evening, I'm able to track Mrs. Covelli down when she isn't busy talking with someone. We exchange pleasantries before Jared yanks me onto the dance floor for the tossing of the bouquet.

"Front and center, Emma," Maggie announces over the microphone.

My heart stops for a minute at her words.

"Come on all you single ladies. Get over here. It's time to toss the bouquet," Maggie says a second time.

I try to hide behind Nǎinai, but she doesn't let me. Maggie counts down from three and before the flowers go flying into the air, I grab Jade and hoist her up in my arms. Seeing the flowers dropping, I instruct, "Catch it, Jade!"

Jade reaches high above her head and grabs the bouquet by the white silk ribbon that is tied around the stems as it goes above us. I know Maggie was aiming for me, but she sent the flowers a little too high.

Chapter Forty Five

Kim, Jade and I stand off to the side of the dance floor as Henry takes off the garter from Maggie's leg. Jared, Nathan, Jimmy and Allen are standing behind me claiming that they are taken. I argue that I'm taken too, by B.O.B., but they tell me that B.O.B. doesn't count. Henry hurls the garter into the air at all of the single men. You can see the disappointment on their faces knowing that Jade is the bearer of the bouquet. A hand shoots up and attains the prize. It belongs to Joe Covelli.

I lead Jade over to the chair that is now back in the middle of the dance floor. As Jade gets settled, Henry gets on the microphone. "Joe will be putting on two garters tonight. One for the lovely Jade who caught the bouquet. And . . . because there needs to be someone of legal age to properly receive the garter, Emma will be getting the other one that Maggie is wearing."

My body freezes and my heart stops. "No!" I protest.

"Our wedding, our rules," Henry rebuts.

My eyes narrow. "I'll remember that."

Jade gets up and lets Maggie sit. Henry reaches up to get the other garter rather quickly this time. More whistles and cheering erupt from the giant crowd. When I lead Jade over to the chair, she insists that I sit with her.

Joe sweetly walks over and kneels before the two of us. "I need your arm," he instructs Jade.

Jade extends her right one.

Joe dances the circular object up Jade's arm and over her shoulder. He lifts her up in the air as everyone cheers and before lowering her to the floor, he kisses her on the cheek. When Joe kneels back down, Jade walks up and kisses Joe. I'm barely able to see it because of all of the flashing lights.

"You ready?" he grins knowingly.

I stick out my arm like Jade.

"No," Joe chuckles.

"The right way, Emma," Henry announces.

Everyone watching laughs.

"You won't get it that high with this dress," I comment.

"Wanna bet?" Joe's grin widens. He removes my right shoe before coming a little closer.

Henry gives a play by play over the microphone as I bite my lip and look away. Joe deliberately torments me, moving ever so slowly inch by inch. As his hands reach the bottom of my knee, I use my left foot to slide back in the chair away from him. I manage to get the chair to go back a few inches.

459

"You can't move," he claims, sliding closer.

I feel the chair get stuck and notice that Jimmy and Jared are holding it in place with their feet. "No moving," they say at the same time.

I hold my breath and wince as Joe tickles my leg with his fingers, heading back up to my knee. In one quick movement, he rounds my knee cap and stops. I look to him thinking he's done, but the wicked smile on his face tells me otherwise. He nudges the garter with his fingers, getting further up my thigh. My lips clench as Joe's hands climb higher. Somehow Joe has managed to reach the middle of my thigh. I shake my head no, hoping that he doesn't dare to go any further. Winking, Joe gives one last nudge before he seductively slides his fingers back down to my ankles and returns my shoe. Joe helps me to stand and plants a kiss on my cheek.

"You're a dead man," I proclaim when we are surrounded by just our friends.

"Ohh come on, Emma. Joe was just having a little fun," Jimmy defends.

"Looked like you were enjoying it too," Allen antagonizes.

"I need a drink," I say, turning to Jared for a rescue.

"Follow me, Kitten." Jared takes my hand leading the way to the bar. "Be thankful it wasn't Lee, Richard or any of the other single and horny men in the room," he comments once we are off the dance floor.

I refrain from replying.

The rest of the night is a blur. We dance, we drink and I watch everyone gab the night away. At some point, I'm not sure when since I don't have a watch, Maggie plops herself next to me. She rests her head on my shoulder and I wrap my arm around her. We sit not talking for a long while, just enjoying the moment.

"What is it with men and babies that is so freakin' hot and sexy?" Maggie exclaims.

I laugh at her comment, but don't verbally agree. I know that she's been watching Henry dance with Rey from her statement. Ironically, my thoughts were on the same thing. I was busy watching Joe dance with Jade.

"Thank you, Emma!" Maggie slides closer giving me a kiss on the cheek.

"For what?"

"Everything. All of this. And, what you said earlier. It means a lot to me, and it means a lot to Henry too," she confesses taking my hand in hers.

"You're welcome." I avoid looking at her because I don't want to cry.

Running her fingers back and forth over the top of my hand, Maggie asks, "Can I tell you something?"

Chapter Forty Five

"Sure," I agree.

"I haven't told anyone . . . not even Henry," she begins.

My attention is caught. I turn to look at her. "What?"

Maggie's face is beaming. No. Glowing. She leans in and whispers, "I'm pregnant!"

"What?!" I blurt in shock.

The music is so loud that no one near us hears me.

"Are you serious?"

"Yeah . . . you're the first to know. I'm telling Henry either tonight or tomorrow. I'm waiting for the right moment, you know."

"Kim knows though, right?" I check.

"No. I haven't had an appointment with her. I have one scheduled when we get back from the honeymoon to find out how far along I am," she confirms.

"Thank you," I say with tears in my eyes.

"For what?"

"Sharing it with me. Thank you," I take a deep breath in to fight the sobs. "I'm so happy for you!" I wrap my other arm around her.

I am. I genuinely am happy for Maggie. I'm happy for her. I'm proud of her. She couldn't be more perfect than in this very moment.

"You can tell Jared after we've already left, but no one else. I want to make it a special thing to tell the rest of the family," she explains.

"Okay," I agree.

The next slow song that comes on, Maggie and I dance together. Jared and Nathan join us about halfway through the song, circling around Maggie and me. Shortly after, Jade wedges herself between our legs, so I pick her up. Henry, Joe, Jimmy and Allen surround Jared and Nathan. As my eyes sweep across all of the beautiful, happy faces around me and to others in the crowd like Amy, Kim, Peter, Eric, Rey, Jet, Mǔqīn, Fùqīn and Nǎinai, I feel — I feel as if my life is complete. It's a family. They're a family. They just aren't a family. They're my family.

Henry and Maggie leave the reception while at least half of the guests continue to dance and celebrate into the night. I hide in a corner, sitting in a lounge area away from the single men who keep asking me to dance or offer me a drink. Jared and Nathan come by first, followed by Jimmy, Allen and Joe. Lee and Richard bring a few stragglers along with them, mostly the men who I've been avoiding.

Jimmy and Allen disappear first followed by Jared and Nathan about a half hour later. I beg Jared to stay, but sex is more important than saving his best friend from a bunch of boys. It doesn't take long before some of the men start to move closer and talk to me. I try my best to be polite until I can't stand it any longer. I need to get away. But how?

"We forgot to give Henry and Maggie the thing," I abruptly announce to Joe.

With a puzzled look on his face, Joe just stares at me.

"Come one." I pull on Joe's sleeve to get him to stand up.

"I don't think now is a good time to bother them," he counters.

"We aren't going to bother them. We'll take it to the front desk and instruct them to deliver it with their morning breakfast," I explain to make my actions sound more realistic to the men around us.

Without question or hesitation, Joe follows me as we duck around corners or rush past open doorways to prevent ourselves from being seen.

"What are we doing?" he asks when we get stuck behind a pillar. "What thing did we forget to give Henry and Maggie?"

"Shh . . . the thing, remember," I inform him, as if he knows what I'm talking about. "We're waiting until it's clear to go by."

"Why? Why don't we just walk by?"

"Shhh . . . I don't want to be seen or heard," I explain.

"Why don't you want to be . . . " Joe's voices trails when I yank on his collar to follow me, dragging him behind me into a staff member service elevator.

"I don't think we're allowed to use this one," he contends, slowing down as I enter the box.

I pull him in and press the button for the doors to close. As soon as we have privacy, I press my body against his and seize his lips. Joe doesn't object, instead, he presses harder into me forcing me back against the wall.

"So, what's the thing we forgot?" Joe questions once the doors open to our floor.

"You'll see . . . " I offer with a smile as we walk casually down the hall to our rooms.

Joe ushers me to my room. I guess he thinks the thing I'm talking about is in my room.

I turn to face him and check down the hallway before I reach into his jacket pocket and pull out the very item I intended to get.

"What are you doing?" he questions as I shift around him and walk towards the other side of the hall.

Chapter Forty Five

Biting my lip, I hold up what I took out of his pocket. Without taking my eyes off of him, I slip the key in the slot behind me and crack open the door. I don't say a word as I push the door open further and turn to go into his hotel room. As soon as the door closes, I hear Joe lock the security latch. There's one light on in the room, but it's coming from the bathroom, causing me eyes to take a moment to adjust.

I walk over to the dresser and gently set down my purse. Joe's body brushes against mine when he places his right hand on my hip and turns on the small lamp that is next to me on the dresser and sets down his ruby cufflinks. Turning my head to the left, I can see Joe out of the corner of my eye. Joe caress my naked arm and I knowingly lean back into his body. Holding my cheek, Joe delicately kisses me as if he's savoring the moment. My right hand rests on his and my left seeks to curl into his hair, not wanting him to stop.

I moan when Joe removes his lips from mine, but I'm pleasantly surprised when his fingers begin to unbutton the back of my dress, taking his time. After the top three are undone, Joe's fingers tease my spine, gradually caressing my skin to the bottom of the back opening. I begin to take care of the few buttons that are at my lower back, but Joe eagerly takes over. My dress is carefully peeled away from my body before it falls and bunches on the floor at my feet. I'm left wearing nothing but my lace thong, the garter and my Jimmy Choo shoes. I slide my hand up and release my hair from its confinements.

About to turn to face him, I immediately stop when Joe's lips reach my shoulder. Inch by inch, Joe's mouth travels across my skin as his left hand slides over my chest. He guides me a step back further into him so my feet are no longer trapped by the dress. When his mouth meets mine again, I spin to face him.

Wanting to feel his naked chest on mine, my fingers frantically undo his vest first. As Joe shrugs out of it, I proceed to his shirt. As I'm halfway down his dress shirt, I can't help but to complain, barely moving my mouth from his. "You have too many layers."

Joe chuckles at my announcement.

As Joe's hands get caught in the cuffs, I set my sights on his belt and pants. Just as his pants hit the ground, Joe clutches my ass and lifts me, delivering us both to the bed. His mouth fondles my neck from one side to the other before he ventures down to my breasts. He sucks and licks each nipple with precision, causing my lips to dampen more. I thrust my hips against him, hoping he takes the hint. Licking and nipping at my stomach, Joe deliberately teases me, making sure he covers every inch of my body before giving me what I want — what I need.

I groan when Joe's mouth avoids my sex on purpose. Our eyes meet and I watch him grab the garter with his teeth. Little by little, Joe tugs the garter down my leg, stopping just above my knee. My hands fondle my breasts in anticipation. Joe taunts me as he creeps his fingers to the garter, and gradually releases it from my leg. Continuing his erotic torment, Joe proceeds to kiss and lick up my leg, bouncing from one thigh to the other until he delivers a single long kiss over my underwear, on my sex. I squeeze my nipples, desperate for him to taste me.

In a single, quick movement, Joe literally rips my lace thong away from my body, as if he can no longer take his own kinky torture. "I'll buy you another pair," he offers sweetly before his tongue licks up the slit of my folds.

"It's . . . okay," I moan with pleasure from his touch.

"No . . ." he objects, keeping his skin to mine. "I really liked that pair." His mouth devours my entire sex.

My back arches, thrusting my hips into his face as I gasp, overwhelmed by his manipulation of my body.

"I'll buy you at least one pair . . . ." His mouth eagerly delivers another round of pleasure to my clit. "Maybe a couple . . . so I can rip them off again . . ." he suggests, sliding a finger or two inside my wet, eager cave.

Another sharp gasp escapes my mouth. "Mmmmmm . . . hmmmm . . ." I agree, not wanting him to stop.

Joe continues to pulse his fingers in and out, in and out, in and out, as his tongue seduces my clitoris. I can feel myself on the cusp of climax.

"More . . ." I beg on a breath out. "More."

"More what?" he searches.

"You . . . your . . . fingers . . . " I barely mutter. "Yes . . ." I confirm as I feel more of him deep inside me and my fingers squeeze into the sheets below me. "God . . . yes!"

Like a roller coaster, my body is on a constant uphill climb on the verge of the peak. Joe's hand slightly moves, striking the very spot I need for the roller coaster to be let loose on the tracks.

"Right . . . there . . . " I instruct, wanting to cum all over his fingers.

"Here?" he checks hitting the spot again.

"Yes . . . !" I moan. "I'm . . . going . . . to . . . ."

After several more thrusts of his hand, I beg, "Harder . . . ."

He complies instantly.

"Yes . . . mmmmm . . . mmmmm . . ." my voice whimpers as I get closer.

Chapter Forty Five

My left hand grabs the back of his head a few seconds before the sweet release washes over me, drenching his fingers, as I grind my hips into his face. "Don't stop . . ." I command, wanting it to last, convulsing as if I was getting shock therapy.

My body continues to shake as Joe licks his fingers and moves up my body. I moan my protest when I see that he's licked his fingers clean. Taking his face with my hands, my tongue seeks the flavor of my cum in his mouth.

A sudden urge, perhaps need, rushes through me. I roll over, placing Joe underneath of me. Once I'm sure I've gotten all of me from his mouth, my lips begin their exploration of his body. Joe moans when I kiss and nip at his neck, fisting his hands in my hair. Then, I taste his sweaty chest and bite his nipples, getting him back for the exquisite torture he gave to me.

As my lips round his stomach, Joe protests. "No . . . ."

"Why?" I search as I taunt him further with my lips slipping down his body.

"It's been a while," he informs me trying to sit up.

I force him back down. "So . . . all the more reason," I grin. My mouth rounds the ridges of his hip bones.

Joe tries to sit up as my fingers curl into the edges of his boxer briefs to release his erection. Before he gets all the way up, my mouth consumes his penis from tip to base.

"Fuuuuuuckkkkk . . ." Joe exhales, flopping down on the bed.

I hum with delight at rendering him both speechless and motionless as I continue my desired pursuit to make him cum just like he did with me. Sliding my mouth up and down, my tongue flicks along the seam of his hot, thick organ. Taking a quick break for some air, my mouth skillfully ravages his balls before it slides up in one single, fluid stroke to the tip of his head. Hearing him moan with satisfaction, I repeat licking him like an ice cream cone three more times before I inhale his erection back into my mouth.

"Shit . . . Emma," he groans through gritted teeth.

With just a few more glides up and down his shaft, I can feel his penis getting harder, readying to erupt. I slow my pace down just enough, allowing him to reach further in the back of my throat. My slowed pace is perfect because by the sixth time my mouth is stuffed full of his cock, Joe climaxes.

Before I get the chance to slurp up every last drop that tries to slip out through the corners of my mouth, Joe cups my face, tasting his cum on my lips and tongue.

"Mmmm . . ." he hums, rolling us over to where he is on top again.

Breathe In

In all of my years of having sex with men, I've never wanted to give oral sex. Not like I just did with Joe. This was sudden. Do I enjoy oral sex? Yes! Hell, yes! Maggie and I do it every time. I never bothered with men because after the first few guys that I did sleep with, who only took and never gave after receiving, ruined it for me. Why should they get two releases let alone one when they never took the time to really help get me off? I've had a few guys try to give me oral stimulation, but after a few minutes, they plunge right in with their dicks. They'd get their release and I would have to take care of myself. Most of them didn't like it when I would rub myself while they were inside me, but then they never offered to do anything for me after they came or if they did they were unsuccessful and I'd have to fake it.

Along with always feeling sexually frustrated, I've never had a guy want to kiss me so eagerly after having his cock, let alone his cum, in my mouth.

Joe's erection never goes away after I suck him dry. It just keeps twitching on my belly as he kisses me.

"Don't move . . ." he commands after a slow, lingering kiss.

I watch him get up and head to the bathroom. Is he going to pee?

Ten seconds later, with his cock at full mast, Joe strides back into the room. I swear both he and his cock confidently stride around the bed, stopping at my feet. Joe tosses something at the dresser before he lifts his hand to his mouth. My eyes try to watch the object flying in the air, but my head snaps to look at him when I hear the tear of a condom wrapper.

Keeping his eyes on me and a grin on his face, Joe rolls the condom on as if it's nothing. There's no effort or attention needed to his action. Once it's on, Joe crawls over me on his hands and knees. I try to sit up, but he yanks me to the side by my waist, repositioning me on the bed. He lowers himself on top of me before I can move to get on top of him.

Joe's mouth returns to mine, exploring it with his tongue with deep, rhythmic strokes. His mouth shifts to my neck again, which just primes the pool of wetness between my folds.

"Fuck . . . me . . . " I whimper, unable to wait any longer.

"Not yet," he insists. He strategically dips just the tip of his penis inside me.

I moan my protest.

Waiting a second, he slides in a little deeper.

"Mmmmm . . . fuck . . . me!" I groan, begging again.

"Not yet," he repeats into my ear with that voice that gets me every time.

I gasp when he thrusts in, filling me completely. "Mmmmmm . . . ."

Chapter Forty Five

With measured pulses, Joe slides in and out of me. My hips rock in the opposite direction to his, ensuring optimal penetration. He kisses me, groaning each time he's completely inside. A moan escapes my throat each time he thrusts in and I revel at the sensation. My mounds are so sensitive that I don't think that it will take me long to cum again, which surprises me. When Joe's mouth returns to my neck, my fingers scale down his back until they are low enough for me to grab his ass. My hands push, as if they'll help him get further inside me.

Joe suddenly quickens his pace and my body immediately responds, clenching down and around his hard shaft inside me. We both moan with pleasure, feeling the moment building again.

"Harder . . ." I request.

He obliges.

"Yes . . . like . . . that . . ." I praise.

Joe's thrusts quicken even faster and I can feel the ecstasy swirling inside me. My muscles clench more each time they're stimulated by his penis rubbing them.

"Don't . . . stop . . ." I command.

So close. I'm so close to cumming.

"Cum for me," he exhales into my neck.

"Yes . . ." I agree.

I want to cum so badly.

Joe keeps his stride as I get closer and closer.

"God . . . I'm . . ." I wail as the pleasure surges through my veins, more intensely this time. My body convulses, more contented that satisfaction has been met again.

Joe slows his stride, but I know that he has not finished yet. He's just waiting for me to catch my breath. Regaining self control and strength, I roll us over to where I'm on top. Kissing me, Joe slides us up to a seated position, resting his back against the headboard, which gives me something to hold on to.

Joe's lips bounces between my mouth and neck as I rock back and forth over his even harder cock. Just as I find the urge to touch myself, Joe's hand dips to the front of my hips and circles my clitoris with his thumb.

"Mmmm . . ." I moan my satisfaction at his touch. My back arches and I feel his slick tongue playing with my nipples. "Mmmmm."

With the aid of his thumb, the very tip of Joe's cock strikes a particular node in my cave, making me wetter and closer to another orgasm. My hand tightens on the back of his neck steadying my body as I wiggle deeper, harder on him.

"Cum for me," he seduces into my neck.

"Yes . . ." I answer, wanting to give into his request and capture the euphoric feeling once again.

I've needed this for so long.

"What . . . about . . . you?"

"You first . . ." he confirms his intent.

"Mmmm . . . Joe . . ." I pant.

"Cum for me, beautiful," he urges with the sexy voice.

"Yes . . . Mmmmmm . . . ."

Taking the other side of my hip, Joe thrusts up into me.

"Mmmmm . . ." I moan, getting closer. "Again."

With slow rhythmic pulses, Joe eagerly gives me what I want.

"Mmmmmmm . . . Joe . . ." I whimper as I gloriously orgasm, soaking his penis completely.

With his hands pulling on my hips, Joe encourages me to keep rocking until I've been completely satiated. We sit quietly, taking in the moment as we exchange slow, enduring kisses to each other's lips.

"You're turn," I offer with a grin.

In a split second, Joe's on top of me. He pulls back for his first thrust since he never left my body, eager to take care of himself. Joe, however, still manages to pay attention to my needs; touching me, kissing me, licking me, the whole time. I rock my pelvis into him each time he comes charging down deep inside me. As his stride quickens, I'm surprised to feel my body get closer to another orgasm. Harder and harder, deeper and deeper he pushes inside.

"Don't stop . . ." I plea when his pace slows a little. "Fuck me . . . fuck me until you cum . . ." I direct.

Joe immediately returns to his previous pace, with my body confirming that a sweet release is within reach. Right as his penis hardens, hitting deep inside of me, an orgasm rushes over me like a geyser.

I cry out in elation. "Joe . . . ."

"Emma . . ." Joe shouts, confirming his climax.

Chapter Forty Five

He continues to pound me, like he's making sure he squeezes ever last drop out of himself. Just as I catch my breath from my orgasm, another one rushes over me, completely taking my breath away.

Joe's face buries in my neck, our chests heave and my head spins as we lay motionless. We both groan when he slips himself out of me and rolls to the side, pulling me into him. Joe props my left leg over his hip before sweeping wet hair from my face and kissing me.

Five orgasms. Five orgasms! My brain can't believe that I just had five orgasms. Was it really that good or was it from not having sex for so long? Shut up, Emma. It doesn't matter. Just enjoy the fact that you just had five wickedly awesome orgasms.

At some point, I feel Joe uncurl himself from me and get off the bed. He returns quickly, applying a warm, damp cloth to my sex and then covers me with the blankets. He's snuggling in behind me not long after. My eyes, feeling like sand bags, staying closed as my brain and body succumb to utter exhaustion.

Forty Six

I wake with the most unpleasant pain in my lower abdomen. The need to pee.

My eyes are heavy, unable to open. I hear the breath of another person in the room. It's not Sadie. Who is it? Maggie? Jared?

My eyes open into slits so I can try to see where I am. It's too dark, even with the small bit of light to tell where I am.

The room smells of sex. Glorious, steaming hot, sinfully delicious sex. Yum. Wait! Where am I? Who is that next to me? Memories quickly flood my brain. I'm not dreaming. It wasn't a dream.

My eyes spring to life. Shit! Did I fall asleep? I look for a clock in the room. It's two twenty-two in the morning. Shit! I did fall asleep. I never fall asleep. I always leave. Shit. Shit. Shit!

Sliding to the edge of the bed, I feel Joe pull me back into him. He groans with disapproval. "Where you going?"

"I need to pee," I whisper.

I don't think he's actually awake. He's was like this a few times in the past when we've shared a bed. If you talk to him, he'll talk to you, but he's not actually conscious.

"You comin' back?" he mumbles.

"Mmm hmm . . ." I lie.

"K . . ." he utters before kissing me on the head and releasing his grip.

I rush to the bathroom. As much as I don't want him waking up to find me leaving, I really do need to pee. I can't hold it.

When I'm finished in the bathroom, I close the door more behind me to prevent most of the light from coming through. As much as I need the light to see, I don't want to wake Joe. On my hands and knees, I scour the floor for my clothes after I get my purse off the dresser. I find my shoes and the dress but nothing else. Shit. Damn it!

Not wanting to take any more time, let alone deal with trying to get the dress on just to get across to my room, I grab Joe's white button down shirt and shrug it on. This will have to do. I hold it closed in front of me as I pick up my things. I tiptoe to the door, carefully undoing the security lock, and slowly lower the door handle until it clicks open. I open the door just wide enough for

Breathe In

me to get through it sideways. I watch the room, making sure Joe doesn't get up. Once I have the door closed, I wince at not thinking about checking the hallway. I listen before I look. No one is there. I'm safe.

My hand trembles as I search for the room key in my purse. Come on. Come on. I know it's just a matter of time when he wakes up. Careful to not let the door slam, I spin flicking on the light surveying my options.

Panic engulfs my chest. I quickly text Jared that I'm heading home, unable to sleep and wanting to sleep in my own bed. I grab my bags, change my clothes and stuff the dress in. No need to worry about it getting wrinkled now. I dart to the bathroom to check my appearance. No need to look like a complete and utter mess, giving away to anyone I see that I just had sex. I brush my hair, wash my face and then stuff my bathroom things into the toiletry bag.

I press the button on the room phone. After a pleasant greeting, I inform the receptionist that I need to have a cab waiting for me downstairs. The woman from the front desk informs me I'll have to wait about fifteen minutes. Sitting on the edge of the bed, I chide myself for not calling first.

With my knee vigorously shaking, all I can do is sit and wait for the desk to call me back to let me know that the cab has arrived. The minutes click by painstakingly slow. I swear that time is traveling backward just to spite me.

I dart out the door before getting the call that the cab has arrived. I'm hoping it will be there waiting by the time I get to the lobby.

As quickly and quietly as I can, I hurry down the hallway to the elevators. I push the button several times, hoping that it will coming faster. What is taking so long? Everyone should be asleep. The elevator should be here by now.

What feels like five minutes later, the elevator dings and gradually opens. Getting myself situated, I take a deep breath, hoping it will calm my nerves, and then I press the button for the lobby. The doors don't close right away. I press the button that is supposed to make the doors close sooner, but nothing happens. I try again.

The sound of knocking on a door down the hall gently echoes into the elevator. My eyes fly wide open and I don't blink.

A voice whispers followed by the knock again. "Emma?" the voice says a little louder this time.

Close damn it. Close! Why is this elevator not closing?

I don't tip my head to the left when I hear my name called slightly louder a third time.

Ding. The elevator door begins to slide closed at what feels like five seconds per centimeter.

Chapter Forty Six

My phone chirps at half volume in my purse. My body freezes, unable to move.

The doors seal shut.

I hurry across the lobby to the front doors where I'm greeted by the cab driver who just arrived and offers to take my bags. There's no need to check out since I did that over the phone with the desk and left my room key on the dresser in the room.

The cabbie politely opens the back door for me before he takes my bags to the trunk. Just as the driver turns the car on, I swear I hear my name being called. Not looking back, I instruct the drive where to take me.

Right as the vehicle pulls away from the St. Regis, my phone chirps again. Don't look back, Emma. Don't look back. When the car reaches the end of the circle driveway that leads out onto the main road, I continue to fight the urge to look back. My phone chirps again. Pulling it out of my purse, my eyes confirm that it's Joe calling. Unable to deal with the situation, I turn my phone off.

An ugly feeling stirs in the pit of my stomach. A feeling I've never felt before. I feel nauseous. On top of the nausea, there's a tightening pain forming in my chest that is making it hard to breathe. What the hell is happening? A single tear trickles down my right cheek and I quickly wipe it away. My mouth feels like it's getting dryer by the second as moisture builds up in my eyes. No. No tears. No crying. What the hell is happening to me?

Breathe, Emma. Just breathe.

CPSIA information can be obtained
at www.ICGtesting.com
Printed in the USA
FSOW02n0935030616
21124FS